BOOKS BY MARGARET WEIS

THE
DRAGON'S SON

MARGARET WEIS

TOR®
fantasy

A TOM DOHERTY ASSOCIATES BOOK
NEW YORK

This is a work of fiction. All the characters and events portrayed in this book are either products of the author's imagination or are used fictitiously.

THE DRAGON'S SON

Copyright © 2004 by Margaret Weis

Edited by Brian Thomsen

A Tor Book
Published by Tom Doherty Associates, LLC
175 Fifth Avenue
New York, NY 10010

www.tor.com

Tor® is a registered trademark of Tom Doherty Associates, LLC.

ISBN-13: 978-0-7653-4391-8
ISBN-10: 0-7653-4391-6

First Edition: July 2004
First Mass Market Edition: October 2005

Printed in the United States of America

0 9 8 7 6 5 4 3 2

To Bayne and Bette Perrin,
with a daughter's love and respect

PROLOGUE

MELISANDE CLOSED HER EYES. SHE DREW IN A labored breath, breathed it out in a sigh. The twisted grimace of pain relaxed, smoothed. Her head lolled on the pillow. Her eyes opened, stared at Bellona, but they did not see her. Their gaze was fixed and empty.

Bellona gave an anguished cry.

Beneath the bed, the two babies lay in a pool of their mother's blood and wailed as if they knew.

Melisande's sons.

One of them human, born of love and magic.

One of them half-human and half-dragon, born of evil.

Both of them hidden away. One in plain view for all the world to see. One in the tangled forest of a grieving and embittered heart.

None of this had turned out as any of the dragons had planned.

"Killing the mother was folly," raved Grald, the dragon father of the half-human son. "Your women were supposed to capture her, bring her to me. She was unusually strong in the dragon magic, as proven by the fact that she bore my son and both she and the babe survived. I could have continued to make use of her, to breed more like her."

"You have found others who are serving the same purpose. As for Melisande, she *was* unusually strong," Maristara stated coldly. "The threat she posed far outweighed her usefulness. She was the sole human on this earth who knew the truth about the Mistress of Dragons."

"A threat she posed to you," Grald grumbled.

"A threat to me is a threat to us both," Maristara returned. "Without the children of Seth, you would have no city, no subjects, no army."

"We do not yet have an army."

"We will. Our plans can go forward now that Melisande has been removed," said Maristara, with a dig and a twist of a mental claw.

"What about the Parliament?"

"The Parliament of Dragons will do what it has done for a thousand years. Talk and debate. Decide not to decide. Then fly back to their safe and secret lairs and go to sleep."

"And the walker. Draconas." Grald growled the name and mumbled over it, as if it were a bone the dragon would like very much to chew. "You must concede that he is—or could be—a threat."

"That is true and we will deal with him, but all in good time. As he so cleverly arranged it, he is our only link to the children—the sons of Melisande. Your son in particular. Kill him and we kill any chance of finding them. Besides, if he were to suddenly turn up dead, think of the uproar. The Parliament might actually be inclined to do something. Best to lull them into complacency. Let the Parliament slumber and let Draconas walk the world on his two human legs."

"So long as we keep track of where those human legs of his take him," said Grald.

"That is a given," agreed Maristara.

Draconas heard two babies crying. Not an unusual sound for human ears to hear, for every second that passed on earth was heralded by a baby's cry, as some woman somewhere brought forth new life. The cries of babies might be said to be the song of the stars.

What was unusual was that Draconas—the walker, the dragon who had taken human form—heard the cries of these two babies in his mind. The babes themselves were far away, but the dragon blood in both linked them, all three, together.

He stood beside the cairn he had raised over the body of their mother and listened to the wails and spoke to her, who would never hear the cries of those she had brought into the world.

"There are some of my kind who believe it would have been better if your children were now lying dead in your arms, Melisande. Better for us. Better for them. In that instance, we dragons could yawn and roll over and go back to sleep and wake again in a thousand years. But, the children lived and so does the danger from those who brought all this about. We dragons must remain awake and vigilant. Your children were born of blood and death, Melisande, and I believe that is a portent."

He placed his hand upon the cold stone and wrote in flames of magic the words:

Melisande
Mistress of Dragons

Picking up his walking staff, Draconas left the tomb. The cries of the babies sounded loud in his mind until each fell asleep, and the wails died away.

1

BELLONA SENT THE BOY OUT TO CHECK HIS RAB-
bit snares. this was one chore he never minded, for he was
always hungry. When he found that he'd caught nothing, he
was only mildly disappointed. He did not have to worry
about his next meal this day. Bellona had brought down a fat
doe the week before and there would be fresh meat in the
house for some time to come. His mind was not on food. Today was the boy's birthday and he was preoccupied with the
memory of what had happened this morning.

He'd experienced five birthdays up to now. Today made
the sixth. He remembered clearly his last three birthdays and
he might have been able to remember the birthday before
that, but he could not be certain if he was actually remembering the birthday or if he had formed the memory out of
those birthdays that had come since.

The boy dreaded his birthday and looked forward to it, all
at the same time. He dreaded the day for the awful solemnity
that attended it. He looked forward to the day, too, for on his
birthday, Bellona would sit him down and speak with him
directly, an unusual occurrence. There were just the two of
them—the boy and the woman—but there was little commu-

nication between them. The two would sometimes go for days without saying more than a few words to each other.

At night, especially in the winter, when darkness came so early that neither of them was ready for sleep, Bellona would tell stories of ancient days, ancient warriors, ancient battles, ancient honor and death. The boy never felt as though she was talking to him when she told these stories, however. It was more as if she was talking to them, those who had died. Either that, or talking to herself, as if she was the same audience.

On his birthday, however, Bellona talked to him, to the boy, and although the words were terrible to hear, he valued them and held them close to him all the rest of the year, because on his day they were his words and belonged to no one else.

The boy had an imperfect sense of time. He had no need to count the days or months and he remembered the years only because of this one day. He and Bellona lived deep within the forest, isolated and alone, just the two of them. The passage of time for the boy was marked by gentle rain and the return of birdsong, the hot sun of summer, falling leaves, and, after that, snow and bitter cold. Bellona counted the days, however, and he always knew when his birthday was coming, for she would begin to make ready their dwelling in order to receive the special guest.

Bellona always kept the dwelling neat, for she could not abide disorder. She kept their dwelling in repair, working to make it dry during the spring rains and the summer thunder and warm during the harsh winter. Beyond that, she paid scant attention to it, for she was rarely inside it. Four walls stifled her, she said. She could not breathe inside them. She would often sleep outside, wrapped in her blanket, lying across the door.

The boy slept inside. He had a liking for walls and a roof and snug darkness. His favorite place in the world, apart from their dwelling, was a cave he had discovered located about a half mile from the dwelling. He visited the cave often, whenever he could escape from his chores. He felt safe in the cave, secure, and he would come there to hide away. He had come to the cave now, to think about his birthday.

Yesterday, the day before his birthday, Bellona swept the floor of their one-room hut, then laid down the fresh green rushes he'd gathered from the marsh. She cleaned the ashes from the fireplace and sent him to the stream to wash up the two wooden bowls and two horn spoons, the two eating knives and the two pewter mugs. She shook the dried grass out of the pallet on which he slept and burned it and stuffed it with fresh. She cleared away her tools and the arrows she had been tying from the table, which was one of only three pieces of handmade furniture in the hut. The furniture was not very well made. She was a warrior, she said, not a carpenter. The table wobbled on uneven legs. There was a tipsy chair for her and a low stool for him, a stool that he was fast outgrowing.

Her cleaning done, Bellona stood inside the small hut, her hands on her hips, and looked around with satisfaction.

"All is ready for you, Melisande," Bellona said. "We are here."

That night, the night before his birthday, Bellona remained inside the hut, keeping watch. Whenever he woke, which was often, for he was too nervous to sleep, he saw her lying on her side, her dark eyes fixed on the dying embers, the embers glowing in her eyes.

That morning, first thing, she sent him out to gather flowers. He knew how important the flowers were to her and they had become important for him, too, as being part of the ritual of this day, and he had taken to searching out places where grew the spring wildflowers, in order that he would be prepared.

He brought back two fistfuls of the bright blue flowers known by the peculiar name of squill, some dogtooth violets and bleeding heart. He gave them to Bellona, who dunked them in one of the two bowls that she had filled with water. She then set the flowers on the table, and sat in the chair. He squatted on his stool. His claws scraped the floor nervously, bruising the rushes and filling the air with a sweet smell of green and growing things. Bellona looked at him, also something special. On other days, she cast him a glance now and then and only when necessary. The sight of him pained her. He had once assumed he knew why she couldn't stand to look at him, but he had found out on his last birthday that he'd been wrong.

She would look at him today. She would also touch him. Her look and her touch made this day doubly special, doubly awful. He waited, tensely, for the moment.

"Enter, Melisande. You are welcome," Bellona called. The first rays of the morning sun slid in through the chinks in the wooden logs and stole in through the open door. "You have come to see your son and here he is, waiting to do you honor.

"Ven." Bellona turned her gaze full upon him. "Come to me. Let your mother see how you have grown."

Ven's mother, Melisande, was dead. She had died on the day of his birth. Her death and his birth were tangled together, though Ven did not understand how. He knew better than to ask. He had learned, long ago, that Bellona had little patience for questions.

Ven stood up. His claws made scraping noises as he walked across the dirt floor and he was conscious of the sounds his claws made in the silence that was fragrant, smelled of the flowers and the bruised rushes. He was conscious of the sound because he knew Bellona was conscious of it. On this day she heard it, when on other days she could ignore it.

Ven saw himself reflected in her dark eyes, the only time in the year he would ever see himself there. He saw a face that was much like the face of other children, except that his face had forgotten how to smile. He saw blue eyes that were fearless, for Bellona had taught him that fear was something he must master. He saw fair hair that his mother cut short, hacking savagely at it with her knife, as if it hurt her. He saw the arms of a child, stronger than most, for he was expected to earn his way in the world. He saw the body of a child, slender now that he had lost his baby fat, his ribs visible beneath sun-browned skin.

And he saw, in her eyes, his legs. His legs were not the legs of any human child ever born upon this earth. His legs, from the groin down, were the legs of a beast—hunched at the knee, covered all over in glittering blue scales; his long toes ending in sharp claws.

Ven walked up to Bellona. She rested her hands on his shoulders, and pinched them hard, to make him stand as straight as he could, given his hunched legs. She reached out a hand that was callused and rough to brush the fair hair out of his eyes. She looked at him, looked at him long, and he saw pain twist her stern mouth and deepen the darkness of her eyes.

"Here is your boy, Melisande. Here is Ven. Bid your mother greeting, Ven."

"Greeting, Mother," said Ven, low and solemn.

"This day six years ago you were born, Ven," said Bellona. "For you, this day began in blood and ended in fire. For your mother, this day began in pain and ended in death. I promised her, as she lay dying on this day, six years ago, that I would take her son and raise him and keep him safe. You see, Melisande, that I have kept my vow."

Outside the door, a bird sang to its mate. A squirrel chattered and a fox barked. The wind rustled the leaves. Creeping through the open door, a breath brushed Ven softly on the cheek.

"What is your name?" Bellona asked him, beginning her catechism.

"Ven," answered the boy. He didn't like this part.

"Your true name," Bellona said, frowning.

"Vengeance," he replied reluctantly.

"Vengeance," she repeated.

Leaning near, she placed her lips upon his forehead in the ritual kiss that she gave him once a year, her gift to him on his birthday. Her lips were rough, like her hands, and the kiss was cool and dry and dispassionate, yet he would feel it all the year long, feel the memory of it. This, too, he would hold close to him.

"Let your soul rest easy, Melisande," said Bellona. "Go back to sleep."

She let her hands fall from him, took her eyes away from him. Her gaze rested on the flowers and she was sad and far distant.

"You have the rabbit snares to check, Ven. And," she added unexpectedly, "tomorrow we're traveling to the Fairfield faire. We have furs to barter."

He froze the way the rabbits froze whenever he came near. He hated the faire. Once a year, they went to either Fairfield or another town for Bellona to barter fur pelts, exchanging them for salt and flour and tools and whatever else they needed, which wasn't much. At the faire were the children who looked like Ven from the waist up, but were not like him from the waist down. And though Bellona hid his beast's legs beneath long woolen breeches and a long woolen tunic and hid his clawed feet inside leather boots, she could not hide the fact that he did not walk as did other children.

"I don't want to go," he said to her that morning, the morning of his birthday. "I want to stay here. I'll be all right on my own."

He hoped for a moment she might let him, for there was a thoughtful look on her face instead of the scowl of displeasure that he expected. At length, however, she shook her head.

"No. You have to come. I need your help."

That might be true, but that wasn't the reason. She was making him go to torture him, to test him. She was always testing him. Tests to make him strong. He was angry at her and his anger blazed red in his mind and he said words he was surprised to hear.

"Today is my birthday. You made me greet my mother. Why is it I never greet my father?"

Bellona looked at him again—twice in one day—but this time he could not see himself in her eyes. He saw fury.

She struck him with her open hand, struck him a blow that knocked him in a heap to the dirt floor. He tasted blood in his mouth and the green smell of the rushes.

Ven picked himself up. His ears rang and his head hurt. Blood dribbled from his lip and he spit out a baby tooth that had been loose anyway. He did not cry, for tears were a weakness. He looked at her and she looked at him. He understood about his father then. Ven didn't know how he understood, but he did. He turned and ran out, his claws tearing the rushes.

He checked the rabbit snares, which were empty, and then came to this place, his place, the cave, where he felt safe, secure. He thought about his mother, who had given him his face—the face that pained Bellona to look upon because she had loved Ven's mother dearly and grieved her deeply and she blamed Ven for her loss. And, not for the first time in his life, Ven thought about his father.

The father, who had given him his legs—the legs of a beast—and who was the reason for his name.

2

VEN SPENT THE DAY IN THE CAVE. BELLONA
would not miss him. He was free to do what he liked during
the day, so long as he completed his chores. The rule was to
be home by sunset. The one time he broke that rule, ventured too far away, so that he was late coming back, Bellona
whipped him with a willow branch, then made him stand in
the middle of the room all night. If he started to slump or
doze off, she flicked him with the branch.

The cave was not a large one, to Ven's disappointment, for
he often saw visions in his mind of vast caverns with enormous chambers and labyrinthine passages to be endlessly
explored. Sometimes, at night, if Ven couldn't sleep or if the
snarl of the wild cat or the snuffling and pawing of a bear
around their hut woke him, he would imagine he was curled
up safely in the darkest, deepest depths of his cave, so that
no one in the world could ever, ever find him. Not even his
mother.

Ven's cave had only one chamber and had apparently
been used by a bear taking its long sleep in the winter. Last
fall, Ven had been certain that the bear would return to claim

it and he had prepared himself to defend it, for under Bellona's tutelage he was already a deft hand with a small bow. Fortunately for him and for the bear, the animal had smelled his strange and vaguely terrifying scent and sought another refuge, leaving Ven in sole possession of the cave.

Screened by a heavy stand of trees and a jumble of rock, the cave was always in shadow. Ven loved the darkness, for it was not dark to him. For him, darkness was filled with vibrant colors, wild and clashing and dazzling, that blazed across his mind. Alone, safe and protected by the darkness, he could close his eyes and watch the colors, touch them, handle them, shape them, as Bellona shaped the arrowheads or planed the arrow's shaft.

He played with the colors on this day, his birthday. He tossed the colors into the air and caught them as they fell. He used the colors to form an image of his mother, Melisande, giving her his face, for Bellona had told him last year on his birthday that he had his mother's face.

Ven made his mother's face softer than his, forming it to match the faces of mothers he'd seen at the faire. Melisande's face was soft and kind and always sad, for no matter how hard he tried, he could not imagine her smiling at him, as other mothers smiled at their children. He hoped that today she might smile, for it was his birthday, and when he had created her, he reached out his hand to her.

Another hand—a child's hand, like his own—took shape and form in his darkness. The hand was not made up of the colors of his mind, but was formed of colors of another mind. The child's hand reached for his hand. . . .

Startled, Ven lost control. The colors swirled about and the image of his mother and the strange hand vanished in the confusion. He sat hunched in the cave in the darkness and wondered what had happened. Another mind had touched his, that much he knew. As he and Bellona talked with words, the other mind talked with colors. Ven had heard a voice within the colors, but he hadn't been able to understand what it said.

The experience jarred him. He didn't know whether he

liked it or not. In some ways, it was pleasurable and exciting, and in some ways terrifying. He sat in the darkness, keeping the colors carefully subdued. He wanted to hear the voice again, to try to understand it.

He thought about the rabbit snares.

Ven summoned the colors and painted his mother's face, used her face to bait the trap. He opened his mind to the vast darkness and waited, impatiently, expectantly, for the other hand to reappear. When it did, he would grab hold of it and find out who it was.

A claw, not a hand, reached out of the darkness. The claw seized hold of the colors and would not let go. The claw tore open his mind, as it might have torn open a rabbit. The claw roamed around inside him, upended him, dumped out the contents, turned him inside out. The claw lifted him up. A face filled his mind—a face with a long snout covered with blue-black scales, snapping jaws and sharp teeth, red reptile eyes that looked straight at him.

"Where are you?" The words were flame and they burned Ven's mind. "Tell me where to find you. . . ."

The pain was unendurable and Ven writhed in agony. He could not run away, for the claw held him fast, but the darkness could run to him and it did, flinging its blanket over him, burying him deep.

Ven woke to a pounding headache, sickness, and terror of the beast that had attacked him. He pressed his cheek to the cold stone floor. The chill helped ease the nausea. He lay there, shivering and sweating, afraid to leave, afraid to stay.

Another face filled his mind. Bellona's face, twisted in anger. Her face was real and so was the willow branch. The other face—the dragon's face—was starting to recede. Wobbly-legged, Ven crept out of the cave, moving slowly, stealthily, pausing every few steps to look and to listen.

Nothing came after him.

Ven broke into a run and did not stop until he reached the stream that ran near their hut. He realized then that he was thirsty, with a terrible taste in his mouth. Falling to his knees, he scooped up the water with his hand, then halted, staring at his reflection.

The sight of his face shocked him. He was deathly pale, his eyes wide and wild. The moment Bellona saw him, she would suspect something had happened and she would ask questions he did not want to answer. Ven splashed cold water on his face and pinched his cheeks to bring the blood back. The hour wasn't as late as he'd feared. The sun hung from the lower branches of the trees, hadn't yet dropped to the ground. He sat in the sunshine and let it warm him and banish the memory of the dragon.

Ven didn't know why a dragon was hunting for him, and there was no one to ask.

He knew better than to mention it to Bellona. Last year, at the faire, he'd watched a troupe of actors putting on a show about a prince and a damsel and a dragon. The dragon came on stage in the last scene, for the prince to battle. (The dragon was not real, of course; even a five-year-old could see that.) The battle raged. The prince slew the dragon. Ven returned to their tent and, when Bellona asked him where he had been, he told her or started to tell her.

When he came to the word "dragon," she rose to her feet. Her face was as pale as his face had been in the stream. She did not hit him, though he thought she was going to. Her hands twitched; then the fingers clenched. She turned her back on him, walked away, and stayed away all that night, leaving him to fend for himself. They left the faire early that year and lived the poorer for it that winter.

The sun dropped off the last branch and fell into the horizon. Ven reached the hut just as night's first shadows darkened the doorway. He found Bellona seated at the table, fletching arrows. She cast him her usual cursory glance, making certain he was still living and breathing; then she looked back to her work and never took her eyes off it until it was time for their meal and their beds.

That night, Ven could not sleep. He could hear something snuffling and pawing outside the hovel, something huge.

When he went out the next morning to see what sort of tracks the beast had left, he saw no marks in the dirt.

The night had been quiet, Bellona told him, when he asked. That morning, they set off for the faire.

The Fairfield faire was one of the largest in the kingdom of Idlyswylde. The city of Fairfield, located on the river Aston, south of the capital, Ramsgate-upon-the-Aston, was noted for the faire held yearly on the vast piece of level ground that gave the town its name. Every other day of the year, the town's eight hundred residents went about their business in a somnambulant state, rousing for births and deaths, weddings and the occasional war, but mostly sleepwalking their way through life. On the week of the faire, the townspeople opened their eyes, sat up, and looked around at the world.

People from all over their kingdom and surrounding realms poured into Fairfield, swelling its population by a thousand, filling every inn and the abbey guesthouse, and spilling out into a colorful, temporary city of tents. Booths and stalls blossomed on the newly rolled green, their colors outdoing the spring flowers, their dealers tempting children with sticky treats and gentlemen with sticky games of chance. Merchants traveled with their goods by barge down the river Aston or journeyed overland, their pack mules laden with everything from silk gloves to pet monkeys.

Ven and Bellona did not keep a mule—a luxury too dear for them to afford. They loaded up the fur pelts in a pushcart to make the fourteen-day journey to Fairfield on foot. The trip was slow and tedious, especially at the beginning, for they had to haul the cart through the woods where they made their home, dragging it over a trail that Bellona had hacked out of the wilderness. No one else ever ventured on this trail, for Bellona did not tolerate visitors and, indeed, she had built their dwelling so deep in the forest that only the most dogged visitor could have found them. Since they used this trail just twice a year—for the spring faire and the fall—the trail was overgrown with weeds and brush and difficult to navigate.

Sometimes they found that a tree had fallen across it and then, if they couldn't move the tree, they had to either haul the heavily laden cart over the obstruction or drag the cart through the brush. This arduous task required both of them, one pulling and one pushing. Ven was unusually strong for a child of six and he did his share of the hard labor. That was why when Bellona had said she needed his help, he could not argue with her.

Leaving the forest, they struck the King's Highway, and the going was easier, for the road was well maintained. Bellona could pull the cart herself and she ordered Ven to ride in the cart, perched among the furs, where his deformity would not be so noticeable. Ven could walk fast and run faster on his beast's legs, but he had a strange gait, a loping spring, that brought strangers up short, evoked rude stares or ruder remarks. And if Ven spent too much time walking, the sharp claws on his scaled feet would pierce through the soles of his boots. Any of their fellow travelers who saw shining white claws instead of pretty pink toes would do more than stop and stare. They would descry Ven as a demon and slay him on the spot, or so Bellona told him.

Ven helped Bellona push and shove and wrestle the cart through the forest, a laborious task that cost them two full days. They made the journey in silence for the most part, except when Bellona would bark an order or swear savagely beneath her breath. Ven was used to the silence. He had come to prefer it, for it allowed him to retreat to his "mind-cave." He was leery about going there now, however, after the awful experience of yesterday when his cave had been invaded. He avoided it, and, with nothing to occupy him, he found the journey through the forest long and dull.

He was glad when they struck the King's Highway, for it at least provided diversion. If people stopped and stared at him during those times when he walked alongside the cart, he could stare back and sometimes have the pleasure of seeing them flush in embarrassment and quickly avert their eyes. There was lots to see and think about. Bears with iron collars and chains about their necks lumbered alongside their handlers. Noble lords in sumptuous clothes rode past, carrying hooded falcons and hawks upon their wrists, sometimes stopping along the way to let them fly. Their ladies came behind, riding in sedan chairs or on dainty palfreys. The ladies laughed and sang and sweetened the air with their perfume. A tinker's wagon rattled past, his pots banging and clattering. A party of monks walked the road, their heads bowed and their eyes fixed on the ground, so that they would not look upon a woman. A troupe of traveling actors rolled their gaudy wagons past, drawing attention to themselves by beating a drum and blowing blasts on an off-key trumpet.

Sometimes fellow travelers would call out greetings to Bellona. She never responded or even looked at them. She trudged the road in stoic silence, pushing the heavy cart, where Ven rode, brushing the fur pelts and smoothing them with his hands to make them shine and to keep off the dust of the road. The only people to whom Bellona deigned to speak were those who stopped to look at the furs and try to wangle a deal.

Since she was going to the faire, Bellona could afford to refuse to bargain, and though most shook their heads at her demands and turned away, now and then some wealthy merchant or noble lord would pay her what she asked or barter with her for something she needed.

At these times, Ven was forced to clamber out of the wagon and stand beside it. His wool trousers and tunic hid the scales, but they could not hide the fact that he did not walk or stand like a normal boy. Depending on their quality and breeding, the customers either would pretend not to notice him; regard him with kind, but pitying smiles; or coarsely laugh. Ven knew enough not to answer back, for, as Bellona said, their coin was good if their manners were not.

Ven didn't mind the looks that consigned him to nothingness. He didn't really mind the rude stares. The looks he hated were those filled with gentle pity. He would rather have them knock him down.

The deal concluded, Bellona would put the money in a leather bag she carried inside her tunic and lift the handles of the cart. Ven would climb up onto the furs and they would start once more on their way.

At night, when he lay on a mattress of pelts, blinking drowsily at the stars, he would wander into his cavern, there to relive, in the soothing darkness, the clamor and the voices and the looks. This day had been a long one, the journey tiring. He decided to risk venturing into his cave. He was half-asleep when he heard something snuffling about his mind, peering and poking and prodding at the chinks.

Fear gripped him, jolted him to wakefulness. Colors filled Ven's eyes. The dragon called to him, urged him to answer.

"Son," the dragon said, his colors pretty and wheedling, his claws hidden. "My son. Tell me where to find you."

Ven did not want the dragon to find him and so he curled up in a tight ball in the very center of his cave and, eventually, the dragon grew frustrated and went away.

The dragon—his father.

3

"WHERE IS HE, MINISTER?" DEMANDED THE OLD dragon irritably. "Draconas is late."

"He is on his way," Anora replied, her colors conciliatory. "The summons was unexpected. He required time to travel here."

"The reason it was unexpected is that he has cut himself off from us," Malfiesto continued, his colors red and angry.

"Can you blame him?" Anora returned, frost blue. "Two of us are dead. His own life is in peril. He believes it is for the best—and I agree—that we have as little contact as possible. It was with great reluctance that I called this meeting of the Parliament."

Draconas, who was the subject of this conversation, could hear it clearly as he walked the winding and twisting corridors that led to the secret cavern far below ground. The path he walked was pitch dark, but he needed no light. Although his eyes had the appearance of human eyes, he could see in the darkness far better than any human. His human legs could run faster, his human arms were stronger, for Draconas was not human. He was a dragon who had been magically given human form and then sent by the dragons, who were the true rulers of this world, to live among humans, keep an eye on them, and report back to the Parliament all the doings of their short and chaotic lives.

By Parliamentary decree, Draconas was forbidden to intervene in those lives, either for good or for ill. He'd recently been ordered by the Parliament to break that law, because another dragon had broken it first. Unfortunately, in trying to mend the crack, the dragons had shattered the pot. And they were leaving it to Draconas to pick up the pieces. They had no idea what havoc they had wrought in the lives of the humans.

They were about to find out.

One member of Parliament knew—the dragon who was the spy for Maristara, the female dragon who had first broken the Law of Dragonkind by seizing a human kingdom and holding it in thrall. Her spy was a male dragon and, so Draconas believed, a member of the Parliament. He deduced this from the fact that Maristara knew more about the goings-on of the Parliament of Dragons than did most of the dragons who actually came to the meetings and who generally dozed through them.

Draconas had warned Anora of this, when she had summoned him to attend Parliament and make a report. She had agreed with him, but there wasn't much she could do. As the current Prime Minister, she was being pressured by the other dragons, who no longer slumbered through the meetings, to find a solution to this problem. The other dragons were understandably nervous—two of their kind had been murdered, presumably by other dragons. Such heinous acts had not happened since the Dragon Wars centuries ago.

Anora was being pressured by dragons like Malfiesto, the dragon who had complained about Draconas being late. For all she knew or Draconas knew, Malfiesto might be the murderer, might be the spy. Precisely the reason Draconas had argued vehemently against holding a meeting of the Parliament. The Parliament had nothing to say to him that he wanted to hear and there was nothing he could tell them, lest it go straight back to their enemy.

Anora insisted, however.

"If Parliament is not to be consulted in this—our greatest emergency since the end of the Dragon Wars—then we might as well disband the Parliament and fall back into the old ways of governing," she told him, the colors of her mind dark-tinged with fear. "The old destructive ways."

Draconas was forced to grudgingly concede that she was right.

He entered the enormous cavern, its ceiling far above him, lost even to his far-seeing dragon sight, lost in darkness so profound that it might have been the ending of the universe. The eyes of the assembled dragons fixed on him. He could hear their fear, hear it in their inability to keep still—claws clicking against the stone, the nervous thumping of a tail, the snap of teeth, the rustle of wings. He could see the fear in the colors of their minds: ugly greens and yellows, shot through with streaks of black.

The dragons blended their thoughts to gray, mastered their emotions. Draconas looked searchingly at each of them, thinking that perhaps he might find a clue to the identity of the spy in the slant of the eyes, the twitch of a nostril, the flick of a head. He concentrated especially on the males, for it had been a male who had attacked him and Melisande, a male so crafty and cunning with his magic that he had fooled Draconas completely.

Of the twelve Houses of Dragonkind, five were ruled by males, the rest by females. The dragon who had been complaining—Malfiesto—was well over a thousand years old, the eldest male member of the Parliament. His scales, once a vibrant blue, had darkened to almost black. His teeth were yellow and his eyes clouded. His joints creaked when he moved. Draconas could almost discount Malfiesto as Maristara's cohort, but for the fact that every creak could be an act.

Malfiesto considered himself clever. He had been furious when Anora had been chosen to lead the Parliament instead of himself and he was quite capable of deciding that he was above the law. Draconas disliked Malfiesto, whose acid still burned on his tongue, if no longer in his belly.

Litard was a middle-aged male, hale and hearty in his late eight hundreds. He sported flashy green scales, of which he was very vain and took great care. During previous meetings of Parliament, Litard had spent much of the time preening and grooming himself, to the ire of the other dragons. He was looking a bit seedy these days, Draconas noticed, as if he had other matters on his mind. Litard refused to meet Draconas's eye.

Mantas was the age of Draconas, a relatively young dragon, and a mystery to everyone. He kept his colors dark, as the saying went among dragons, rarely sharing his thoughts, never speaking unless forced to do so by some direct question. He was an observer, not a participant. He seemed to have a great many secrets hidden beneath his blue-purple scales and, because he was such a very obvious suspect, Draconas had almost written Mantas off. Mantas had no trouble meeting Draconas's eye. He held his gaze so long that it was Draconas who looked away.

Jinat was another elderly male, though not as old as Malfiesto. Red in his youth, his scales had darkened to burgundy. He was mild and unassuming and always seemed laden with some heavy sorrow, as though bearing the weight of everyone's sins upon his shoulders. He did not make a very good suspect unless, Draconas thought, the weight Jinat bore was that of a guilty conscience.

The last of the males was Arat, a sharp and intelligent dragon of early middle age, cunning and selfish. His scales were red-orange and his thoughts almost always tended to that color, his brain afire with schemes and plots. He made no secret of the fact that he despised humans. He went out of his way to avoid having anything to do with them and he sat through the meetings with a curl on his lip, to show that he considered all this namby-pamby care of these insignificant creatures a waste of time. He ranked high on Draconas's list.

Once the dragons had settled themselves—though the

darkness was still restless with their movement—Anora opened the session by relating the terrible events that had precipitated this crisis.

Anora told how the dragon Maristara had, several hundred years earlier, broken the Law of Dragonkind by seizing Seth, a kingdom of humans located in an isolated valley surrounded by mountains. She had taken human form—not by magic, as was done in the case of Draconas—but by murder. Down through the years, Maristara had murdered countless human females, torn the hearts from their still-living bodies, then used the images of those bodies to rule over the kingdom of Seth. She had again broken the Law of Dragonkind by giving human females dragon magic, teaching them to use this magic to defend against dragon attacks. Thus she and the humans who served her were able to stave off the members of Parliament, who had tried several times to enter the kingdom in order to remove her.

Maristara had a companion in her evil—a male dragon who acted as Maristara's spy and informant, and who received payment in the form of all the male children born to the women of Seth who possessed the dragon magic. The male dragon had also taken human form, undoubtedly by murdering his victim. His name was Grald and he ruled over another kingdom—one that was hidden away from the sight of humans and of dragons. Here he raised the male children who had been born with the dragon magic, teaching them to use their magic to fight dragons and other humans.

"Hoping to stop Maristara," Anora continued, "Draconas formed a plan. He recruited a human male and transported him to the kingdom of Seth. There this human male was supposed to find the human female known as the Mistress of Dragons and spirit her away from the kingdom. Draconas hoped that by questioning this female, we might be able to discover Maristara's plans and find a way to thwart her.

"The plan was a good one, but it went awry. Maristara nearly caught and killed the two humans. Draconas rescued them, took them from the kingdom. He then devised another ingenious plan—"

Breaking all the rules, Draconas interrupted the speaker. "Do not credit me, Anora," he said, using his human voice, his words grating. "The plan may have been mine, but I later advised against it. You and Braun decided it should be implemented."

"Without consulting Parliament," Malfiesto stated testily.

"The danger was too great," Anora returned. "As evidenced by the fact that poor Braun was killed not long after."

"All this is spilt milk, as the humans say," said Draconas, "and the cat is licking its whiskers. The plan was that the human male would impregnate the human female. Since she possessed the dragon magic, we assumed that her child would also be gifted in the dragon magic. She and her child were to be brought here, to be cared for by Anora, until the child grew to an an adult. Then he would be sent to deal with Maristara.

"It was a fine plan," Draconas added wryly. "It had the benefit of delaying any action or decision-making for at least twenty years, while we waited for the child to grow up. After all, what is twenty years to the life of a dragon? An eyeblink, nothing more. Maristara had other ideas, however. She discovered the plan through her spy, Grald. He lured me into a trap and there he delved into my mind, tore it open, saw everything. He located the female and raped her, impregnating her with his child.

"The female gave birth to two sons—one human, the other half-human, half-dragon. The mother died, but both boys survived. They are now about six years old."

"You should have brought them to us," Malfiesto insisted. "Let us raise them."

"We've been through this once," Draconas said impatiently. "I see no reason to go through it again."

Malfiesto sucked in a breath, about to launch into a harangue.

Draconas swiftly forestalled him. "Madame, Honored Members, there has been a new development."

The dragons stirred uneasily. They did not like the word "new."

"What is that?" Anora asked.

Draconas conjured up the image of a human face, a lovely face, that of Melisande, the human female who had been in his care, the human he had so grievously failed. He created the image of a child's hand—one hand and then two hands—reaching through a prison wall to touch each other.

"What are you trying to convey to us?" Anora demanded, her colors sharp-edged and steel-pointed.

"Exactly what you see, Prime Minister," returned Draconas, keeping the image alive in his mind for all to see. "Because of our unfortunate intervention, two human children have been born with the ability to use dragon magic as we do—to communicate as we do. Mentally. Mind-to-mind. I know this because the two children have been in mental contact with each other."

The dragons all spoke at once, the images in their minds swirling about Draconas in a flaring vortex.

"Humans! Communicating as we do! The only barrier that has kept the savages from destroying themselves and harassing us is their inability to properly communicate their thoughts. The need to take their thoughts and shape and mold them into words that must then be taken by the hearer and shaped and molded back into thoughts. Imagine what havoc they would weld if this process were eliminated, if they could see clearly into each other's minds!"

Draconas made himself the eye of the storm, the calm, the empty center. He had set this trap for the spy and now he watched each male dragon, trying to find the one who was shamming, the one who already knew what had happened. The one whose claw had torn apart the children's dream.

Draconas watched closely, but he was disappointed. The colors of the male dragons were the same as those of their female counterparts: expressive of shock, outrage, fear.

Anora attempted to bring the outburst to a halt, threatening at one point to disband the Parliament if the members could not control themselves, and, at length, she managed to restore order. She kept the speaker's wand for herself, however, ignoring the many demands being made for it.

"Did the father of Melisande's sons intend this consequence, do you think, Draconas?" asked Anora. "The ability of the human children to communicate mind-to-mind?"

"You'd have to ask him," said Draconas wryly. He made a frustrated gesture. "I don't even know for certain why he felt the need to father a dragon child. The most obvious reason is that he wanted to punish Melisande, prevent her from returning to Seth to tell the people the truth—that they are being ruled by the very monsters they've been taught to hate. But, if that was all he wanted, he could have simply killed Melisande when he found her. He has some dark purpose in mind, of that I have no doubt. I just don't know what it is."

"My question—" Anora began.

"Yes. Sorry, I wandered down the wrong path. To answer your question, Prime Minister, I do not think the dragon intended for this 'consequence' to happen. In fact, I believe he is as dismayed by it as we are. The ability for the human children to speak mentally is as much a threat to him as it is to us. When the dragon discovered the children had found each other, he reacted quite violently to put an end to their communication. He is not pleased."

"He didn't harm the children?" Anora asked anxiously.

"Not physically. He cannot find them. He is searching for them, however, and sooner or later, because he can now enter their minds, he will discover them. Therefore, I again bring up my original proposal. I have been looking for Grald's kingdom, the human realm where they have been hiding the stolen babies. I cannot find it. Powerful magic— most likely dream magic—guards it. But if all of us were to band together and search—"

Waves of slate gray and storm black, purple and indigo and green, crashed and beat against him. Anora did not even bother to try to restore order. Draconas let the fury roll over him. He had known before he made the proposal what the response would be.

When the outcry had calmed and Anora could make herself heard, she named off the reasons why they could not do what Draconas had asked of them. He had heard the reasons before. He knew them by heart. If dragons attacked a human colony, the word would spread. The humans of every other human colony would hear of the attack and they would panic. Nations would rise up against the dragons, seek them out, destroy them.

Humans would die.

Dragons might even die.

"There are other ways, Draconas," Anora said now as she had said before. "Patience. That is the watchword. Be patient. Give us time to think up a better course of action."

And so on and so forth, forever and ever, amen.

Anora was right, of course. A war between humans and dragons was a terrible prospect, one to be avoided at all costs. Yet, in the end, they might not have a choice. . . .

"Why won't you tell us where the children are hiding, Draconas?" asked Lysira, a young female dragon. A sibling of Braun, she was now the last of her noble House. She was a beautiful dragon, aquamarine, with a long, delicate neck. "Let us protect them."

Draconas's thoughts softened as they touched hers. "I cannot tell you, Lysira. For that would be to tell my enemy."

Lysira bristled in shock and outrage. "How dare you accuse me—"

"I do not accuse you, Lysira," said Draconas. "Any more than I accuse any other member of this Parliament. But the fact remains that time and again, Maristara has been apprised of our most secret plans and, because of that knowledge, she is able to thwart them."

He lost patience. Reds and oranges flared. "If our enemy is here among us, that single question—where are Melisande's children—is the one question he or she most wants answered!"

He bowed stiffly to Anora. "This has been a waste of time, Minister."

Turning on his heel, he walked out before he had been formally dismissed, a serious breach of etiquette. He didn't give a damn. He was angry, frustrated, disappointed. He'd made the trip for nothing, it seemed, except to start a furor.

He could see the dragons' colors flash and flare, their version of shouting. The argument would rage for days and, in the end, they would do what he had known they would do from the start—nothing.

Leaving behind the shifting, clamoring brilliance, Draconas began the long ascent back to daylight.

The two dragons had seen all they needed to see and now they met, mind-to-mind, the moment Draconas departed the underground cavern where the Parliament was in session.

"The walker knows where to find the children," said Maristara, gnawing, frustrated. "If only we knew where to find the walker. Sometimes I am sorry we ever took it into our heads to involve ourselves with humans. I had no idea they would be so much trouble. Who would have thought, for instance, that this wretched boy you fathered would turn out to be able to communicate mentally with another human? This means the others can, also."

"So far, I've seen no signs of it in his siblings. I am keeping close watch."

"We need that boy!" Maristara said, frustrated.

"We will find him. Sooner or later, he will use the magic again and when he does, I will seize hold of him and probe his mind—"

"A pity you missed the first time he used it."

"Human minds are slippery at this age," Grald protested. "I could not hold on to him."

"Suppose we find the walker," Maristara suggested. "Suppose the walker should meet with an accident . . ."

"We've discussed that before and discarded it. Draconas dead. Talk about panic! Parliament would take action then. They would have no choice. Besides, the walker serves our purpose. He is the buffer between us and them. So long as he remains alive, they will be content to let him handle everything. Remove him and they will be forced to intervene.

"Consider this, Maristara," Grald added. "Draconas is our link to the children, the children our link back to Draconas. Find one and you find the other."

"And what if the walker warns the children not use the magic? Then we will have lost all three."

"No need to worry about that," said Grald. "One thing that you can rely upon with humans is that you can never rely upon them. No matter what the walker says or does, Melisande's sons will go their own way and then we will have them."

4

IT WAS LATE AFTERNOON WHEN BELLONA AND ven reached the outskirts of Fairfield. The main street leading into the city was clogged with travelers, all coming to the faire. Those who wanted to enter the walled town had to wait in line to pass through the gates. The fairegrounds were located outside the city, however, and those going to the faire could circumvent the walls and strike out for the smooth sward of fresh mown and rolled grass on which the gaily colored booths were being erected.

Bellona did not have a booth. She did not sell her furs to the public at large. She sold them to dealers in furs, who would take the ermine, the mink, and the white fox back to the kings or queens or princes who employed them, there to show the quality of each pelt and describe how it might look upon the royal robe or royal gown. Bellona had no desire to enter the city proper. She hauled the wagon past the walls, heading for the tent city located on the northern edge of the fairegrounds, where the grassy field gave way to thick forest.

Ven's pulse quickened. By the end of the faire, he would be glad to leave the noise and confusion; glad to return to his quiet, solitary existence in the wilderness. And thus he tended to forget, from year to year, the thrill he always felt when first arriving at the faire.

People were in a good mood at the start of the faire. Merchants anticipated fat profits. The common folk anticipated some fun to brighten their drab lives. The nobility anticipated intrigue, shopping, and gossip. And so, while there was much confusion during the setup of booths and tents, jostling and collisions were taken in good humor. Strangers pitched in to help when a wheel fell off a wagon. The traveling actors, busy erecting a stage at one end of the field, enlivened the work with the music of tambour and drum.

The mood would change by faire's end. Exhaustion, disappointment, pickpockets, and hangovers would take their toll on the fairegoer's good nature. But for now, every man was every other man's brother. The merriment was contagious and Ven felt himself swept up in the excitement and gaiety.

Not so Bellona. She pushed the cart with grim determination, glared at anyone who jostled her, and swore at those who hampered her progress. Most people rolled their eyes and got out of her way. Those who thought they might want to make something of it were usually put off by the speed with which she dropped the handles of the wagon to clasp the short sword she wore strapped around her waist.

Bellona did not look like a woman, nor did she behave like one. By her dress and her walk, she appeared to be a clean-shaven man in his mid-thirties. She wore her black hair cropped short. Her gaze was bold and challenging and unafraid. Her arms were muscular from hard labor, and she handled her sword with practiced ease. All but the most obdurate (or the most drunken) backed down from an encounter with her. Those who persisted in fighting often found themselves lying on the ground, rubbing a cracked head or nursing a broken jaw.

Bellona made no friends at the faire. She wanted none. She made no enemies, either. Most people were glad to leave the dour and half-mad fur trader to her own devices.

She and Ven pitched their small tent made of bear hide at the very edge of the encampment, as far from the other tents as they could manage, while still staying within the established boundaries. The tent was intended more for the comfort of the furs than it was for their own.

They both unloaded the cart; then Ven hauled it away to the nearby woods, where he stashed it beneath a tree. Bellona arranged the furs inside the tent, then both went to their rest. Ven slept inside the tent, lying on the ground so as not to damage the pelts. Bellona slept outside, guarding the tent, her hand on her sword's hilt. Both were so weary from the road that they fell asleep quickly, oblivious of the sounds of raucous merrymaking all around them.

The next day, the faire opened and business commenced.

"If you please, kind sir," said Ven, tugging on his forelock in respect, "my master has arrived with his furs. He trusts that you are in the market for fine pelts this year and, if so, he asks if you would be so good as to favor him with your business."

The busy merchant barely glanced at the boy. He knew Ven from years past. "The usual place, I suppose?"

"Yes, kind sir," Ven replied.

"I'll be there," the merchant promised, and turned back to wait upon his customers.

It was Ven's task to visit all the merchants with whom they'd done business in the past, bringing the word that "Master Bell the Fur Trader" was in attendance. Ven was also tasked with seeking out possible new customers, and he carefully scrutinized all those merchants dealing in furs. Bellona had taught him how to judge the merchant's quality by the quality of the furs he sold and the type of customers he attracted. Ven watched and appraised and noted down two new merchants who looked like potential buyers.

Of necessity, such business brought the boy among the crowds of fairegoers. Walking the fairegrounds was not as bad for Ven as walking the road. The aisles between the booths were packed with people and everyone was busy— buying and selling, gaming and drinking. Even with his pe-

culiar gait, he remained relatively unnoticed. Occasionally
someone would stop to stare or make a crude jest, but, for
the most part, people were having too much fun to pay attention to a crippled child.

As long as Ven did not stray from the fairegrounds and he
returned to their tent by the noon meal to report his success
to Bellona, he was free to do as he pleased. By midday of the
first morning, he had made the circuit of the faire twice, spoken to all their old customers, and taken stock of the new.
His work was done and only half the morning gone. The remainder of the time was his own.

Ven wandered aimlessly, taking in the sights. He paused,
enthralled, to watch a fellow clad in motley (that had seen
better days) dance nimbly upon a rope strung between two
trees. He laughed uproariously to see poor Punch being
hounded by his tyrannical wife. He admired the jugglers, but
passed by the minstrels without interest, wondering what
people saw in them. To his ears, the screeching and scrawl-
ing and howling was bone-jarring, tooth-grating.

The booths that sold sweetmeats held no interest for him,
though the other children thronged to them. He had no taste
for sugared almonds or pastries sticky with honey. The
smell of fresh meat drew his attention, led him to a fire pit
where men were roasting a whole pig on a spit. He sniffed
the air hungrily and looked at the sun to confirm what his
growling gut told him—time to return to the tent for the
midday meal.

He loped toward the edge of the faireground, taking his
time, for Bellona would be busy with customers and he'd
likely have to wait for his supper anyway. Passing by the
bull-baiting arena, he saw no harm in joining the boys and
men gathered to watch the savage sport.

Inside the arena stood a bull, shaking his horns and snuffling and pawing at the ground, his beady eyes keeping wary
watch on a small, squat dog with an ugly face, whose metal-
studded collar was held fast in the grip of a man on the far
side of the arena. Another man gave a shout and the dog's
owner let loose the animal. The dog charged across the

arena, leaped at the bull, and sank its sharp teeth into the fleshy part of the bull's nose.

Roaring in pain, the bull flipped his head back and forth, trying to free himself of the dog. Though the bulldog was being battered and shaken, it held on grimly. Blood spurted from the bull's nose, spattering the spectators, who yelled in glee and made bets on how long the dog could maintain its grip before the bull sent it flying.

Ven reached the fence that surrounded the ring just as the bull managed to fling off the dog, which landed heavily on its side and lay still a moment, before shaking its head and staggering to its feet. The dog was slathered in blood. Its owner retrieved it, collected his wagers. The wounded bull was deemed fit enough to carry on. Another man with another dog took his place at the end of the arena. Ven climbed onto the bottom rung of the fence, peered over the railing.

At the signal, the man loosed the second dog. The animal charged at the bull, then skidded to a halt. Something else had attracted its notice. The dog's owner cursed, urging the dog toward the bull. The dog ignored him. Sniffing the air, the bulldog turned its head and saw Ven. The dog ran straight for him, its teeth bared.

Ven had no time to react. The dog was on him in seconds, growling and snarling. The dog seized hold of Ven's boot and ripped it off his clawed foot.

Grappling with the dog, Ven lost his balance, and tumbled backward off the fence. The dog dropped the boot and returned to the attack, tearing at Ven's woolen leggings and ripping the fabric, trying to sink its sharp teeth into Ven's scale-covered hide.

Ven beat at the animal with his fists, but the dog was used to fighting bulls, and the blows of a child, even an exceptionally strong child, could not halt the animal's furious attack.

The dog snapped at Ven's scaled flesh, trying to find purchase. Its sharp teeth finally managed to pierce the scales. Getting a good grip, the dog shook Ven's leg back and forth in its strong jaws.

The stupefied spectators were at first too shocked to do

anything; then some began to laugh and call out wagers, while others hovered ineffectually over the child and the savage dog, arguing over how to handle the situation. Someone grabbed a club to hit the dog, but the owner of the animal cried out that his trained dog was worth more than a beggar boy. The man with the club persisted. The dog's owner attacked the man with the club and a general scuffle ensued.

An ear-piercing shriek brought everything to a halt. "Demon! A child of the devil! A hell-child!"

Bright sun gleamed brilliantly off blue scales, shone on white claws. Each man staring at the boy realized he was seeing something that should not be. Eyes widened, mouths gaped.

Leering, horrid faces thrust themselves at Ven. The pain of the dog bite was minimal; the animal could not harm the hard scales of his leg. Fear made him sick and dizzy. *They will call you a demon,* Bellona had often told him. *They will burn you at the stake.*

Someone shouted for a priest. Someone else for the sheriff. Rough hands seized hold of him. Ven fought and bit and scratched.

"Let him go!" said a commanding voice. "Clear off!"

Few would have obeyed, but the order was accompanied by thwacking sounds—a staff thumping heads, necks, and backsides.

The hands let go of Ven. The myriad faces disappeared. Ven stared up at blue sky and a man's face, dark-avised, with cool, dispassionate eyes. The man stood protectively over Ven, gripping his staff in his hands, waiting to see if the crowd was minded to have another go at him. No one was, apparently. Someone again suggested summoning the sheriff and several ran off to do just that. The others backed away, though there were still cries of "Demon spawn!" All the while, the dog continued to worry Ven's leg, snapping and snarling and slavering.

The man rested his staff on the ground within easy reach. Keeping one eye on Ven and another on the crowd, the man seized hold of the dog. He prized the dog's jaws apart, forced the frenzied animal to release its grip, and flung it aside. The dog stood panting, considering another run at Ven. The man lifted his staff. The owner surged in, grabbed hold of the dog, and carried the squirming animal away.

Ven raised himself up.

The man lowered the staff, rested his hand on Ven's leg.

"Lie still," he said in a low, calm voice. "No one's going to hurt you."

Ven knew better. He knew what would happen and he was right. They could see his beast's legs. They believed him to be a demon or perhaps the devil himself. The cries for a priest increased. Someone suggested slaying him on the spot.

"Here!" a man shouted. "Here is a holy sister!"

"Save us, sister!" a woman screamed, hysterical, falling onto her knees. "Save us from Satan!"

The black fabric of the sister's wimple lifted in the wind. Her hands tightly clasped, her gaze fixed on him, she started walking toward him.

"I said lie still," the man's voice ordered, sharp as a whip-crack. His grip on Ven's leg tightened, and Ven had no choice but to obey. "Let's have a good look at that wound."

The man moved so that the crowd could get a good view of Ven's leg. Shrieks and cries dwindled to mumbles that tailed off in bewilderment. Those standing around Ven shook their heads and muttered and eyed his leg askance.

Ven looked back at his leg and saw flesh—pink flesh—ripped and torn from the dog's mauling. Blood, oozing from the wound, soaked through the tatters of his wool pants.

The man with the staff picked it up and turned to face the crowd.

"Go along now," he said in a pleasant tone. "The boy is not much harmed, as you can plainly see. This show has ended. There's no demon child here. Go watch the actors. I hear they have a man who can eat fire."

"I seen what I seen," insisted an old man with all of three teeth in his head. "He had the legs of a lizard. Covered in scales they was."

"Here, sister, come and look!" another cried. But the holy sister was nowhere to be found. Someone suggested stripping the boy to see for certain.

Ven's protector reached into his purse. Drawing out some coins, he tossed them in the dirt.

"You're drunk, Father, but not drunk enough, apparently," he said, still pleasant. "Take that money and go finish the job. Here, look at the boy's leg. What do you see? Flesh and blood and bone. Feel it, if you don't believe me."

The old man was stubborn enough to do just that. As the others gathered around watching, he gave Ven's leg a poke with a bony finger. The old man grunted, snatched up a coin, and walked off. Seeing their spokesman depart, the others fell on the coins, grappling and clawing in the dirt. The mob that had gathered dwindled away to the ale tents or went back to the bull-baiting.

"We had best get you to the abbey infirmary," said the man. He picked up the maltreated boot, stuffed it into his belt, then picked up Ven.

"No!" Ven gasped. "Not an abbey—"

"Shut up," the man growled in Ven's ear. "We're not out of danger yet. Let me do the talking."

The man lifted Ven in strong arms and slung him over his shoulder. They headed for the edge of the fairegrounds.

"Sir," said Ven, "if you'll just take me home—"

"Keep silent," the man ordered.

Ven did as he was told, more because he was still too confused by what had happened to talk, than because he felt compelled to obey a stranger, even one who had saved his life.

The man did not take Ven to the abbey or go anywhere near it. As soon as they were out of sight of the crowd, the man left the road that led to the city and struck out over the open fields, heading for the forest. A few people stared at them, but, seeing nothing more interesting than a man carrying a blood-smeared child, they went on their way.

The cool and familiar shadows of the forest closed over Ven and he breathed easier, relaxed. The man stopped to peer about to make certain they were alone. Seeing and hearing nothing, he eased Ven down onto a bed of dead leaves. The man held his hand over Ven's flesh-and-blood leg.

A narrow, shifting band of sunlight filtering through the green leaves of the walnut tree shone on blue, glittering scales. The man lifted Ven's leg, examined the scales minutely, then nodded in satisfaction.

"The dog tore a few of them loose, but no serious harm done. You were lucky I happened to be keeping my eye on you," the man added, his voice grim. "Tell Bellona she must take better care of you—"

Ven jumped to his feet and ran. The man shouted something. Ven ignored him. He ran as fast as he could, giving his beast's legs their freedom, loping over the rough, uneven ground; springing off his clawed toes. He heard the man give chase, crashing through the underbrush. Ven was small and he was agile. He dodged in and out among the tree trunks, slithered under tangles of brush and vines, crawled beneath fallen logs, and splashed through streams. He ran until his legs ached and he was forced to halt to ease the pain. Gasping for breath, he listened for pursuit. He could no longer hear the man's shouts or his crashing footfalls and he knew he'd lost him.

Ven had lost himself, too, in the woods, but that wasn't a worry. He knew his way around a forest. Far off in the distance came the faint cries of the hawkers, shrill laughter, hoarse calls and shouts—the sounds of the faire. He had only to follow the sounds and he would find his way out. He didn't intend to go out, not for a long while. He wanted to remain here in the forest, in the silence, away from the staring eyes and the gaping mouths and the human voices. He would be in trouble with Bellona, but he would deal with that.

He stared at the jagged hole in his breeches, at the blue scales glistening in the sunlight. He closed his eyes and saw what he had seen back at the bull-baiting ring: torn pink flesh; fresh, bright blood. For one wild, irrational moment, Ven had known a miracle. He'd known joy.

He opened his eyes. The scales were back. There was no

miracle. The joy was gone and the despair that came now was worse for having known it.

Ven curled up in a ball, his beast's legs pressed tight against his human chest, and he lay quite still and listened to the howling silence.

5

AFTER HE'D FINISHED MENTALLY KICKING HIM-
self, draconas stood at the edge of the woods and wondered
what to do. He knew better than to try to continue chasing
after the dragon's son. With Ven's sharp senses able to detect
Draconas's every move, the boy would play at hide-and-seek
until Draconas gave up the game. He took back what he'd
said about Bellona. She'd done her job well. She'd raised the
boy to be able to take care of himself, at least under ordinary
conditions.

Conditions were no longer ordinary.

Draconas had decided during the meeting of Parliament
that he had to find the dragon's son. He had to find the boy
and Bellona, warn them both that the dragon-father was
searching for them and that they needed to hunker down and
lie low.

The day the child was born, Draconas had given the baby
to the reluctant Bellona, warned her to hide the child away,
keep him safe from both humans and dragons at first. Bellona had heeded his warning.

Altering his appearance, which he could at will, Draconas

had secretly kept an eye on Bellona and the newborn baby. He had never approached them, not disturbed them. He watched over them in secret until he determined that Bellona was a good guardian for the child, if not the ideal mother. Then, fearing that he might put them in danger if he continued to hover over them, Draconas deliberately turned his back on mother and child and, for five years, he had not set eyes upon them.

Draconas had, instead, kept watch on those who might also be watching for the dragon's son. He roamed the countryside around the kingdoms of Seth and Idlyswylde, searching for the mad monks—human males who possessed the dragon magic. Acting under Grald's orders, they had pursued Draconas in Seth and, so he reasoned, they were the most likely to be sent on the hunt for a child with dragon blood in his veins. But church brethren were always traveling; making pilgrimages, working or visiting. Draconas encountered a great many monks and, without direct confrontation, he could not be certain whether he was seeing real monks or false. He would have to find the boy. He dared not enter the forest for fear he was being watched. He would have to wait for Bellona to come out.

Bellona was a soldier, not a farmer. She would have to sell or barter her skills for food and other supplies and that meant leaving the shelter of the wilderness and going where there were those who would be able to provide what she required. The annual faire at Fairfield was her logical choice. Closest to her forest home, the faire and its crowds of people provided cover and protection. What was one more crippled child in that mass of humanity? Asking around, Draconas discovered that she had been there before. She would likely go there again. At least, the faire was a good place to start.

Draconas arrived at the faire a week before it opened in order to familiarize himself with the grounds and the people. He made discreet inquiries about fur-sellers, received descriptions and recognized a couple that might fit Bellona.

Draconas had last seen the child at about one year of age

and he hadn't seen much of him then. Draconas pictured to himself what the dragon's son would look like at age six—a normal-looking little boy, except for the legs. Bellona would disguise those, but she would not be able to disguise the fact that the son of a dragon walked differently from the son of a human.

When the crowds began to arrive, he kept an eye out for her and for the boy. He spotted the child the very first morning, his attention caught by the way the boy walked. Young dragons, only a few months old, use that same loping gait when they try to walk upright on their hind legs. Intrigued, wondering how he was going to approach the boy, Draconas followed him. Catching a good look at the boy's face, as the child gaped at the jugglers, Draconas was confirmed in his suspicion. The boy was Melisande come back to life.

As he watched the boy, Draconas watched for anyone else watching the boy.

He spotted the holy sister.

She aroused his suspicions for several reasons. The other nuns he saw strolling about the faire went in groups. This holy sister was alone. She seemed to go out of her way to avoid meeting other members of the sisterhood, for she would turn aside if any came near her, ducking her head and retreating behind the black folds of her veil. She appeared to be taking an unusual interest in the boy, for, as Draconas tailed the child around the faire, he noted that wherever the boy was, there she was. This included the bull-baiting—not the sort of entertainment that generally attracted nuns.

The sister's behavior at the bull-baiting confirmed Draconas's fears. She reacted normally when the dog attacked the child, staring in shock, seeming paralyzed by horror. Recovering, she ventured close to look at the child's injuries. But she did not hasten forward to help him, to pray over him and succor him—actions a holy sister might be expected to take. She remained in the background, watching, until Draconas arrived. He tried to keep an eye on her, but he was forced to focus his attention on the boy while casting his illusion spell, and he lost track of her. When the crowd dispersed, she was gone.

Did the nun have other urgent business at the faire? Or was she hastening off to alert her cohorts that she had found the dragon's son?

Draconas mulled over his predicament. He was not well pleased with himself. He'd lost both the nun and the boy. He could try contacting the boy through the use of the dragon magic. He banished that idea as far too dangerous. If the child opened his mind to Draconas, the boy might inadvertently open himself to Grald.

Draconas decided to confront Bellona. Leaving the woods, he went in search of her. He'd been provided with a couple of locations where she might be camping and the first proved accurate. He found her exhibiting her pelts to a customer, a man who knew his furs, to judge by his knowledgeable questions and the swift, deft way he sorted through the pelts. Their business was soon settled. They shook hands upon the deal. He promised to send his apprentice with the money to pick up the pelts. Bellona promised she would be here to receive him, and the two parted. Draconas stood to one side, watching. When the customer left, he stepped forward.

"Well, sir?" said Bellona, gruffly polite. "What is your business here? I don't recognize you—"

She stopped talking. Her eyes narrowed. Turning, she entered her tent and yanked down the flap.

"We have to talk, Bellona," called Draconas, standing outside the tent. He kept careful watch, looking all around, among the other tents, into the woods, across the fields. "Something happened to the boy at the faire. Something you should know about."

At first no sound came from inside the tent. Then, thrusting aside the flap, Bellona emerged.

He barely recognized her. Six years had passed since their last meeting and not even humans aged a great deal in only six years, but each of those years might have been ten, for the marks they had left upon Bellona. Hardship and toil had melted the flesh from her body. She seemed made of nothing except bone and sinew. Her face was gaunt, her expression hard and stern and hostile. She was young still, maybe only in her early thirties, but her hair was streaked with gray.

"Where is Ven?" she demanded, glaring at Draconas. "It is past his suppertime."

"I told you. Something happened to him."

"Where is he?"

"The last time I saw him, he was safe. He's tough, that child. What is that name you call him?"

"Where is he?" she asked a third time, her dark brows lowering, her eyes glinting. "What have you done to him?"

"I haven't done anything except get him out of a nasty scrape," said Draconas, exasperated. "Do you want to listen to me or not?"

Bellona hesitated, then gave an abrupt and grudging nod.

Draconas related the incident with the bulldog and the crowd of people that saw, for an instant, a child with the legs of a dragon. He watched, as he spoke, for some sign of distress, of fear, of worry. Her face was iron, cold, and hard. Her eyes took in, did not give out.

"I cast a magic spell on his leg," Draconas explained. "A spell that created an illusion similar to the one I used when we were attacked that day his mother died; the spell that made it look as if the window was still shuttered, even though in reality the shutters had been chopped to kindling."

He paused, expecting some response. Bellona had nothing to say, however, and so he continued.

"I made it appear to the onlookers that his leg was the leg of a normal human child, torn and bloodied from the attack by the dog. A few doubters remained, but they found it hard to argue with their own eyes, and eventually they left."

"Did the dog bite harm him?" Bellona asked gruffly, and she seemed to resent having to ask that much information of him.

"No. Those scales of his would turn a dagger's blade. The dog's teeth managed to loosen a couple, but they will heal. He is a quick healer, I think?"

He waited for a response, got none, and went on. "I carried him into the woods, away from prying eyes. I wanted to talk to him, to explain what I had done. He ran away before I had the chance. I went after him, but I lost him."

Bellona smiled, tight-lipped, and for the first time, he saw what might pass for maternal pride. "You'll never find Ven," she said. "Not unless he wants to be found. He is both swift and strong. And, as you say, a quick healer."

"You're not the least bit worried about him, are you?" Draconas observed.

Bellona shrugged. "Ven can take care of himself. He'll come back when he gets hungry. If you're expecting thanks," she added caustically, "you're not going to get it. What he is, you made him."

"He is in danger, Bellona. I came to warn both of you—"

"He has been in danger since the day he was born. I know it. No need to tell me about it now."

She rested her hand on the hilt of her sword. "Leave us. And don't come back."

Bellona was not a threat to the dragon. Draconas could fuse her sword's blade to the scabbard or cause it to melt and ooze into a puddle on the ground. He could do many things with his magic and he was tempted to do all of them to the infuriating woman. People were roaming about among the tents, however; a person who looked to be another furrier was making his way up the hill, heading toward her cart. Draconas swallowed his ire. There would be talk enough around the faire over this day's deeds as it was. No need to give them anything more to discuss.

"I saved him today, Bellona," he told her as he left. "But I won't always be around to protect him. Take better care of him."

He stalked off in ill humor, heading back toward the fairegrounds. As he went, he glanced surreptitiously over his shoulder, certain that she would leave to go search for the boy herself. If she did, he would follow.

Bellona turned away, but only to talk to the new customer.

Draconas stomped though the tall grass, cursing the stupidity of humans.

Bellona's face came to mind and with it her words. *What he is, you made him.*

Her accusation brought him up short. He was forced to admit that was true, at least in part. And if Bellona was careless of her charge, perhaps that was because he'd never fully explained to her the danger. He'd thrust the newborn babe, still drenched in the mother's blood, at Bellona and bid her take the child and hide him away in the wilderness. He'd never told her who she was hiding from or why; never warned her about the magic that blazed inside the child's head; never told her about the false nuns.

"Yet how could I know how the magic would affect him or his brother?" Draconas asked himself, frustrated. "How could I have told her what I didn't know myself? And I might have led Grald straight to them."

Well, it was all the cat's milk now. No use crying over what he hadn't done or berating himself over what he should have done. He had to assume the worst. He had to assume that the holy sister was one of the false nuns, sent to locate the dragon's son.

He focused his thoughts on the holy sister—middle-aged; plump, motherly figure; puckered mouth and eyes. Keen eyes, alert, penetrating. Where would she go to search for the boy?

To the place where Draconas had announced he was taking the wounded child. She would go to the abbey.

Built to honor some obscure local saint, the abbey in Fairfield was small and humble, compared with its grander cousins in more major cities. Its priests and lay brothers lived quiet lives, spending their time in prayer, working their fields, assisting the poor, and maintaining a small hospital for the sick and injured. Since the abbey stood outside Fairfield's protection, it had its own fortifications. A gray stone wall surrounded the gray stone abbey and its various outbuildings. A porter stood in attendance at the main gate. His duty was not to keep people out—for the brothers welcomed all to enter and worship freely—but to direct them to where they needed to go once they were inside.

Usually a quiet place, the abbey was busy during the faire. Their small guesthouse provided accommodations to wealthy patrons who had a claim to the abbot's hospitality. In addition, the abbey also provided shelter and food for the train of beggars and cripples who hoped to share in some of the faire's wealth. Draconas passed a veritable army of men, women, and children, squatting or lying, sitting or standing along the road that led from the faire to the abbey, holding out their hands or their begging bowls.

He made his way past the line of misery to the abbey's main gate, where the porter sat basking in the afternoon sunshine, taking his ease and refreshing himself with a meat pasty in one hand and a mug of ale in the other. At the sight of a visitor, he put his meal aside, and rose to greet Draconas.

"A fine day, sir. A day God made. And what is your business with the abbey, Master?" asked the porter with a broad smile, unconscious of a blot of gravy on his chin.

"I come seeking information, good Porter," said Draconas. "A young lad was injured this day at the bull-baiting contest. A torn and bloodied leg. He was a brave lad and bore his injury like a soldier. I was much impressed with him and I thought that since I was passing, I would stop to make inquiry. How does the lad? Is he mending?"

"Now that is strange that you should ask, Master," said the porter. "You are the second person who has made inquiry after such a boy. What is all the more uncommon is that no such lad ever came here."

"Are you certain?" Draconas feigned surprise. "Perhaps you were off-duty and did not see him."

"No, I have been here the livelong day. I've seen all who came and all who went and not a boy among them, let alone a boy with a hurt leg."

"Well, then, he must not have been so badly hurt as I feared," said Draconas, adding offhandedly, "Who was the other who made inquiry about him?"

"A holy sister. She seemed right put out that he was not here. Insisted that he was and would not take no for an answer. She went in to look for herself. She left here in high dudgeon and when I wished her good day, she cast me such a look as it was a wonder did not roast me where I stood."

"She was probably worried about him," said Draconas. "Did you know her?"

"Oh, no, sir," said the porter. "But then, it's not likely I would. We are an out-of-the-way place most of the year, with few visitors."

"I suppose that is true. Well, I will not keep you longer. That pasty looks too good to let go to waste. Return to your dinner, good Porter," said Draconas. He fished about in his coin purse. "And thank you for your information. Please put this toward feeding the poor, will you?"

The porter accepted the money with a blessing and settled himself down with his pie once more.

Convinced that his fears for the boy's safety were justified, Draconas made his way back to Bellona's campsite. With any luck, he'd find the boy with her, for the afternoon was waning toward evening and a young stomach would demand to be fed. Draconas was well aware that his reception would be chill. He'd make the two of them listen to his warning about the nun, if he had to spell-bind them to do it.

Draconas arrived back at the place where Bellona had pitched her tent, but he didn't find the boy.

He didn't find a tent.

He didn't find Bellona.

No tent, no furs, no boy, no cart. The spot where the tent had stood was empty. He told himself that perhaps he had remembered wrong, that this was the wrong site, but he couldn't fool himself for long. Ruts from the cart's wheels were plainly visible in the ground, alongside a patch of yellow, flattened grass corresponding to the shape of the tent.

"She fooled me," he muttered, torn between rage and admiration. Admiration for her, rage for himself. "She fooled me completely. I thought she didn't give a damn, when, in truth, she was scared witless. So scared that she packed up and left."

What about the boy? Maybe he'd been there all along, hiding inside the tent. Or perhaps Bellona had gone seeking the boy in the forest, knowing that she could find him when no one else could.

"At least, I *hope* no one else found him," Draconas said gravely.

He scanned the landscape—the bright green of the rolling hillsides, the deeper green of the forests, the fairegrounds splashed with the speckles of booths and tents. The road was crowded with people, coming and going.

If only he could take dragon form! Spread his wings, dig his hind claws into the ground, and propel himself into the air with his powerful, heavily muscled hind legs. If only he could reach with his wings to seize hold of the sky and pull himself up among the clouds. He could soar over the hills and fields and roads far below, searching with his keen eyes until he spotted them.

Fleeing safety. Rushing headlong into danger.

A wonderful image, but that was all it was or ever could be. Too many humans about. The babble of their voices surrounded him. Their smell filled the air. He pictured himself transforming, flaring up from among the grass in a blaze of orange-red, sun-fired scales—a creature of dreams, a monster of legend, a dragon of wrath and death and destruction. He pictured the panic, the chaos.

Draconas looked down at his dust-covered boots—the toes scuffed, the heels worn down after only a few months' wear. He was the walker and this was how he came by his name. He spent more money on shoe leather than on anything else in this world of humans.

With a grim sigh, he set off walking, tracking the ruts made by the wheels of a cart being hauled with haste through the grass.

6

BELLONA HAD DONE ALL THAT DRACONAS HAD
envisioned, with one exception. She had not taken the cart.
More frightened than she could have ever imagined at hearing of the disaster that had befallen Ven, she lost her head
and acted rashly and impulsively. Such behavior was not
usual with her and she was astonished by it, even as she gave
in to it.

Bellona had once been a warrior for the kingdom of Seth,
the same kingdom where Melisande had been high priestess.
Both of them unwittingly served the dragon Maristara. Bellona had trained as a warrior from an early age, and part of
that training included learning to keep her shield raised, her
sword arm steady. Bellona had believed herself secure behind her shield, safe in the knowledge that since Melisande's
death the weapon had not been forged that could penetrate
her defenses.

Then came Draconas and his tale of what had happened to
Ven at the faire, and suddenly fear's sharp point slipped past
her shield, struck her to the heart.

Bellona was surprised to feel pain, for she had imagined

she could not feel anything. The pain of her grief had been so agonizing that she had never wanted to feel anything, ever again.

Bellona had not known until that moment how much she cared for Ven. She had not cared for him at all when he'd been a babe in arms, forced upon her by the untimely death of his mother, her beloved Melisande. Bellona would have refused to take him, but she had made a promise to the dying Melisande to care for her sons—both this child and his human twin—and Bellona had been taught to honor any promise she made to the dead.

She could not look back on those first few months with the infant Ven without experiencing again the burning ache of loss that had nearly suffocated her. She could not draw a breath without feeling her grief catch in her chest. The pain was so terrible she often thought it would be easier to die than to go on bearing it, and she might have died, if it had not been for Ven. She had to live for the baby's sake. He was so utterly dependent on her and she was such a poor substitute for a mother.

At that, he nearly did die, for she knew nothing about raising babies. He almost starved to death, until she found a peasant girl willing to serve as his wet nurse in return for food. Bellona was able to keep his lower extremities wrapped in swaddling bands, so that the girl, who was dull-witted as it was, never suspected the child she held to her breast was anything other than a pretty, fair-haired, blue-eyed babe. Once Ven was weaned, Bellona carried him deep in the forest, and there they had lived ever since.

She named him Vengeance, because she fully intended that he would grow up to avenge his mother's death. In order to do this, he would have to enter a world of normal humans, and Bellona raised him for that, or tried to. She trained him to be self-reliant and fearless and she gave him a shield like her own, a shield against feeling. She did not know he was hiding behind that shield, because she did not realize she was hiding behind hers.

After hearing Draconas's story of Ven's mishap, Bellona had only one panicked thought—escape.

Escape the faire, escape Draconas.

She blamed him for the tragedy that had befallen Melisande and she did not trust him in regard to Ven. Bellona was the only human in the world who knew the truth about Draconas—that he was a dragon who had taken human form. He had told her the truth on the day Melisande died. He had told her because, he said, she had a right to know.

In those hard, early days, Bellona had often hoped that Draconas would come to take the burden of the dragon's son from her. Her feelings had changed. She would do all in her power to keep him away from Melisande's child.

She sold the remainder of her pelts at a loss to a happily astonished furrier and when he said he could not take them at that moment, but would need to find a vehicle to transport them, she threw her cart into the bargain. Anything to get rid of him.

She helped the man load, flinging the pelts into the cart in haste, and fidgeting with impatience while he carefully counted every coin twice before handing over the agreed-upon sum. She dismantled the tent and was packed up before he was halfway down the hill. Slinging the tent roll over one shoulder, she hurried into the woods to find Ven and take him home.

Day was drawing to a close as Bellona entered the forest. The abbey bells were ringing the call to Vespers, though that meant nothing to Bellona. She had been raised to worship the Mistress of Dragons, the woman who defended Bellona and her people from the dragons. Betrayed in that belief, Bellona had never sought another. For her, the bells rang the tenth hour, which meant she had two or three more hours of daylight left.

Searching the fringes of the woods, Bellona came across Ven's boot lying beneath a tree. Draconas had claimed he'd brought the boy into the woods to examine the wound. Thus far, it seemed he was telling the truth. Bellona saw traces of the boy's flight. He'd cut a wide swath through brush and fern. He must have been terrified.

"Poor kid," she said, surprising herself, for generally she spared sympathy for no one. She carried his boot with her.

Tracking him through the tangle of trees and undergrowth, she took care to move as stealthily as if she were tracking some wild beast. Instinct warned her not to call out his name. Like a wounded animal, he had crawled off to be alone. He might well run from her.

She came upon him lying curled in a ball on a pile of dead leaves. He was so pale and lay so still that fear smote her, lanced through her heart, robbed her of breath. She had to wait a moment for the sensation to pass before she could trust herself to examine him.

She touched his forehead and found his flesh warm. The pulse in his neck was strong. He was not dead. Worn out, he had fallen asleep.

Bellona reached down, roughly shook him.

"Ven, wake up!"

He slept so soundly, he didn't hear her. She flicked him hard on the cheek with her nails.

At the sharp, stinging pain, he woke up and sat up all in one movement, staring confusedly about.

His eyes found her and left her, searching for another. Seeing no one else, Ven looked back at her and his eyes flickered.

"I know what happened," she said, to spare him. "Does it hurt? Where the dog bit you?"

He shook his head.

She tossed his boot at him. "Put that on then."

She stood over him, her arms crossed, her expression stern. She was nervous, ill at ease. The snap of a twig made her jump.

"Hurry up," she said impatiently, as Ven fumbled at the boot, tugging it over his clawed foot.

"I won't go back," Ven stated defiantly, meaning the faire.

"No," she said. "Neither will I. We're going home."

He looked up at her, surprised. "But the furs . . ."

"I've sold them. We didn't make much, but we'll get by. Damn it, I told you to hurry!"

She seized hold of him by his arm and dragged him to his feet. She started to give him a tug, to pull him along. To her astonishment, he jerked his arm free and drew back from her when she tried again to take hold of him.

"Why am I like this?" he cried, a cry that came from somewhere deep inside him, ripping and tearing through him. He was bleeding inside, his face ghastly white, his eyes pale blue with pure flame. "Who made me like this?"

"You wouldn't understand," Bellona said brutally. She didn't understand. How could she explain it to him? "I'll tell you when you're older—"

He leapt to his feet, rushed past her, limping through the brush.

The muscles of his injured leg had stiffened, were bruised and sore, and Bellona easily caught up with him.

"Very well," she said coldly, "if you want—"

He came to a stop, looked up at her. "I changed my mind. I don't want anything. Except to go home."

He held out his hand.

Fear and anxiety softened her. Taking his hand, she looked down at him and saw how small he was and how lonely and forlorn.

"Me, too," she said simply.

7

BELLONA STEERED CLEAR OF THE FAIREGROUNDS, made a wide detour around them. She did not enter the city of Fairfield, but avoided that, too, following a circuitous path that led south along the river. They traveled several furlongs away from the city before Bellona deemed it safe to return to the road. She was growing increasingly concerned over Ven. He made no complaint and he managed to keep up the swift pace she set, but his limp was worse. The bruised leg was obviously causing him pain.

Bellona glanced to the west, to the sun sinking gently into a feathery cloud bank of purple and saffron. Night would be on them soon. She toyed with the idea of halting for Ven's sake, but she wanted to put as much distance between Ven and Draconas as possible. They could walk another couple of miles before darkness forced them to make camp. Ven could keep going a little longer. After all, Bellona reasoned, he'd have all the night to rest his leg.

The two of them had the road to themselves. What few travelers they met were all heading toward the city, making haste, so as not to be benighted in the wilderness. Bellona had no fears on that score. Danger lay in the hot and noisy city, not in the quiet, cool darkness. When the last vestige of the sun's afterglow faded from the heavens and the evening star shone bright against blue-black, Bellona began to search for a place to camp. The night was hot, oppressive. There would be rain before morning.

The highway dipped down a steep hill, then dove into a thick woods. She could not see the river that was off to her left, but she could hear it.

"We will camp beside the riverbank," she announced to Ven.

"Excuse me," came a woman's voice, panting from exertion, quite close to them. "But aren't you the boy from the faire?"

Startled, Bellona whipped around, her hand on her sword's hilt. She had kept close watch on the road and she could have sworn that there had been no one either ahead of them or behind them.

She faced a holy woman dressed in the clothing of her faith—plain black robes, a black wimple that hugged her plump face. She had been running, which perhaps explained why Bellona had not seen her.

Hand on her breast, gasping, the nun added, "You are swift walkers. I have nearly run my legs off, catching up to you. I was concerned about the boy, you see."

Her face and her hands were all that were visible of her in the darkness, a pale blur in the lambent light. She was a stout woman and her broad bosom heaved from her exertions.

Bellona turned away. "No need. He is fine, as you see. Come along, Ven."

Ven did as he was told, but he turned his head to stare at the holy sister over his shoulder.

The sister did not take the hint. She hastened after them, her wimple billowing out behind her in the freshening breeze.

"I saw that ill-favored man carry him off and I was very worried. I thank God that the boy is safe, though I see he is limping. After the mauling he took, I am surprised he can

walk at all. I have some knowledge of the healing arts. Why
don't you let me examine his wound? We don't want it to
putrefy."

The sister did not say this all at once. After each sentence,
she was forced to catch breath enough for the next. Bellona
quickened her pace. By the way she was wheezing, the stout
sister wouldn't be able to keep up with them for long.

The sister proved dogged, persistent. She waddled on,
prattling away. "There is a shrine just ahead. A clear spring
runs there. Its waters are in truth the tears of the blessed
Saint—"

Cloaked and muffled figures wielding cudgels sprung up
out of a ditch.

The nun gasped then shrieked. "Help! Merciful saints defend us!"

A blow struck Bellona on the back of her head. Pain
blazed yellow behind her eyes. She staggered, her hand
clutching at her sword.

Her blurred eyes found Ven. "Run!" she gasped. She
started to draw her blade. Another blow across her shoulders
drove her to her knees. A blow on her right arm cracked it
and she cried out in pain and anger.

The men aimed first at Bellona's head and her sword arm;
then, when she was dizzy and weak, they hit any part of her
they could reach. They beat her even after she was down,
clubbing her about the head and shoulders and savagely
kicking her.

Ven heard the sister scream and Bellona curse and then
darkness took shape and form and the stench of sweat and
filth. A man seized hold of him and flung him out of the way
to get at Bellona.

The holy sister caught Ven as he stumbled and dragged
him across the road, away from the battle. She held him fast,
pressed against her ample form, and he could feel her body
tense and quivering. He watched them beat Bellona senseless, beat her into the ground. They stopped only when she
lay still and had ceased to moan.

Another man emerged from the darkness. He was a huge

man, with rounded, hulking shoulders and an overhanging brow. He was the biggest man Ven had ever seen, even counting the so-called giant posturing in the freak show at the faire. The huge man had taken no part in the attack. He eyed Ven as he walked over to Bellona's limp and bloodied body. Only then did he wrench his gaze away from Ven. The man poked at Bellona with the toe of his boot.

"Find the money," he ordered his men.

A last kick, to make certain she wasn't shamming, and two of the thieves rolled Bellona over. One thrust his hand inside the breast of her wool tunic.

"You will burn in the fires of hell for this," cried the holy sister, her voice shrill. She kept fast hold of Ven.

The huge robber barely glanced at her. "I was hell-bound from birth, Sister. This only greases my way."

His cohort was still fumbling about beneath Bellona's tunic.

"I can't find it," he muttered.

"He's not looking. He's having too much fun playing with her boobies," said another with a snigger.

"I don't plan to stay here all night watching you getting your jollies, Watt," said the big man in acid tones. "Be quick, before someone comes."

Clouds blotted out the starlight and thunder drowned their voices. Lightning flared across the sky and Ven reached out with his mind and took hold of it. The bolt crackled and sizzled in his grasp, blazed in his vision, so that he was blind and dazzled. He flung the lightning at the man who was mauling Bellona.

The bolt struck the man, sent him flying backward. He landed heavily on the road, his body jerking and twitching. The smell of burnt flesh brought Ven fierce joy.

"I was right, Grald," said the holy sister. The nun's hands, resting on his shoulders, tightened. "He is the dragon's son."

Draconas crouched beneath the trees, the river at his back, the boy and the nun before him, so close that Draconas could have reached out his hand to touch them. Draconas remained hidden in the darkness, still and unmoving, barely breathing, watching and waiting.

Having followed the trail of the cart, Draconas had ended up back at the fairegrounds standing in front of the cart and its load of furs and swearing. By the time he realized that he'd been an idiot, Bellona and Ven had a long head start. Draconas set off along the southern road. He gave their descriptions to travelers heading into the city, and received confirmation that the two were ahead of him and not that far ahead, either. Although he had raced after them with his dragon strength and speed, he had arrived too late to save Bellona. He could try to save the boy.

Draconas had been about to make his move when Grald stepped out of the darkness onto the highway. Draconas hunkered down, forced to rethink his plans.

Grald was a dragon in human form, much like Draconas. The two had met before in a bone-crunching contest that had left Draconas half-dead. Draconas had been looking forward to the day when they would meet again, for now that he knew Grald for what he was, Draconas knew how to fight him. Unfortunately, this was neither the time nor the place for two dragons to battle.

Draconas was still considering what to do when Ven unleashed his thunderbolt and the holy sister made her pronouncement.

"The robbery was a ruse," Draconas realized. "You had to be certain this child was the right child and so, as a little experiment, you beat to death the only mother he's ever known right in front of his eyes. Well, you have your answer."

He glanced at the smoldering remains of the "thief." The stink of burning hair and flesh was strong in his nostrils.

Ven twisted his head to look up at the holy sister.

She carressed Ven's shoulders and said in soft and urgent tones, "Come with me, now, child. There is nothing more you can do for your mother except to pray for the repose of her soul. Come away with me. I will take you to a place of safety."

"She's *not* my mother," Ven said harshly. He shook himself free of the nun's hands and backed away from her.

"G'away," he ordered, his voice thick and half-choked. He waved his hand. "Leave me alone."

He limped over to where Bellona lay in the dirt. He stared down at her and then awkwardly knelt beside her, and put his hand out to touch her.

"My child—" the holy sister began in dulcet tones.

"Someone's coming," warned Grald, his head jerking around to peer down the starlit road. "I hear horses. We don't have time to coddle the boy. Step aside. All of you."

Folding her hands in her habit, the holy sister moved a safe distance away, as did the remainder of the "thieves." Grald stretched out his hands. Thin filaments of light sprang from his ten fingers and extended toward the boy. Twining and twisting together, the filaments of light formed a web— a burning and biting web meant to jangle the boy's nerves, incapacitate and paralyze him.

Draconas moved. Bounding onto the road, he thrust his staff into the magical net, caught hold of it, and jerked it out of Grald's astonished grasp. Draconas twirled the net in a flaming arc, then cast it back at Grald. Amazed by this unexpected interference, the dragon had no time to evade it. The glowing, entwined filaments settled over him, and Grald's human form collapsed to the ground, screaming and writhing.

The holy sister opened her mouth. Draconas had no idea what she was about to say, but feared it must be some sort of magic. He brought the staff around and gave her a clip on the side of the head. The holy sister toppled over in a heap of black.

The last remaining attacker leapt on Draconas's back, sought to throttle him. Draconas flipped the man over his head. He landed heavily on the road, groaning in pain. Draconas kicked him in the temple.

"That's for Bellona," he said grimly.

He could hear the approaching riders—men, laughing and talking. They were in no hurry, riding along at a sedate clip, but coming nearer. He couldn't be caught here with a bloody body, an unconscious nun, a burnt thief, and a boy that was half-dragon.

Ven had not moved from Bellona's side. He had not even looked around.

"You have to come with me," said Draconas. Reaching down, he took firm hold of the boy's hand. "Now."

Ven looked up at him and recognition dawned.

"What about Bellona?" he said.

Draconas cast the body a glance. "I'm sorry. There's nothing I can do."

"I'll stay with her," said Ven, hunkering down in the dirt.

Draconas didn't have time to argue. He scooped up what he thought was a corpse in his arms, only to feel Bellona shudder in pain when he lifted her.

"Keep close," he ordered Ven, "and don't make a sound."

The boy nodded. Draconas slipped back into the woods and hid in the brush. Bellona began to moan and he spoke a whispered word of magic that sent her into a deep slumber. Ven put one hand protectively on Bellona's shoulder and took his place alongside Draconas.

Two knights, well armed, and accompanied by well-armed retainers, cantered along the road. One of the horses whinnied and shied at the body lying in the road. Dismounting, their swords in hand, the knights went immediately to the aid of the nun, exclaiming in angry tones at footpads who would dare harm a holy sister.

"What do you make of it?" asked one, scratching his chin, as his servant tried to revive the holy sister.

"Thieves fall out," answered his friend. "They attacked the nun, robbed her, then began fighting over the spoils."

"But this one's burnt to a cinder, my lord," said the servant, awed.

"Witness God's wrath," intoned the knight sternly. "And let it be a lesson to you."

"This bastard's still breathing, my lord," reported one of the retainers, bending over Grald.

"He's a big brute," commented the knight. "We'll have to

build an extra-strong gallows to hold him. Bind him fast, Reynard, and keep your sword at his throat."

Hidden among the trees, Draconas made a slight gesture at a field that could be seen from the road. One of the retainers turned his head, looked in that direction.

Shadowy figures could be seen haring over the freshly plowed earth, running for their lives.

"My lord! There, in the field! Some of the rascals, trying to escape!"

"By holy Saint Dunstan, this promises to be a more exciting evening than we had planned," cried one of the knights, leaping on his horse and galloping off in pursuit of the will-o'-the-wisp of Draconas's magic. The other knight followed after him. The servants roused the groggy nun as the soldiers bound Grald with bowstrings, and Draconas breathed an inward sigh of relief.

He would have liked to settle his score with Grald and maybe even unmask the dragon. Another time, however, when there weren't humans watching and a half-dragon child on his hands. Draconas did gain some amusement out of the thought of Grald waking to find himself in a dungeon, awaiting the hangman's noose. He'd find a way out, of course. With his magic, Grald could walk through the walls, leaving the bewildered humans to scratch their heads, none the wiser. Still, it would put the dragon to no small amount of trouble, Draconas reflected with satisfaction. And by the time Grald finagled his way out of jail, Bellona and Ven would be safely away.

The servants were preoccupied with the holy sister. The soldiers laughingly discussed what to do with the thief's remains, suggested making him crow bait. Draconas nodded to the boy, who rose to his feet. Quietly, stealthily, they left their hiding place and crept deeper into the forest, heading for the river.

Draconas and Ven crossed over the river on a narrow bridge leading to a sheep pasture. In the starlit distance, a grove of trees was a dark mass against a paler background of grassland. Draconas headed for the grove and, once sheltered beneath thick branches, he deemed it safe to stop. He eased Bellona onto a bed of dead leaves.

"Will she be all right?" Ven asked.

"She's not dead," Draconas replied cautiously. "Which is more than I expected. Her leather helm saved her from a cracked skull. I need water. Go fill this." He handed Ven his water skin. "We need to keep her warm. Can you build a fire?"

Ven nodded, not wasting time with words. He fetched the water, then left to search for dry wood. Draconas took advantage of the boy's absence to examine Bellona's wounds. He was relieved to discover they were not as serious as they had first appeared. Once a human has started down the road to death, not even his dragon magic could save her. He could not fully mend her broken bones, but he could splint the arm, ease her pain, stanch the bleeding, and alleviate shock. He had Bellona resting comfortably by the time Ven returned with an armload of wood. The boy tended to business before asking any more questions. Only when the fire snapped and crackled, and Draconas could feel the warmth of the blaze, did Ven come over to Bellona.

Draconas washed the blood from her face. A faint flush of life returned to her pallid skin. She ceased to moan and her breathing evened out.

"She is a strong woman," said Draconas. "That was a horrific beating she took, but all she has is a broken arm and a couple of broken ribs."

"The thieves couldn't find the money," Ven said as if he felt he needed to provide explanation. "They looked in the wrong place."

Draconas glanced at the boy. "You don't have to pretend for me, Ven. I saw the attack. Both attacks," he added pointedly.

"I don't know what you mean." Ven turned away, and walked to the fire. Crouching down, he poked at the glowing wood with a stick to stir up the blaze. "They were thieves."

Draconas shrugged. So that was the game.

"I heard Bellona call you 'Ven,'" Draconas said in friendly tones, to put the boy at ease. "That's an unusual name, one I've never heard before. What does it mean?"

"It's short for Vengeance," the boy said offhandedly.

Draconas sat back on his heels, surprised and not surprised. What a dreadful burden, he thought. Still, he supposed he could understand.

"The best cure for Bellona is sleep," Draconas said briskly. "You must be hungry. I have food in my pack."

Ven shook his head. Squatting on his beast's legs, he continued to play with the fire. He did not look at Draconas or at Bellona. He kept his gaze fixed on the flames.

"Are you tired?" Draconas asked. "Ready for sleep?"

Again, Ven shook his head.

"Good," said Draconas pleasantly, easing his back against a tree trunk. "That gives us a chance to talk."

Now Ven looked at him, peering out warily from beneath a mass of lank, fair hair. He frowned. "I don't want to talk."

"But I do," said Draconas. "We need to talk about what happened back there on the road. About why you killed that man."

Ven poked at the fire. Sparks flared, drifted upward with the smoke. "I didn't kill anyone," he said in calm, matter-of-fact tones. "How could I?"

"Like this." Draconas seized a bolt of lightning and, taking careful aim, threw it at Ven.

The bolt struck the ground right next to the boy. The blast bowled him over. The flaring light blinded him. The white-hot heat singed all the hair off his arm.

Shocked, burnt, and dazed, Ven lay on his back, gasping and panting.

"You can lie to humans, Ven," said Draconas. "You have to lie to them, in order to survive. You can try lying to me, though I'll tell you now it won't work. Never lie to yourself. You killed that man and you know it."

Ven said nothing.

"I'm not saying he didn't deserve to die," Draconas continued. "But you killed for the wrong reason. You killed out of fury, out of rage. You killed because you lost control. You killed because it felt good to kill."

Ven sat up slowly, nursing his burnt arm.

"Dragons kill for one reason, Ven. Dragons kill to survive. And, even then, we don't kill humans."

Ven stood up, tossed his stick into the fire.

"Where are you going?" Draconas demanded.

"My arm hurts. I'm going to put cold water on it." Ven walked off, heading back toward the river.

"You heard the holy sister say that, didn't you?" Draconas told the boy's back. "You heard her call you 'the dragon's son.' "

Ven paused, but he didn't turn around. "I didn't hear her say anything."

He limped away, favoring his injured leg. Draconas watched him, his dragon vision seeing the red warmth of the human part of the boy, following him with his gaze to the riverbank. Ven squatted at the water's edge, dunked his arm into the swift current and let the chill water flow over the wound, easing the pain.

Draconas could imagine the pain burning inside Ven. Nothing could ease that. Except maybe telling yourself it wasn't there.

Ven lingered beside the river a long time. He kept glancing up the hill toward the grove of trees. Perhaps he was hoping Draconas would go away.

Draconas stayed put and eventually Ven had to come back. He had his excuse ready. "I'm tired. I'm going to sleep."

"I have to talk with you about this, Ven. If I don't, your father will. He'll never give up looking for you. Either he or his people will find you and next time I might not be there to help. Next time they might kill Bellona."

Ven circled around to the opposite side of the fire, as far from Draconas as he could manage. The child flung himself down, curled up in a ball, his beast's legs drawn up to his chin. He hugged his arms around him, closed his eyes.

"Ignore it, then," said Draconas, rising to his feet. "Maybe the fear will go away. I guess I can't blame you for trying."

He shook out a blanket from his bedroll, draped it over the boy's thin shoulders, tucked it around the dragon-scaled legs.

"When you're ready to face the truth, go to your mother's tomb. I will meet you there and I will tell you the story."

Draconas picked up his staff. "I have to leave now. So long as I'm here, I put you in danger. It's doubtful Bellona will remember the attack. You can tell her what you want and she'll believe you. Rest easy. I'll keep watch from a distance. No further harm will befall you—this night, at least."

Ven did not move. His breathing was soft and even, his cheeks flushed, his hair tousled. He might truly be asleep.

With a shrug and a sigh, Draconas left the grove, and struck out across the open fields.

Ven waited until the sound of the man's footfalls had ended, then cautiously opened his eyes a slit and peered around to make certain that the man was truly gone. He was alone with Bellona. The fire was dying.

Throwing off the blanket, Ven tossed on more wood. He went to check on Bellona. Laying his small hand on her forehead, he felt it cool and damp. She was deep in sleep.

He thought he would go back down to the river, to soak his arm, which burned and stung. As he walked to the edge of the grove of trees, movement caught his eye and he froze in the shadows.

Draconas stood in the center of the field. As Ven watched, the man lifted up his arms to the night and the sparkling firmament reached out its hands to him. Wings, thin and delicate, so that the starlight shone through them, spread out from his human arms. Scales, shining red, overspread his human body, obliterated it. A long neck, graceful, curving, stretched up to the sky. A head with eyes of flame lifted its gaze to the stars. Catching hold of him, the stars pulled him up into the heavens.

The dragon sprang off the earth and took to the skies. Ven followed its flight, watching the dragon soar higher and higher, until his tears washed it away and all he could see was a blur of cold, white starlight.

He stumbled back to his bed. Stuffing the blanket into his mouth, so that no sound should wake Bellona, the dragon's son gave way to his fear. The blanket muffled his choked and aching sobs.

8

DRACONAS KEPT WATCH FROM THE SKIES UNTIL ven and Bellona reached their isolated forest home in safety. He waited tensely for Ven to use the magic again, but perhaps the incident had frightened the boy. Ven kept his colors dark. Once assured that they had not been discovered, he immediately set out for Idlyswylde, to see what could be done to safeguard Melisande's other son, her human son, born with royal blood in his veins.

The blood of kings and the blood of dragons.

Draconas had also kept circumspect watch over King Edward's son during the six years since his birth, traveling to Idlyswylde periodically to catch up on the local gossip concerning the child. Draconas customarily timed his visits to Idlyswylde to coincide with the anniversary of the boy's birth. The birthday of the prince was always celebrated with the month-long festivities due a royal child, and if there was news of young Prince Marcus, for good or for ill, Draconas was sure to hear it at this time.

He entered the prosperous city of Ramsgate-upon-the-Aston through the main gate, his thoughts going back to another time he'd entered that gate, proclaiming himself a "dragon hunter." Now he told people he was a traveling merchant, newly come from the Fairfield faire, breaking up the tedium of his journey by seeing the wonders of the capital city. Draconas strolled the streets, eyes and ears open. What he saw disturbed him. Or rather, what he didn't see.

No garlands put up in doorways to honor the birth of the prince. No bunting in the royal colors draped over balconies. He wondered if he'd got the date wrong—dragons have very little sense of the passage of time—and he stopped into an apothecary's shop to check the date. He was right. This month was the natal month of Prince Marcus, youngest son of King Edward and Queen Ermintrude, or, at least, youngest son of King Edward. Gossip chewed hungrily on the subject of the boy's mother.

Troubled, Draconas forewent visiting his usual haunts, instead going straight to an alehouse whose proximity to the castle made it popular with off-duty guardsmen. No matter what his dress, Draconas could, by a change in speech, air, and manner, become any sort of human he wanted. He could speak knowledgeably of war implements with a soldier, trade sea stories with a sailor, or converse with a seamstress on the best way to sew a feathered hem stitch.

He paid for his ale, then carried his mug to an out-of-the-way table in a corner and sat down alone. From the way he walked and his manner of speech, the patrons of the tavern took him for a former military man of the common sort. He was like themselves, wounded perhaps, unable to return to duty, pensioned off. They liked the fact that he did not try to butt in on their conversation and they rewarded him with nods before turning back to their talk.

One man, bored with his companions, picked up his mug and sauntered over to the table. "What parts do you hale from, friend?"

"Bramfell," Draconas answered, naming a town to the north. He answered a few polite questions regarding his home, but the soldier wasn't really interested, and Draconas was able to end that topic and glide with ease onto the next.

"I came to Ramsgate on family business and to see the festivities for the young prince's birthday. But I must have mistaken the month, for I see no signs of a celebration."

The guardsman took a pull at his ale. The men standing at the bar ceased their talk and exchanged glances. One said he must return to duty and took his departure. Picking up their mugs, two others walked over to join Draconas.

"You do not have the date wrong," one said.

"It is the lad's birth month, but there will be no celebration," added his comrade.

"Not dead, is he?" asked Draconas, sipping at his ale.

"Maybe. Who knows?" said the first, with a shrug. "Naught's been seen or heard of the boy for nigh on six months now."

"Here, now, Robert, you know well that he was sent to visit his grandfather, the King of Weinmauer, and that the boy's living a fine life in the royal court there," argued his friend.

Robert grunted, watched the foam settle on his ale.

"So the boy's with his grandfather," Draconas remarked.

"Maybe," said Robert. "Maybe not."

"Watch your tongue, Robert Hale," warned his comrade.

"Now I'm curious. What is wrong?" asked Draconas. "Has there been murder done then? What?"

"Not murder," said Robert, taking a pull at his ale.

"You don't know anything," his friend told him.

"I know that servants talk," returned Robert in an ominous tone.

"And that's all it is. Talk. I'm leaving." His friend stood up. Taking his ale mug, he walked over to join another crowd of soldiers standing at the far end of the bar.

"You've about finished that," said Draconas, eyeing Robert's empty mug. "Let me buy you another."

"Naw, I've had enough," said Robert. He stared in silence out a mullioned window into the sunlit street, then said abruptly, "The lad was a good lad. He always had a pleasant word for a man. There's more than me wonders what's going on."

"What do the servants say?" Draconas asked, adding, "I do love a good gossip."

Robert turned his gaze to him. He was a sun-burnt veteran of about forty years; a big man, with long, curly black hair. His face was open and honest.

"The servants tell of a wing in the palace where no one's permitted to set foot and a room that's always kept locked."

"Ah, well, as your friend says, it's probably just talk," said Draconas. "I'll pay for the ale."

"I pay my own way," said Robert and tossed a coin onto the table. He rose to his feet, started to leave, then turned back. "Our king, God bless him, was never one for secrets. This one is eating him up inside. It's high time something was done."

He walked out the door and let it slam shut behind him.

Draconas continued drinking his ale, more for show than because he tasted it. He thought over Robert's words, assigned various meanings to them—most of them sinister—and pondered what to do.

His thoughts were driven clean out of his head by an enormous boom that shook the ground, the building, and the chair in which he was sitting. The blast rattled the walls and set a stack of crockery mugs clicking like chattering teeth. Draconas jumped, spilling his ale, and peered out the open window to see the approaching storm, which must be a terrible one.

No thunderclouds, as he'd expected. Blue sky and bright sunshine. He looked back to find the soldiers all grinning at his discomfiture.

Knowing that humans delight in thinking themselves superior, Draconas played up his shock and astonishment.

"What was that awful noise? I thought it was thunder!"

"That was our cannon," answered several soldiers proudly. "We have the best in the world. We can knock a dragon out of the skies."

Cannons. Draconas had seen these monstrosities before. Some were made of low-grade bronze and were so large and cumbersome and heavy that they had to be manufactured by bronze-smiths who cast the bells for cathedrals. Others were constructed of strips of iron welded together lengthwise and bound with iron hoops to keep the thing from blowing apart, which it usually did in any case. No matter what they were made of, cannons had to be mounted in one fixed location, generally on a castle wall. Shifting them about even a few inches required teams of sweating men, straining and hauling to manhandle the monster into position.

We can knock a dragon out of the skies. Draconas grinned inwardly at the thought. A dragon such as himself could do flip-flops in the sky overhead while the men were wrestling with the gun, then flap leisurely away by the time the iron beast was ready to fire a single shot.

Then another boom went off, causing him to flinch, in spite of himself.

"His Majesty is testing his new cannons and training the crews right now," said the soldier. "Just feel how she shakes the floor!"

"You can watch, if you've a mind," said another. "There's always a big crowd gathers when they fire off the guns."

"Perhaps I'll do that," said Draconas, using this as an excuse to leave. "I was hoping to visit an old comrade of mine at the castle. He used to serve there, seneschal to the king. Gunderson is his name. I trust he is well?"

"Gunderson has gone gray and his joints are stiffening up on him, but he is well. And he is still seneschal," was the answer.

"That's good to hear," said Draconas, privately thinking it was very bad to hear.

Gunderson had threatened to kill Draconas if he came around King Edward again. And Draconas knew from experience that Gunderson was a man of his word.

No help for it. Draconas had to find out why no one in Idlyswylde was celebrating the young prince's birthday.

Arriving outside the castle walls, Draconas found a large throng of idlers and gawkers gathered to watch the wonderful cannon exhibit its prowess. At each firing of the behemoth, the crowd would gasp and applaud in admiration. The cannon was mounted on the wall high above where he stood, but Draconas could still get a fairly good view. What he saw both amused and troubled him. Amused because, although Edward had obviously made advances in the design of the cannon and its use, he still had a long way to go before, as the soldier had boasted, it could knock a dragon out of the skies. Troubled because Draconas could see that, with very little more effort, Edward might actually achieve that goal.

The cannon was half again as long as a tall man. Its cold black elongated form stood out against the gray stone of the battlements. The cannon was made similar to ones Draconas had seen before—iron strips welded together, then bound with iron bands. This cannon used maybe twice the number of bands at the stress points, making it stronger and more powerful. It was the positioning of the gun, however, that gave Draconas cause for concern.

All other cannons Draconas had seen were set in a fixed position so that they fired a projectile straight ahead. With this cannon, an iron-reinforced wooden mount attached to pivots cast at the midpoint of the barrel allowed the cannon's muzzle to be winched up until it could fire straight into the sky. Steel arms, affixed to both sides of the mount—front and back—added stability to the rear of the cannon and helped absorb some of the recoil, while those in front supported the winches and pulleys that controlled the raising and lowering of the muzzle. The contraption had been built on a movable, circular platform. At a word from the commander, men operating the platform could turn the heavy cannon with relative ease, reposition it and change its angle of fire in a matter of seconds.

What Draconas found troubling was that Edward was obviously seriously and even obsessively pursuing the goal of using cannons to battle dragons.

I guess I can't blame him for hating us, Draconas reflected somberly. *After what we did to him. And he doesn't know the half of it.*

Draconas pushed his way through the spectators, who

oohed and aahed at every fiery belch, and went to try to bully, beg, or brazen his way into obtaining an audience with the king, all the while keeping a wary eye out for Gunderson.

This time of the year, the anniversary of his youngest son's birth, was always a difficult time for Edward King of Idlyswylde. He ordered the boy's birth month celebrated for the boy's sake, and made the ceremonies as merry as he could, although it required an effort on his part. For him, springtime was not a time to celebrate, but a time of mourning, regret, recrimination, and guilt. And now, added to that, this spring brought grief and fear. Opening his eyes this morning, Edward shut them again and wondered how he would find the strength to go on.

He did find the strength. He did go on. He had to. He had no choice. Life went on and especially the life of a king, for his life did not belong to him. His life belonged to his people. Edward found solace in his work and he spent most of the day engrossed in the complex business of running the kingdom. He supervised the firing of his newly designed cannon and took some grim pleasure in the fact that his innovative design was producing the desired results.

His pleasure was short-lived, however. Firing the cannon was expensive, both in shot and powder and manpower, not to mention making reparation to various shopowners who claimed that the reverberations from the gun had broken windows and cracked crockery. Edward could fire off only a few rounds, and then the gun was silenced. He had to go back to being a king and, more difficult, a father.

Queen Ermintrude knew better than anyone what this time of year meant to her husband. She offered him sympathy, but since she was partially the cause of his guilt, she knew that her sympathy brought him more pain than comfort. She had her own burden of grief and unhappiness to bear, made worse by the fact that it had to be kept concealed. No one must know the terrible secret hidden inside the royal palace. No one must suspect that anything was wrong. She had to smile. Her dimples had to flash as brightly as they had on past birthday celebrations for her youngest child. For even though Marcus was not her child by birth, he had become her child. Hers to love as she loved her own. Hers to weep over in the dark hours of the night when no one could see.

Her other three boys were away from home. Her eldest, Crown Prince Wilhelm, thirteen, was living in the court of his grandfather, the king of Weinmauer. The two younger boys had been sent off with their tutor for an extended holiday in the north of the kingdom. She was glad that they were not here, forced to participate in the lie, although their absence left an aching silence in the room when she and Edward were alone—each so very alone—together.

Ermintrude had dismissed the few women she kept about her, ordering her ladies-in-waiting to go enjoy this lovely late-spring day in the palace gardens. Seated in the solar near the window to gain the benefit of the sunlight for her needlework, she was silently wiping away the tears she had resolved not to cry, when she caught sight of Gunderson striding across the courtyard, heading for the palace. Ermintrude could not see his face from this angle, for she was looking down upon the top of his gray head, but she could tell by the rigid set of his shoulders and the swiftness of his walk that something was amiss.

Jabbing her needle into the fabric, Ermintrude hastened to the hall in order to intercept Gunderson before he could reach the king. He was too quick for her, however. She just missed him. He was already stomping up the stairs that led to the king's private chamber.

Ermintrude was about to call out to him, then thought better of it. She followed after him, moving as swiftly as she could. Since she was inclined to plumpness and much encumbered by her heavy, voluminous, hooped skirt, corset, chemise, and petticoats, climbing the stairs required time, care, and a stop on the landing to catch her breath. She reached Edward's rooms well after Gunderson had been admitted and was talking in urgent tones to the king.

The seneschal had left the door ajar, and Ermintrude lingered outside, waiting for a propitious time to enter. From her vantage point, she could see that Edward's careworn face had gone quite grim. She had not followed Gunderson with the intention of eavesdropping, but she couldn't very well barge in on the conversation now, and she was determined to find out what was going on, for Edward's sake. She waited just outside the open door, listening in dread to hear what terrible thing had happened. Since Gunderson had a good, strong carrying voice and Edward's was deep and resonant, she could not help but overhear them.

"—threatens to cause trouble, Your Majesty."

"I don't care, Gunderson," said Edward harshly. "I will not see him. Send him away."

"I tried that. He refuses to leave. He says he will camp outside the walls, day and night, until you admit him. And he says he will start talking," Gunderson added dourly.

"Then have him arrested and escorted to the border by armed guards. Tell him if he dares to return, he does so on pain of death."

Ermintrude knew all now, or guessed it.

"On the contrary, Gunderson," she said, sweeping into the room with a defiant rustle of petticoats, "tell him that we will see him. Bring him here, to His Majesty's chamber. Or to my own, if His Majesty persists in his refusal."

Edward frowned. "My dear, this does not concern you—"

"But it does," Ermintrude said, calmly refuting him. "You speak of Draconas, don't you, Gunderson?"

The seneschal made no response, other than a noncommittal bow, but Ermintrude didn't need his response.

"I was not spying on you, so don't give me that look, Edward. I guessed who it was the moment I saw Gunderson come up here. If you must know, Husband," Ermintrude continued, "I've been hoping Draconas would come."

"You are mad," said Edward, turning away.

"I am not mad," Ermintrude cried, her voice shaking, "but I am nearly driven so. He might be able to help, Edward. He might!"

Gunderson glowered and Edward shook his head emphatically and made an impatient gesture of dismissal. "Go back to your women, my dear—"

Ermintrude held her ground, which, considering the amount of room her hooped skirts took up, was considerable.

"We owe it to the child, Edward," she said emphatically. "We owe it to him to find out if there is anything that can be done."

"And what makes you think Draconas knows any more than I do—his father?" Edward demanded angrily.

"I'm not sure," Ermintrude faltered. She laid her hand on her breast. "But I have a feeling here, in my heart. Call it a woman's instinct, if you will, but please see Draconas, Edward. See him and tell him . . . tell him the truth."

She drew near him, stretched out her hands in supplication. "For the boy's sake, Edward. For the sake of our son."

He looked at her and for a moment his anger still burned. She clasped her hands over his, held them fast, and looked into his eyes. His anger, which was more truly fear than rage, could not withstand her loving gaze. He bowed his head.

"You always say 'our' son," he murmured brokenly.

"And so he is, Edward," whispered Ermintrude, tears sliding down her cheeks. "And so he is and always will be."

"Tell Draconas we will see him, Gunderson," said Edward.

Gunderson hesitated, not wanting this, disapproving it. He longed to urge the king to follow through on his first command and have the "dragon hunter" marched to the border in chains. Gunderson looked pleadingly at his king, at the man who was so much more to him than king, dearer than son.

Six years ago, Edward had been a youthful king in his thirties; open, earnest, handsome, with hazel eyes and a charming smile. Then Draconas had entered Edward's life and carried him away to a strange kingdom and a terrible adventure, that had left him with a son born of death.

Now Gunderson saw Edward stagger beneath the heavy burden of this terrible secret. Gunderson realized then that unless something changed for the better, the burden would crush the king. He would fall beneath it and with it, the kingdom.

Shaking his head, Gunderson headed for the door.

"Gunderson," called Ermintrude.

"Your Majesty?" He turned.

"Do not bring Draconas here," she said. "Bring him to the room."

Gunderson glanced at the king.

Edward closed his eyes. A spasm of pain constricted his face. When he spoke, it was without a voice. His lips formed the words. "Do it."

"Yes, Your Majesty."

Sighing deeply, his heart full to bursting, Gunderson left to obey his king's command.

9

HIS EYES WERE PRISMS, HIS MIND A FRACTURED rainbow.

All day, all night, Marcus gazed in rapt fascination on colors unimaginable. If such colors existed in the world at all, they came as unexpectedly as the rainbow and faded away before anyone could capture them. Anyone except Marcus. He held the colors trapped in his mind, admired them, played with them, danced among them. The sun shone through the perpetual stained glass of his fancy by day. The stars shone through a night that was bright and vibrant with moon glow and white fire.

People were nothing, food was nothing, sleep was nothing. He was nothing. The colors were all and everything.

As beautiful and amazing as the colors were, they could be horrifying, too. There was something dreadful in the colors, something alien and bestial and terrifying that wanted him, that was trying to find him, and he knew that he didn't want to be found. He would hide himself amid the colors and they would cluster thick around him and the fear would go away, leaving him again at peace to play and dance along the rainbow.

He had once seen a face, a woman's face, made out of the colors. The face looked upon him with such love and understanding that he reached out his hand to touch hers and another hand, like his, reached out of the colors to him.

The face splintered. Sharp fragments of pain lanced his mind, so that the colors could not protect him. Everything went dark—a cool and soothing darkness. For a long time, he'd been afraid to leave. And then a mote of vibrant orange flitted into this darkness, and with it new-leaf green and goldfinch yellow, and the colors enticed him out once again to play. He did not see the face or the hand again.

He sometimes heard voices from the world outside, a world that was gray and colorless compared with his world. He had once listened to the voices, but now they grew more remote and distant every day. He had long ago forgotten what it was to touch an object, to taste food, or smell a flower. His mind brought to him the only world he wanted, the only world in which he was happy.

He looked on the vibrant, sparkling, dazzling colors and he knew that one day, very soon, he would dissolve into a drop of rainbow brilliance and shine brightly among them for a single breathless moment, and then fade away forever.

"He sits like that," said Ermintrude, her voice choked with pain. "For hours on end. Not moving. Just staring at nothing."

"Most of the time, Marcus is quiet and docile, as he is now," added Edward. "But sometimes he grows violent and flings himself about and screams in terror. If anyone tries to touch him, he goes berserk. He has hurt himself, on more than one occasion, and hurt others in his wild frenzies."

"He doesn't mean to," Ermintrude said defensively. "He doesn't know what he's doing, poor lamb. Once, he tried to climb through a stone wall. His little hands were bruised and bleeding and he broke several toes kicking at it. Two strong manservants had to restrain him—"

"—and they came out of it looking as if they'd been battling wolves," finished Edward grimly. "What else could we do but lock the child up? We feared one day he might throw himself off the parapet or seriously injure someone and then we could not keep the matter quiet."

"He will no longer eat, Draconas," said Ermintrude. "We have been feeding him as one would feed a babe, and he used to take food willingly, though it was plain he had no care what he was given, and would have eaten sawdust as readily as chocolate. But now, he turns his head away or spits it out. He grows thinner every day and I fear . . . I fear . . ."

She could say no more, but clasped tight hold of Edward's hand. Her tears fell silently, unchecked, down her cheeks.

"Marcus will die of starvation," said Edward bluntly. "Unless we can find some way to reach him."

Draconas looked through a small window set in the heavy wooden door to see a six-year-old boy, sitting on a stool in the middle of the turret room, staring at nothing. His too-thin arms rested on spindly legs. His hands hung flaccid. He sat quite still. The only part of him that moved was his wide-open eyes, and they roved constantly, shifting from one point to another, bright with awe and wonder. He had bruises on his wrists. His caretaker was forced to bind his hands in order to feed him.

The boy was kept as clean as they could manage, for he took no care of himself. The woman who had nursed him as a child tended to his needs. She remained in the room with him constantly, watching over him, cleaning him and feeding him, making certain he did not hurt himself when the fits of violence came over him.

"Those have been less frequent," Edward said. "We used to thank God for that, but now I consider it an ominous sign. I fear he is slipping away from us and we can do nothing to stop him."

"When did this lunacy begin?" Draconas asked.

Edward winced at the word. He looked to his wife to answer.

"Marcus was a normal child, or at least almost normal, up until the age of five," said Ermintrude, resolutely wiping away her tears.

"What do you mean by 'almost normal'?"

"He would sometimes stop playing and stare at nothing for long periods of time, wearing a rapt smile, as if he were witness to some incredibly beautiful sight. He would say, 'Don't you see it, Mother? Don't you see the colors? How wonderful they are!' I would look, but all I would see would be sunlight on the stone floor or a sparrow on the window ledge. I would say I did see it, just to please him. I think he knew I was lying, though, for his smile would fade. He drifted in and out of this world and whatever world he sees inside his head, until the day came a month ago when something happened to him, something horrible."

"It was on his birthday," said Edward. "We wanted to make the day so happy. . . ."

"You don't know what this something was?" Draconas asked sharply.

Ermintrude shook her head. "He began to scream in terror and pain. He clutched at his head, tearing his hair out by the roots so that his scalp bled. Then he collapsed and was unconscious for many hours. When he came around, he appeared to have no idea where he was. He seemed to have left this world completely."

"Before that, was he happy?"

"Yes," Ermintrude answered, a little too promptly. "Marcus was always a quiet child, not rambunctious, like most boys his age. He didn't like the rough games his brothers played. He preferred to go off by himself."

"What about his brothers? How did they treat him?"

"They loved him as a little brother. They were kind to him and treated him well, but they had their own interests," said Edward. "They couldn't always have Marcus tagging along and, in truth, he didn't seem disappointed that he wasn't included."

Draconas noted that they both spoke of the boy in the past tense.

"People know he's your bastard, Edward," said Draconas bluntly. "Did adults or children tease him, taunt him?"

Edward's face darkened. His brows furrowed in a frown.

"No," said Ermintrude firmly. "No one would dare." She placed her hand on her husband's arm. "Marcus was my child from the moment I held him in my arms. I loved him as I loved my natural-born children."

Her tone faltered. "You seem to be implying that this is our fault, but I don't know what more we could have done! We don't understand what is happening to him. We thought you might."

Draconas peered again through the iron grate. Turning away, he shook his head. "I'm sorry. I didn't mean to blame you. You are, in truth, blameless. There is nothing you could have done differently. The dragon magic in his blood is the cause of this madness."

Edward glanced uncertainly at Ermintrude, as if he would say something, but feared it might pain her.

She smiled at him reassuringly and pressed his hand. "Speak freely, Ned. You do not hurt me. Especially if it can help our son."

Edward brought her hand to his lips, kissed her palm, and kept fast hold of her. "The boy's mother was not like this, Draconas, and you said the dragon magic was very strong in her."

"The magic manifests itself differently in males and in females, or at least so I believe," Draconas replied. "Do you remember that false monk who attacked us on the road to Bramfell?"

"The fellow with the wild look in his eye who pointed his finger at you and sent you flying halfway across the road. Yes, I remember," said Edward with an edge in his voice. "You passed it off, but I wondered at the time how he managed such a feat."

"If I had told you the truth then, Your Majesty, you would have thought *me* a raving lunatic. And, to be honest, I myself didn't know what was going on. What I know now, I've learned over the past few years. The dragon magic in women such as Melisande affects the woman only when she wields the magic and even then the effect is relatively mild. The magic acts like a fever in the blood, making the woman weak and sick for the moment, but the illness lasts only a short time. The women of Seth call it 'the blood bane.' In men, however, the effect of the dragon magic is much different, much more drastic, probably because men can use the magic to kill, whereas women cannot."

Edward glanced through the grate at his son. His expression grew troubled. "As I recall, that poor monk looked to have been beaten and half-starved."

"Yes, I wondered about that at the time," said Draconas. "Do you remember the baby smugglers?"

"The women disguised as nuns we saw carrying babies out of that cave? Yes, I remember," said Edward darkly.

"Melisande told us they were stealing away male babies born to the women who served the Mistress of Dragons—the women with the dragon magic in their blood. The dragon in Seth used the women with dragon magic to guard her and her kingdom. The male babies were taken away to be raised to use their magic in much the same way. Only the plans of the dragons went awry. The magic in the blood of human males drove them insane."

"But why mistreat the wretches?" Edward asked. "Especially if you've gone to all the trouble to steal them and raise them. For that reason alone, it seems to me you would take care of them."

"Unless you couldn't," said Draconas, struck by a new thought. "Unless circumstances forced you to . . ."

His voice trailed off. He stared through the grate at the child, who stared through his mind at wonders only he could see. Draconas made his decision.

"I can *try* to help him," he said, laying emphasis on the word. "I warn you that we may be too late. If you agree, I will take him with me this night."

"Why must you take him?" Ermintrude demanded.

Draconas shook his head. "You have to trust my judgment. I have to take him away from the palace, somewhere far away."

"No," said Ermintrude immediately and Edward spoke in the same breath, "No, I won't permit it."

Draconas shrugged. "Then you may as well measure him for his coffin."

Ermintrude moaned and Edward gave a slight gasp, but neither said a word.

Turning, Draconas left them holding onto each other outside their son's prison. He walked over to where Gunderson stood silent guard at the head of the spiral stairs leading up to the turret room.

Gunderson regarded him with enmity, his gnarled hand fiddling longingly with the hilt of his sword. The old seneschal would obviously have dearly loved to bury his blade deep between Draconas's shoulder blades.

Draconas didn't much blame him. He had given Marcus's unhappy parents a choice that was no choice. They had an agonizing decision to make.

"Wait, Draconas," called Edward.

Draconas waited.

"Where will you take him?" Edward asked bleakly. "What will you do with him?"

"Save him, I hope."

"How? What is this magic doing to him?" Ermintrude wrung her hands, helpless and bewildered. "If we understood, perhaps we could help him."

"I am the only person who can help him," said Draconas. "And I make no guarantees. He may die anyway."

Ermintrude covered her face with her hands. Edward put his arm around her. He said something to her, spoke to her quietly. She murmured brokenly, shook her head.

"If it was up to me," said Gunderson in a savage undertone, his single eye glittering, "I'd run you through the gut and let you die by inches, just like you're doing to them."

"If it was up to me," Draconas replied, "I'd let you."

"Very well," said Edward, his voice thick with unshed tears. "You can take him. How . . . What arrangements . . ."

"Dress him warmly," said Draconas, brisk and businesslike. "Dose him with wine laced with honey and poppy.

That will cause him to sleep. Fill a wagon with straw and put him in the wagon bed. He'll slumber through the journey."

"When he wakes, he'll be alone in a strange place," said Ermintrude, her voice quavering.

Draconas thought back to the child, his eyes shifting from one dazzlingly beautiful image to the next.

"He is already in a strange place," Draconas said. "He needs to find his way home."

They did as Draconas ordered. When night fell, Ermintrude dismissed the nursemaid—not an unusual procedure, she told Draconas. Ermintrude often stayed with Marcus at night, for sometimes, by holding him and rocking him, she was able to coax him out of his trancelike state. She swaddled him in blankets and, in the dead of night, when everyone in the palace was asleep, Edward smuggled Marcus out of his tower chamber. Edward carried his child through a series of secret passages that had been built hundreds of years back, when the castle had been little more than a fortress for a barbaric chieftain with many enemies. The tunnels led beneath the outer walls, emerged some distance from the palace. Here Gunderson waited with a horse and wagon.

Horses did not like Draconas, for they sensed the dragon in him. For Draconas, the feeling was mutual. He would have dispensed with the wagon, but he needed to take supplies with him, for the boy must be fed and clothed. Draconas and the horse eyed each other. The horse flattened its ears and snapped at him, but it did not immediately bolt and dash off, which he took for a good sign. At least driving a horse would be preferable to riding one.

Edward carried Marcus in his arms, with Ermintrude walking closely alongside, holding fast to the boy's limp hand. Edward placed the child gently into the wagon. Ermintrude fussed over the blankets, and piled the dry straw about him. Both parents leaned over the wagon's side to kiss the child's forehead.

The boy was drowsy, but still stirring. The poppy had yet

to take full effect. He even opened his eyes a little, stared about him.

"Go with God, son," Edward said softly.

Draconas, mounted on the wagon's seat, saw Gunderson's eye glint and his mouth twist. Clearly Gunderson considered that the child was going off with God's opposite. Both parents drew away from the wagon, holding tightly to each other.

"You'll bring him back to us," Ermintrude said. "Even if it's for . . . for . . . a proper burial." Her voice failed her on the last words, but Draconas understood.

"I will bring him back," he promised.

Gunderson had been holding the horse's head. He let loose. Draconas released the brake on the wagon's wheels, and gave the reins a flick. Horse and wagon moved slowly.

The night was clear and chill for spring, the sky iced over with stars. Draconas clucked to the horse and flicked the reins on its rump. The horse broke into a trot and they rattled off down the road. Draconas wanted to put distance between himself and the king, in case Edward changed his mind.

Glancing back to check on the boy, Draconas saw to his displeasure that the child was still awake. He realized irritably that if his parents had given him poppy juice, as he had instructed, either it wasn't enough or it wasn't having the desired effect.

He looked at Marcus. Marcus looked at Draconas.

And then Marcus did more than look. The boy walked straight into the lair of Draconas's dragon mind, a place no human had ever been, a place no human knew existed.

"I don't like you," said Marcus coldly and distinctly. "Go away. Leave me alone!"

10

A HUMAN ABLE TO ENTER THE MIND OF A DRAGON?

In the six hundred years Draconas had lived and worked among humans, he had never received such a shock. Fortunately Marcus drifted into a drugged sleep moments after he'd made his startling appearance, so that Draconas was once again alone with his thoughts—thoughts that were reeling and tumbling like a performance given by some motley fool.

A human able to enter the mind of a dragon.

At least, Draconas thought he could now guess what was going on in the boy's head.

Marcus was eavesdropping on dragons.

The "pretty colors" that Marcus could see were dragon conversations, dragon thoughts, dragon dreams. The magic in the child's blood had reacted in a way no one could have anticipated. It had given him the ability to slip into the dark shadows of a dragon's inner lair as an uninvited guest.

Marcus was a quiet, unobtrusive observer; the child sitting silent and unmoving on the dark staircase that overlooked the banquet hall, watching the adults dance and talk and laugh. Alone and noiseless, he roamed the streets of dragon consciousness, pausing beneath a window to hear what was going on inside a house or standing outside a door to listen. No dragon ever noticed him—tiny mite of a human child—for no dragon would have ever dreamed in a hundred years of slumber that such a catastrophe was even possible.

Draconas was bound by dragon law to contact Anora immediately and provide the Minister with this astounding news. He knew exactly what would happen when she found out. She would command him to bring the child to her and he would have no choice but to obey. If he refused, the Parliament would punish his defiance. They would take away his humanity and, much as he sometimes wearied of his human form and sometimes cursed it and sometimes even loathed it, he found that he could not bear the thought of losing it.

Nor could he bear the thought of shutting this child inside a prison. For that would be Marcus's fate. The dragons could not dare take a chance on letting this human roam the world when at any moment he might cease to be a passive eavesdropper and do what he had done to Draconas—enter a dragon's mind and tell it to "go away."

There was another consideration—Grald.

"His first instinct will be to slay the boy, for he is an immense threat. His second might be to leave him alive," Draconas reflected. "Make use of him. What more potent weapon could Grald use against us? Those wretched monks of his are not able to penetrate a dragon's mind. Not yet, at least. If Grald could capture this child and study how he is able to eavesdrop on dragons, then Grald could teach his monks to do the same. The damage such humans could do to us would be incalculable.

"And Grald will find out the truth about Marcus. Sooner or later, Grald will discover the boy wandering about *his* mind—if he hasn't already."

As the wagon rolled and bumped over the ground, Draconas glanced back over his shoulder at the slumbering child. The night was clear and crusted with stars and a sliver of moon. He could see the child by the lambent light of night, a gray light that washed away all color, so that the boy was corpse-white. He observed the boy's thin, pallid face; the wizened arms, the eyes that continued to rove even beneath fast-shut eyelids.

"Creating him was wrong," Draconas said softly, vehemently. "We dragons wronged his parents. We wronged this child. The most merciful thing I could do for all of us would be to stab the boy through the heart now, while he sleeps. And then I should find his half-dragon brother and do the same to him."

Draconas slid his knife out of the scabbard. He eyed it thoughtfully, eyed the sleeping boy.

"Merciful. But not logical." Draconas slid the knife back into its sheath. "Grald is not the only one who can make use of Melisande's sons. Nor"—he reflected—"is he the only one to break the laws of Dragonkind. I will not tell Anora. I will not tell Parliament. I will do this on my own."

Dragons are a solitary species. They live most of their long lives internally: thinking, dreaming, studying, pondering. When they converse with each other, they do so mentally, speaking a silent language woven of threads of colors. They live their lives in serene isolation, wanting no contact with even their own kind. All that wing rustling, scale twitching, claw clicking disrupts thought and scatters dreams. The worst years of a dragon's existence are those spent in breeding and raising its young, one reason there are so few dragons in the world.

Because dragons require solitude, they almost always choose to dwell in caves. On first leaving the nest, a young dragon roams the world until it discovers a cavern that suits its needs—one that is large, far from human lands, and far from the cave of another dragon. Once the dragon has taken over the cavern, the dragon begins working to build the defenses that serve to protect it during slumbers that may last a hundred years. Dragons do not defend themselves not against humans—puny creatures. Dragons defend themselves against other dragons. Although the Dragon War had ended centuries ago, the memory of those terrible days when dragon blood stained the rivers red lingers in dragon dreams and dragon memory. A lair's labyrinthine passages, illusions, traps, and secret passages are created to confuse and deter a dragon invader, not a human one. Dragons have little fear of humans. It is difficult to fear something one has seen evolve from pond scum.

A dragon's children are born in darkness and spend their early years in darkness, seeing no light but the light of the magic inside their own minds. When they are ready to leave the nest and enter the world, dragonlings must be introduced to sunlight gradually. They find the experience unpleasant and intensely painful at first, which perhaps explains a dragon's natural aversion to sunlight. Eventually, the dragons grow accustomed to the light, finding it useful for such pursuits as hunting. Given a choice, a dragon will always seek out darkness because he feels safer and more secure in the darkness. Knowing this, Draconas took the child with the dragon blood into darkness. He took the boy to a cave.

Draconas was at a disadvantage with Marcus. Draconas could understand and empathize with Ven, the dragon's son, who had been born with a dragon's grasp of the brilliant magic that flared across his mind. Ven was, in many ways, a younger version of Draconas, learning to wield the magic by playing with it, tossing it around as the human part of him tossed a ball. In Ven's case, the magic had turned lethal, but that was the fault of the human passions that raged inside him. Ven would have to learn how to control both the dragon magic and his human passions, a feat that was going to be difficult since he was refusing to admit to either.

With Marcus, Draconas had no idea how to break magic's grip on the human child, the magic that was opening doors that should never have been opened. Draconas guessed that Maristara and Grald had faced the same problem when they first started raising children whose blood burned with the dragon magic. The dragons must have raged to see potentially valuable commodities devolve into babbling lunatics, enthralled by the wondrous sights they could see in their minds, sights more beautiful and fascinating than anything in the bleakness and harshness of their daily lives. Like Marcus, these humans had entered the world of dragon magic and never returned. Many hundreds, perhaps thousands, must have suffered and died over the centuries as Grald and Maristara experimented with their human breeding programs, trying to find the perfect mix of dragon blood and human.

They had partially succeeded in those experiments. Grald had managed to keep alive some human males with dragon magic in their blood, raise them to adulthood. And now Draconas knew how that had been achieved and also why the "mad monks" looked and acted as they did.

"These men are half-starved because, like Marcus, they have no way of sustaining their bodies when they are in the grip of the magic." Draconas had developed a habit over the years of talking to himself, a remnant of his dragon days. Dragons talk to themselves all the time, preferring not to dilute their own thoughts by mixing them with the thoughts of others. "And these men are whipped and beaten because the dragons discovered that physical torment could jolt the humans back to reality . . . but pain brings the humans only partway, leaves them half in and half out of sanity.

"Such humans have little control over the magic and less control over themselves. Pain isn't the answer. Not the complete answer, anyway. Still, it's a start."

Draconas drew his knife, whetted it so that its point was razor sharp, and waited for the boy to wake from the drugged sleep.

As Marcus stirred and his eyes opened, Draconas observed the boy's reaction. The last the child knew he had been inside a small room, warmed by a fire, surrounded by people who loved him. He woke to find himself alone in a chill cave in the dark with a stranger. Any other human child would have been terrified. Marcus only seemed vaguely confused. He blinked once or twice, and then his gaze turned inward. He caught sight of some bright, drifting dragon dream and he focused on that. Reality held nothing for this child, not even fear.

"Because you're not in a cave," Draconas told him. "You are in a wondrous realm of light and beauty. Well, my boy, that is about to end."

Draconas took hold of the blankets that had been wrapped snugly and lovingly around the boy and roughly yanked them off. He opened the child's frilled shirt at the neck, shoved up the long sleeves, leaving his chest and arms exposed. Marcus's flesh shivered in the sudden chill. Marcus's mind never noticed.

"But you will notice this," Draconas promised.

He placed the knife's point on the child's arm and made a small cut, not deep, but enough to start the flow of blood.

Marcus winced. His gaze wavered. His attention cracked, and Draconas was able to walk inside the child's playroom.

A man stood in the little room, frowning down at him.

Marcus glowered and jumped up from the little chair where he sat by the fire.

"I told you to go away," Marcus shouted angrily. "Go away and leave me alone."

The man didn't go away. He stood there, looking around the room, making himself at home.

"Nice world you've got here, Marcus," the man commented.

He looked back at Marcus and his gaze was stern and severe. "But this is killing you and I want it to stop."

"Get out," Marcus ordered. "This is my room. I didn't invite you to come inside."

"I didn't invite you inside my mind, either," the man returned. "Yet in you walked, just as if you owned the place."

"You left the door open," said Marcus defensively.

"Maybe I did—" began the man, and then he paused, listening.

Marcus heard the noise, as well. He'd heard it before— the snuffling and snorting of a dragon trying to find a way inside his room. Marcus saw the colors of the man's mind darken.

"You are in danger, Marcus," said the man. "You have to come with me—now."

"Go away," said Marcus.

If he left the room, the dragon would grab him. He hunkered down in his chair, pretended the man was not there.

The man did not play fair, however. He waved his hand and a staff appeared. He moved the staff in an arc across Marcus's mind. Wherever the staff touched the radiant colors, those colors vanished. Marcus's chair slid out from under him, dumping him on the cold floor in a cold and ugly darkness. The man was the only color, the only light.

Marcus shivered. His arm stung and burned. His belly cramped with hunger. He wrapped his arms around his thin, frail form, hugged himself, and whimpered, "I want my mother."

"No, you don't," said the man. "If you did truly want her, you would have never left home."

Marcus was startled, wary. He knew this to be the truth, but no one else was supposed to know it. He'd spent a lifetime hiding it.

He shut his eyes, trying frantically to regain the beauty, but the man blocked it. The man was inside his head and he was more real in that inner darkness than he was in the cold darkness that chilled the child's flesh.

"I don't want her, because she doesn't want me." Marcus whimpered again. "Neither does my father. They both hate me."

"Why do they hate you?"

"Because people whisper about me."

"And when you come in here, the whispers stop."

"I don't hear them. I don't hear anything."

"Yes, you do. You hear voices. Not your parents' voices. Voices from inside. Voices like mine that speak in colors and pictures."

Marcus decided he didn't like this man and he backed away from him, retreated deeper into the darkness. He wasn't going to answer, but he felt a sudden sharp prick on his flesh.

"Maybe," he said to make the pain stop.

"What do the voices say?"

"I don't know. Most of the time I can't understand them."

"Most of the time?"

Marcus was silent. He hadn't meant to say that.

"When do you understand the voices?"

"I won't tell you."

Another prick, this one more painful.

"I saw a face," Marcus mumbled. "A woman's face. She was beautiful and she held out her hand to me and there was another hand, a child's hand. I thought this child might be someone I could play with. Someone who wouldn't laugh at me. I reached out to him, but he wasn't there."

"And then something happened. Something horrible. What was it?"

"Nothing happened. Go away. I don't want to talk to you."

"I'm not going away. And you are going to talk. What else did you see?"

Marcus searched for a way out. He ducked his head and turned and twisted, but everywhere he looked, there was the man. Again, the pricking sensation on his skin. Tears stung his eyes.

"I saw a dragon. A horrible dragon, like the one that attacked our city before I was born. The dragon was huge with eyes like fire and a voice like the cannon when it goes off and it scared me. The dragon told me that the woman was my real mother. The dragon would take me to her if I would tell him where I lived. Part of me wanted to, but another part of me was afraid, and I ran away."

"Did the dragon try to follow you?"

"Yes. I could hear its wings beating and it growled at me, but I kept running and running and the darkness hid me."

"The dragon is searching for you now. You hear it, don't you? It's getting very close. If it comes, I won't be able to protect you. Give me your hand, Marcus, and come walk with me in the sunshine. Quickly, before the dragon finds you."

Marcus shook his head and crawled and squirmed his way deeper into the darkness.

"If you come with me," the man bargained, "I'll give you this."

He swung the staff and the colors reappeared inside Marcus—sheets of wondrous colors that twisted and warped and billowed out. The man reached out and seized hold of the colors and molded them and shaped them. He opened his hand and there was a ball made of motes of fire held together by strands of rainbow. The man tossed the ball up into the air and when it fell, he caught it, tossed it up into the air again.

"I'll give you this toy, Marcus," said the man, "and I'll teach you how to play with it. But you must come with me."

Marcus stared at the wondrous ball. He had never imagined anything so enchanting. He'd often tried to touch the colors and even command them, but they darted away from his grasp, like the little green lizards that sunned themselves on the garden wall.

The man tossed the ball lightly from one hand to the other. He made the ball dance, caused it to hang suspended in the air between his two hands. Marcus watched, dazzled. The man asked him again to come out to walk in the sunshine. Marcus didn't answer and the man took the ball between his two hands and clapped and it disappeared.

"Bring it back," pleaded Marcus.

"Only if you come with me," said the man.

"I'm afraid," Marcus said, again whimpering. "You hurt me."

"Life hurts you, Marcus," said the man. "And it will keep on hurting you, for you are different from the rest. I can't stop the pain, but I can give you armor that will help to protect you and I can give you weapons that will help to defend you. You have to do the rest. You can either choose to live, Marcus—pain and all—or you can choose to die."

"Die?" repeated Marcus, his voice quavering.

"Yes, die," said the man, and he was very cool about it and uncaring. "For you are killing yourself. And you know it."

Marcus did know it. It was his secret, that he hugged to himself with gleeful pride.

"Your mother and father will be sorry when you're dead," the man continued. "They will feel the hurt you feel. You will punish them. It's their fault that you were ever born. . . ."

The secret had once seemed very bright and shiny, so clear that Marcus could see himself reflected in it. He could still see himself, but he could see behind him the empty darkness. Compared with the dazzling ball, the secret seemed shabby and dirty.

He imagined tossing the ball into the air, the fresh air, the spring air, the clean, bright air; not the fetid, twice-breathed air of the cell where he was both jailer and prisoner.

Marcus rose, trembling, to his feet. He could hear the dragon clawing at his cave and he was suddenly more afraid of the dragon than he was of life. He reached out his hand to the man and walked into the sun's bright glare.

The dragon swiped at him with a claw, but missed.

11

ONCE HE HAD BEEN ENTICED OUT OF HIS HIDING place, Marcus regained his physical health rapidly. He had gone without eating solid food for so long that at first he could keep down only gruel and water. His youth and resiliency stood him in good stead, however, and he was soon eating rabbit with a relish. His mental health took longer to recover.

Questioning the boy, Draconas found out that Marcus had been living in two separate worlds since about the age of four. At first, he traveled easily between the two realms, as do children who create an imaginary world with imaginary playmates. Then he started to become aware that the real world—the world of stone and brick, flesh and silk, perfume and steel—was not a very nice place. He began to notice the way people looked at him— some with pity, others with scorn. He had always heard the whispers. Now he understood them. Reality brought him pain. The magic in his mind brought him pleasure. Small wonder that he'd made the choice to abandon one in favor of the other.

Marcus did not tell Draconas his secrets immediately.

Draconas had to drain them out of him slowly and carefully, as one drains the infection from a putrid wound. All the while, Draconas was learning about the way the magic worked in this child's mind and possibly in the minds of all the others possessed by the dragon magic. He came to the realization that the minds of those humans who had inherited the magic were not completely human.

They were part dragon. A very small part, perhaps. Not like Ven, who was half-human, half-dragon. Perhaps he was not the first to be born like this. Although perhaps he was the first to have survived . . .

But that was all speculation and conjecture and Draconas didn't have time for either. He'd done what he could to warn Ven about using his magic and either his words had reached the dragon's son or the incident with the "thieves" had scared him because Ven no longer came near the magic. If Draconas could not contact Ven, then neither could his father, which was some comfort. Ven could not hide from himself forever. Hunger would drive him back into the world, whether he wanted to go or not. But for the moment though, the dragon's son was safe.

Melisande's other son was not.

"Scoop up the clay in your hand," Draconas told Marcus. "You're going to shape it—"

"You promised me I could play with the magic." Marcus sat back on his heels and regarded Draconas with a bold, defiant air.

"Go ahead," said Draconas, shrugging. "I'm not stopping you."

Marcus blinked at him. "But . . . you have to give me the magical ball. You have to make it for me. I can't do that myself."

"Yes, you can. That's what I'm trying to teach you. Pick up a handful of clay."

"I don't want to play with clay," Marcus said petulantly.

He and Draconas were relaxing on the bank of the river.

They had spent the morning fishing and splashing in the shallow water near the shore. Marcus cast a contemptuous glance at the wet, reddish gray silt beneath his grimy knees.

"I want to play with the magic."

"You can, but I'm not going to give it to you. From now on, you have to create it yourself."

"But I can't," Marcus complained. "I don't know how."

"You weren't born knowing how to walk, I suppose," observed Draconas.

"Maybe I was," Marcus returned, slyly grinning. "Mother says I am very precocious."

Draconas found himself smiling back—a rare occurrence for the walker, who hadn't had much to smile about lately.

"You're a good kid, you know that," Draconas said. "Or you would be, if your parents hadn't spoiled you rotten. And you're not that precocious. You crawled, like everyone else."

"I know my parents spoil me," said Marcus forthrightly. He shook the hair out of his eyes, gazed steadily at Draconas. "It's because they're afraid of me. I still remember the look on Mother's face when I described the colors and light and shapes I could see in my mind. I thought it was something everyone could do and then I looked at Mother and I saw fear in her eyes. I knew then that she was afraid of me."

"And that gave you power over her, didn't it?" said Draconas.

Marcus's cheeks reddened. "Yes." A glint of defiance returned to the hazel eyes. "But I needed that power. My older brothers are always doing such great and wonderful things. They make my parents proud. And I . . ." He pressed his lips together, fell silent.

"You frighten them."

Marcus nodded.

"And you think that they are being nice to you just because they are afraid of you."

Marcus lifted his eyes, looked at Draconas. "Aren't they?"

"They are afraid *for* you, Marcus. Not *of* you."

The river flowed sluggishly, the swift waters of the spring melt and runoff a distant memory. The early summer sun shone down though the leaves, casting shadows that shifted with the gentle breeze. The clay, covered over by a thin layer of water, was warm in the sunshine and sparkled with a faintly metallic sheen. Marcus gazed out over the river, in the direction that Draconas had told him was home. His eyes grew unfocused, but he wasn't seeing the magic in his head. He was seeing his parents, listening to *their* voices, maybe for the first time.

"I never thought of it that way," he admitted. "I guess you're right." He looked back at Draconas. "I hurt them a lot, didn't I?"

"Almost as much as they hurt you." Draconas reached out to shove back the bangs that kept falling into the boy's eyes.

Marcus was a comely child. He would be a handsome man, very much like his father, but lacking the light in Edward's hazel eyes. Marcus's hazel eyes would always be haunted by the shadows of his little room.

"You'll be home soon and you and your parents can all start fresh." Draconas pointed to the clay. "Now you're going to crawl. Once you've done that, I'll teach you how to walk."

Sighing, Marcus dug both hands into the clay and scooped out a large, dripping mass.

"Now what?" he demanded.

"Form it into a ball. Think about how the clay feels in your hand, how it looks and smells. Feel the tiny granules that make it rough and notice how those contrast with the slippery, smooth texture. Feel the warmth of the sun-warmed water and the coldness of clay that has been lying beneath it. See the tiny, broken shells of the little creatures that once lived in it. Smell the wet smell, the earth smell, the fish smell, all mingled together."

"This is more fun than I thought," announced Marcus, with a small boy's enjoyment of playing in the dirt.

He molded and shaped enthusiastically, slapping the clay and laughing gleefully when he splashed water all over Draconas. Marcus made a ball, smooth and round. Then he made a duck, modeling it after a real duck paddling among the reeds. The finished product looked like no duck Draconas had ever seen, but he praised it to the skies.

They spent the afternoon on the riverbank. Marcus pinched and shaped the clay, learning how to transfer the image in his mind to his fingers. He was often frustrated, but he was patient with himself and his mistakes; rolling the clay into a ball and trying again.

"Good," Draconas commented both inwardly and aloud. "Very good."

They returned to their camp when the sun dipped down among the tree limbs and the boy started to shiver. After dinner, as Marcus sat with his arms wrapped around his knees, staring into the flames of their cook fire, Draconas said quietly, "Go into your little room. Look into your mind. Summon up the colors. You don't need me. You can do this yourself."

Marcus's gaze turned inward. A smile that was soft and tenuous and awed parted his lips. His eyes darted about, following the shimmering swirl of the magic.

Draconas drew in a deep breath, let it out slowly. He had been dreading this moment, but he couldn't put it off any longer.

"Reach out," he instructed, "and scoop up the magic, as you scooped up the clay. Not with your hands. Reach out with the hands inside you."

"I don't understand," protested Marcus. "I don't have hands inside me."

"Your soul has hands, though they are not made of flesh. They are made of dreams and hope, of fear and despair, of beauty and of ugliness. Find the hands of your soul and use them to seize the magic."

"You're not making sense," said Marcus scornfully. He shut his ears to Draconas, concentrated on the magic.

"Stubborn little brat," Draconas muttered. "All right. You asked for it."

Draconas reached into his own magic, grabbed hold of a blazing handful of fire, and flung the glob of flame at Marcus. The fiery ball burst through the door of the little room, coming straight at the terrified boy.

In an instinctive effort to protect himself, Marcus raised his hands and, to his astonishment, he caught the glob. He stared at it a moment, at the blue and yellow flame that burned in his palms, yet did not burn his flesh. Awe blazed inside him, the fire of wonder shining brighter than the sun. In wild delight and excitement, Marcus threw the fiery ball back at Draconas.

He did not catch it. He coolly stepped aside.

The magical flame struck a sapling. The tree caught fire and blazed up, burned fiercely. Sap oozed from the burning wood, sizzled in the heat, and then the tree was gone, reduced in an instant to a pile of hot, smoldering ashes.

But that was not what Marcus saw. He saw what Draconas meant him to see—the horror that Ven had seen: a living person burning to death. Blood oozing from charred and blackened flesh. The screams of the dying in his ears and the smell of burning hair and sizzling flesh.

Marcus stood paralyzed with shock, his face gone livid. He was so pale that Draconas feared the boy would pass out or, worse, that he would retreat back into himself and never come back.

"It's not real," Draconas cried, grabbing the boy by the shoulders. "It's not real. You're seeing what I made you see. Come back to me, Marcus. It was a tree. Only a tree."

Marcus gasped and shuddered and blinked and then he was back, standing on the riverbank. He stared at the ashes.

"I did that," he said, watching the smoke rise.

"Yes," said Draconas. "You did that."

Marcus licked his lips. "I didn't mean to. I thought it was a . . . a game."

"Do you think it's a game now?"

Marcus shook his head. Tears slid from beneath his lashes. He flung his arms around Draconas.

The walker reached down, lifted the boy's face, looked into the tear-drowned hazel eyes. "I'm sorry, Marcus. I didn't mean to hurt you. But I had to make you understand your own power. I had to make you understand the danger that comes with the power. You've grown used to wandering about the streets of dragon minds, eavesdropping, listening in on thoughts that are not your own. The dragons haven't noticed you, because you are small and insignificant and they aren't looking for you. But I found you easily enough and if I can, others will, too. Especially now that they know you're out there."

"Will they catch me?" Marcus asked, his voice quavering.

"Not if you're careful. Anytime you use the magic, you open the door to your little room a tiny crack. If a dragon sees the light shining through that chink, he'll try to barge inside. You must be ready to shut the door and bolt it behind you."

"I don't understand. I'm frightened." Marcus shook his head. "I don't want to use the magic ever again."

"You have to learn how to use it in order to defend yourself."

"I don't want to! I didn't know the magic could kill."

"A sword can kill, can't it?"

"I guess," said Marcus, not about to commit to anything.

"Your father knows how to use a sword. Does that mean he goes around all day killing people with it?"

Marcus refused to answer. He watched the smoke rise from the tree.

"Your father wields a sword in order to defend himself and others. And that's why you have to learn to wield the magic."

Marcus looked back at him, his face strained. "It's not always about death, is it?"

Draconas relaxed. "No, Marcus. In truth, the magic is about life. I'll prove it. Reach your hands up to heaven and catch hold of a star or a bird or a cloud. Whatever you want. They are all yours."

Marcus stared at him, stared beyond him. Tears dried on his lashes. Slowly, glory and triumph lit his eyes from within and the hazel shone golden. His hands took hold of airy nothing and began to mold it and shape it as they had molded the clay, and then his flesh-and-blood hands fell, forgotten, as he shaped wonder with the hands of his soul.

Draconas sat down, settled his back against a tree trunk.

He should have been pleased with himself, but he felt only emptiness.

"I know what lies ahead of you," Draconas told the boy silently. "I know the path that you will walk, because I'm the one who is going make you walk it." He sighed deeply. "Where will the bright, shining joy be then?

"Like that tree, burnt to ashes."

Three months passed. During those months, Marcus made rapid progress in the handling of the magic, so much so that at the end of that time, Draconas deemed the boy ready to return home.

Marcus was excited at the prospect, but also trepidatious.

"I haven't really been home in a long time," he said to Draconas. "My parents don't know me and I don't know them. It will be like going to live with strangers."

He looked at Draconas and the hazel eyes glinted. "Why don't I come live with you?"

"Because you have much to learn that I have neither the time nor the patience to teach you," Draconas answered. "Your reading is a disgrace and a common crow can cipher better than you can. You must learn swordsmanship and chivalry, falconry, music, dancing, and much more before you are ready to take your place in this world as a king's son."

Marcus frowned, but he did not argue. The mention of chivalry recalled the young knights who came to visit his father's castle. He remembered watching them with longing and envy, dreaming of the day when he had the skill and the right to take his place among them. He remembered, too, as something long forgotten, that his father had promised him a pony of his own for his birthday. That birthday had come and gone. Perhaps the pony was waiting for him.

"I guess I am ready to go home," Marcus stated.

Still, when the day came that Draconas drove the wagon within sight of the shining white walls of Idlyswylde, and Marcus saw the turrets and spires of the castle glisten on the hilltop, his heart beat so that the rushing blood made him dizzy. He put his hand on Draconas's arm.

"Stop, please," he said in a smothered voice.

Draconas pulled back on the reins and looked at the child, flushed and trembling.

"You haven't changed your mind, have you?"

Marcus shook his head, gulped.

"Draconas," he said, his breath squeezed, "the woman's face I saw in the magic. Who was that?"

"Just a face," said Draconas.

"And the hand?"

"Just a hand."

"The dragon told me she was my mother," he said softly. "My *real* mother."

"Believe what you will," Draconas returned. "But keep the notion that you saw this face to yourself. You know what I told you—"

Marcus began kicking his boots against the side of the wagon. He repeated in a singsong the mantra he'd heard every day since the two had been studying together. " 'The magic is secret, between you and me. The magic is secret, between you and me.' We can go on now."

Draconas held the reins still, did not move.

"The magic *is* secret, Marcus. Between you and me. Look at me when I'm talking to you."

Marcus lifted his head.

"The secret is a dangerous one. For you, Marcus, because you've seen the dragon who is out there searching for you, trying to find you. If the dragon does find you, he will take you away from your family and your home, take you so far away that you would never be able to find your way back."

Draconas wanted the boy to be afraid, wanted him to remember his fear for years to come, when it all would grow so much harder.

"And not only the dragon," Draconas continued, relentless. "There are people in this world who do not understand the magic. They will claim that you are possessed by demons or worse. They would bring harm to you *and* your family. Your father and mother, your brothers. We've talked about this before, but I need to make certain you understand."

"I do, Draconas," said Marcus earnestly. "I will keep the magic secret."

"You must not use it, not even to communicate with me. Not unless the situation is dire. It's too dangerous."

"I know," said Marcus, his gaze level. "I promise."

Draconas looked deep into the child's eyes, into his mind, and beyond. He sighed inwardly. Marcus meant what he said. He would try to keep his promise, but he was human. So very human. And so very young.

Draconas slapped the reins against the horse's back and the animal started moving.

"You live in a world of secrets, don't you?" Draconas said, after a moment, glancing at the child at his side.

Marcus said nothing. His hand made a quick swipe at his eyes.

"I would tell you about your real mother—"

Marcus lifted his head hopefully.

"—but the secret isn't mine to tell," Draconas finished. "The secret belongs to your father and he must be the one to reveal it."

"He won't," said Marcus, again kicking the side of the wagon. "One day I asked my father what being a bastard meant. He got really angry and told me that I mustn't pay attention to vicious gossip, that Ermintrude is my mother, and I wasn't to say anything about it ever again, because it would hurt her. I know that isn't true, because when I asked her, she wasn't hurt. She hugged me and said I was her boy and that they would explain when I was older."

"I'm sure they will," said Draconas. "When they think you'll understand."

"Maybe," said Marcus, but he didn't sound convinced. He turned his head. "Will you tell me, if they don't?"

"We'll see," said Draconas, using the sop that has been thrown to children throughout the ages and has been universally reviled by them down through those same ages.

Marcus made a face. "I have a question. *If* it's not a secret. Why is the dragon looking for me?"

"Oddly enough—because he is afraid of you."

Marcus's eyes widened. "Truly? Is that the reason?"

"Yes, truly," said Draconas. The boy needed to be afraid, but he needed confidence, as well.

Marcus pondered this, glanced sidelong at Draconas.

"I have one more question."

"This is the time to ask it," said Draconas, striving for patience. He wondered how human parents managed, day in, day out.

"You might not like it," Marcus tempered. "It might make you angry."

Draconas shrugged. "That's a risk you'll have to take."

"All right." Marcus drew in a deep breath, let it out slowly, then said, "Why is it that when I look at you I see a dragon? Oh, I don't see fangs or a tail on you or anything like that," he added hastily, seeing that Draconas was astonished and mistakenly thinking that was the reason. "I mean that when I look at you, I see a dragon behind you, like it's your shadow. And please don't say you'll tell me when I'm older. I'd rather have you angry at me."

Draconas was completely taken aback. Of course, Marcus had been able to enter his mind. Perhaps that had given the boy the ability to see through the illusion that was one of the strongest dragons could cast.

"That is because I *am* a dragon," Draconas answered. "My human form is the shadow."

Marcus nodded.

"You don't seem surprised," said Draconas.

"I think I knew all along. But you're different from that other dragon. The horrible one who wants to find me. Why is that?"

"Just as humans are different, so are dragons."

"That's not an answer."

"It's the best you're going to get," Draconas returned.

Marcus sighed and then eyed him shrewdly. "One more question?"

"One more," said Draconas.

Marcus hesitated, then asked, "Am *I* a dragon?"

Draconas shook his head. "No. You are human. But you do have dragon blood in you."

"I won't grow scales and a tail, will I?" Marcus asked, alarmed. "I won't turn into a monster?"

"No," Draconas answered, thinking of Ven. "You won't turn into a monster."

"Whew! That's a relief. But how—"

"Look there," said Draconas, pointing. "You can see the spires of your father's castle. You're almost home."

"Home!" Marcus repeated softly, and he had no more questions.

During his time away, Marcus had put on weight, filled out, and grown at least an inch. When Draconas drove the wagon to the castle's front gates, the guardsmen didn't recognize the boy as the prince. They took him for some peasant's son, much to the boy's enjoyment, and almost wouldn't let them pass.

It was Gunderson who, with a gasp and an oath, recognized His Royal Highness and that only after Marcus jumped from the wagon's seat to fling his arms around the older man and hug him.

The entire court was roused now. Never mind where the prince had been or what had happened to him. The talk about that would start later and would be squelched by explanations from the palace. For now, everyone expressed joy at his return, safe and sound. Gunderson bore Marcus in state to the palace. Queen Ermintrude ran with open arms to clasp him to her bosom. His father snatched him away from her tearful embrace, but only to hold his son in his arms.

"You promised me a pony," Marcus said.

"In the stables," Edward answered, his voice choked. "Waiting for you."

He carried his son inside the palace, to be kissed and fed and made much of. Ermintrude was about to follow, when she realized that they had not thanked Draconas. She turned to look for him, but he was gone.

Draconas was walking rapidly across the courtyard, heading toward the palace gate, when he heard Gunderson call his name. Pretending to be deaf, Draconas kept walking. Gunderson, huffing mightily, caught up with him.

"Their Majesties want to thank you for bringing their son back to them. They invite you to stay in the palace—"

Draconas shook his head, kept walking. He didn't want their thanks, for he didn't deserve it.

The soldiers were firing off the cannon again. First came the boom, then the oohs and aahs of the crowd.

Edward—working to perfect a weapon that would kill dragons.

Draconas—doing the same thing.

12

A DRAGON BLINKED ITS EYE AND TEN YEARS passed. Humans laughed and cried and lived and died and ten years passed. Ven roamed the forest and checked his rabbit snares and raced the wildcat on his loping beast's legs and ten years passed. Marcus practiced with his fencing master and his dancing master and studied with his tutor and fell asleep over his lessons and ten years passed. Grald and Maristara plotted and schemed and searched and ten years passed.

Draconas walked and watched and waited for those ten years to pass . . .

"I'm going to the faire with you this year," Ven said abruptly.

Bellona looked up from her sewing in astonishment. He'd made his announcement and then returned to his work, seemingly uninterested in her reaction. His eyes were lowered, concentrating on the fletching of his arrowheads, making good use of the dwindling light before night set in. She could tell by the red flush on the back of his neck and the rigid set of his jaw what pain this decision had cost him.

She went back to her work.

Bellona was not a good seamstress. The hands that wielded a sword with such skill were clumsy and impatient with the needle. She had no choice, however. She sewed the clothes they wore and they constantly required either making or mending. Ven had grown rapidly in the past ten years, and it seemed that she had no sooner sewn him a pair of wool breeches or a wool tunic, but that he had split out the seams in the thighs or could no longer fit his muscular arms into the sleeves.

Jabbing the needle in the cloth, she said evenly, "I will be glad of your help."

He lifted his head then, regarded her from beneath his lowering brows. He was suspicious, thinking she accused him.

She raised her gaze to meet his.

The flush spread from the back of his neck to the front and extended up into his face.

"I am sorry," he said gruffly. "I know I have not been much use to you these past few years."

Bellona lowered her gaze to the thread, tugged it through the hole. "I understood."

"Did you?" he demanded, challenging.

She raised her eyes again. "Yes."

He lowered his before her steady gaze. He went back to his work, then impatiently shoved the arrows aside, stood up, and walked out the door. She watched him lope down the path, watched him with the eyes of strangers, those they would meet on the road, traveling to the faire.

As Ven grew older, his body altered. If his legs were disguised, he could almost pass for a normal human youth. He tended to spring off his long, clawed toes, rather than placing his heel down first and rolling forward on the foot, as do humans, and he practiced long hours at walking like a human. His legs were still the legs of a beast and he still had a peculiar gait—as though he walked with slightly bent knees—but his gait could be viewed as an oddity, not a deformity.

At age sixteen, Ven was a comely youth, from the waist up. His upper body was well developed from hard, physical labor and daily practice with bow and sword and spear. His blond hair had darkened to russet gold. He kept it cut short for ease. His eyebrows were thick and brown and formed a bar across his face—a bar that was, to Bellona's fancy, like a heavy wooden bar dropped across a door.

He had no beard. No hair grew upon his chest or groin, and it was becoming apparent to Bellona that it never would. She knew he felt the lack and was pained by it, for she often saw him staring at himself in the still waters of the icebound pond, rubbing his jaw, which was strong and gaunt and jutting, and yet smooth as any maid's.

His eyes were the same blue as his mother's, made darker by the heavy brows, so that where her eyes had been flame, his were shadow.

Bellona watched him until he vanished among the twilight-dappled trees.

After that disastrous experience at the faire when he was six, he had refused to go with her to the faires anymore. He remained in the forest by himself. Bellona compared the danger of leaving a little child alone in the forest with the danger of taking him to the faire, and she opted for the former. She understood his reason for not wanting to go back among people. And she understood why he made the decision to return to the world now. She had seen the restlessness growing on him for years, seen him wrestling with himself, his need fighting with his fear. She understood the need, as she understood the fear. She did not know what to do about either. She felt helpless when it came to Ven. She did not know what to say to him, what to do for him. She'd felt this way for ten years.

Bellona did not feel a mother's love for Ven, but she had always believed there was a bond between them—that bond was Melisande, the mother he had never known. Bellona had taken it for granted that Ven must love his mother. She had been disabused of this notion ten years ago on their return from that diastrous journey to Fairfield.

Bellona had regained consciousness with only a vague memory of the faire itself. She remembered nothing of the attack. She questioned Ven about it, but his answers were vague. He said only that they'd been waylaid by thieves.

One day shortly after their return home, she found Ven standing beside her, watching her. She looked into the blue eyes, in which she was accustomed to see her image reflected back to her, and she did not see herself.

She saw Ven.

Bellona had once been stranded by a blizzard in the mountains of Seth. Seeking escape from the blinding snow and the flesh-numbing cold, she sought shelter in a cave, only to discover that the cave was already inhabited. She had no light, so she had not been able to see what kind of wild animal lurked in the darkness, but she knew it was there. She could feel the anger at her intrusion and the threat and she left the cave, willing to risk death in the blizzard, rather than being torn apart by savage claws.

Ven's eyes were the cavern. Inside was darkness.

"What do you want, child?" Bellona demanded, recoiling.

"Am I my mother's curse?" Ven asked, his voice quavering.

Bellona stared, aghast. She remembered his question in the forest. *Why am I like this? Who made me like this?* He had not wanted to hear the answer then, but he'd been thinking about it. He had come to the conclusion that he was the product of a twisted passion. His mother's curse.

Bellona knelt down in front of Ven, to be at eye level. No need to explain the act of copulation to him. He knew how baby squirrels and rabbits and foxes came into being. He'd seen deer rut, wild cats mate, robins tumbling over each other in a flurry of red bosom and black feathers. He knew what he was asking and now Bellona understood his anger. She told him in a few blunt and brutal words of the rape. She spared him nothing. She told him how she had found his mother after the dragon had finished with her—found her torn, bleeding, terrified, ashamed.

"Melisande had no need to be ashamed," said Bellona harshly. "What happened was not her fault. You are *not* your mother's curse."

The words "You are your father's" were left unsaid, but Ven heard them.

After that, their lives continued on much as they had before, with one exception. The next year, as Bellona started to perform Ven's customary birthday ceremony, she summoned Ven to stand before her and drew in a breath to invoke Melisande.

Light flared suddenly, like the striking of quickmatch, in the cavern of Ven's eyes. Bellona saw in the blaze the soul crouching there—wary, raging, threatening.

Melisande's name sighed out of Bellona, drifted into the birdsong silence of the spring day, and was lost. She never again celebrated Ven's birthday, nor was it ever mentioned between them.

Bellona tore her thoughts from Ven to return to the detested sewing. She wielded the needle as she might have wielded a sword against a foe, battling with grim determination to finish the task at hand.

Ven would need these new breeches and a new shirt, since he was going with her to the faire.

Leaving the shack to Bellona and her needlework, Ven sought refuge in his cave. Now that he had said the words, he found himself shaking from the reaction. To speak his decision aloud had made it real, given it shape and form and substance. He could not go back. If he did, if he stayed hiding in his cave, as part of him longed to do, Bellona would take him for a coward, and she despised cowards. Worse, he would despise himself. And so would the other—the voice that urged him to go out into the world and make the world his own.

Ven never answered his father's voice. He never communicated with the dragon or with Draconas, though both had tried at various times during these past ten years to communicate with Ven. He had never spoken with the third voice, either. The voice that was distant and rarely heard and seemed not to be speaking to him, but to itself. He liked that voice, for it was not a dragon's voice. He didn't know whose voice it was or why he could hear it, but he liked it. The voice wanted nothing of him and, although it did not talk with him, the sound of the voice made him feel less alone. He never answered it. He never answered any of the voices. To do so would be to admit that he was the dragon's son, and that was something he did not choose to admit.

He repudiated his dragon father as he repudiated the dragon half of his body. He seemed almost to believe that if he willed himself to be human, the cold, dry, blue scales would melt into soft, warm flesh. He knew deep inside him that this was not going to happen, but he had some vague sense that conceding to the dragon part of him would weaken the human. He determined that he would be human—or at least be taken for human—no matter what the cost.

As for the dragon magic, he had not used it since the day he had killed that man.

The killing had shaken Ven. It had been so easy. It had felt so good. The way a dragon feels, he thought, when it slays a human.

Ven carried the fantastical images, the beautiful colors and shapes he saw in his mind, into the darkest part of his cavern and flung them into a deep crevice. The magic was still alive down there. Sometimes, he would see the images trying to claw their way up from the depths. Sometimes he would hear them whisper to him temptingly, as he heard his father's voice. He turned his back on them. Resolutely, he ignored them. He concentrated, instead, on being human. He would make the human world his own without help from anything dragon.

Yet how much it had cost him to say the words *I am going with you to the faire.*

Ven lowered his head into his hands. His fingers clawed at his skin and his hair, so that the pain brought tears to his eyes. He was afraid.

He was afraid of leaving the forest in which he'd hidden all these years. He was afraid of staying.

He was afraid of the staring eyes, the sneering lips, the smug pity. He was afraid of his loneliness.

He was afraid of the sexual urges that flooded his body with warmth and bliss and then, when they drained out of him, left him restless and dissatisfied, for his dreams were airy nothings and he wanted to feel, to clasp, to hold and to be held. He wanted to give achingly of himself and be received with aching pleasure. In his fantasy, his legs were flesh and blood, the illusory legs that Draconas had conjured up for him that day at the faire. The legs that twined with a woman's legs were never the legs of the dragon.

His longing overcame his fears. The longing and the need to prove himself to himself. He'd said the words. There was no going back. He rose to his feet, the clawed feet, the feet of a dragon, and he shook himself, shook off doubt and torment.

The sun had set.

Night had fallen in the forest.

The animals that hunted by day sought their own dark sanctuaries. Those that hunted by night were out and on the prowl. He could sometimes see the yellow eyes staring at him from the tangled undergrowth, freezing into stillness until he passed. He walked easily in the darkness, for he had the dragon gift of sight that changed night to twilight, and he feared nothing here.

The bear, the wolf, the wild cat all feared him.

He went back to the dwelling place to get what sleep he could, for he and Bellona would be up before the dawn, loading the furs onto the wagon, to have a full day of sunlight in which to travel.

13

THE FAIRE THEY WERE ATTENDING THIS YEAR
was not a country faire, as was the faire at Fairfield. This was
a city faire, one of the largest on the continent, held in the
cathedral city of Rhun, the capital of Weinmauer. Bellona
had attended this faire for the first time last year and it had
proved to be most profitable. And, she figured, there was
safety in numbers. The more eyes there were, the more
sights there were for eyes to see. The less likely those eyes
might find Ven.

Bellona had not forgotten Draconas's warning about Ven's
father. She had not forgotten his tale of holy sisters who
were far from holy and monks who were mad. The years had
blunted the warnings, however. She had been to many faires
during that time and kept close watch and she had seen nothing to make her suspicious. Admittedly, she had not brought
Ven with her, but she didn't see why that should make a difference. If there were mad monks searching for him, she
must have run across them at some time. She looked intently
at all she met and even broke her customary silence to speak
to some, and they were what they appeared.

She kept watch for Draconas, too, but she did not see him either. He had seen her, but she never knew that.

Besides, Ven was no longer a child of six. He was a man now, strong and formidable, trained in handling sword and dagger, bow and arrow. He had the means and the skill and the courage to defend himself against any foe—any foe armed with steel, that is.

The mad monks were still out there, still searching for Grald's son, but not in any great number. Grald had not been able to coerce or seduce Ven into talking to him, but the dragon was able to see Ven far more clearly than Ven imagined. Grald saw Ven hiding in his cave, refusing to come out into the world of men. Grald saw Ven's desires and fears and torments. As far as the dragon could, he fostered them. They would drive the young man out one day, as the flames and smoke of the forest fire drives out the rabbit.

Patiently, Grald waited. His people were in place, ready.

Located on one of the continent's major rivers, the Urb, only thirty miles from the sea, Rhun was easily accessible by water and by the kingdom's well-kept roads. The faire was held every fall at harvest time in honor of the saint for whom the city was named. The saint did well by his city, for though Father Rhun himself had lived a life of poverty and self-sacrifice and died a martyr, he was seeing to it that his city was blessed with wealth and granted every self-indulgence.

The kingdom of Weinmauer and its neighbors were currently at peace and had been for many years. The absence of armed troops marching about meant that people could travel the roads in relative safety, and crowds poured into the city. The inns were sleeping three to a bed and charging double for the privilege.

Ven and Bellona arrived at the faire without incident on the road. They set up their tent, working from it as usual, and they did extremely well for themselves. Ven sold out his small stock of handcrafted bows and arrows in the first day. Bellona did her usual brisk trade in pelts. She was right in her thinking that Ven would not stand out in the crowds. He roamed the fairegrounds and the teeming streets of the city from morning to night, a silent, watchful observer, avoiding speech with anyone, rebuffing friendly advances with a shake of his head. Few glanced at him twice.

Ven enjoyed watching the crowds, though he felt more isolated among the masses of people than he did in his solitary life in the forest. He looked with bitter envy at the wealthy young men sauntering about in bright-colored hosiery that showed off their shapely legs. He felt the difference between himself and them acutely, as he imagined the looks of horror on their faces should they see the scales and claws beneath his crude trousers. Sometimes the thought made him smile maliciously. Most times he writhed in shame.

He especially avoided the women, many of whom cast a favorable eye on the comely youth and favored him with a come-hither glance and smile. Most of these were whores, plying their trade and wrongly thinking by Ven's crude manners and plain dress that he was a witless bumpkin.

Ven did not need Bellona's warnings to be put off by such women. He witnessed several in the act of earning their pay in the alleys behind the taverns, stopping to observe the gropings and squeezings and jouncings with a throbbing fascination that left him feeling disgusted and wanting a bath.

The aching longing in Ven grew, but he wanted love to come to him shyly and sweetly, not spreading her legs in an alley.

Ven imagined himself alone among the throng, but he wasn't. One man spotted Ven early on. Ramone was the man's name and he was not connected with Grald or any of Grald's mad monks. Ramone worked for only one person's best interests and that person was Ramone. He was thirty years old, handsome in a slick, dark way, with an ingratiating smile and quick, deft fingers. He was always involved in many schemes, most of them illegal, though not so illegal that he might endanger his own skin, which was very dear to him. He was a pickpocket, albeit not a very good one. He was better at swindling, filching, petty theft, and rolling drunks.

Ramone had a predator's instinct for choosing his victims and he had been spying on Bellona and Ven ever since sighting them pushing their pelt-laden cart through the narrow city streets toward the fairegrounds. Ramone took it by their rough clothing that they were barbarians, members of a savage race who lived in icebound lands somewhere to the north and who had once, centuries ago, attempted to invade the city of Rhun.

Ramone knew all about barbarians because he had just watched a miracle play relating the story of the city's patron saint, who had turned aside the barbaric hordes by standing before them and telling them that, in God's name, they could not enter. The barbarians had responded by shooting the pious Father Rhun full of arrows and hacking his body to pieces. While indulging themselves in this light entertainment, the barbarians put off invading the city, allowing time for the king to summon reinforcements. The barbarians were slaughtered, the city saved, and Father Rhun began his journey down the road to sainthood.

Ramone added this barbarian to his list of sheep meant for shearing and kept his sharp eyes open. Ramone observed Ven wandering the city streets; aloof, friendless, fondly imagining that he was keeping himself to himself. Ramone lingered about his tent, keeping track of fur sales on the first day, and he was pleased to see that they did well. He meant to share in their success.

Ramone was kept busy for two days with certain other matters. These having gone well, he decided it was time to check on the barbarians. He found the cart of furs empty and his mouth watered. He kept their tent under observation all that afternoon and, as the day was waning, he was fortunate enough to observe Bellona handing over the day's proceeds to Ven.

The youth deposited the coins in a leather purse that was already well filled. Mindful of pickpockets, Ven tied the purse around his waist, beneath his leather jerkin.

Bellona said something about going to bed early, for they were leaving when the sun rose on the morrow. She entered their tent and Ven started to go in after her.

Ramone gnashed his teeth.

"No, lambkin, no," he muttered beneath his breath. "It's too early to go to bed yet. You'll just lie awake, staring into the darkness. Come out and have a good time with Ramone."

Almost as if he'd heard the man, Ven paused at the tent's entrance, and looked around. Loud and boisterous laughter drifted on the air.

"That's right," Ramone said softly. "They're having fun down there, lambkin. You and I could be having fun, too."

Ven hesitated a moment longer; then Bellona's voice called out something. He turned back toward the tent. Ramone had seen the wistful look at the sound of that laughter. He had watched the young man wandering the city streets, alone and aimless, for the past three days.

Ramone slithered forward. "Ven is your name, isn't it?" he called in friendly tones. "Don't go to your bed yet. I would do business with you."

The young man eyed the visitor with cool appraisal. "The hour is late, sir. What do you want?"

"One of your fine bows," said Ramone, striding up to stand in front of the young man. "I am shooting in the tourney tomorrow, before the king himself, God save and keep him. With one of your marvelous bows in my hands, I am sure to win."

Ven glanced at Ramone's meager chest and skinny arms. Bowmen were strong men, well built. Ven started to turn away.

Ramone laughed. "Ah, I know what you are thinking. This man does not have the build of an archer." He flexed an arm muscle. "I am thin, but I am wiry."

Ven shook his head. "I have sold all my bows."

"A vast pity," said Ramone, heaving a sigh. "Why, just this day, I saw a man use one of your fine bows to win the prize in the queen's archery contest. He gave the bow and the bowmaker the credit. 'His name is Ven,' he said, 'and he has a tent upon the hill.' He pointed this way. I knew you would be besieged by customers on the morrow and so I made haste to reach you tonight. Still"—he sighed again—"I am too late after all."

Ven glanced around. "A man won the tourney with a bow I made?"

"He did indeed. A fine match it was, too. I never saw better."

"Tell me about it," said Ven, interested.

Ramone lowered his voice. "I will, gladly, but I fear we might wake your father if we talk here. Come, let us take a walk. Though I cannot have the bow I want, at least allow me the honor of buying the maker a mug of ale." He added, in a conspiratorial whisper, "It is fine for older folk to go bed with the chickens. But the night is early yet for the young."

Ven looked back at the tent. He had spent many nights lying awake in the stifling warmth, listening to Bellona mumble in her sleep and seeing in his mind slovenly girls with their backs to the wall, their breasts bare and their skirts hiked up to their waists, with men clutching them, heaving and sweating and grunting.

He had never tasted ale before. His bow had won a tourney and he wanted to hear about it. And he did not want to wake Bellona.

"I'll come," he said, adding, "Just let me fetch my sword."

Ramone was about to say that were going out for a drink, not to do battle. Then he noted that the young man's sword, through plainly made, was of good quality.

Ramone smiled and stroked his mustache.

The city of Rhun had outgrown the walls built long ago to protect it. The city was divided into Inner City and Outer City, with Inner City containing the famous cathedral, the royal palace, the theaters, government buildings, hostels and inns. Outer City was residential, with markets and shops and taverns. Ramone headed for Outer City where there were several taverns that he frequented. He chose those whose front doors faced busy streets and whose back doors opened onto dark alleys.

For this night's business, Ramone selected the Rat and Parrot, a name that tickled his fancy, for he was the rat who meant to pluck the parrot. Pausing in the doorway, he sent a quick, searching glance about the tavern.

"Everywhere I go, I am besieged by my friends," Ramone complained with a shrug. He smoothed a thin, black mustache with a slender finger, as his sharp eyes took note of every face. "It is hard to find a quiet table to talk to a companion without being constantly interrupted."

Not seeing any of his former victims, Ramone sauntered into the tavern. Ven hung back, not certain he wanted to enter. His was the solitary nature of the dragon. He did not like this crowded, stinking place.

Lit by candles that melted on the tables and by a desultory fire, over which several drunken youths were roasting a capon, the tavern teemed with people and shadows. Faces suddenly leaned into the candlelight, to be brightly illuminated, then just as suddenly returned to the darkness. Smells of ale and vomit and unwashed bodies mingled with hot wax and roasted meat and burnt pinfeathers. There was laughter and hooting, giggling, and swearing. Most of the customers were busy with their own affairs and few paid any attention to the newcomers. Those who did took stock of the situation and exchanged knowing winks or grins.

Ven started to back out the door, but Ramone—sensitive to his sheep as a mother to a sick child—said in a loud voice, "Come in, my friend, come in and have a drink. What is the matter? You are not too good for this establishment, I hope?"

Conversation stopped. People turned to look.

Ven's skin burned.

He could not leave now.

He walked inside the door. Feeling clumsy and oafish, he slid into the first empty chair he found. His sword banged against the chair and his flush deepened. Ramone sat down and ordered ale. A woman started toward the table. Ramone scowled and jerked his head, warning her off. She stuck out her tongue at him and returned to her seat by the fire.

"We're here for a drink, not a tumble, eh?" Ramone said to Ven, who had not seen the woman and who had no idea what the man was talking about.

The ale arrived, served in two dented pewter pots. Ramone's plan was simple. He would get Ven staggering drunk, steer him into the alley on the pretext of helping him home, and then bash out his brains and rob him.

Ramone lifted his pot in a toast. "Try the ale. You'll find it excellent here. The best in the city."

Ven took a sip and made a face. "It's bitter," he said.

"But it quenches the thirst," urged Ramone. "Swallow it quickly. Gulp it down and you will not notice the taste." He set the example by drinking off half his pot.

"I'm not thirsty," Ven said. He shoved the pot away. "You were going to tell me about the archery match."

Ramone was dumbfounded. He eyed the young man and considered seizing him, prizing open his jaws, and dumping the ale down his throat. Such a course of action lacked subtlety, however.

"Archery match?" Ramone repeated irritably. He was so rattled he'd forgotten his ruse. "Oh, yes. The archery match. Let me recall all the details. I want to get this right."

His brow furrowed in thought, Ramone slid his hand into the top of his boot. His fingers closed over the small vial he kept with him in case of emergency. He flicked off the cork with an expert thumb and secreted the open vial in his palm.

"Six arrows in the black. One right after the other. The last three arrows," said Ramone, who knew nothing about archery and hoped that his companion didn't either, "struck one on top of the other. The second arrow split the first and the third split the second. We were all amazed—"

He paused in his story. Casting a significant glance over Ven's head, Ramone gave him a sly wink. "You have a face the ladies love, lad. Look at that wench there. The fine one with the red hair. She has been watching you since we came in. Perhaps that is why you are not thirsty, eh?"

Ven did not look around. He stared at the table. His fingers drummed nervously.

"Come, lad. Smile at her," said Ramone testily. He was rapidly losing patience. "You do not want to hurt her feelings."

Ven cast a brief glance over his shoulder.

"More to the right," Ramone insisted. "She is worth the trouble, I tell you."

Ven turned his head and finally saw the red-haired woman. She leered at him and scratched herself.

Ven turned back.

"There, you see, she adores you." Ramone nodded toward the pewter pot. "Drink up. Or you will hurt my feelings."

Ven put the mug to his lips, took a swallow.

Ramone relaxed, sat back in his chair, and crossed his legs. "I will go on with my story. When the archer made this miraculous shot, the crowd cheered its head off. The queen herself and all the royal court came down out of the stands to stare at the target and Her Majesty cried out, 'Tell me the name of the man who made that bow. I will commission one thousand for my archers on the spot. . . . ' "

Ven blinked. He was having difficulty focusing his eyes. Ramone wavered in his vision, then dwindled, then grew and expanded, and then, amazingly, split apart. The buzzing of hundreds of bees thrummed in his head. Ven could no longer feel his hands and when he tried to stand up, he couldn't find his feet. He started to speak, his lips had gone numb.

His head was too heavy for his neck to support. He rested his cheek on the cold table and watched the wall become the ceiling become the floor until it all swirled together into a green, nausea-tinged cesspool.

Ramone had poured only a small amount of the opiate into the ale. He was going to lure the young man from the tavern into the alley and, being naturally lazy, Ramone didn't want to have to work any harder than was necessary. He certainly did not want to have to lug a comatose barbarian around. Ven slumbered. Ramone sat at his ease in the tavern, drinking a couple of more pots of ale and waiting for the night to deepen and the streets to empty.

Everyone in the tavern knew or guessed Ramone's game. None took pity on the stranger or came to his aid. Life was hard. Their lives were hard. No one took pity on them or came to their aid. Let the stranger look to himself.

Closing hour came for the Rat and Parrot. The rats that gave the tavern part of its name slunk off. The parrot, stuffed, regarded Ramone with a dead, glassy eye. Ramone lifted Ven's head by the hair and splashed the remainder of his ale into Ven's face.

Ven's eyes opened. Blinking and gasping, he stared about in blank confusion. Ramone tugged at the young man's arm.

"You've had enough, my friend," Ramone said loudly. "Time to go. I myself will escort you. It would be a shame if some unscrupulous person were to rob you on the way home."

The bartender grinned and snuffed out the last candle.

Ven tried to stand up, leveraging himself off the table with his hands. He overbalanced, staggered backward, and knocked over his chair. Ramone slid his arm around the young man's waist to support him and, at the same time, locate the purse.

"This way, my friend. We're moving toward the door. No, no. That way is the fire pit. This way is the door. Merciful Mother of God, you are one heavy son of a bitch!"

Ven shuffled along, leaning on Ramone, so that the thief, who was about half Ven's weight, was forced to practically walk on his knees.

Gasping, sweating, and swearing under his breath, Ramone maneuvered Ven out of the tavern and into the street. Here the thief had to pause for a breather. Ramone had never worked so hard in his life.

"You had better make this worth my while or I'll slit your throat for the trouble you've caused me," he grunted, then staggered halfway across the street in the wrong direction as Ven lurched into him.

Ramone manhandled the reeling Ven into the alley and dumped him thankfully into the gutter. Ramone collapsed against a wall.

"You've ruined me," he groaned, nursing a part of himself that was tender. "I've ruptured something. Bastard."

Ramone kicked Ven a couple of times in the ribs to relieve his feelings.

"Lumbering oaf! Piece of dog turd! Why do you weigh so much? I hope it's because of all the money you're carrying, you load of horse dung."

Ramone eyed Ven warily. The young man lay on his back in the muck. Occasionally he would groan and twitch. Satisfied that his victim was not going to put up a fight, Ramone limped to the end of the alley and peered up and down the street. Seeing no one, he returned to business. The moon, being about three-quarters full, was generous with its light. Ramone didn't really need it. He did most of his work by feel anyway.

Ramone removed the sword belt and sword, then hiked up the wool tunic the young man wore, laying bare his stomach and torso. The money bag and the belt to which it was attached were hidden beneath Ven's breeches. Ramone seized hold of the breeches by the drawstring cord that held them around the young man's waist and gave them a yank, pulling them down past the groin.

Ramone gasped and staggered backward.

"By the blessed liver of Saint Rhun, did I accidentally drink my own poison?" He rubbed his eyes, but the astonishing sight did not go away.

From the waist up, the young man was a normal man. Below the waist, he had the normal appendages of a normal man but that was where the similarity ended. His thighs glittered blue in the moonlight, sparkled brightly as if encrusted with sapphires.

"Some sort of fancy stockings?" Ramone asked himself, dazed. "No, no. Don't be a dolt." He struck himself on the head. "This lout is no orange-sniffing dandy, mincing about in bejeweled hosiery. What is this? What could it be?"

He was about to touch Ven's buttocks, then had second thoughts.

"Maybe it's leprosy!" Ramone snatched back his hand.

He considered the fact that he'd seen lepers before now and none of them had ever glittered.

"It could be some other disease." Ramone gnawed his lip. "But the young man is healthy as a horse. I know. I carried him on my back."

Reaching out his finger, Ramone gingerly poked Ven's thigh, then scrambled backward, blessing himself rapidly over and over. "Mother of God!" he breathed. "He has the skin of a snake!"

Crouching a safe distance from Ven, Ramone regarded the young man thoughtfully. Ideas fomented in his mental cauldron. Stirring the pot, he ventured back and, keeping an eye on Ven for signs of waking, yanked off his boot. Ramone shuddered in horror and shivered in delight.

A beast's foot. A beast's foot with three large toes, ending in hideous, sharp claws, and one smaller claw in back. The foot and the ankle were the same blue snakeskin as the thigh.

Shaking in excitement, Ramone dragged off Ven's other boot. Seeing that both feet were the same, Ramone very nearly burst into tears.

"Our fortune is made, Evelina!" he cried. "We will never work another day in our lives. Yes, yes, that is all very well," he said to himself to calm himself down. "But what do I do now? What to do? Plan. You must have a plan, Ramone, my wealthy friend."

His first wild thought was to hoist Ven onto his shoulders and haul him off. Ramone abandoned that immediately. He would rupture something else. But what to do with the monster? What if someone else saw him like this? Found him? Stole him for their own?

Panicked at the thought, Ramone leapt to his feet and dashed out to once again look up and down the street. Still no one, but the patrols would be by soon. He dashed back to his prize and frantically slid the boots over the clawed feet. He pulled up Ven's breeches, made certain the drawstring was fastened tightly, and gave the knot a solicitous pat. That solved one problem, but did not solve the others.

The monster and his father had been talking about leaving the faire tomorrow. Ramone had to make certain that did not happen.

Gnawing the end of his mustache in frustration, Ramone remembered the money bag. His mental cauldron boiled over. Drawing his knife from his boot, Ramone cut loose the pouch and stuffed it beneath his own shirt. He added Ven's sword to the night's take—it would fetch a few pence and sheep had no need for weapons anyway. Making a quick dash to the local well, Ramone ladled out a dipperful of water. He carried it carefully back to the alley, and tossed the chill water into the monster's face.

Ven coughed and started to sputter his way back to consciousness. Ramone pricked his ears. He could hear in the distance the slogging march of the night watch. Often Ramone had cursed that sound. Now he blessed it, calling on all the saints of heaven to light their path. They would see to it that Ven found his way back to his tent, where he would remain safe until Ramone had everything ready.

"Until tomorrow, monster," Ramone promised, and he padded softly into the night.

Ven peered around, dazed and groggy. He sat up, lifted an unsteady hand to his head, which ached and throbbed. As he tried to stand, his stomach lurched. Ven groaned and vomited.

He lay still a moment to settle his stomach, then staggered to his feet. He wavered a bit, but with the help of the wall, he managed to stay upright. Wiping his mouth, he gulped in air, and looked up and down the alley. He was extremely puzzled as to what he was doing here.

The terrible light of understanding shredded the fog of the opiate. Ven fumbled beneath his tunic and reached down to his waist to where he'd secreted the money bag. He gave a bitter curse and lifted up his shirt in the bleak hope that somehow he'd missed it. He saw, lying at his feet, the leather thong that had once held the money bag.

Cursing himself for a fool, Ven groaned and slumped against the wall. Here the city guard found him and, with kindly words that Ven took very ill, they escorted him safely back to his tent.

14

"I WILL RECOVER THE MONEY," SAID VEN.

Bellona pressed her lips together. Fearful of saying too much, she ended up saying nothing. She was angry, deeply angry, not just at the loss of the money—which for them was a devastating blow—but at the blind stupidity that had led to it.

Ven saw the anger in her tight-drawn mouth. He could have borne with her fury, but he saw also, in her dark eyes, dismay, bleak despair. They needed that money to buy the staples and supplies that would see them through the winter. The pelts were sold. They had nothing left. A year's worth of work gone wanting. A winter of starvation, deprivation.

"I know the man who robbed me," said Ven. "I'll find him and drag the money out of his hide if I have to."

He left her, walking swiftly down the road that led toward the city.

Bellona watched him go and her gut shriveled. A voice inside her urged her to call out to him, *We'll make do. We'll get by. You're young. The young make mistakes.*

Her anger argued down the voice that came from the soft,

woman's part of her. The boy lacked discipline. He had got himself into this mess through his own foolishness. Let him get himself out. The lesson would do him good and, who knows, he might actually recover their money.

Ven did not look back, but walked with long and determined strides down the hill.

Go after him, urged the voice. *He didn't even take a weapon.*

Bellona snorted and entered the tent, pulling the flap shut with a sharp and angry snap.

"I will not do it," Evelina told her father. "And that is final. This monster might kill me! You don't care about me, though, do you, Papa? All you care about is your precious gold. I mean nothing to you."

"Evelina, my dearest daughter, you know that is not true," said Ramone in wheedling tones. "You are the world to me. I would not ask this of you, but, truly, I can think of no other way."

Ramone doted on his daughter, and Evelina was fond of him in her spoiled, petty way. The two were much alike. Both were completely lacking in morals and both were willing to sell anything—including each other—to gain what they wanted.

Evelina's mother had run off with a soldier when the child was six, leaving father and daughter to fend for themselves. Ramone had fretted over the burden of a child, but had soon realized that she could not only earn her own way, but help him earn his. The little girl was pretty and she was clever. She had realized from an early age that she could wind people, including her father, around her baby finger. She had imbibed deceit and lies with her mother's milk and her father had taught her everything else she needed to know.

"I need a woman of beauty," continued Ramone, holding out pleading hands. "A woman with a talent for seduction."

Evelina sniffed. Sitting on the bed in their shabby lodging, she stared out the grimy window and pouted.

"Using you was not my idea," Ramone continued. "If you must blame someone, blame Glimmershanks. He refuses to take my word—"

At this, Evelina heaved a sigh and rolled her eyes.

"—but insists on viewing the goods for himself before he buys. He came up with this role especially for you, my dear. You know how much he admires you. . . ."

Evelina did know. She smiled to herself and deigned to shift her gaze from the window to her father.

"The plan is quite clever," Ramone urged, "for it accomplishes two objectives—it gets the monster alone and out of the city."

Evelina said nothing. She tapped her foot on the floor.

"The monster is not monstrous to look at, I assure you, Daughter." Ramone sidled closer to her, peering through the mass of blond curls to try to see by her expression what she was thinking.

Evelina averted her head.

"He is quite handsome—" Ramone went on desperately.

"From the waist up," said Evelina in scathing tones. Rising, she went to stand before a piece of broken mirror she had found in the street and hung up on the wall. "It is the waist down that concerns me."

"As well it should, my dear," said Ramone slyly. "As well it should."

She cast him a withering glance. "I'm glad you find it amusing, Papa. I hope you will laugh heartily when you discover my poor body, torn to shreds—"

"No, no, Evelina," said her father petting her, soothing her. "Nothing like that will happen, I assure you."

Evelina examined herself critically, arranging and rearranging the heavy blond curls that fell over her shoulders in a bright mass.

"Hand me my veil," she ordered her father, who was quick to do her bidding. He brought the silken veil and, playing lady's maid, carefully draped it over Evelina's head. She adjusted the veil to best advantage as she talked. "I will want something for myself."

"My dear, the money—" Ramone began.

"I'll take my share, of course," said Evelina. "But I want something more. I want to join the troupe. Glimmershanks has made vague promises before, but now he can jolly well act on them. It's that, or you can do this on your own," she added petulantly.

"I'll talk to him this afternoon. I'm sure he'll agree," said Ramone, fawning over her. "And now, my dear, you really should be going. This monster is not one to let grass grow under his claws—"

"And what do I do if he doesn't show up?"

"He will," said Ramone. "And, if not, you'll go to him."

Evelina regarded herself in the mirror. She was young in years, only fifteen, though wise enough in the ways of the world to have been thirty. With shrewd business sense, she and her father had seen to it that the flower of her youth had not been squandered on those who would not properly appreciate it. The rose might not be fresh off the vine, but neither was it wilting or crumpled. She could be taken for a unspoilt blossom under the right circumstances.

Evelina gave the veil a final tweak. She smoothed her skirt—a castoff of some burgher's daughter—and tugged on the tightly laced bodice so that it would reveal more bosom. She longed for a golden circlet to hold her veil in place and promised herself that this would be her first acquisition, once she had her share of the money. Lacking the circlet, she tied the veil with a ribbon. She gave her veiled face a full-lipped smile, nodded in satisfaction, then turned to her parent.

"How do I look, Papa?"

"A little too good, my dear," said Ramone anxiously. "He'll never believe your story."

"Don't worry," Evelina assured him. "I'll take care of that."

Ven began his search for the thief at the Rat and Parrot. He had some vague hope of finding Ramone there, celebrating his victory. If he could not find the thief at the tavern, Ven intended to ask questions, discover all he could about the man—where he lived, where he was likely to be found. Ven knew what he was doing was dangerous. The guard had warned him last night.

"You came off lucky, lad. Most of the time we find young fools such as you dumped in the alley with a knife between their ribs. These bastards are clever. Let the sheriff find the thief who stole your money."

Ven saw the look in Bellona's eyes, the look that said she despised him. She could not despise him any more than he despised himself, however, and he was determined to prove his worth to both of them. Ramone had played Ven for a fool once. He would not play him so again.

In trying to follow the twisted, tangled city streets to the Rat and Parrot, Ven immediately lost his way. He continued doggedly on, walking up and down the streets and byways of a most disreputable part of the city until he eventually found objects that seemed familiar. At length, he saw the sign—a parrot holding a squirming rat by the tail. His pulse quickened.

As he walked toward the tavern, noticed a pretty young girl lingering in the street as though waiting for someone. The girl was so very pretty that she seemed out of place in such rough surroundings, and he could not help but stare at her. Drawing nearer, he saw she was nervous. She shrank away from the tavern's customers as they came for their morning ale, blushing and lowering her veiled head at their crude remarks. Still, she waited, looking closely into the faces of all who passed her by.

Ven could not take his eyes from her. He had come to view everything in this city as ugly and it was a joy to him to see something beautiful. He did not lose sight of his goal, however, and he would have entered the tavern without saying a word to the girl. To his astonishment, she came up to him, timidly blocked his way.

"Pardon me, sir," she said in a low, sweet voice, "but are you called Ven?"

"I am," he said, more startled than ever.

She laid her hand on his arm and he felt her trembling.

"Oh, thank the good God, young sir, that I have found you. I hoped you would come back. I . . . I . . . you see . . . Oh! How can I say this? I am so ashamed!"

She slid her hands beneath the veil, covered her face, and began to sob.

Ven was completely undone. He'd never seen a woman cry before and he had no idea what to do. He gazed at her helplessly, afraid to touch her.

"I'll go get help," he said.

He didn't quite know how it happened, but the girl had her arms around him. She raised her eyes, her face pale and drawn with terror.

"No, don't, sir. Please. He'll find out and he'll kill me! Ah, me, I am in such sad straits!"

She began to sob again. Ven didn't know what to do. She was sweetness and warmth and tears, clinging to him. He was dumbfounded.

"I have to talk to you," she said, or at least that's what he thought she said. It was hard to hear her, through her sobs and the golden curls. "Not here. I'm afraid he'll see us together. Go to the plaza. Wait for me at the well."

She sprang away from him and shoved him away from her.

"Go, sir," she pleaded with him. "For my sake. Meet me at the well!"

Drawing her veil over her face, she looked about in terror, then hastened off down the street.

Mystified, charmed by her beauty, and convinced that this strange assignation had something to do with his money, Ven did as he was told. He crossed the street to the plaza where a line of women and children, armed with buckets, waited to draw water at the public well. Ven roamed about the plaza and soon the girl joined him. She led him to a stone wall, shaded by a branching linden tree, whose leaves were just starting to yellow and fall. She sat down, inviting him to sit beside him with a pat of her hand upon the wall, and a shy look from her brown eyes.

Ven had never seen such beauty. She had blond hair that

hung unbound in shining ringlets down to her waist. Her eyes were large and open wide to the world, giving up all the secrets to her heart. When she smiled, a little dent appeared in one cheek. Her hands and feet were small and dainty as a lady's, though she was not a lady by her dress, which was plain, but neat and clean.

She lifted her veil and Ven saw that one cheek was bruised.

"Someone hit you," said Ven.

She blushed and hurriedly lowered her veil again. "It's nothing," she answered, confused.

"Who was it?" he demanded.

She shook back her hair, placed her hand on his arm. He was the one who trembled now, at her touch.

"Please, let it go. We don't have much time. My name is Evelina. My father is"—she paused, bit her lip, then gasped out in a rush—"the man who robbed you last night."

Ven stared at her, amazed, not knowing what to say.

She drooped her head. A tear slid down her bruised cheek and fell on his arm. The tear's touch was cool and burning so that he flinched.

"My father bragged about it! I could not believe he would do such a thing. I told him he must return the money to you, but he refused. I . . . I tried to take it from him, but he . . ." She swallowed, shook her head.

"He hit you," said Ven angrily.

Her hand clenched spasmodically on his arm. "Papa is not a bad man," she said pleadingly. "He has never done anything like this before, I swear! We have no money. Still," she added, lifting her chin, her eyes flashing, "I would rather starve to death than eat bread bought by stolen money. And that is why I'm going to help you get it back."

"Just tell me where to find your father," said Ven grimly. "I won't have you involved."

"I don't mind," she returned, leaning into him.

Her movement caused her veil to slip from her hair. She

was rose scent and pale skin and enticing fullness and shadow beneath her chemise.

"Especially now that I've met you. I want to help you and I want to save my father. Do you know the penalty for theft? Hanging! They will hang him. Poor Father. You won't tell anyone, will you kind, gentle sir? Promise me you won't."

"I promise," said Ven. "Please calm yourself, Mistress."

"Not Mistress," she said shyly. "I am not a fine lady. My name is Evelina."

"Evelina," he repeated, and he wondered that the sparrows pecking at bugs at his feet didn't burst into song.

"Here is my idea," said Evelina. "Father and I plan to leave the city tonight. We're traveling to Ausden, where they say there is work to be had. Father wanted to leave today, but I told him I couldn't, I had something I needed to do. He was afraid to stay in the city, for fear the sheriff might be looking for him, and so he left. We have arranged to meet tonight at a little shrine on the road east of here. He'll be alone. If you come with me, I'll see to it that he gives you back your money. But you must promise me that you will come alone and that you won't . . ." Her chin quivered. "You won't hurt him very much."

"I won't hurt him at all," said Ven. "I just want my money. It's all my mother and I have to live on for the winter."

"God bless you, sir," Evelina said, pressing his arm. "I'll meet you here tonight at twilight."

She drew the veil over her face. With a wave and a smile, she walked away. He watched her until he lost sight of her in the crowded streets. Feeling as if he were dreaming, he left the plaza, led by force of habit to walk back in the direction of the fairegrounds.

Halfway there, Ven halted. He didn't want to go back to the tent. He didn't want to meet Bellona or tell her anything about what had happened. He didn't want to talk about Evelina, especially with Bellona. He wanted to keep Evelina's face and words pure in his mind, there to dance and sparkle and blaze like the magic, to hold her image as he held the magic in the hands of his being and feel her tingle in his blood and burn in his bones.

Ven altered his direction. He walked toward the thick trees of the forest. Feeling at home in the woods, he sat by himself beneath the branches and kept his eyes on the sun. That orb seemed so reluctant to disappear from the sky that he wondered impatiently, more than once, if something had happened to stop it.

15

VEN RETURNED TO THE PLAZA LONG BEFORE SUN-
set. he sat on the wall next to the well, watched the sun
teeter on the chimney tops, and waited impatiently for it to
fall. With agonizing slowness, the sun descended from
chimney to rooftop, languished behind the buildings for an
eon, then, finally, sank into a puddle of its own radiance and
was extinguished.

Evelina came to him in the soft blue-purple of half-night.
Ven saw her the moment she entered the plaza and he never
took his gaze from her. She walked with the grace of the
bending willow. The evening breeze, scented with late roses,
ruffled the few curls of hair that escaped from the demurely
draped veil. She did not find him so easily as he found her,
but located him at last and smiled at him.

He met her with the awkward, uncomfortable reserve of
one who has been thinking and dreaming of nothing else but
this meeting.

Evelina appeared embarrassed and blushing. She was too
shy to look directly at him, but glanced at him from beneath
modestly lowered lashes. She was the poet's dream of the innocent maiden, something Evelina had never been.

Life held no secrets from this girl. As a child, she slept in the same room as her father and whoever his companion happened to be that night. She fell asleep to a lullaby of grunts and gasps. But Evelina had seen innocence, if she'd never experienced it. She had a spy's talent for observation, an actress's talent for mimicry, and a dog's instinct for doing whatever it took to please the one who handed out the food.

Evelina saw innocence in Ven. From the first moment she met him and felt his strong body shudder when she touched him, she knew exactly the sort of girl she needed to be. She reveled in her role and in her power over him, enjoying herself, though she could not help but feel some doubt about this plan. Ven was, as her father had said, very comely to look upon. She found it difficult to believe he was the monster her father had described. Evelina, who did not trust her father in the least, began to wonder if Ramone had been the one to imbibe the opiate.

"If that's the case, Papa dear," Evelina muttered to herself, "what fools we will look! I hope Glimmershanks beats you senseless. If he doesn't, I will."

True, Ven did have a peculiar way of walking. Evelina noted this oddity about him as they left the plaza. He moved with a graceful lope like an animal. He had an animal quality about him, one she found quite attractive. She eyed him askance, as they walked, remembering the feel of her hand resting on his arm; the movement of strong, hard muscle beneath the sun-browned skin. He was different from any other man she had ever met. He smelled of leather and wood smoke, not grime and cheap ale. Although undoubtedly a rube, he was more a gentleman than the supposed "gentlemen" she met in the alehouses, who made grabs for her bosom or tried to slide their hands up her skirts. Evelina imagined his hands lifting her skirts and her heart lurched. Playing the demure young virgin with Ven was going to be harder than she had imagined.

"I brought some food," she said, folding back a corner of the cloth from the top of a basket she carried, revealing some bits of broken meat, bread, and a jug of wine. "I thought you might be hungry."

Ven had not eaten all day—he'd been too enraptured to think of anything so mundane. He frowned at the sight of the jug.

"You need not fear the wine," Evelina added hastily. "It was not the ale you drank last night that made you sick. My father put some sort of drug in it. The wine is safe, unless you think"—her cheeks flushed in shame—"unless you do not trust me—"

"I would never, ever think that," Ven returned gently.

"Good." Evelina rewarded him with a smile. "We will both drink the wine and then you will know it is safe."

Night had fallen in earnest by the time the two left the city and struck out on the road. The moon was near full and made the darkness almost as bright as day. Ven suddenly remembered, as they walked, that Bellona would be expecting him to return to their tent at his usual time. He had never before absented himself like this, and he was troubled that he was doing so now. She would be extremely angry.

He looked at Evelina, her hair silver-gold in the moonlight, and he caught her stealing a glance at him. The welcome thought came to Ven that when he returned with the money, Bellona would have nothing to complain about. Besides, as she was always telling him, he was a man now, not a little boy.

Evelina's hand accidentally brushed against his hand. He felt a thrill tingle through his blood and, disturbed by his unseemly feelings, he moved apart from her, so that he would not sully her with his rough touch.

To his surprise, Evelina sidled nearer him. "It's frightening, being on the road alone at night. I'm glad you're with me."

Her fingers, so slender and fragile, twined with his.

Bellona spent the day nursing her anger and worrying over what they would do if Ven did not recover the stolen money. They needed salt to preserve the meat so that it would keep through the deep winter, when game grew scarce. They needed flour and potatoes to stretch out their meager meals, and onions to ward off scurvy. They needed to purchase essential tools, such as axes and knives, to replace those that were worn past mending.

"If there is a harsh, long winter, we will likely either starve to death or die of disease," Bellona said to herself.

She rehearsed in her mind what she would say to Ven on his return, how she would impress upon him the folly—the fatal folly—of his actions, whether he recovered the money or no. She was so intent upon his return that she never thought of what she would do if he failed to come back this night, as he had the last.

Bellona had not missed him the previous night. The faire was always a strain on her. Accustomed to a solitary life in the forest, she found it difficult to merge back into society, where she had to mingle with people, talk to them, be polite to them. After a long day spent dickering and haggling with her customers, she was worn out. She had thrown herself on her blanket last night and gone to sleep immediately. The next thing she knew, she was wakened in the early morning to find Ven, bruised and battered and weaving like a drunkard, in company with the sheriff's man.

When darkness fell this night and the cook fires sprang up around the tent city and the smell of roasted meat wafted through the air, the feeling of foreboding that Bellona had experienced that morning returned to her in double measure. Whether it was a mother's instinct or a soldier's, she knew that something had happened to Ven.

"What was I thinking? Letting him go off like that alone. My rage overcame my judgment. Just as it did with his mother." Bellona sighed bleakly. "Melisande, I am sorry. Be with your son and watch over him until I can find him."

She buckled her sword around her waist, slid a knife into the top of her boot, and left the tent, heading for the city and a tavern called the Rat and Parrot.

Ven and Evelina had the road to themselves. The shrine where they were to meet Ramone was not frequented by travelers, unlike those of more popular saints, Located a good distance from the road, the shrine was lost to sight and memory amid a tangle of undergrowth. Ven and Evelina had to slog their way through weeds and brush, following the dim traces of an overgrown path. The shrine was old, by the looks of it. The pious friar Rhun might well have made offerings here.

As they drew near it, Evelina's long skirt caught on a thornbush. Ven bent down to release the cloth and was rewarded for his pains with a glimpse of bare leg. His chest tightened and his throat burned. Rising, he looked into her eyes. She looked into his and her breath came fast.

Evelina lowered her head in maidenly confusion.

"There is a clearing behind the shrine," she said, pointing. "No more of these thorns. We can sit down and eat our meal and wait for Father."

"How did you ever come to find this place?" Ven asked curiously.

Evelina wondered that herself.

The thornbush provided the answer.

"Blackberries," she said. "I heard from an old woman in the city that they grew around here and I came picking them this summer."

Ven had picked blackberries and would have readily believed her story, but that he wasn't really listening to her answer. He heard nothing but the music of her voice, played to the cadence of his heartbeat. Ven tramped about, flattening the long green grass of the clearing, which was half in moonlight, half in the shadow of the trees that surrounded it.

Evelina settled herself on the crushed grass, carefully arranging her skirts around her. Ven remained standing, as he thought he should.

The dragon's son had no knowledge of courtly manners. He had never been around a young woman before. He could not read or write, for they had no books, and Bellona had never been much inclined toward study anyway. She told tales to while away the long, dark winter nights; tales that came from long ago. Tales of a city destroyed for the love of a beautiful woman, tales of a king blown off his course home by the breath of vengeful gods and the faithful wife who waited for him, tales of love and loss, honor and betrayal. This night was a tale come to life for Ven, born of moonlight and a silken veil covering gold-spun curls.

"Will he be long, do you think? Your father?" Ven asked abruptly.

"Why?" Evelina said, teasing. "Are you eager to be rid of me?"

Ven reddened. He was not accustomed to jests; Bellona was not a jocular person. He thought Evelina was serious and didn't know how to answer. Her father could stay away all night, as far as he personally was concerned, but there was another matter.

Having impaled him on this dilemma, Evelina was kind enough to remove her horns.

"I'm sorry," she said. "That was cruel. Of course, you are concerned about your money. I do not blame you."

Removing the veil from her head, she shook out her hair, causing it to glisten in the moonlight.

"Father may be some time, I fear." Evelina looked up at Ven. "You had best come sit down."

As Ven took his seat beside her, lowering himself to the grass with an animal's ease, Evelina heard a rustle in the brush behind her, the snap of branch, and a muffled "shush."

She froze, certain Ven must have heard. She waited for him to react.

Ven could not hear very well, however, for the throbbing of the blood in his ears and other parts of his body. He did not react, but sat with his head bowed, absently pulling out the grass by the roots. The noises were not repeated, and Evelina breathed again.

The two shared the food and the wine, drinking out of the same jug, handing it back and forth. Ven liked wine better than ale. Wine was sweeter to the taste and warmed the blood and it gave a radiant luster to Evelina's dark eyes. The wine made it seem entirely natural that she should lift her face to his, press her soft body against him, and kiss him on the lips. He tasted the wine on her mouth and its sweetness was trebled.

Evelina did not forget the business part of this deal, but she felt she deserved some pleasure for herself out of this, and so she did not rush matters. She was aroused by Ven and also by the knowledge that her father and Glimmershanks were lurking in the bushes, watching. Seeing that Ven was too far consumed by his wine and passion to be thinking clearly, she dropped the role of the virginal maid and gave herself to him with sensual abandon.

He was an exciting lover, unpracticed, instinctual, rough as an animal, yet with an underlying tenderness that made her respond in kind, arching her body to meet his, yielding to his touch, sighing with his sighs. She was so caught up in her own pleasure, she almost forgot about the money.

Almost.

Evelina could tell by the feel of him that the moment of truth was soon to be upon them. She hiked up her skirts, revealing her naked legs, and spread them wide.

"Take me!" she whispered urgently into his ear and pulled him down on top of her.

She could feel him fumbling at the flap on his breeches, undoing the buttons that held it shut. Damn him to hell and back! He was going to leave his pants on!

"Oh, my love," Evelina purred, running her hands over his bare back. "Let me feel your flesh against my flesh."

Ven pretended not to hear her. He'd been wondering how he would manage this. He'd seen the men at the tavern walls taking their pleasure without dropping their drawers and he knew it could be done. Kissing her hard, he pressed her into the ground with his body. He was going to have her and nothing could stop him.

Evelina realized she'd lost control. Pushing at his chest with all her strength, she gave a desperate heave, rolled him partially off her, giving her room enough to wriggle out from under him. Taking hold of his breeches, she grasped them with both hands and jerked them down past his butt cheeks, clear to his thighs.

Blue dragon scales gleamed in the moonlight.

Evelina shrieked in horror. Torchlight flared. Two men came crashing through the undergrowth.

"What did I tell you?" Ramone gabbled with excitement. "What did I tell you? A monster. A beautiful monster. Wait until you see his feet! Three toes, all with claws."

Ven knew the moment Evelina screamed that it had been a trap, that she had used him. The wine and his passion fuddled his mind. Rage robbed him of his faculties. He scrambled to his feet, his breeches tangled around his ankles, and lunged bodily at Ramone, his hands grappling for his throat.

Ramone screeched. Evelina cried out and leapt at Ven, to try to drag him off her father. Her nails raked his back, left bloody trails in his flesh. He paid scant attention to her. He concentrated on choking the life out of Ramone.

Glimmershanks entered the fray. Catching hold of Evelina, he pulled her off Ven and flung her aside. He was armed with a club and he struck Ven a blow on his head.

Ven collapsed on top of the pitifully groaning Ramone.

Glimmershanks grabbed hold of Ven's inert body and hauled him off his friend. Cursing her father for a fool one minute and soothing him the next, Evelina assisted the half-strangled Ramone to his feet.

Ven lay on his belly in the dirt. Pain blurred his vision, but could not blunt his rage. He tried to rise, only to be clubbed again. As he sank beneath the second blow, he heard Ramone croaking, "Don't kill him! He's worth more alive than dead!"

But it was Evelina's chill voice that followed Ven into pain-glazed darkness.

"Hit him again, Glimmershanks. Don't let him up. Hit the beast again. . . ."

Bellona disliked cities intensely and avoided them when she could. The citizens of Rhun and its many visitors were taking advantage of the full moon's light to loiter about the streets, chatting with neighbors, frequenting the taverns and alehouses. Musicians played on street corners, accompanying impromptu dancing. The jostling crowds made her feel as if she could not find air; it was being sucked into so many noses, exhaled with all its poisons by so many jabbering mouths.

Not knowing her way around, Bellona had no idea where to go to find the Rat and Parrot, but she was not afraid to ask. The city guard was out in force. Bellona stopped one, followed his instructions until she knew she was lost, then stopped another. In this way, she eventually came to the Rat and Parrot, though she lost half the night doing so.

She could tell at once, on entering, that the tavern was a repository for the dregs of humanity, who settled to the bottom of such containers until something happened to shake the container and dump them out into the streets.

Bellona did not enter the tavern, but remained standing at the door. She had no intention of turning her back upon any of these people. She cast a swift glance about, but did not see Ven.

Everyone was staring at her. She met their eyes boldly, stared them down. The patrons took her for a man, thin but muscular, who was undoubtedly capable of using the sword that rested so easily on his hip.

"I am seeking information," Bellona announced loudly from the door stoop.

She waited for silence to fall, which it did eventually, everyone now curious to hear what she had to say. "I am looking for a young man of about eighteen years, well built, dressed in clothes such as I am wearing. He was with a man called Ramone. Has either of them been in this place tonight?"

Glances flashed among the patrons. Some took a swig from their mugs. Others smiled knowingly and turned away. One woman—the red-haired whore who had been repulsed by Ramone the night before—spoke up.

"No, they haven't been here this night, but they were here last night."

Bellona fixed her attention on the woman, who was seated on a man's lap, one arm draped over his shoulder, sharing a mug of ale.

"Can you tell me where I can find this Ramone?"

"Keep out of this, Bets," warned the man. "It's no concern of yours."

The woman lurched drunkenly to her feet. Stumbling, she sagged against the table, peered at Bellona.

"What'll you pay me for what I know?" she leered.

"I have no money," said Bellona. "That's why I am seeking this man. He robbed me and my son. If I find him, however," she added, seeing the woman start to turn away, "I'll give you a reward."

"You'll never see it, Bets." The man grabbed hold of her forearm, gave it a twist. "Sit back down and behave yourself."

"It don't matter," said the woman sullenly. "That daughter of his thinks she's so high and mighty, looks down her nose at me. I owe him one and her another." She jerked her arm away, turned back to Bellona.

"Ramone lives in an inn overlooking an alley off the south end of Church Street. Follow Church Street 'til it dead-ends at a wall. If you end up in the church," she added with an ugly, beer-soaked laugh, "you've missed him."

"There, now, Bets, you've done your good deed," said the man, pulling her back down on his lap. "Now do a bad one."

He began to kiss her neck and fondle her. She took another pull at the ale and went back to business.

At the word "daughter," Bellona's heart sank. She guessed immediately what had become of Ven. Knowing she would get nothing more out of the woman and thankful she'd found out this much, Bellona left the tavern and set off in pursuit of Church Street, using the same means to locate it that she'd used to locate the tavern.

She found the street and the alley and the wall. The term "inn" implied more than what it was—a ramshackle structure of wood and plaster, held up on either side by adjacent buildings. Bellona knocked and beat upon the door and kicked at it with her boot, but there was no answer. She backed up a pace, craned her neck to look up at the windows.

"Ramone!" she shouted.

Heads poked out of windows. Angry voices told her to go

away or they would summon the guard. Bellona persisted in yelling for Ramone and at last a shutter on the ground-level opened a crack. A fox-faced man glared out at her from beneath his nightcap.

"You're wasting your breath," he said. "He's gone."

"What do you mean 'gone,' " Bellona asked.

"Gone!" repeated the man irritably. He waved his hand. "How many other meanings does the word have? He's gone and his whore of a daughter with him. Packed up and sneaked out before sunrise. If you find him, let me know. The filthy pig owes me four months back rent."

The man slammed the shutters. The heads in the windows withdrew, went back to their pillows. The echoes of Bellona's voice, that had rattled among the tall buildings, faded away.

She stood in the silent street. She had come literally to a dead end. There were a thousand holes into which these rats might run, a thousand things they could do to Ven, and all of them terrible.

She could waste days, weeks, months searching for him, and all the while he might be dead, his body buried in some shallow grave or thrown into the river.

Bellona had no idea where Ven was or what had befallen him. But she knew the person who might. She set out that night, walked until dawn, and then kept walking.

16

GLIMMERSHANKS HAD NOT BEEN BORN WITH SUCH
an outlandish name. He had bestowed it on himself, after
overhearing one noble lady remark that he was so graceful a
dancer that his legs seemed to "glimmer." That same noble
lady had been his patron, for a time. Her patronage meant
that his troupe of traveling players could wear her livery and
paint her coat of arms on their wagons and exhibit her writ
of authorization when they arrived at castle or manor house
or faire. Her name gained them entry when they would have
otherwise been turned away.

Sadly, word of thefts occurring at castles and manor houses
and faires honored by the presence of Glimmershanks's
troupe eventually reached the ears of the noble lady, causing
her to withdraw her patronage in high dudgeon. Nothing
daunted, Glimmershanks conceived that this was a mistake
on her part and continued to bandy about her name and wear
her livery until her soldiers descended upon the troupe,
ripped the livery from their backs, and set fire to the wagons.
Glimmershanks was still rebuilding following that disaster.

His father and mother had been gypsies, traveling the
continent with a dancing bear and a son. His parents thought

far more highly of the bear than they did the boy, for the bear brought them money and the boy did little but eat. Glimmershanks was taught to dance in order to perform with the bear. He was better than the bear, but few in the crowd noticed. He ran away at fifteen to join a troupe of traveling players, perfected his skill at dancing, added rope walking and juggling to his routine, and became head of the troupe when its founder died of eating bad eels.

Glimmershanks lost several members of the troupe during the encounter with Milady's guards, including his stilt walker and his ventriloquist. Lacking patronage, he was no longer welcomed into the noble houses; cities and faires relegated him to the fringes. Always an opportunist, he was able to capitalize on his banishment by putting it about that he could exhibit what other, more respectable troupes did not dare to. He replaced the ventriloquist with two brothers who had been born joined at the hip and the stilt walker with a full-grown man who was only two feet tall. As he came across other "freaks" he took them into his show, including a man whose body was covered with thick hair. He became the "bear man" and he wrestled all comers and ate raw meat, to the delight of the crowds. Then there was the girl who could bend her body into knots and kiss herself in places nature never intended.

Glimmershanks no longer danced. He was too busy being the troupe's business manager and promoter. He kept himself fit, however, for had a fondness for the ladies, and his shapely legs and gypsy eyes and languid grace rarely failed to win him a fair partner to share his bed. He was doing well for himself these days. His tawdry troupe, with its freaks and contortionists and dancing girls, was a popular diversion for gawking peasants and gullible middle-class burghers. The addition of a bona fide monster was certain to outdraw even the two-headed midget.

When Ven had been clubbed into unconsciousness, Glimmershanks bound him hand and clawed foot.

"The boys are waiting with the cart on the highway," Glimmershanks stated. He looked at the monster; then he looked at Ramone. "You'll have to help me carry him."

"He nearly smashed my windpipe," Ramone whimpered, massaging his scrawny neck.

"He didn't hurt your back or break your arms," Glimmershanks retorted. "You take his shoulders—"

"That's the heavy part," Ramone pointed out sullenly. "Besides, where's my money?"

"You'll get paid," said Glimmershanks.

"Now," said Ramone.

"Do you think I carry that much on me? You take the feet then."

"I'll help carry him," offered Evelina. She started to approach Ven, then stopped, eyed him warily. "If you're sure he's not going to wake up."

"If he does, I'll give him another clip with the club. You handled yourself well there, Mistress." Glimmershanks favored Evelina with an admiring gaze. "Your father tells me you've a mind to join the troupe. I'm thinking we could use someone with your talent."

"I'm going to be a dancer," said Evelina.

"And so you shall," Glimmershanks promised.

"On my terms," Evelina stated.

Glimmershanks stroked his mustache and quirked an eyebrow, intrigued. "What would those be?"

"I'm not going to dance on the stage by day and in some man's bed by night. I mean to do courtly dances. I'm to be dressed in fine clothes with ribbons in my hair. For, you see, sir, I plan for a wealthy gentleman to see me and fall in love with me. . . ."

She glanced at Glimmershanks from beneath her long, dark lashes. He recalled what he had just seen of her body, bare in the moonlight; her yearning, yielding abandon.

"Perhaps some wealthy gentleman has already seen you 'dance,'" he said. "Perhaps he'd like to see more."

Evelina favored him with a smile, then bent down to lift up the monster's feet. Ramone sighed, relieved. His daughter might do worse than become Glimmershanks's mistress and he was certain to get his money now that Evelina held the hand that held the purse strings.

"Grab his other foot, Papa," Evelina ordered irritably. "I'm not going to carry him by myself!"

"Devil take me!" Glimmershanks grumbled, lifting up Ven by the shoulders. "I didn't know monsters were this heavy."

"You're getting your money's worth, you see," Ramone grunted.

The three stumbled through the brush, half dragging and half carrying the unconscious Ven to where two men waited on the road with a horse and cart, ready to load up the monster and haul him back to the troupe. As they manhandled Ven into the cart, Glimmershanks eyed the blue-scaled legs and the clawed feet, and he came near salivating as he thought of the loot this would bring. His one regret was that the monster didn't have a tail.

"I could charge double for a tail," he said accusingly to Ramone, as though it were his fault the monster came up lacking.

Still, tail or not, he was a beautiful monster, as Ramone said. And he had just acquired a lovely young bedmate, who would fetch a good price when he tired of her.

Not a bad night's work, Glimmershanks reflected in satisfaction.

Jolted by a sense of danger jabbing at him from the darkness, Ven worked hard to regain consciousness.

The sun was shining brightly, which was odd, for he remembered it being nighttime. His head throbbed with pain and when he tried to open his eyes, the light made the pain so much worse that he gagged and shut his eyes against the knife-sharp brilliance. He tried to remember what had happened, but he was stretched out on some sort of unsteady bed that rocked and shook beneath him, bumping and jouncing him so that he found it difficult to think. If he could just be still a minute, memory would come to him. The jolting continued, however, making him sick to his stomach and jumbling his thoughts. He sank back into unconsciousness.

When next he woke, he was in the same place and he

forced himself to open his eyes, despite the pain caused by the bright sunlight. His vision was blurred, at first. He had an impression of iron bars, and his pain-muddled mind told him that he must be standing outside a prison. As his head cleared, he realized, with a thrill of horror, that the iron bars surrounded him. He was inside, not outside. He was the one imprisoned.

The shock dulled the pain and sharpened his senses. He could see now that he was locked inside a cage on wheels rolling down the highway, rattling and jouncing over bumps in the road. He looked out from behind the iron bars to see the countryside sliding past him. Glimmershanks's bully-boys, armed with stout clubs, walked on either side of the cage. The floor of the cage was covered in straw, as if it housed some wild beast. When he struggled to sit up, some of the men grinned and laughed and pointed at him.

Looking down, Ven saw that he was naked. The blue scales of his dragon legs gleamed in the sunlight. Manacles were locked around his wrists and ankles. Chains ran from the manacles to a bolt in the center of the rumbling wagon. The chains permitted him to move only a step or two in any direction. Understanding struck Ven a more terrible blow than any he'd yet received.

The cage did house a beast—him.

Rage and fear and shame stripped off Ven's humanity, as Glimmershanks had stripped off his clothes. Ven's one thought was to free himself. He seized hold of the chains and, in a burst of strength, ripped them from the bolt. The heavy iron chains dangling from his wrists, he lunged at the bars, hitting them with such force that the cage swayed and seemed likely to tip over. The men who had been grinning stopped grinning and fell back, raising their clubs. The draft horses pulling the cage flinched and swiveled their heads around and the drover shouted that unless the monster stopped his gyrations, they were all going to end up in the ditch.

Ven gripped the bars and gave a heave. The iron began to bend in his strong hands.

"Sweet Mother, do you see that?" one of the men gargled, backing up still further.

"Glimmershanks, your monster's escaping!" several bellowed.

Ven pulled with all his might at the bars and they gave way several more few inches. Another heave and he would have a hole big enough for him to force his body through. He was ready to give one more try, when one of the wheels rolled over a stone in the roadway, causing the wagon to lurch.

The drover shouted an urgent command and dragged the horses to a halt. Five men rushed the cage and wrenched open the iron-barred door. Two of the men, wielding clubs, jumped inside, while three remained on guard outside.

Ven took hold of the chain that was still attached to his wrists and lashed out. The heavy iron chain caught one of the men across the jaw. His face exploded in blood and he toppled backward out of the wagon. The other man was on Ven before he could shift his attack. The man struck Ven a savage blow that drove him to his knees. Blood dribbled into his eyes. He feared he was going to pass out again and he fought against the darkness.

He could not remain in this cage, on exhibit, for all the world to see, to gawk over and leer. He surged to his feet.

The man, standing over Ven, clubbed him again, opening last night's wounds and causing new ones.

Ven sank onto the floor of the cage. The straw underneath him soaked up the blood.

Glimmershanks had been riding at the front of the troupe. Hearing the shouts, he galloped back to the rear to find out what all the commotion was about. At his side, riding a small gray palfrey, was Evelina. She was dressed in fine clothes (stolen from the aforesaid patron). Evelina looked sleek and smooth and sleepy. Her night had been a long one.

"What's the trouble?" Glimmershanks demanded.

"Your beast-man tried to get out," reported one of his bullyboys.

The man inside the cage jerked Ven's arms behind him and bound the wrists tight with rope. He tied his feet at the ankles, above the manacles, which were still attached to the chain. The guards were taking no chances. They had carried off their friend half-dead.

The man cast Ven a surly glance. "The beast's strong, I'll say that for him. Tore apart those chains like they was made of bread dough."

"He's a marvel, isn't he," said Glimmershanks, enthused. "Why, look at him. Near beaten to a pulp and he's still awake. You'd like to get at me and rip out my throat, wouldn't you, monster," he called, rallying. "Puts me in mind of that lion we had a few years back."

"That cage won't hold him," his man stated. He continued to eye Ven warily. "He's safe for a bit, now, I reckon, but we should stop at the next town and have stronger chains made for him and repair those bars."

"Good idea," said Glimmershanks. "Well, all seems to be under control now. Let's get this caravan moving. We've wasted enough time, as it is. Are you coming, Evelina, my dove?"

"In a minute," she said coolly.

Evelina gazed through the bars at Ven. He saw himself in her brown eyes, saw his naked body. He remembered everything then—her lips, her touch, their lovemaking, and he stared at her dumbly, wanting to believe her innocent.

Evelina smiled at him. "Monster." She hissed the word. "Be a good monster or you will get no supper."

She cast Ven a last, taunting glance; then she reached out her hand to take hold of Glimmershanks's hand and the two of them rode off together. They took the place of honor at the head of the column of Glimmershanks's Traveling Troupe, which lacked a patron, but which had a real-life, honest-to-god-touch-him-my-noble-lords-and-ladies-if-you-don't-believe-it monster. Their fortunes were made.

Shame and despair roiled inside Ven, the bile so strong that it sickened him. His stomach muscles spasmed. Chill sweat covered his body and he began to shake. His bowels gripped. He retched and then was too weak and dizzy to be able to roll out of his own vomit, so that he retched again.

The drover started the horses moving. The iron-banded wheels bumped over the rough surface of the dirt road. The cage shook and swayed, but it was strongly built (its former occupant had been that same lion, whose moth-eaten remains were now exhibited to the wonder of small children).

Ven lay on the floor of the rocking cage, his eyes closed tight shut to blot out the sight of the iron bars. Darkness started to drag him away again and this time he let it. He hoped it would take him and keep him.

"Help me," his soul cried.

A voice answered.

Ven roused. He had never before listened to that voice. He had always hated the sound of it, but now it soothed him.

He had long avoided the cavern of his mind. He knew how to find it, however, and he sought it out.

As he entered, he found the dragon—his father—waiting there, waiting patiently.

17

FEW EARS HEARD VEN'S ANGUISHED PLEA FOR help, for most are not attuned to the voice that comes from the soul. His cry echoed among the caravans of Dragonkind, however, and there Grald heard it and recognized the voice of his son and exulted. Draconas heard the cry and he likewise recognized Ven's voice.

Draconas did not exult. He cursed.

His vile words, spoken in their own language, startled and offended the three elderly men who sat near him. Clad in richly embroidered tunics worn over loose trousers, their heads covered with expertly wound turbans, the elderly men and Draconas, who was dressed much as they were and looked very much like them, sat at their ease among cushions spread over the floor of a large tent. The three men and the disguised dragon held small cups of thick, sweet, black coffee, from which they would each take a delicate sip.

The old men were discussing magic, as it was practiced by their desert-dwelling people. Draconas did not participate in the discussion, though he had led the way to it. He listened carefully, hoping to find out if any of Grald's people with their dragon magic had appeared among these desert nomads, infected them.

Draconas heard tales of djinn and giants and enchanted lamps, clever princesses and charming thieves, evil sultans and wise sheiks, and carpets that flew like dragons. Nothing about dragons or dragon magic, however, much to his relief.

It was in the midst of one of these tales that Draconas heard Ven's cry and he cursed aloud. His rude interruption brought the speaker to a startled and offended halt.

Bowing, Draconas rose to his feet. Bowing again and gesturing, he begged the storyteller's pardon many times. He claimed that a sudden indisposition had seized hold of him and he must leave immediately, lest he offend them further. Draconas could tell that the old men were still indignant, though they murmured the proper words and pretended not to be, for a guest in the tent is always accorded hospitality, no matter how strange his behavior. Draconas would not be welcomed into their midst again, but that was the least of his worries.

The dragon's son was in danger—they were all in danger—and Draconas was half a world away.

His excuses made, Draconas flung open the tent flap. His unexpected and unannounced exit caused the guards to think he had committed murder at the very least. Two clapped their hands to the hilts of their curved-bladed swords, while a third seized Draconas and held his knife to his throat. Draconas kept perfectly still, made no move to defend himself. At a sharp command from the sheik, the guard released him.

The old man politely tried to dissuade Draconas from roaming the desert in the heat of the day. Draconas thanked him, but was adamant. The old man shrugged and went back inside the tent.

"Sunstruck," he muttered to his friends, who shrugged and soon forgot the bizarre behavior of their guest. Only the guards watched Draconas walk away. They kept their suspicious eyes fixed on him until he vanished behind the dunes.

Heat rose in shimmering, suffocating waves from the

windswept sand, a vast change from the dark, cool interior of the tent. The wind whipped Draconas's enveloping robes around his ankles, hampering his movement. He walked until he could no longer see the caravan and the oasis around which it camped among the undulating dunes. He hoped they could no longer see him. He looked searchingly about, fearing one of the guards might have been sent to follow him. He saw no one. Probably they thought him mad, and were just as pleased to be rid of him.

Like his shadow, the dragon's body was always with him. Draconas summoned the magic and his human body flowed into the dragon's and now it was the human body that was the shadow, insubstantial and wavering in the glaring sunlight. Draconas took wing and flew swiftly westward.

Draconas skimmed high above the world that turned beneath him, slipped past him into minutes and hours that were here and gone too soon. The dragon's massive wings beat the air. Stroking down to catch and hold the wind beneath him. Swooping up to free the trapped air and fling himself forward into heaven. Stretching out his neck and reaching upward for the stars, then the downbeat again. He drew air into his lungs with the upward stroke, exhaled with the down, maintaining the rhythm so that his body would perform without his being conscious of it, achieving maximum efficiency.

And all the time, the waves of the vast wind-rippled ocean seemed frozen beneath him. He knew with every upstroke and downbeat that he would be too late.

"Anora!" His urgency was blaze-orange, flaring red. "What we feared has occurred. The dragon has found his son."

"Then deal with it, Draconas," Anora returned, gray and sharp-edged.

"I am half a world away. I cannot reach him in time."

"Whose fault is that?" Anora was cold.

"I cannot be in two places at once!" Draconas fumed, frustrated. "It was you who sent me on this mission."

"True." Anora sighed. Her thoughts splintered, became disorganized, hard to follow. "I suppose we must take some responsibility. It's just . . . so much is happening in the world . . . Now this . . ."

Draconas was alarmed. He'd never known Anora to be indecisive, distracted.

She is showing her age, he thought, and immediately, guiltily, he buried that thought deep where she would not see it.

"By law we dragons cannot intervene," she said at last. "Not directly. You know that, Draconas. That is why you are the walker."

"Damn the law!" His answer was blue-black as thunder. "For once in your life, damn the blasted law!"

"The law *is* our life, Draconas," Anora returned sternly, rebuking. "And the lives of those under our care."

Of course it is. Of course. He knew that.

She was gone, and he was left to continue his solitary flight across the vast ocean.

18

GLIMMERSHANKS'S TRAVELING TROUPE, NOW boasting a monster. rolled along the King's Highway, heading for the nearest major city with all possible speed. Glimmershanks was in haste not only to exhibit his monster and recoup some of the money he'd laid out on him, but also to have a blacksmith forge chains that would hold Ven securely. Glimmershanks would never admit it, but he'd been more than a bit shaken to see the broken chains and the bent bars, not to mention his guard's broken face.

Still, the monster—even comatose—attracted so much attention that Glimmershanks could afford a little danger. Travelers they met on the road stared, open mouthed, at the Snake Man (as Glimmershanks was thinking of billing his prize). Many ran after the caravan, shouting and calling out to others along the way, until such a crowd gathered around the cage that they were starting to impede the troupe's progress.

"To say nothing of the fact," Evelina pointed out caustically, "that they are getting to see the monster for free."

Struck by this, Glimmershanks ordered a halt for the

night. His bullyboys drove away the gawkers, while other members of the troupe, under Evelina's direction, draped the cage in canvas.

As twilight smeared the sky with orange, Glimmershanks contacted the local lord to offer a private showing. The lord was laughingly skeptical, but he and his friends had nothing better to do, and so they rode over to view the monster. Glimmershanks drew aside the canvas. His Lordship was impressed. He tweaked and gouged Ven's scales, to make certain they were real and not affixed by spirit gum. Convinced of the monster's validity, the lord handed over a sack of coins, stating that the show was well worth it. He then led his noble lady forth to see.

She and her ladies gasped in pleased horror at the monster, tittered over his nakedness, and afterward teased each other with titillating references to snakes and asps.

Fortunately Ven was spared knowledge of this, for he had not yet regained consciousness. He had been unconscious for so long that Glimmershanks began to fear for his investment and he persuaded the troupe's leech—on pain of a beating—to enter the cage. The leech examined the monster. He gingerly felt the skull and pronounced it intact. Emerging from the cage, the leech stated that in his opinion, the monster was suffering from melancholia and would likely die of it.

Glimmershanks was sick with gloom, until Evelina pointed out that he could make money off the stuffed corpse of the Snake Man, with less trouble and expense.

Thinking this over, Glimmershanks concluded she was right. After all, His Lordship had paid handsomely to see a slumbering monster. A dead one would do just as well. Glimmershanks was enchanted with Evelina. He'd never met a woman with so much sense.

After the lord and ladies departed, Glimmershanks shut himself in his wagon to stash away his money and take some pleasure with Evelina.

The deepening night was warm and pleasant. Laughter came from Glimmershanks's wagon. The other members of the troupe passed around jugs of raw wine and made bawdy guesses as to what was happening in the master's bed.

Around midnight, the wine jugs were empty and those who had not passed out were thinking groggily of their own beds. Glimmershanks emerged from his wagon, wearing only his breeches, and went to check on his investment. He found the monster unconscious, but still breathing. Yawning, Glimmershanks was traipsing back to his wagon when he caught sight of a halo of bright light moving in his direction.

Glimmershanks had been born on the road. He'd visited every major city and most of the villages and towns in this part of the world. He'd seen plague, fire, famine, flood, and war, and he'd lived through it all. His instinct for trouble was finely honed, and that blaze of light approaching his caravan raised his hackles and pricked his fingers.

"What is it, Boss?" asked one of the drovers.

"A mob," said Glimmershanks shortly.

"Headed this way," the drover opined.

Glimmershanks glanced around. "How long will it take to hitch up the wagons?"

"Too long," said the drover. "They'll be on us by then."

"I'll go alert everyone," said Glimmershanks. "You stay here and keep an eye on them."

He ran through the camp. "Douse that fire! You, girls, pretty yourselves up."

"What is it?" Evelina demanded, as Glimmershanks came bursting into the wagon. "What's wrong?"

"A mob, headed this way."

"A mob?" Evelina repeated in disbelief. She caught hold of a shawl, wrapped it around her naked body, and peered out the open door. "But where did they come from? The nearest town's ten miles away. And why? We haven't done anything."

"A mob doesn't need a why," said Glimmershanks. "Hand me my shirt."

In truth, there were so many possible "why"s that he would have been hard pressed to have picked just one. There wasn't a town or village in these parts that he hadn't visited in the past few years, leaving pregnant girls and cheated tradesmen in his wake.

"You better stay in the wagon," he added, seeing Evelina drawing on her chemise. "I'm going to have to talk our way out of this one."

"Then you will need my help," she said.

"Boss!" The drover appeared at the door. "It's not a mob! It's—you're not going to believe this—it's a group of holy men and there's a nun with them!"

"Holy what?" Glimmershanks paused in the act of thrusting one knife up his sleeve and tucking another into his boot. "Are you sure?"

"There must be twenty of 'em, Boss. All dressed in brown robes, their shaved heads a-gleaming. The nun's all in black and she's at the head of the line. See for yourself."

"How strange," said Glimmershanks, frowning. "There isn't a monastery within a hundred miles of here."

"They're likely on some pilgrimage or other," suggested Evelina. Now that the excitement was over, she sank back on the bed with a yawn, her skirt half on and half off. "They're just passing by here on their way somewhere else."

Glimmershanks was not so sure. His fingertips still prickled and the back of his neck itched. Snatching up his hat, to make himself appear as respectable as he possibly could, he left the wagon and went out to the road to where the rest of the troupe had gathered, chatting and wondering. He could see the group clearly in the torchlight and there was no doubt that they were holy brethren of some sort. There was also no doubt but that they were walking toward the caravan.

The monks and the nun were in no hurry. Their progress was slow, solemn, and inexorable. They did not have the look of a friendly audience. Glimmershanks could not imagine what he had done to draw the wrath of a group of holy men, for he made it a practice never to go near a church. He put on his best manners, pulled off his cap, and went to meet them.

"Brothers," he said, bowing humbly, not being exactly certain how to address them. He bowed again to the nun.

"Sister. You are welcome to our camp. Please, come, seat yourselves by our fire. We are a troupe of poor players and we do not have much, but what we have is yours."

He cast a worried glance over his shoulder at his troupe, but they knew the way of the world as well as he did. The women, who had been dressed for bawdy comedy, saw that they were going to be in a miracle play and changed their costumes to suit the action. They scrubbed the rouge off their faces, threw scarves over their heads, and covered up their bosoms. Evelina, accompanied by Ramone, and looking very much the virginal daughter, came to stand meekly beside Glimmershanks. She dropped a graceful curtsy and demurely crossed herself. The bullyboys sobered quickly. Dropping their clubs, they stood twisting their hats in their hands, looking uncomfortable.

The nun was at the head of the procession and she was the one who advanced to receive Glimmershanks's homage. She was stout, middle-aged. Her expression, bound by the wimple, was severe.

Glimmershanks made a welcoming gesture toward the fire. "Please, Sister, Brothers . . ."

The line of monks came to a halt. The nun cast a look around the caravan. Her gaze fixed on the cage covered in canvas. She turned glittering eyes back to Glimmershanks.

"We hear that you are harboring a demon in your midst," she said gravely. "Where is it?"

Glimmershanks gaped. He could not for the life of him imagine what the woman was talking about.

"D-demon?" he stammered, looking at Ramone for inspiration.

Ramone shrugged and shook his head.

The nun pointed a plump finger at Glimmershanks. "Speak, man! Tell us where to find the demon. Every moment that passes puts you and all here in peril of your immortal souls."

Glimmershanks was beyond mystified. "I am sorry, Sister, that you have come all this way for nothing. We have a man with two heads and a—"

Evelina elbowed him in the ribs. "The monster, you ninny," she hissed.

Glimmershanks cast a nervous glance at the draped cage. He was reassured to see that the canvas was drawn tight-shut.

"Your Holiness, we may be actors, but we are god-fearing men and we would never—"

The nun turned her head to speak to the monks. "Brother Jon, Brother Mikal. Search the wagons."

"Now see here, Sister," Glimmershanks said heatedly, moving to intercept the two monks, "you have no right—"

"You would do well to stand aside, sir, and let us proceed." The nun's eyes narrowed. "I would not like to think that this fiend of hell has seized hold of you and speaks through your mouth. There are ways of removing the devil from a man." The nun calmly folded her hands, one over the other, inside the sleeves of her habit. "These ways are not pleasant. Stand aside."

Accustomed to performing before unfriendly crowds, Glimmershanks was used to thinking on his feet. He did as he was told, with a great show of humility.

"Ramone, escort the brothers to the first wagon," said Glimmershanks in defeated tones. "Show them *everything.*" He laid emphasis on the word. "We have nothing to hide."

Ramone took the hint. The wagons were parked in a haphazard horseshoe around the fire. The prop wagon was at one end of the horseshoe. The cage holding the monster was at the opposite. Knuckling his forehead, Ramone bade the monks accompany him. The prop wagon to which he led them held the stage sets, the costumes, and the troubadour's instruments. It would take the monks a long while to sort through the tambours and cymbals, drums and wigs and petticoats, castle walls, a bright orange sun and a shabby moon that had seen better days.

Glimmershanks looked back at the nun. She stood alone, aloof, her gaze fixed now on nothing, her eyes unfocused. She might have been listening to a distant voice.

"Daft old bitch," muttered Glimmershanks. "I'll just go see how they're getting along, Sister," he said aloud.

As he turned away, he made a motion to his bullyboys. Each man slipped his cap back on his head and, moving slowly and silently, picked up the club he had let fall. Evelina, who had been fidgeting in the background, saw the gesture, understood its import.

"Are you crazy?" she demanded, pouncing on her lover. "You can't beat up a nun! It's . . . it's . . ." She wasn't sure what it was. "Bad luck."

"Bad luck for her, not for me," growled Glimmershanks. "We made twenty sovereigns off the monster this one night alone. I'll be damned if I lose that kind of money!"

"But suppose she's right?" Evelina whispered nervously. "Suppose he is a demon who's here to steal our souls? We might all be damned!"

"He's welcome to my soul if he can find it." Glimmershanks grabbed hold of her, pulled her close to whisper, "I'll stall them. You fetch a blanket and throw it over the monster's legs." He fumbled in his pocket. "Here's the key to unlock the cage."

Evelina cast a trepidatious glance at the cage. It was all very well to taunt the monster when he was on one side of the bars and she on another. But to be in the cage with him . . . And if he was a demon . . .

"I don't know—" she faltered.

"Hurry, damn you!" Glimmershanks gave her arm a painful twist for emphasis. "Before you're missed."

Evelina looked at him and then at her father, who stood near the wagon, watching the monks and wiping sweat from his forehead. She took the key, gripped it tightly in her hand, and, rubbing her arm, turned to walk back toward their wagon.

"Where is she going?" the nun demanded, her eyes focusing suddenly and unpleasantly on Glimmershanks.

"To open up the other wagons for inspection," he replied. He pressed his hands together in a prayerful manner. "Would you like something to eat while you wait, Sister?"

The nun did not deign to answer.

Glimmershanks stood with his arms crossed, one hand

toying with the hilt of the knife in his sleeves. The two monks had entered the first wagon. There came the tinny clatter of a cymbal falling and a bang as a prop toppled. Glimmershanks hoped it fell on their tonsured heads. He kept Evelina in sight out of the corner of his eye. She had entered their wagon, grabbed up a blanket, and now stood hesitating on the stairs. He scowled and made a jerk with his head, to urge her along.

Another bang and a clatter drew the nun's attention to the prop wagon. Evelina dashed out the door and ran behind the next wagon in the line. Glimmershanks lost sight of her. He turned back to the nun, favored her with an ingratiating smile.

"Are you certain you wouldn't like to sit down, Sister? This may take a while."

Clutching the blanket, muttering imprecations against Glimmershanks and stomping on him with every angry footfall, Evelina circled around behind the wagons. She was not accustomed to being ordered about, nor was she accustomed to being manhandled. Her father had never dared lay a finger on her. She'd have an unsightly bruise on her arm by morning.

"The bastard will pay for this," she promised.

She had difficultly seeing in the darkness, for the wagons blotted out the light of the torches and she stepped ankle-deep into a puddle of slop thrown out of the twins' wagon. This did nothing to improve her temper. Evelina threatened her father, her lover, and everyone else who had gotten her into this mess and the cage holding the monster was on her before she knew it.

Evelina drew up short. Shrouded in canvas, its misshapen bulk looming large against the cold light of the stars, the wagon had an awful look to it in the night. Evelina clasped the blanket to her chest and slowly walked around the cage to the rear. She held her breath, listening. She could hear nothing; no sounds came from inside.

"The monster must still be unconscious," she said to herself. "Unconscious or asleep. Or dead."

She didn't want to do this. She lingered outside the wagon, building up her courage. The fact that she could hear no sounds of life coming from inside helped her—that and the thought of the money, which, in her fit of temper, she'd forgotten. Twenty sovereigns, Glimmershanks had said. Evelina gingerly lifted up the flap of canvas that covered the bars of the cage and slipped beneath it.

The folds of the heavy canvas fell down around her, pressed her against the cage. Beneath the canvas, the darkness was absolute and stank of urine and blood, leather, and wet straw. Evelina had smelled worse in her time and she paid scant attention to the stench. She could not see the monster, but then she could not see her own nose in the pitch darkness. The monster made no sound. Not even breathing. She fumbled around in the dark, trying to find the lock, and eventually was forced to thrust the canvas aside in order to let in some light. Drawing in a welcome breath of fresh air, she glanced back over her shoulder at the camp.

Glimmershanks and the nun stood near the fire. The monks were searching the other wagons. For all the commotion, the night was eerily silent. The monks did no talking. The players kept their mouths shut. Ramone wandered about aimlessly, twisting his hat in his hands.

Ruin of a good hat, Evelina thought irritably.

No one was looking at the monster's cage. A glimmer of light from the distant torches dimly illuminated the iron bars. She adjusted a fold of the canvas so that she had a clear view of the lock and thrust the key inside. Before she opened it, she took another wary look at the monster. His eyes were closed. He lay unmoving in the matted, filthy straw.

"And what is in that wagon?" The nun's voice was loud in the stillness.

"Which one, Sister?"

"The one covered with canvas."

Evelina froze, the key in her hand.

"Ah, that one," said Glimmershanks. "We had to lock up a member of our troupe, I am sorry to say. I hired him on in the last town. Too late, we discovered the man was a thief.

We are honest folk, Sister. Traveling players cannot afford to be otherwise. We planned to hand him over to the sheriff at the next stop. He found out and he went berserk. He attacked one of my actors. Perhaps you saw him? The man with the broken nose?"

Evelina couldn't see Glimmershanks but she could almost hear him shrugging his shoulders.

"We had to confine him and the only place we had was the empty cage where we used to keep the lion."

Evelina smiled sourly. A convincing liar, that man. She gave the key a wrench. The lock clicked. Grabbing hold of one of the bars, she hoisted herself inside the cage. She shook out the blanket and started to throw it over the monster's lower body.

She looked up.

Eyes looked back.

The monster's eyes—open, dark and empty, save for two points of flame that burned too steadily, were too unwavering to be a reflection.

Evelina shrank back against the bars of the cage. Terror, stark and numbing, closed off her throat. She was helpless. The scream that would bring them all running to save her was the scream that would ruin her. The monks would find their demon. Glimmershanks would blame her, cast her out, and her father with her.

The monster made no move. He said nothing. He had no need. His eyes spoke for him.

Twenty sovereigns.

Her lip curling, Evelina took a step nearer Ven and tossed the blanket at him. She missed her aim. The blanket only partially covered him. One knee and a shin, with its glistening scales, were bare.

He might have covered himself up, but he lay still, looking at her.

Evelina drew in a breath. Bending down, she grabbed the corner of the blanket and twitched it into place. If any monk peered into that cage, he would see no demon. Nothing but a grubby, stinking thief.

"It's in your best interests to keep quiet, monster," Evelina hissed from her curled lip, "and play along. Else you will be burned at the stake!"

The flame in the monster's eyes did not waver. The eyes did not blink. No expression altered the face that was half in shadow. Evelina shuddered, uncertainty pricking her. From the way the monster looked, he might embrace burning, as some of the martyred were said to do to hasten their own deaths, reaching out to the searing flames with half-charred arms. Evelina thrust open the cage door and jumped out.

She trembled; her hands shook. She had to pause to calm herself, quiet the beating of her heart, and recover before she could walk back into the torchlight.

"Twenty sovereigns," she repeated to herself, telling them off in her mind as if they were beads on a rosary. Feeling better, she ducked beneath the canvas, taking care to keep to the side of the wagon that was in shadow. She sauntered over to stand beside Glimmershanks and smiled at him in confident assurance.

19

VEN WRAPPED IN DARKNESS. INSIDE THE CANVAS covering, he could see nothing. He could hear voices, but they were muffled and indistinct. He concentrated, listened closely, trying to make out what was being said.

The words brought only fear, not reassurance. Fear that was half-remembered, yet sprang from somewhere hidden deep inside the cave of his being.

"Demon . . . devil . . ."

He was a child again and his breeches torn and his leg exposed, blue scales glistening, and the horrified whispers, all around him. . . .

He tensed, raised himself up on one elbow.

There came the crunch of feet outside the cage and the click of a key in the iron lock. He smelled perfume. He heard her voice, muttering to herself. He closed his eyes.

The barred door opened. Evelina pulled herself up into the cage. He opened his eyes, looked at her.

She went pale. Her eyes widened in terror. She shrank back against the bars.

Ven took grim and bitter pleasure in her fear, but her terror didn't last long. Disgust curled her lip. Her mouth moved, but he couldn't hear what she was saying for the blood pounding in his ears. He watched her until she left and even when she was gone, he watched where she had been, her afterimage burned on his eyes, as when one stares too long at the sun.

"See for yourself, Your Worship." Glimmershanks took hold of a corner of the canvas and drew it back from the bars of the cage. Ever the showman, even with his livelihood at stake, he could not help but indulge in a bit of theatrics. His gesture at Ven came complete with a bow and a flourish. "As you see, Sister. No demon. Naught but a thief and an inept one at that."

Ven propped himself up on his elbow.

The monks gathered around the wagon. The light of their torches blinded him and Ven raised his hand to shield his eyes. At first he could see nothing but flaring flame and black, indistinct shapes merging together in a smoky haze. His eyes focused. The shapes were faces, separate and apart and distinguishable: Glimmershanks with his unctuous smile, Evelina scornful and aloof, Ramone afraid.

The nun approached the cage, her hands folded in her sleeves. She came to a halt at the iron-barred gate, standing directly opposite Ven, separated from him by the length of an arm. The light of a torch carried by one of the monks shone directly on her.

Ven knew the nun. He didn't know how he could know her, but he did. He knew her face, knew the features of her face, knew the eyes and the sound of her voice. The thought came to him that she was someone he'd run across at the faire or in the city, but that seemed unlikely. The face did not conjure up images of faires or cities. The face conjured night, loneliness, blood, death.

Transfixed, Ven stared at the nun. Her lips moved, forming words that only Ven could see and hear.

"Dragon's Son."

Ven knew her then.

The night on the road. Bellona beaten, bleeding, dying. The holy sister holding him fast in her smothering, black-robed grip. His rage, his terror hot in his mind, coursing through his blood, bursting out of his fingertips. The horrifying scream and the sickening smell of burnt hair and flesh and the satisfaction of the kill.

The holy sister smiled at Ven, a secret smile, for just the two of them. With a rapid movement, she reached into the cage and took hold of the blanket that covered Ven's legs. The nun proved that she, too, appreciated a good show. She hesitated just long enough to allow Glimmershanks to break out into a sweat, then she gave the blanket a yank.

The blanket slithered off Ven's legs. The monks held their torches high, so all could see.

Scales glittered in a smoky halo. The white claws on the toes glistened.

The nun turned to Glimmershanks. "Not only are you harboring a demon, but you attempted to conceal the fact. There can be only one reason." The nun sounded sorrowful. "You have bartered your soul to the devil, my son."

"And I made a damn good bargain, Your Holiness," returned Glimmershanks with a laugh. He could see, out of the corner of his eye, his men on the move, clubs in their hands, slipping up on the hapless monks. "Twenty sovereigns off the monster this night alone."

Evelina clapped her hands. "Bravo," she shouted, mocking. "Bravo, my love."

Emboldened, Glimmershanks thrust out his jaw in a grinning leer. "I'd make money off the devil himself if I could keep him penned up."

"Godless man!" The nun's voice stalked the hillsides with the rumble of a gathering storm. "Your soul is lost! Would you drag down the souls of others?"

Glimmershanks raised his voice. "Shall we save our souls tonight, lads, or our purses?"

Growling ominously, his bullyboys raised their weapons and moved in. The monks appeared oblivious to their danger. The nun laid her hand gently on Glimmershanks's breast.

"I call upon the devil to leave you," she said softly.

Glimmershanks started to strike aside the hand that rested on his beating heart. His hand jerked. His mouth gaped, his eyes bulged in shock. His body went into spasms. Starting at his rib cage, the spasms jolted through his arms and legs and snapped his head back. Glimmershanks stared at the nun with eyes in which life had already fled, then toppled over, stiff as a stone statue, dead.

Evelina's gleeful mockery gurgled into screams, her cries rending the fire-filled night. The rest of the troupe stared at the corpse, their leader. They stared at the nun, who had not moved, beyond the outstretching of a lethal hand. The stares shifted wildly after that, some going to Evelina, some to the monster, and many, in growing terror, to the monks. All the thoughts of each person seemed to coalesce in a single moment. Without a word spoken, the members of the troupe dropped their weapons and fled. The first off the mark was Ramone, whose self-serving thought process had moved a bit more quickly than the others.

"Slay them!" cried the holy sister. "For they, too, have consorted with the devil. They cannot be permitted to live."

The monks reached up to the torches. Grabbing handfuls of fire, they held them, blazing, in their palms. Each wrapped his hand around the flame, shaping and molding the fire. Selecting a fleeing target, each monk hurled his gob of flame. Trailing fire like comets, the balls streaked through the darkness and smote their targets squarely.

The flames whirled around the writhing bodies of the players. The fires spread rapidly, fanned by the winds of dragon magic. Ven could see the flames reflected in his scales, tiny people dancing a death dance in each one.

The horrifying screams of the immolated lasted only moments before the charred bodies collapsed into heaps of black, greasy ash.

The holy sister turned to Evelina. She had not run away, but had remained standing over the ruin of her dreams. Her face drained of blood, she began to shake, her teeth chattering so that she bit through her tongue. Blood dribbled out of her mouth.

One of those piles of ash was her father.

"Hand me the key, girl," said the nun.

Evelina stared at the holy sister without seeming to comprehend her words. Then, with a sudden movement, a spasmodic jerk of her hand, she flung the key into the woods, flung it as hard and as far as she could. Ven could hear the faint tinkle of iron as it struck a stone or a tree. The sound and the key were swallowed up by darkness.

Evelina laughed—tight, thin, terrible laughter that echoed strangely in the night. Still laughing, she sank onto her knees and crouched there, clutching her arms around her breast, and rocking back and forth, laughing.

The nun made a gesture to Ven, who stood impatiently waiting for freedom behind the locked door.

"Stand back, Dragon's Son," she said.

Ven obediently stepped back a pace. The nun passed her open palm near the lock. Blue light sparked and the lock burst asunder with a sound of splintering metal. The cage door slowly sagged open. Ven jumped lightly out of the cage to land on the ground. His claws dug gratefully into the cool, dank earth.

The monks bowed to him, bowed their tonsured heads. The torches sputtered and smoked, the flames flickered.

"Dragon's Son," they whispered softly.

The holy sister's gaze flickered from Ven to Evelina. "If you want this girl for your pleasure, Dragon's Son, take her. We have time," she added in cool nonchalance.

Evelina ceased to laugh. Huddled on the ground, she looked up. Her eyes fixed on Ven, who stood staring down at her with a calm and terrible impassivity. Drawing herself up, Evelina clasped her blouse and chemise over her breasts—a flimsy blockade—and regarded him with disdain that was not feigned, not bravado. She knew her power. Every man she had ever known had withered before it.

"You dare not touch me, monster!" she cried.

Ven reached out, took hold of her arm, and dragged her close.

Evelina quailed. She saw in his eyes her own reflection, yellow in the firelight, and she saw herself withering in the fire, like the dying martyrs in the books she could not read, but could only enjoy the pictures. Her disdain burnt to ashes, she shrank from him, tried to pull away.

"Ah, Sister! Don't let him harm me!" she pleaded. "He's a demon. . . ." Her voice died.

The holy sister had turned her back. The monks had re-formed their line and were walking back toward the road, taking their torches with them. Evelina was left in the dark with Ven, with the monster.

She began to sob and beat on him frantically with her free hand. He held her fast, his dragon eyes seeing her flesh glimmer pale as moonlight in the darkness.

It was pleasing to think: *I can take her. I can have my revenge on her. She made me love her and then she laughed at me.*

The thought, unbidden, came to him, *What grotesque creature will I begat? What kind of wretched child will come wailing into this world to live what sort of wretched life?*

Suddenly sickened, Ven flung Evelina away from him. She stumbled and fell, landing on her hands and knees, sobbing and moaning.

He turned his back to walk away and then felt something strike him. He glanced over his shoulder. She had thrown a clod of dirt at him. Crouched like a beast on all fours, she shouted curses at him, filthy curses, fit for the brothel.

Ven continued walking to join up with the monks. The holy sister glanced at him, as he fell into loping step beside her.

"You do not want her?"

Ven shook his head. He felt sick to his stomach.

The nun made a gesture. "Brother Mikal, kill her."

"No, don't," Ven said quickly. "Don't kill her."

"Wait, Mikal!" The holy sister intervened. "The Dragon's Son has spoken and we obey." She turned to Ven. "What would you have us do with her?"

"Let her go," Ven said, glancing back at the pale, slobbering girl. "What harm can she do?"

"A great deal," said the nun gravely.

She seemed to be silently communing with someone. A spark flared in her eyes, dimmed, and was extinguished.

"If we do not kill her," she said, after this pause, "then we must take her with us."

Ven scowled. "I don't want—"

"She knows too much," the holy sister stated in the flat tones of finality. "She would talk. Fetch her along."

When Evelina saw the monks coming for her, she leapt to her feet and tried to run. Her skirts tangled around her ankles. She staggered, tripped, and fell flat. The monks seized hold of her by the arms. Evelina gave a muffled cry, then sagged in their grip, her body going limp, flaccid.

"She's fainted," reported Brother Mikal.

"Just as well," said the holy sister. "She'll be less trouble." She gestured to a handcart that the troupe had used for hauling about barrels of ale. "Put her in there and bring her along."

They tossed Evelina into the back of the cart. Ven pretended not to watch, though he cast worried, sidelong glances at her when he thought the holy sister wasn't looking.

At a gesture from the holy sister, one of the monks untied a bundle he had been carrying and brought out a brown robe, such as they were all wearing. He handed the robe to Ven to cover his nakedness. They had also brought along leather boots, to hide the clawed feet.

Ven slipped his arms into the loose sleeves of the robe and pulled it over his head. The rough cloth covered his bare flesh, fell in folds over his scales. He tugged on the boots, then straightened to his full height, once more hidden, comforted.

"I want to fetch my sword," said Ven. "It is probably in Ramone's wagon."

The holy sister shook her head. "You must appear to be a man of peace. Wearing a sword is out of the question. Why is that a problem?" she asked, seeing Ven frown. "After all, you do not need weapons of steel to kill a man, do you, Dragon's Son?"

"I don't know what you are talking about, Sister," he said, his voice even, level. Shrugging, he added, "If I may not wield a sword, then at least let me carry a knife."

The holy sister regarded him steadily.

Ven met her gaze, held it.

At last she said, "If you feel the need. Brother Mikal, fetch the Dragon's Son a knife."

"Where are we going?" Ven asked, eager to leave the camp of the ill-fated troupe of actors. Eager to leave the greasy piles of ash, that were already being picked up and scattered by the hands of careless night.

"Your father is eager to meet you," said the holy sister in response.

Ven understood by this that he was not to know their destination. He pulled the hood up over his head, so that the fabric blotted out the wagons and the cage and the drifting ashes, as the shadow of his father blotted out the other voice, the voice of Draconas, who had told him who and what he was.

But not the why.

"I am eager to meet my father," Ven said.

20

THE RAIN HAD BEEN FALLING FOR THREE DAYS. not a pounding. driving rain, that made the creeks rise and caused people to eye the river nervously. This was a nurturing rain, the type of rain the farmers liked, for it fell so gently that it had time to soak into the ground.

Marcus stood at the window of his father's study and watched the raindrops slide down the leaded panes of glass. One after another, they spattered against the pane, dissolving into each other, rippling along the thick glass that distorted everything he saw through it, so that the rain blurred an image that was already wavery. All he could really see were colors. The dark slate of stone walls and the stone courtyard below. The sodden blue of the cloaks worn by the king's guards, who huddled beneath eaves and overhangs or stood miserable in corners, trying unsuccessfully to stay at least moderately dry. The dull green of grassy hills. And over and above everything the feathery gray of the clouds that rolled with steady, boring monotony over the land. The clouds obsured the city of Idlyswylde, so that Marcus could see nothing of it and it was not that far away.

The palace was silent, except for the rain sounds, and those had become monotonous, so that one did not hear them anymore.

He pushed open the window, which operated on hinges, and breathed in the moist gray air. Water gushed from the mouths of the gargoyle drain spouts, spewing out the rain in small waterfalls. That amusing sight could entertain Marcus only so long, however, and eventually he turned from the window with a sigh.

He'd been closeted with his tutor all morning, conjugating the verbs of languages that no one spoke anymore, because the people who had once spoken them were dead. Undoubtedly of boredom. His tutor was gone, but the verbs still wandered about in Marcus's head, dull as the dripping rain. He needed something to clear the moldy taste of them from his brain, something to brighten the gloom of this day.

Marcus's body remained standing by the window, near the desk where his father's astrolabe collected dust and spiders. Marcus's mind left the study and entered a place known only to himself—a small, round room that had no windows, furnished with nothing but a small chair—a child-sized chair.

Usually he was alone in this room. Only one person was ever allowed to enter it with him, and that was a person he'd never seen, a child he knew only by hand and voice, and that voice rarely heard. Marcus kept all others out, for he recalled quite vividly Draconas's warning about the dragon who was waiting somewhere, hoping to enter and seize him. Marcus could sometimes hear snuffling and sniffing and scrabbling outside the door to the room, as of some great beast prowling about. When that happened, he sat quite still in the very center of the room, let no one know he was there, and the prowler always went away.

Marcus did not remember the tower room in which he'd been kept prisoner as a child; he remembered very little of his childhood, nothing much before the arrival of Draconas. Looking back at that time was like looking through the wavery glass into the rain-washed landscape—a blur of colors and images, reality gone over with a damp sponge. The wing

of the palace where the room had been located had been re-
furbished during Marcus's absence and nothing had been
said to him about it on his return. He did wonder, though,
why he sometimes felt a strange reluctance to go into that
part of the palace.

The room where he went in his mind to work his magic
was the exact replica of that physical room, although he
would never know it.

Inside his room, Marcus sat down in the chair that was a
child's chair, yet always large enough to accommodate him.
He spun the colors in his mind, the way the spiders spun
their webs in the astrolabe, and he caused the rain to stop
and the clouds to part. He brought forth sunshine and it
sparkled and crackled through the leaden panes. He could
see the city with its church spires and thatched roofs and colorful banners. The rain-soaked dead verbs drowned in the
sunshine. Motes of dust danced in the air.

Pleased, Marcus embellished the dust motes with wings
and gave them heads and arms and legs and little hats made
of the tops of acorns. . . .

A scream and a crash jolted Marcus out of his chair. He
turned around to see one of the maidservants standing amid
shards of crockery. The maidservant had her eyes screwed
tight shut and her mouth wide open, screaming.

Before her danced hundreds of playful dust motes, each
with a little hat.

"Oh, dear god!" Marcus gasped.

He approached the hysterical servant with some intention
of soothing her, but when she saw him coming, she flung her
apron over her head and fled the room, still screaming.

The ludicrous side of the situation struck Marcus and he
started to laugh. A rustle of petticoats and puffing outside
the door caused his mirth to evaporate. He hastily banished
the dust motes and began contritely picking up broken
crockery.

His mother stood in the doorway, regarding him with a
look of affectionate exasperation.

"I'm sorry, Mother," Marcus said hastily, before she could

speak. "I didn't realize—" He paused, then amended, "I thought I was alone."

His mother shook her head and gave a deep sigh.

"Is the girl . . ." Marcus had to work to keep his lips from twitching at the memory. "Is she all right?"

"Oh, I suppose so," said his mother. "Fortunately, she's a bit addlepated. Cook will be able to convince her she was seeing things, which she apparently does on a regular basis anyhow or so I'm given to understand. . . . Now, don't you start laughing, young man. It's no laughing matter."

Ermintrude looked as severe as her dimples would allow.

"I know, Mother," said Marcus, sobering. "I'm sorry."

Marcus had promised Draconas he would not make use of the magic for this very reason.

Danger to him.

Danger to his parents.

He swallowed his laughter, washed it down with regret. It was a promise he had trouble keeping. The magic was so enticing, so tempting. The magic made of this gray and washed-out world into which he had so mistakenly been born a fantastical realm of his own creation. His little room was a realm he ruled, a realm he controlled. In his room, no one looked at him askance or whispered behind his back or sneered. . . .

Walking over to his mother, Marcus took hold of her hands and kissed her on her dimpled cheek. She had grown plumper over the years, something she did not mind, for as she was wont to say, "Better a double chin than one that looks like turkey wattle." Even though she was somewhere in her forties—just where she would never say—gallant courtiers still wrote poems praising her dimples, which flashed as winsomely now as they had done in her youth.

"I am truly sorry, Mother," Marcus repeated. "It won't happen again. It's all so boring. Verbs and rain, raining verbs." He smiled, hoping to make her smile.

Ermintrude was forced to look up at him for he was taller than her by several inches. He was sixteen, so young and so handsome in his youth, with his fair hair, strong body, and finely molded face, marked by strong will, intelligence, and a roguish sense of humor that sparked in his hazel eyes.

Everyone liked Marcus, yet he had no friends.

He was the king's bastard, that was true. But being born on the wrong side of a royal bed was no impediment to advancement in a royal household. His grandfather, the king of Weinmauer, had made one of his bastards a chancellor and another a bishop. Nor were bastards shunned or looked upon as less than desirable marriage candidates. A king's son was a king's son, no matter the bar sinister. But when the tourneys and revels were held at Castle Idlyswylde and the nobility gathered for merriment and play, the young men laughed and drank and danced, the young ladies whispered and giggled and danced, and Marcus roamed the windswept castle walls alone.

They thought him "odd." People whispered that there was something "peculiar" about him, not quite right. One young lady-in-waiting had actually used the word "fey" to describe him. Ermintrude had immediately banished that young woman, sent her back to her parents on some manufactured pretense.

It is his eyes, Ermintrude thought. *Charming, laughing. Disconcerting. Look into his eyes and you see dreams, glimpses of other realities. He does not look at you, but through you and above you and around you and beyond. He sees you and he sees so much else besides. You wonder if you mean anything to him or if you are just another dust mote, adorned with an acorn hat.*

Ermintrude loved Marcus dearly, this child that she had not borne, this child who was her husband's shameful secret. She loved Marcus more than she loved her own sons, much as she was ashamed to admit it. She loved him because he needed her. Her other boys were normal, healthy lads, who had let go of her hand at age two and toddled forward into life without ever looking back. Marcus was different. She had walked through darkest hell alongside him, only to feel his little hand slip out of her grasp. She had watched helplessly as he wandered into a dream world where she could not follow. Although he had no memory of that terrible time, he did remember the hand that held fast to his through the long night of his insanity. The two of them were close, with the closeness of those who share a special secret.

Edward loved Marcus, but his love was a love born of duty and self-recrimination. Marcus was a constant, living reminder to Edward of his downfall and, although the king accepted his punishment with a good grace, whenever he looked into Marcus's eyes, he saw reproach.

"My son," said Ermintrude, her grip on him tightening, as if once more she felt him starting to slip away, "don't go back into that little room of yours. Promise me. You are always saying that these incidents will not happen again, but they do and they will. Last month, it was a stableboy who was frightened half to death by the sight of a mermaid in the horse trough, and before that a guard. Shut the door to the little room, my son. Lock it and throw away . . ."

Her voice died, her words sighed to an end.

Marcus still held her hand. He still looked on her with the same affectionate smile, but mentally he had turned his back on her and left her, perhaps going into that same small room.

He squeezed her hand, to assure her of his love, then, letting go, he turned away from her to gaze out the open window. The wind had risen slightly, blowing a fine mist of rain into his face. He'd hurt her and he knew it. She'd hurt him and she knew it.

Ermintrude smoothed the silken folds of her voluminous skirt and tried to think of words that would smooth over what she'd said, make amends. They'd had this pain-filled conversation before. Afterward one or the other or sometimes both at once would reach out, apologize. This time, he was the one. Something was happening in the courtyard and he was swift to make use of it to ease the tension.

"Barbarians at the gates, Mother," he said lightly, gaily. "I believe we are being invaded."

Grateful to him, Ermintrude prepared to take up the proffered olive branch. She moved to the window with a rustle of petticoats.

She looked down on top of the grizzled head of Gunderson, the old seneschal, escorting a prisoner. Gunderson was wrinkled and crippled now. His gnarled limbs might have belonged to an old oak, they were so bent and twisted. He was as tough as an old oak and seemed likely to be as long-lived. The person being marched along behind him might well have been one of those ancient people responsible for the death of the verbs Marcus had been conjugating. The person was middle-aged, with long dark braids that straggled out from beneath a crude leather cap. A leather vest covered a sodden wool shirt and breeches. An empty sword belt hung around the waist; the guards having confiscated the weapon at the gate.

By the sword belt and the breeches, most people took this person for a male. Ermintrude did too, at first, but she changed her thinking.

"That is a woman," she said astonished, not quite certain how she could tell, yet positive it was so.

Perhaps it was a graceful flow to the walk, a lilt to the long neck, the set of the slender shoulders and muscular arms. A woman wearing a sword belt being escorted to the castle under guard. . . .

Ermintrude grasped hold of her son's arm, a clutching grasp, desperate and keeping.

"What is wrong, Mother?" he said, startled. "Your hands are like ice!"

Not only her hands, but her heart, chilled to stillness.

Ermintrude knew the woman crossing the courtyard in the rain with her long, determined strides. Knew her well, though Ermintrude had never before seen her. Perhaps it was the description Edward had given of her, though he'd caught only a fleeting glimpse of her, seated astride her horse, drawing back the bowstring, loosing the arrow. Perhaps it was instinct. A mother's instinct. Or perhaps it was the fear that had festered in Ermintrude's heart from the moment Gunderson had laid the tiny, squalling newborn babe in her arms.

Fear that someday, this woman would come to claim Melisande's child.

"Mother," said Marcus, chafing her hands to warm them. "Please don't be upset with me. I'll think about what you said, Mother. I truly will. It's just that . . . the magic is a part of me . . ."

Ermintrude managed a smile for him, though not the dimples. "I know, dear. I should not have said anything. You are so precious to me. So precious." She was rattling. She felt herself starting to lose control.

"I don't dare send up another servant," she added, hearing her voice and not recognizing it, hoping he didn't notice. "Pick up the pieces of the pitcher, will you, dear? Toss them in the dustbin. I'll send . . . someone . . . to fetch it."

She hastened to the door, her hooped skirts swinging, the trailing hem sweeping up bits of broken crockery and carrying them after her, scraping across the floor. Impatiently, she caught hold of her skirt, shook the bits free.

"There's a love," she said, and was gone before he could say a word. She shut the door so quickly that she nearly caught her skirts in it.

He stared after her, bemused, then glanced down at the shattered crockery that was now strewn all over the room. He grinned again at the memory of the dust motes. The grin vanished in a twinge of conscience.

"I love her best of anyone in the world," he said to the rain, remorseful. "Yet I hurt her more. I don't mean to. I just do."

Mentally pummeling himself, he swept up the pieces, threw them away, and then flung himself down at the desk, intending to perform penance by going back to raise the ashy verbs from the dead, thinking gloomily that they were starting to take on vampiric life, sucking his soul dry.

"This woman won't give you her name," said Edward, looking up from the text he was reading. "She won't tell you why she is here. And yet you say that I should give her an audience."

"Yes, Sire, I do," said Gunderson steadily.

"In the name of salvation, why?" Edward demanded irritably.

He was in his solar, in a comfortable chair before a crackling fire, a cup of mulled wine at his hand, and a new book on astrology, with what were said to be revolutionary theories about the orbital paths of the planets, open on the reading stand before him.

Gunderson sucked on his lip a moment before answering. "Because I've seen her before, Sire."

Edward tensed, wary and alert. "Where?"

"In the house, Sire"—Gunderson paused—"where your son was born."

Edward closed the book, rose to his feet.

"You said she would not say why she had come. Then how did she manage to enter the palace grounds? She must have said something to somebody."

"She told the guards that she was here to see you on urgent business. Dressed as she is—and she is a sight, Sire," Gunderson added, shaking his head—"they would have turned her away, but she told them that if you did not see her, you would be sorry. She said that on purpose, Sire, because she knew she would be arrested and brought to the palace dungeon. When I saw her, I knew her. When she saw me, she knew me." He shrugged.

"And you truly advise me to see her?" Edward asked.

"It's not her sword that worries me, Sire. It's her tongue. She has a tale to tell, if she was of a mind to tell it."

"Who would believe her?"

"Your enemies, Sire," said Gunderson.

Edward looked away, looked back at the book. His fingers absently traced the raised gilt letters on the leather binding.

"Weinmauer, you mean. I—My dear," he added, turning to see Ermintrude standing in the doorway. "This is not a good time—"

"You must see her, Ned," said Ermintrude emphatically, sweeping into the room, her hooped skirts swirling around her, making her the eye of a silken storm. "She is here to take our son. I know it. You must not let her!"

Her face was flushed, her eyes bright, pleading. She

clutched her missal in her hand, as if keeping fast hold of God.

"Talk to her, Ned," Ermintrude urged. "Tell her she cannot have him. Tell her!"

"No one will take him, Wife." Edward put his arm around her, felt her trembling. "No one will take Marcus. I promise you that. I will see her, Gunderson. Bring her here to this chamber. Dismiss the servants."

Gunderson bowed and made his way out. He moved slowly these days, for his knees pained him, especially in wet weather, and he was gone some time. Neither Edward nor Ermintrude spoke. She slipped out of his embrace to stand before the fire, holding tight to the missal, once bringing it to her lips to kiss it in silent supplication.

Edward stared into the memories that were rushing at him like foes on the attack, memories that knocked him from his saddle, rode him down, jabbed at him with their spears, drawing blood. He started to take a drink of wine, feared he could not swallow, and set the cup back down.

The door opened. Gunderson entered, followed by the woman. He shut the door behind him and placed his back against it. Outside the rain fell. The gargoyles drank it up and spit it out into the courtyard. The woman was wet to the bone, her leather vest giving off an unpleasant, animal odor.

"She says her name is Bellona," announced Gunderson.

She stood straight, her shoulders back, her chin high, for she had been a soldier and a leader of soldiers, and she was not intimidated by kings, she who had loved a high priestess.

"He knows who I am," Bellona said.

"I do, as a matter of fact," Edward returned, determined to keep his voice steady, his demeanor calm. "The last time I saw you, you were aiming an arrow at Melisande, trying to kill her."

If he hoped to gain some advantage, he failed. The woman accepted the accusation with nothing more than a slight inclination of her head. Her eyes went to Ermintrude, then flicked away, returned to the king.

"Melisande died in my arms," Bellona said. "She died moments after the birth of your son. Did he tell you the story?"

"Did Gunderson tell me? No—" Edward began.

"Not him." Her voice was scornful. "He came too late to do anything except take away the child. I mean the other one who served you. Draconas."

Edward shook his head. "He told me nothing."

"Did you even ask?" Bellona's lip curled.

"No, I did not," Edward replied, adding with quiet dignity, "Melisande made it a condition that I never try to find out. She made me swear it, as a holy vow, in return for allowing me to take and raise our child. I have kept my promise to her."

His voice hardened. "What do you want, Bellona? Why are you here? Do you want money—"

He might have struck her. Her face went livid, her eyes flared. Her hand grasped spasmodically at her empty scabbard and though the guards had taken her weapon, she burned with such a fierce, pale light that Gunderson half drew his sword. At a glance from Edward, Gunderson slid the weapon back into its scabbard. But he kept his hand upon it.

"I do want something," said Bellona in a voice that was tight, squeezed by her anger. "But not money. I want to talk to Melisande's son."

"Out of the question," said Edward brusquely.

"He has a right to know his mother!" Bellona cried, her hands clenching.

"He knows his mother," Edward returned. He held out his hand to Ermintrude, who moved slowly to stand beside him, but did not take hold of his hand. She kept fast hold of the missal, her gaze on Bellona. "He has no need to know the story of his birth. It would do no good and might do great harm. I think you had better leave, Mistress Bellona."

He gave a nod to Gunderson, who reached out his hand to take hold of her arm.

She shook loose, pulled back. "I will not leave until I have seen him and talked to him."

"Then I will have no choice but to have you thrown into the cells, Mistress," said Edward.

Bellona crossed her arms over her chest. "Then that is what you had better do."

Edward made an impatient gesture. "Take her to prison, Gunderson, if that is what she wants."

"Edward, perhaps—" Ermintrude began.

He rounded on her, his face a face she did not know, had never before seen. "No, Ermintrude. This time I will *not* be persuaded. This woman will go to prison and stay there until she rots."

He stalked out of the room. Gunderson again laid his hand on Bellona's arm and this time she did not shake him off. She looked intently at Ermintrude. Two women, utterly different. One soft and plump, shored up with steel bands sewn into the fabric of a corset, bulwarked by velvet and silk, jewels and lace. The other sinew and muscle, bone and skin and leather. Neither could ever understand the other's life. Yet, in that moment, something passed between them.

Unspoken, simple, basic, not found in everyone, but once found, recognized—the knowledge of what is right.

Gunderson gave Bellona a none-too-gentle tug and dragged her off. Bellona did not defy him, though her head turned as she stumbled after him, her gaze still fixed on Ermintrude. Until she was removed from the room, Bellona looked nowhere else, and even after she had gone, Ermintrude still saw the woman's eyes.

Ermintrude stood in front of the fire, holding fast to the missal. She did not pray. She knew what she had to do and so did God. No need running after Him, tugging on His sleeve, when He had so many other worries. She might have begged Him to spare Edward from hurt, but it was too late for that. The hurt had happened. For years, the wound had festered. Either this would help heal it, or he would hate her forever.

The possibility of his hatred grieved her, for she loved him dearly. But before her was right alongside wrong and if she turned from right, she was not worthy of anyone's love or trust, whether he ever understood that or not.

Ermintrude wriggled her bulk around inside the corset, adjusting the stays so that they did not pinch her—or rather, pinched less. She grasped the missal, clasped her hands over her stomacher, drew in a breath, and advanced.

21

BELLONA PACED THE SMALL PRISON CELL THREE steps in each direction, her feet scattering the straw that had been strewn over the floor. The cell, located far below ground level, was as dark and cold as the sixteen-year-long night of her grief. The cell door had a small grate for the use of the jailer, who could open it, peer through it to make certain that the prisoner had not hanged herself, then close it again, shutting off the light. The prison was rat-infested, but then so was the palace. Vermin were a fact of life. Bellona paid the rats no attention, except to kick one that got in her way.

She paced because she had to be doing something. If she had been at home, she would have been mending clothes or making arrowheads or sharpening knives. As it was, she had nothing to do with her hands and so she occupied her feet. She did not doubt that the young man would come. She only wondered when. She trusted it would be soon. A fortnight had passed since she had lost Ven and she had to face the fact that more time would pass before she could start searching for him. Still she felt keenly each moment that slipped away.

Voices—barely heard, muffled—came from somewhere in the distance, echoing among the stone corridors.

Bellona halted, listened tensely.

The grate slid open. Light flared, blinding Bellona. She raised her hand to block it, trying to see. The cell went dark; the jailer's bulk momentarily blotting out the light. A moment's silence, and then the key rattled in the lock. The heavy door swung open, pushed inward. Light flared again, and cast the shadow of a man onto the floor at Bellona's feet. She could not see his face, which was in darkness, but she could feel his wonder.

"I am Marcus, prince of Idlyswylde. My mother said I am supposed to talk to you."

He remained standing in the doorway, his shadow touching the tips of her boots. Melisande's son.

"Alone," she intoned.

The young man hesitated, then turned to the jailer. "Leave us. Wait at the end of the corridor. I will call out if there is need. You have the queen's command in writing. And the queen's gold in your pocket," he added wryly.

This argument carried the day. The jailer thrust the flaring torch into an iron sconce on the wall of the cell, lit another torch for himself, then departed, shutting the door behind him and locking it. They heard him walk away, his footfalls loud in the silence that stood between them. The torch light flickered. The cell was alive with shadows. Bellona saw Melisande in every part of the young man and her heart ached so that she could not speak.

"What do you want with me?" Marcus asked finally.

"To make amends," Bellona answered in a low voice.

He stared. "For what?"

"For your father and for myself. We have both failed her."

"Failed? Who did you fail?" He was perplexed, bewildered.

"Your mother."

No need to say which mother. He knew. He flinched.

Bellona swallowed, went on. "I swore to do something and I failed. I didn't keep my vow because I was afraid. Afraid of losing him."

She made a sad, bleak gesture with her hands. "But I lost him anyway. Maybe because I didn't do what I had promised. And now your mother is disappointed in me and in your father. For the same reason. He, too, is afraid."

She lifted her gaze, met the eyes that pierced her heart. "I must make amends."

Marcus was silent, absorbing. She expected him to protest, to ask where, who, how. But all he said was, "You talk of my mother as if she were alive. She isn't, is she."

Bellona shook her head and he nodded his slowly, sadly.

"I didn't think so. But I always hoped . . ."

He let the words trail into silence. He met her gaze, his own steady and unwavering. "You want me to go somewhere with you. To do this thing you left undone."

"And your father," Bellona insisted belligerently, determined not to let Edward off blame's hook. "You father is at fault, too."

"Very well," said Marcus. He turned to lift the torch from the sconce. "Let's go."

His sudden decision caught Bellona completely by surprise, although it shouldn't have. Melisande had the same capacity to make swift decisions, to act without hesitation, so that it often appeared as if she were impulsive, behaving recklessly or rashly. The truth was, as Bellona had come to learn, that Melisande had the ability to access a situation swiftly, think it through, reach a decision, and act on that decision immediately—a trait her son had apparently inherited.

Bellona saw him about to bellow for the jailer and she grabbed hold of his arm.

"Wait! I doubt the queen's command or the queen's gold can free me from this prison cell."

"That's true," Marcus admitted, looking back at her in a thoughtful manner. He suddenly smiled and his smile was his father's—ingenuous, infectious. "That won't be a problem, however."

He glanced around the cell, considering. "My mother told me your name is Bellona." He paused, added gently, "My other mother. The one who told me to trust you." He pointed at something. "Sit over there, will you? On that straw pallet by the wall."

"What are you—"

Marcus raised his hand. "I didn't ask you questions," he reminded her.

Shrugging, Bellona sat down on the pallet.

Marcus studied her intently, as if committing her to memory. He raised his hand and smoothed it over the air between her and him. The air shimmered in front of Bellona like a wave of heat rising from the ground.

Marcus gestured. "You can stand up now. Come over here, beside me."

Mystified, Bellona did as he told her.

"Look there," he said, gesturing.

Bellona standing stared at Bellona sitting.

She gasped and fell back, bumping into him and nearly knocking him down. He held on to her, steadying them both. The seated Bellona did not move.

"I'm sorry I startled you," he said.

"No, you're not," Bellona retorted. "You enjoy startling people with your magic."

"Ah, you know about it then?" Marcus sounded disappointed.

"I've seen in before," she said coolly. "There is one called Draconas who can do the same."

Now it was Marcus who gave the start.

"You and I have a lot to talk about" was all he said.

Bellona looked back at the illusion of herself. She had not seen her reflection for a long time and she was surprised to see how old she was, how much she had changed since the days when the leader of the warrior women of Seth had regarded her face with pride in the bright metal of her shield. She had not cared about how she looked, not cared since the day Melisande had died in her arms. Time had marched on with Bellona's body, carrying her, wounded, from the field of battle. But time had left her soul behind in a ditch, forgotten.

"I'm afraid I can't do more than make you just sit there

like that," Marcus apologized, thinking that was why she was staring so long at the illusion. "If I were here with it, I could manipulate the magic, make you stand up or lie down, for example. But once I leave, I have no control over the illusion. It will remain static."

"Won't the jailer see through it?"

"Oh, Burt will figure it out eventually." Marcus grinned. "The third or fourth time he looks through the grate and sees that you haven't moved, the cobwebs in his brain will part and he'll enter the cell to check. He'll let out a yell and people will come running and my parents will know what I've done. We'll be well on the road to wherever it is we're going by then."

He mused, scratched his jaw, deep in thought. "Spiriting you out of the cell and away from the palace is going to be a bit trickier."

Bellona quit looking at herself. The image disturbed her. She focused instead on Marcus, tried to find something of Ven in him.

That was difficult, because he wasn't a monster.

Marcus was handsome, well groomed, well fed, well educated, well mannered, well spoken. Everything was well with him. The world was well with him. Bellona felt a stirring of jealousy for Ven.

If she had known of Marcus's past history, she might not have been so bitter, so vindictive. But she knew nothing of the locked room, the tormented dreams. She saw only that he was beautiful and that his beauty had gained him everything he had ever wanted.

Yet, his beauty is Melisande's. How can I hate him? she asked herself. *Why do I feel I want to drag my nails across that perfect face and leave it ruined? Yet, I do. And I do not understand.*

"I have an idea," Marcus said, interrupting her tangled logic. "But you must do exactly as I tell you. Will you?"

"That depends," she growled, not in a mood to grant his every wish.

Marcus smoothed his hand over the air in front of her. He

walked around her, shaping the air as if it were clay. When he finished, he eyed her critically.

"That's good. Not perfect, so you'll have to be careful. But it's good. I can't see you and yet I know you're there."

"What do you mean? You can't see me?"

"I have used the magic to make you one with the darkness," said Marcus proudly.

Bellona looked back at the illusion of herself.

You're not as clever as you think you are, she told the young man silently. *It doesn't take magic to do that.*

"And keep out of the light," he cautioned her. To give emphasis to his words, he doused his torch in the slop bucket. "Stay in the shadows. Not because people will be able to see you if you step into the light. They can't, even then. But if they expect to see something and suddenly they can't see it, then they start to get suspicious. Do you understand?"

"No," she said, impatient to be gone. "But I will keep out of the light and I will not talk and I will move quietly and not bump into anything. Summon the jailer!"

He began to yell for Burt.

The jailer opened the door. "I was starting to get worried, Your Highness. What happened to your light?"

"Dropped my torch," Marcus explained.

"You should have called me, Your Highness," Burt said, rebuking. "No telling what that savage might've done to you in the darkness."

"I did call, Burt," said Marcus lightly. "And here you are. No need to worry. All well, as you can see."

He pointed to the seated Bellona.

Burt stood aside, his back against the door, allowing just enough room for the prince to squeeze pass the jailer's pudgy gut. Marcus walked out the cell and into the corridor. Burt cast a perfunctory glance at his prisoner. Seeing that she wasn't going anywhere, he started to shut the cell door. Bellona could have made a mad dash, but she would bump into the jailer and she did not need any of Marcus's patronizing explanations to know that this would be disastrous.

She experienced a moment's panic that was swiftly consumed in anger. Marcus had played her for a fool. He was using this means to escape her.

She was about to take matters into her own hands, grapple with Burt, brain him if necessary, when Marcus said, "Oh, wait a moment, will you, before you shut the door? I seemed to have dropped my gloves."

He brushed past the jailer and stepped back into the cell, where he peered down at the floor, searching all around.

"I can't see in this confounded murk, Burt. Hold the light for me."

Burt obeyed, lifting the torch high. Marcus moved deliberately near the wall, forcing Burt to shift the torch and his protruding gut away from the door. Bellona slipped past the jailer, moving as quietly as she could. The slight rustle of straw was covered by Marcus, rummaging around in the search for his gloves.

"Ah, here they are." He held them up in triumph, slipped them into his belt.

Burt grunted. Marcus walked back out into the corridor. He cast an oblique glance around for Bellona and it was then, for the first time, that she felt as if he must have truly caused her to blend in with the shadows, for his gaze passed over her twice before he found her. He flashed her a conspiratorial grin and she saw what she should have seen earlier, if she had not been so preoccupied. This was a game for him. He was enjoying this—the daring, the intrigue, the secrecy, the ability to use his magic, show it off. This was a break from the dull routine of being prince.

Play your game, then, Your Highness, she said silently. *So long as you plan for us to win, it is all the same to me.*

Burt slammed shut the cell door, thrust the large key into the padlock, and turned it. He led the way down the corridor, the torchlight flaring and smoking, casting Marcus's shadow on the wall. Marcus chatted easily with the jailer, discussing the firing of the famous cannon. His arms and those of the shadow moved as he talked, indicating with broad, sweeping gestures how far the cannonball had flown that day, doubling his fist and punching at an imaginary dragon to indicate the damage it would have done. His shadow glided over the cold stone walls, surrounded by a halo of light.

Bellona walked after him. She was her own shadow.

Marcus saddled and bridled his horse. The stablehands, sleeping in the loft above the stalls, slumbered through the entire process. Pulling Bellona up behind him, he guided the animal quietly over the cobblestones, casting a nervous glance up at the windows of his parents' rooms. No light flared. His father would be asleep, but perhaps his mother stood there in the darkness, looking down on him. He blanched at the thought of her sorrow. The fun was not quite so much fun. She was the one who had sent him, however. He looked up at that dark window, bid her silent farewell, and rode on toward the gate.

The guards were highly amused at Marcus's earnest tale of riding out alone to visit a "friend," especially when he implored them to keep his departure secret and assured them he would be back before daybreak. Laughing, they let him pass.

"Boys will be men, it seems," said the commander with a knowing wink.

"It's about time he showed some interest in wenches," stated one of his troops. "Should we tell Gunderson?"

"Naw, let the lad have his tumble." The commander grinned. "Like as not, the Old Man knows all about it anyway and he won't thank us for waking him."

The guards went back to their watch, whiling away the long, dull hours to dawn, which would not be dull—sadly for them—for the prince would not return.

Edward had never been so angry. His rage burned in his gut. Hot words bubbled in his throat, so that he could taste them, bitter, on his tongue. He kept himself under control, for his father had taught him that a king who ranted and raved and took out his temper on those who did not dare strike back was not a true king, nor even a true man. Edward did not give voice to his anger, but it was plain to see in his livid face, his dilated eyes.

Ermintrude stood before him, her hands clenched tightly over her stomacher, her own expression resolved and un-apologetic. She believed she had done right. He believed she had committed a terrible wrong. It was the worst moment of their marriage, the worst in their lives.

Their love had never been one of wild passion, such as the poets celebrate. Politicians, not chubby angels armed with bows and arrows, had manufactured their romance. They had met each other on the day they were wed and been whisked into bed almost before they knew each other's names. If they didn't find the love of the ages in each other's arms, they did find affection, caring, and mutual respect.

Ermintrude had known deep pain only once in her marriage, and that was the day Edward confessed, in tears and broken words, his infidelity to her, the infidelity with Melisande that had resulted in a son. Ermintrude had never been disloyal to Edward, never given him cause for pain before now. In his own way, he felt as much betrayed as she had felt then.

"How could you do this?" he demanded, when it was safe to speak, when he was certain the hot, vile words would not come spewing out like the rainwater from the mouths of the gargoyles.

"It was right he should know the truth," Ermintrude an-swered, quavering a little, for she was truly grieved to have hurt him, yet steadfast in her determination.

"No, it was not right!" Edward cried, slamming his clenched fist down onto a table. "*You* had no right! He is *my* son—"

"And hers," said Ermintrude, her voice low, throbbing. "His mother. Melisande's."

Edward could find no immediate answer and, making an emphatic gesture negating the entire argument, he turned his back on her.

"His mother has a claim on him," Ermintrude went on, advancing. "A claim on you. She has never made it before now—"

"His mother is dead," he said impatiently.

"Not to him, Ned! She lives in him. Half his blood is her blood. Half his heart is her heart. You cannot reach inside him and rip her out. He knows you, but he doesn't know her. He needs to know her, Ned. He wonders about her, all the time—"

"Bah! He's never said anything—"

"Not to us. He fears upsetting you and hurting me. I've seen it in him, though, many times. Whenever he stops his reading and lifts his head and stares out the window, into those distant mountains where the kingdom of Seth lies hidden in the clouds, he's thinking of her. He's wondering who she was and why she abandoned him and if she loved him or hated him. She has reached out from the grave to take her rightful hold of him and if we try to break that hold, he will be the one who suffers."

"He will suffer." Edward turned around again, his eyes alight with his fury and he was not listening because he did not want to hear. "He will suffer and die, perhaps, at the hands of that savage female!"

He flung wide the shutters, leaned out the window.

"Saddle my horse!" he shouted at the startled faces, who, with craned necks, peered up at him. "I leave in ten minutes. A flogging for all of you if the horse is not ready in time!"

"Edward—"

"I know where she will take him," he said thickly. "I'm going to bring him back."

Ermintrude started to intervene, but changed her mind. The ride would do him good, clear his head, give him a chance to think. He slammed out the door and she could hear him racing up the stairs to his room. She went to the window and waited and eventually he came, booted and cloaked and armed, into the courtyard, where Gunderson stood with the horse. She saw Gunderson say something to the king, probably also trying to dissuade him, for Edward shook his head and mounted. He looked up at the window, where he knew she would be standing. He made no sign, however, but looked away.

Gunderson stepped hurriedly back to avoid being ridden down, and Edward rode off with a clashing of hooves on the cobblestones.

22

ALL THIS WHILE, VEN AND THE MONKS WERE traveling east toward an unknown destination. Ven asked several times where they were going, but the monks made no reply—they rarely spoke to him or among themselves. The holy sister did talk, but only if talk was absolutely necessary, and then their conversations were brief.

"All in good time, Dragon's Son," she would say. "All in good time."

Since Ven was not given to idle conversation himself, he found the silence of the party suited him. As to their destination, he came to realize that it didn't matter. He was bound to go there, as a babe in the womb is bound to be born.

Evelina was going there, too, whether she wanted to or not. She was no longer being hauled about in the pushcart. The holy sister had found her a nun's habit, which she donned without protest. Ven had no idea what the nun had said or done to Evelina, but she walked along quietly enough, never speaking a word, keeping her head cast down. Perhaps her compliance lay in the fact that one of the monks was always at her side. When she needed to make her ablutions, the monk accompanied her. She was never alone, either by day or by night, when the monks posted guard over their campsite.

Once, early on in their journey, Evelina tested the monk's resolve. Ven woke to a commotion in the night. He started to rise, but the holy sister told him sharply to go back to sleep, all was in hand. The next morning, he caught a glimpse of Evelina's face, hidden in the shadows of the wimple. Her lip was cut, her nose bloodied. The left side of her face was badly bruised, the left eye swollen shut. There were no further incidents in the night.

Ven stayed away from Evelina. He did not speak to her or acknowledge her existence. If she walked at the head of the line, he walked at the rear. If she was in the rear, he walked up at the front with the holy sister. The nun gave Ven to understand that in preventing Evelina's death, he had exhibited a weakness that had displeased his dragon father. Ven had the impression that Evelina had been brought along as some sort of test for him. Testing his willpower perhaps.

Ven's weakness displeased him, as well. He reminded himself over and over how Evelina had deceived him, sold him, caged him, mocked him. He went to sleep every night telling himself how much he loathed her, only to wake in the darkness, sweating and aching from dreams of her. Whenever he stole a glance at her, saw her trudging along the dusty road, her head bowed, reliving, perhaps, the gruesome death of her father, Ven knew intense guilt. When he saw her beaten and brutalized, he felt responsible.

"If I had not come into her life, she would be dancing somewhere in the sunlight," he said to torment himself.

His feelings were irrational, of course. If her father had not robbed him and then conspired with his daughter to ensnare him, Ven would have never come into her life. Love and desire are at constant war with the rational and Ven very quickly vanquished logic. He was not foolish enough to think that one day she would come to love him. He was a monster, after all. But he did nurse the feeble hope that she might come to care for him, if only just a little.

And so the days passed. The journey continued, until one day they reached a wide river that the holy sister told Ven was named the Aston. The nun pointed out a mountain range to the north. She told him that there was a city hidden in those mountains, a city named Seth, and that the river flowed down from those mountains. The party took to rowboats when they came to the river, paddling upstream toward the mountains, only to veer off to the east when they reached a fork in the river.

They paddled the boats into a slot canyon, rowing beneath towering cliffs until they came to a cave that was partially submerged under the water. Oars shipped, the boats let the current carry them into the cave, into darkness that was cool and refreshing to Ven, after the hot glare of the sunlight off the water.

His dragon eyes were still compensating for the darkness when a tall man walked out from the shadows and came to stand at the water's edge. The man was massively built, with hunched shoulders, a thick neck, and heavily muscled legs. Ven recognized him immediately. The leader of the "thieves" who had attacked Bellona.

"Sister, you and the Dragon's Son remain here with me. The rest of you, go," the man ordered, waving his hand. "I will meet you downstream."

The boats containing the monks and Evelina continued on through the cavern. Ven could not help but cast a glance at her, still in her disguise, as the boats pulled away. She did not look at him, but kept her head lowered.

The monk rowing the boat that held Ven and the holy sister steered toward the shore. The man eyed Ven, who boldly returned the scrutiny.

"My name is Grald," said the man. "I serve the dragon, your father."

You are the dragon, my father, Ven thought, but did not say. Bellona's story of his mother's rape and her description of the human male who had been the conduit for the dragon's seed was a portrait Ven hung in his mind's lair. Ven had no idea how the dragon could take over a human body; that was something Draconas might have told him, if Ven had cared to listen. Ven didn't care. He caught himself scratching the scales of his legs and stopped.

"My name is Ven," said Ven, "and I serve no one."

"We all serve the dragon—" the holy sister began in a tone of rebuke.

Grald motioned her to silence. "Ven," the man repeated with a half grin, half leer. "That's a strange name."

Ven shrugged. "Strange or not, it is my name." He saw no need to explain the derivation.

"And what is your brother's name?" asked Grald, conversationally.

"Brother?" Ven stared, startled. "I have no—"

The denial hit a wall.

A little room. A small chair. His mother, holding a child by the hand. The child reaching out that hand to Ven, inviting him into the little room, to come play with the rainbows. . . .

"No one told you," said Grald.

"No," said Ven.

"But you've been in contact with him."

"No."

The dragon came sniffing and snuffling around the cavern of Ven's mind. Anger darkened Ven's colors, for he resented this interrogation. He did not lash out, for that was what the dragon wanted him to do. Lash out. Come out. Come out of his lair. Ven held still, kept silent. The dragon probed with his claws, jiggling every rock Ven had piled up in front of the entrance, testing them all to find the slightest chink or crack. The dragon would find none.

Dragons spend years on the construction and design of their lairs, laying out the labyrinthine corridors meant to confuse an intruder, placing the traps intended to dissuade him from going on. So Ven had worked for years on protecting himself in his own cavern, the one deep inside him. He had not used the dragon magic since that day he'd killed the man. He had remained hidden deep in the center of his lair, where no one could find him. Ven shut out everyone. Bellona. Draconas. His mother. The dragon.

The brother he had never and always known.

Ven stood alone in the center of his lair, imbued with white, the absence of all color.

"Don't you want to meet your brother?" Grald asked.

"Not particularly," said Ven.

Grald accompanied them to their destination, which was not far, he assured Ven, who had not asked. Both Grald and the holy sister appeared put out by Ven's rectitude, for he saw them exchange glances; Grald frowning, the holy sister shrugging.

The submerged cavern had an opening at the back, through which the river flowed funneled through the cave to become a narrow stream that wandered into a thick and tangled forest. Trees lined the banks, their roots crawling into the water, their intertwined branches reaching out over the water, clasping hold of each other, so that it seemed to Ven that they had left a cavern of stone and entered a cavern of leaves. The leafy walls were dark and quiet as stone. The air beneath the canopy of branches was still and humid. The only sound was the splashing of the oars dropping into the water, lifting out, dropping in.

Grald led the way, rowing his boat with swift and powerful strokes so that the monk rowing the boat holding Ven and the holy sister was hard pressed to keep up. The distance they traveled was short. Rounding a bend in the stream, they came upon the other monks and Evelina, standing on the shore, waiting for them. The monks had pulled their boats out of the water and lined them up neatly on the north side of the bank. Evelina stood among the boats, one of the monks at her side. Ven hoped she might lift her eyes to meet his gaze, but she kept her face averted. He noted that Grald looked at her, as well. Looked at her intently.

Ven climbed out of the boat and helped the monk haul it to shore. He saw no signs of a camp, as he had expected, yet the nun had indicated to him that this was where they all lived. She had not spoken of this place much and the monks had not spoken of it at all. Still Ven was left with the impression that they had built some sort of fortress or stockade in the wilderness. He concluded that it must be located deeper in the woods, which meant that they had a trek through the forest ahead of them. He searched, but saw no signs of a trail.

The monks looked expectantly at Grald, as did the holy sister. The dragon's hulking human body walked over to the stump of a felled tree, the remnants of which lay sprawled across the bank, the tree's dead leaves half submerged in the water. Grald climbed onto the tree stump. He pushed outward with his arms, as if he were thrusting open a heavy door. Stepping down off the tree stump, Grald walked forward into the forest. The monks filed along behind him. Evelina's guard seized hold of her arm and brought her with them.

Ven looked at the holy sister.

"This way, Dragon's Son," she said, with a half smile, and motioned for him to follow.

Ven had no idea what the dragon's gyrations on the tree stump had been about, but apparently Grald had found a trail. They walked some distance through the forest and then . . .

Once, while walking in his forest home, Ven had placed his foot onto what he thought was solid ground, only to have the earth give way beneath him, plunging him into a sinkhole. He had felt then as he felt now.

He stepped into deep shadows cast of an enormous willow and found himself emerging onto a city street in glaring sunlight. He stared around in disbelief.

Behind him rose an immense stone wall. Twice his height, the wall was constructed of huge chunks of rock that appeared to have been scooped out of the earth, then brought here to be stacked one atop the other. The wall had a glassy sheen to it in the sunlight. No grout held the individual stones in place. The rocks had been fused together by fire. Fire so hot it could melt stone. And he had just walked right through it.

Around him was the clatter and rattle of carts, the clamor of voices punctuated by a shout or loud laughter, someone hawking wares. People bumping into him, staring at him.

One moment a river and silence beneath thick trees. The next moment a wall and the hubbub of life. A city in the forest. A city that had not existed until Grald summoned it forth—or so it appeared.

"Welcome, Dragon's Son," said the holy sister, smiling at his discomfiture. "Welcome to Dragonkeep."

Unlike humans, who construct buildings as works of art, made to honor God, king, or country, the dragon viewed construction in terms of its functionality. Creating dwellings in which to house his humans bored the dragon, who raised the buildings as swiftly as he could to be done with it. Dragons are not accustomed to constructing. Dragons form their lairs by deconstructing—delving and digging into mountains, gouging out the rock, shaping it. Generally, the only construction dragons do on their lairs is building the nest meant to house their eggs and, later, the young dragons.

This nest, made of stones and darkness, is built by both dragons during the elaborate mating ritual. The nest is strong and well built and magically guarded, for it has to protect and shelter the fragile eggs and the equally fragile young. The nest's elaborate defenses are a holdover from the ancient Dragon War when the young were primary targets.

Dragons come together rarely to mate—some might do so only once in a lifetime. Wiping out a dragon's offspring was considered an immense triumph by the enemy, for such an act might well wipe out a dragon family that had been in existence for thousands of years. The nest for the young is built as a last line of defense, in case both parents are slain. The nest is made of rock fused together with dragon fire and concealed by the most powerful illusions.

Thus, the Dragonkeep could well be considered city of the dragon's nest, for its buildings and the enormous stone wall that surrounded it were similar in function and construction to the nest created for young dragons, as was the powerful illusion magic that hid it, an illusion so wonderful that Ven had difficulty telling which was real—the silent forest or the clamoring city.

"The city is real and so are its inhabitants," the holy sister assured him. "The illusion of the forest surrounds the city, guarding it and our people from those who might do us harm."

"You mean enemy armies?" Ven asked. "But why should anyone attack you? No one knows you're here."

The nun smiled indulgently. "Not armies, necessarily. Originally the wall was built to keep out dumb animals, who are not fooled by illusion, as are humans. In the early days all manner of wild beasts, such as bears and wolves, would come blundering into our city, bringing harm to themselves, as well as our people. To prevent this, the dragon built the wall, tearing the stones from the mountainside and fusing them together with the fire from his belly."

The city streets were narrow and crowded. Like a giant child outgrowing its swaddling clothes, the city's swelling population was threatening to break out of the wall that surrounded it. Buildings that had been one story were now two or three. Even the dragon-created mines from which the stone was quarried were being converted into dwellings and shops into which more people were crammed. Slapped together in haste, held together by fire, the building leaned at precarious angles, with not a level plane in sight.

"You say the wall is real," observed Ven. "Yet I walked right through solid stone."

"The wall *is* real," replied the nun. "No part of the wall is illusion."

"Yet we entered, Sister," he said.

The nun seemed reluctant to reply. Finally, she said, "There are gates within the wall that only the dragon has the power of opening."

Ven cast a look over his shoulder, back at the wall. He was aware of the sister's keen eyes upon him, aware of the dragon probing and prodding.

"And so those who live inside this city cannot leave unless the dragon wills it?"

"The wall is in place to protect our people, not imprison them. Our people possess the dragon magic and that makes them different from other humans. As you know full well, Dragon's Son," the holy sister added, "the world is not very accepting of those who are different. Thus, for their own protection, we keep our people inside."

Ven said nothing. The holy sister led him on through the crowded streets, pointing out the sights. Ven paid scant attention. He wondered what had become of Evelina. On entering the city, the monks had hustled her away, and Ven had no idea what they had done with her, and he was worried. He recalled the look Grald had given her. He wasn't certain how to find out about her without revealing himself and he was mulling over this question when he became gradually aware that the people in the street were stepping aside to allow him passage. He noticed then that many lowered their heads or dropped a curtsy or made some other gesture of respect.

"You should acknowledge their homage, Dragon's Son," said the nun in low tones. "A certain detachment on your part is advisable, of course, but you must not allow your subjects to think that you are arrogant and unfeeling."

"Subjects?" Ven repeated, startled. "What subjects?"

"Your subjects. Your people. Their homage is for you," replied the holy sister. She indicated a group of brown-robed monks standing on a street corner, who bowed low as Ven passed.

He shook his head. "They must have mistaken me for someone important."

"You are the Dragon's Son," said the holy sister, and her tone was rebuking. "You will be their ruler one day."

Ven was intrigued. "I don't understand."

"Your father will explain. I have said too much, as it is."

"And when will I have a chance to talk to—" He tried, but could not bring himself to say *my father.* "When will I talk with the dragon?"

The holy sister's mouth puckered in amusement. "You have talked to him, as you well know, Dragon's Son."

"I have talked with a human called Grald," Ven returned. "I have not talked with the dragon."

"Yet they are one and the same—"

"No, they are not," Ven countered. "I know better. I want to meet the one who"—he paused, then continued, forcing the words through gritted teeth—"made me what I am."

The holy sister was no longer amused. She eyed him thoughtfully. Her face was expressionless. He could not tell if she was angry or displeased.

"All in good time," she said finally in noncommittal tones, and walked on in silence.

"Where are we going," he asked, still trying to think of a way to find out about Evelina.

"We are going to a place the people here call the Abbey. You will find it interesting, for it is one of the oldest buildings in Dragonkeep. You have quarters in the guesthouse there. The young woman in whom you have taken an interest has also been given a room in the guesthouse of the Abbey." The holy sister smiled a sly and knowing smile. "Her quarters are located next to yours."

Ven hated that smile and he hated himself for caring enough to hate it. He couldn't help himself, however. Like a smear of blood in the snow, Evelina was the only color in his mind.

23

EVELINA SAT IN A CHAIR IN A WINDOWLESS room. outside, she heard the rumble of thunder. A storm was brewing. She had seen the lightning flicker from cloud to cloud just before the monks had hauled her into the ugly gray stone building. They took her to a room and shoved her inside. She sat where they had left her—unmoving, stiff and afraid—watching the door, waiting for the monks to return to fetch her, carry her off to some dire fate.

A half hour passed.

A full hour, and no one came.

Evelina rose to her feet and with much hesitation, starting and stopping, she crept to the door. She placed her ear against the wood, listened. She heard nothing in the hallway outside. Touching the wrought-iron door handle, she gave an experimental tug and was surprised beyond measure when the door actually opened. She had assumed that they would lock her inside.

Evelina slammed the door and waited, afraid someone had seen her. No one came, and at last she began to think the unthinkable—she was alone and she was free. After a moment to calm her nerves, she opened the door a crack and peeped out into the hallway.

The corridor was short and narrow. Five doors opened off it, two on one side and three on the other. At the end of the corridor were the stairs that led to the first floor of this place that the monks had called the Abbey guesthouse. Evelina had assumed that "guesthouse" was their jocular term for a prison, but now she began to wonder. This really did look like a guesthouse. She examined the door and saw that there was no lock, only a latch that held the door shut.

No lock, no bolt, no way to keep her inside.

With one eye on the stairs, Evelina left her room and ran across the hall to the door that stood opposite. She listened at the door. Hearing no sounds inside, she opened it. The room was exactly the same as hers, furnished with a bed with a straw mattress, two chairs, a small table, a fireplace, and a slop bucket. She saw no sign that the room was inhabited.

Investigation revealed that two of the other rooms on the floor were like hers. The door to the fifth room—the room adjacent to hers—was different in that it had a lock. She could not see inside. Evelina returned to her own room and shut the door. She took off the horrid wimple and threw it on the floor, then sat down to think about what she should do next.

She had recovered quickly from the shock of seeing her lover and her father murdered by the wrath of heaven. Evelina was not one to waste energy in weeping and wailing over them. As a lover, Glimmershanks had been brutal and abusive. She did feel a certain sorrow for her father, mainly because he was the only person she had ever truly been able to trust and that because she could easily manipulate him. Her major grief was for the death of her dreams and plans. For that death she truly wept and for that she blamed Ven.

As to the strange monks and their awful ability to summon fire and destruction with their bare hands, Evelina cared not a wit. Her own survival was what was important to her and—just as she had done all her life—she concentrated on that to the exclusion of everything else. Evelina swam on the surface of life, clinging to logs and flotsam when she could, striking out on her own if she had to. She saw no need to look down beneath the dark water. She knew she would see—just more dark water, and what was the use of that?

Evelina had been obedient, compliant, quiet around the monks. She had hoped by this to fool them into complacency, so that she could escape. Her first attempt to flee had not worked. They had caught her sneaking out of camp at night and brought her back. She had expected to be punished and she was, but the punishment was mild by her standards—nothing more than a couple of slaps across the face. After that Evelina kept her mouth shut and her eyes and ears open, eavesdropping on every conversation, thinking over every word in the context of how the words related to the only person she cared about—Evelina.

The monks were not a chatty bunch. Evelina had learned nothing from them. The holy sister and one of the monks would occasionally put their heads together, hold low-voiced conversations. Whenever this occurred, Evelina tried her best to be near enough to eavesdrop, and on one or two occasions she had succeeded. Most of their conversations she either didn't understand or didn't bother to understand (those that had nothing to do with her). One, however, was of particular interest to her.

"Why are we hauling about this piece of baggage?" the monk grumbled to the holy sister. By his glance at her, he meant Evelina.

"Have you seen the way the Dragon's Son looks at the girl? He is in love with her."

The monk shrugged. "So?"

"The dragon has detected an independent spirit in his offspring—a spirit he deems might be difficult to control."

"Ah, I understand," the monk replied.

Alone in her room, Evelina went over that conversation in her mind. Some of it was confusing to her—the part about the dragon and offspring and independent spirits and such—

like. She dismissed all that as irrelevant. The relevant part was the fact that Ven loved her. Other men had loved her in the past. She'd always found their love to be highly useful for her, highly costly for them. Ven would be no different.

"I've made mistakes with him," she admitted. "But I can mend them."

She wished there were a mirror in the room. She feared that the trip had been hard on her beauty.

I must look pale and haggard, she thought.

She heard sounds—footsteps on the stairs. Footsteps coming down the hall. The footsteps halted outside her door. She held her breath, fear making her heart beat fast. She waited for the door to burst open, but whoever it was knocked once, hesitantly. By its nature and the fact that the knock was not repeated when she did not immediately answer, Evelina guessed it was Ven.

She had decisions to make and she made them swiftly. Pinching her cheeks and biting her lips to bring more color to them, she leapt out of her chair and threw herself on the bed. She arranged herself to best advantage, all the while making it look unarranged. She wished she was not wearing this detestable black bag of a nun's habit, but there was no help for that now. In position, she called out, quavering, trepidatious, "Who is there?"

There was a moment's silence, then the reply, "It is me— Ven. You do not need to be afraid," he added swiftly. "I will not intrude on you. I only want to make certain you are all right and that you have everything you need." He paused, then said, "Have I your permission to enter?"

"You need not ask for my permission," said Evelina in choked tones. "The door has no lock."

Slowly the latch depressed. Slowly the door opened. Ven stood in the corridor. His legs and feet were concealed by the monk's robes, but she remembered them clearly, remembered the feel of them against her skin. Disgust caused her stomach to roil and she didn't think she could go through with it.

Then Evelina saw immediately that what the nun had said of him was true. His face was impassive, but there was no doubting the expression in his eyes as he gazed at her. He adored her. Evelina relaxed. All was well.

She rolled over on her side and hid her face in the hard pillow and wept. Having no handkerchief, she was forced to use the hem of her nun's garb to muffle her sobs, thus causing her skirts to hike up around her knees, revealing a generous portion of shapely leg. Thinking this might not be enough, poor Evalina was so overcome by misery that she reached down her hand and, in her distrait state, hiked the skirt up even further.

Glancing at Ven from the corner of her eye, to make sure he noticed, she said with a quiver of her chin and a tear in her voice, "You may have your way with me anytime you want me. What can I do to stop you? Imprisoned by those terrible monks, who killed"—she gave a sob, but struggled bravely on—"killed my poor father . . ."

"I didn't mean for that to happen," said Ven. He did not enter the room, but remained standing in the door. "I am sorry for it and for the fact that you had to witness it. That must have been horrible for you."

Evelina gave another sob and a yank on her skirt. She kept watch on him from beneath her long lashes.

"And you are not a prisoner," he added. "You may come and go freely."

"And can I freely leave this city?" she cried wildly. "A city that rises up out of nothing and nowhere, barricaded by a wall of solid stone through which we pass like wraiths. Tell me how am I to leave this city. I do not not know where I am or what is going to happen to me."

She was careful to weep just a little; otherwise her nose would swell and her eyes would turn red. She sobbed only enough so that he would come to comfort her.

Except that he didn't. Evalina peeped at him beneath her fingers. Ven continued to stand in the doorway.

"It is true that you cannot leave the city," he said. "But you may walk its streets freely, speak to anyone, go where you will. You need have no fear on my account. Even though I have been given quarters next to yours, I assure you I will not disturb you. I will never come near you. I will not speak to you again."

He started to shut the door.

Evelina was considerably put out. She'd heard the troubadour's songs in which the lover prides himself on never telling the object of his love that he loves her and then, in celebration of that love, he does away with himself in the last stanza. She'd found the notion silly then. She found it annoying now.

"Wait, Ven," Evelina called faintly, half rising from the bed, her hair falling in cascades over her shoulders. "I have misjudged you. I thought . . . I thought you were like the rest of the men I've known. Like that pig Glimmershanks, who took advantage of my youth and my innocence. I see now I was mistaken."

She held out her hand to him in a pretty, placating gesture.

"Please forgive me, Ven. I am ashamed of myself. I did what I did because they made me. I never meant to bring harm to you. I was afraid of what they would do to me."

She lowered her head. Real tears trickled down her cheeks.

Hearing the door shut, she closed her eyes, smiled a wan smile, and lay back down on the bed in a yielding, helpless manner.

Long moments passed. No heavy body weighted down the bed. No lips sought hers. Evelina opened her eyes.

Ven was gone. The door was shut. He'd walked off and left her.

"You bloody stupid bugger!" cursed Evelina.

Ven turned from Evelina's door to find one of the monks standing in the corridor, watching. Ven didn't like these monks, didn't trust them. Some appeared normal as most men, but others were like this one—gaunt and pale, with a lean, spare body on which his robes hung like laundry from a tree limb.

"What do you want here?" Ven demanded harshly.

"Grald will grant you an audience, Dragon's Son."

The monk's hands were in constant motion, nervous fingers plucking at the hems of his sleeves or picking at sores on his face or tugging at his straggling hair. He watched Ven with eyes that gleamed with an eerie light that had something disquieting behind it. If Ven had not been assured by the holy sister that these monks revered him, he would have called the look one of hatred and loathing.

"I want a bar on this woman's door," said Ven, pointing.

The monk's eyes flicked to the door, flicked back. He said nothing.

"A bar that locks the door from the inside," Ven added.

The monk bowed. "As you will it, Dragon's Son. And now, if you will accompany me. Grald does not like to be kept waiting."

Ven didn't have much faith in the monk's promise. He didn't like to leave Evelina alone, undefended, yet he wanted to talk with the dragon.

Ven turned back to the door and knocked on it. Before Evelina could reply, he opened the door. She sat bolt upright on the bed, staring at him, her eyes red-rimmed and glistening. Drawing his knife from his boot, he tossed it onto the floor beside the bed.

"Do not be afraid to use it," he told her and, shutting the door, he stepped back out into the corridor.

"I will see Grald now," Ven told the monk, making it clear that it was his choice.

He needn't have bothered. The monk merely bowed again and turned on his heel, leading the way.

Ven followed after the monk. They walked down the corridor, then descended the spiral staircase that led from the upper floors of the guesthouse to the ground level. Ven wondered dourly, as he went, what sort of guests one entertained in a city that no one could find.

* * *

The Abbey was the largest building in Dragonkeep, according to the monk, who told Ven of its history in a rambling and disjointed manner that rather resembled the Abbey itself. The first structure raised in Dragonkeep, the Abbey stood at the foot of the mountain whose bones had been used in its construction. The city had grown up around it, expanded beyond it to the limits of the wall, and now burrowed into the mountain itself.

As were all the other buildings in Dragonkeep, the Abbey was simple in design, being made of stones that had been dropped on top of each other with no particular regard to fit, since they were all fused together by dragon fire. Originally only one level—arranged in a long rectangle and topped by logs and thatch—the Abbey had since acquired three additional floors. Its human dwellers had added such undragon-like touches as doors and windows, stairs, and a slate-tile roof. Outbuildings had been constructed over time; some by the dragon, but most by those humans who had been born without the dragon magic in their blood and who therefore served as laborers or nursemaids or guards for those blessed with what the monk termed proudly "the blood bane."

"What is the blood bane?" asked Ven, thinking it had a sinister sound. Rain had started to fall. Storm clouds hung gray over the mountain.

"It is the colors in our mind," the monk answered. "It is the eyes of the dragon, always watching over us. It is the fire that burns within and without. It is the pain and the hunger that saves us from the madness."

Ven could understand the colors of the mind of which the monk spoke and the fire and the ever-watchful eyes of the dragon. Ven was baffled by this talk of the madness, however, though he could see it plainly in the monk's eyes.

Ven wanted to be rid of the wretch, and when they reached the Abbey's main building, Ven informed the monk that he could find his way alone.

The monk would have no part of it. Grald had ordered the monk to bring Ven directly to him, and the monk was bound to obey. Nothing Ven could say would cause the man to budge, and so Ven gave in. He and the monk stepped through a large wooden door banded with iron and entered immediately into a great hall.

"Cavernous" was the word for the hall. Cavelike.

The hall was large—extending the full length of the building—and dark, for it had no windows; the dragon seeing no need for what he considered to be useless breaches in his defenses. There was a large fireplace that had once been used to keep the humans—particularly the babies—warm. Since the humans had moved out of this building over two hundred years ago, the fireplace had been blocked up with stones.

The walls were of exposed rock, not covered over by plaster, as Ven had seen done in the guesthouse. The hall was devoid of decoration, for what need have dragons of tapestries woven of cloth when they can weave far more splendid tapestries in their minds? Iron sconces for torches ringed the walls—a concession to the limitations of human eyesight—and iron braziers stood at intervals along the walls. The only furniture was a large thronelike chair placed at the back of the hall, directly across from the door.

The atmosphere inside the hall was chill and dank as a cave. When the door shut behind them, it shut out all the light.

"Wait here, Dragon's Son." The monk lifted a torch from a bucket that stood inside the door. "I will find Grald."

Ven could see the dragon's human body quite clearly. The warm flesh gave off a radiance that made it seem illuminated from within.

"Never mind that," said Ven. "He is here."

The monk looked at Ven askance, for to his human eyes, the hall was dark as a starless, moonless, fog-bound midnight.

"Get out," said Grald, his harsh, deep voice echoing among the stones, "and leave me alone with the Dragon's Son."

The monk obeyed with alacrity, bowing and muttering to himself, and twitching. Ven was thankful to be rid of him.

"Come closer, Dragon's Son, so that I can see you in this

murk," Grald ordered, grumbling. "This human body that I have appropriated is good for many things, but it lacks the capacity to see in the darkness—a trait I am pleased to note that you have inherited from me."

"I do not want to talk to you, Grald," said Ven, coming to stand in front of the human. "I want to talk to my father."

"You are talking to your father," Grald returned. "The human is my mouth, that is all. The words and thoughts are mine. You don't understand, do you? I will explain. You have met the walker? Draconas?"

Ven thought the dragon was changing the subject. He considered whether or not to make his demand to see his father an issue. He decided that he would let it go. Not forever. Just for now. He gave a brief nod.

"Draconas has taken human form, as I have. But his appearance is a powerful, marvelous illusion that required the work of many of my kind months to create. I did not have the luxury of all those dragon dreams at my disposal. Yet I needed a human body. I found a way to take over a human's body by ripping out the still-beating heart, working my magic on it, then imprisoning the living remains. I keep what is left alive until the aging process takes its toll on this body and I am forced to find another. The body is a shell, nothing more. The mind"—Grald tapped his head—"is mine. What do you say to that, my son? Are you shocked? Revolted?"

"I say that from what I know of the Grald whose heart you stole, he got what he deserved," Ven answered.

Grald laughed. " 'Like father, like son,' the humans say. Our thinking runs along the same lines." He waved a deprecating hand. "You crouch in the darkness of your mind, as I sit in the darkness of this hall. Yet as you can see me, I can see you, my son."

Grald sat back comfortably in his chair, thrust out his huge legs. "Oh, yes, you have defenses. Defenses you have built up over what—sixteen years? Bah! What is that to me? I have slept for sixteen years at a time and considered that little more than a brief nap. If I wanted to, I could tear down your puny defenses and reach inside your lair and rip out your soul, as easily as I ripped out this human's heart."

"Then why haven't you?"

"Because it would destroy you. And I don't want to destroy you. You are my son. You have a great destiny before you. Sit down." Grald gestured to another chair. "We have much to discuss."

"I will stand," said Ven. "My dragon legs do not tire easily."

"I detect a note of bitterness in your voice." Grald sat forward, his shoulders hunched, his eyes intent on Ven. "You should not feel bitter, Dragon's Son. You should rejoice. I made you better than any human ever born. Better, stronger, swifter, smarter. You have the magic of our people, a power for which humans hunger, but one which, when it is given to them—" Grald paused.

"—drives them insane," Ven finished, understanding now the madness of the monks.

"Only the men," Grald conceded. "The women suffer a feverish sickness that soon passes. We are working with our breeding program to overcome these problems and we are making some progress, though not as much as I had hoped. Not as much as Draconas made with your human brother."

Grald said this very casually, but Ven could see the eyes— shadowed by the overhanging forehead—gleam. "I want to meet this brother of yours. I think you know how to find him."

"I only learned I had a brother this morning." Ven shrugged. He wondered for a moment why Grald made such a distinction of saying "human" brother, but then forgot about it in his preoccupation. "How should I know where he is?"

Grald's eyes half shut to slits. "You know."

"And you *don't* know. My brother has defenses, too, apparently."

"You can reach him. He will listen to you. Summon him here and he will come."

"So you can do what? Rip out his soul? Or maybe his heart? Do your own dirty work, Grald. Don't get me involved." Ven turned to leave. "And the next time my father wants to see me, tell him that I want to see him. Not you."

He was halfway to the door before Grald spoke.

"You are not the only one who lusts after the girl, Dragon's Son. The human body I inhabit wants her and there is no good reason why I should not let him have her. He is not gentle with women, as you know."

Ven halted, turned slowly back. "So this is why you brought her here? Because you want her?"

"No," said Grald. "Because you do. Speak to your brother, Dragon's Son. Tell him you need to see him. And the girl will remain safe, to be used for your pleasure alone." Grald sat back. "What do you say?"

Ven considered, then said, with a shrug, "I would say I am looking forward to meeting my brother."

24

THE SMELL OF THUNDER WAS IN THE AIR. STORM clouds climbed on each other's backs, trying to see which could mount higher into the heavens. A gust of wind took hold of the tops of the trees, whipped them, shook them. Ripples darkened the river to slate gray, sent waves dashing up against the shore. Marcus had watched the advance of the storm, rolling in from the west, for as long as Bellona had been talking to him. He had the dreamlike notion that she'd raised the wind and lightning to accompany her unsettling tale of love and birth and death.

"Draconas gave me the dragon's son," Bellona was saying, as the first raindrops spattered against Marcus's cheek. "He told me to take the child and flee with him into the wilderness, because his life was in danger. The last words Draconas said to me were this: 'When the dragon's son wants to know who and what he is, bring him to his mother's tomb.'"

Bellona fell silent, watching the trees that bent and swayed and mourned.

"He asked the question. He asked if he was his mother's

curse." She spoke in dispassionate, emotionless tones. "I told him the truth, but I did not bring him to the tomb."

Marcus listened to her, said nothing. He had been listening for hours, it seemed, standing beside a strange-looking cairn built atop a grass-covered hill, the highest point of land for many miles. He felt dazed and shocked, horrified and dismayed, and, oddly, settled. The questions he'd been asking all his life had been answered. The answers were blood-stained and awful and he needed time to think about them. Still, they were answers.

The rain fell in earnest now, drops hard as the iron cannonballs. He rested his hand on his mother's tomb—a cairn, crudely built, made from chunks of stone that had been ripped out of the earth by some powerful force, then fused together with fire. Breathed into the stone was a fire-seared word, a name: MELISANDE. And below that the words: MISTRESS OF DRAGONS.

The stone was warm from the bright afternoon sun, which had put up a losing battle against the encroaching clouds, but Marcus fancied that the warmth was hers, that she was glad to see him, glad that he was here. His mother's resting place was located near an abandoned village only a few miles from the city of New Bramfels, the second largest city in the kingdom of Idlyswylde. Marcus and his family had relatives in that city and had visited there on more than one occasion. An hour's ride would have brought him to this place, had he known of its existence.

"Why *didn't* you bring Ven?" he asked Bellona.

"Because I knew he wouldn't come."

"I don't understand," said Marcus, and suddenly he laughed. "I don't understand!" He repeated it wildly, flinging out his arms and lifting his gaze to the rain-soaked heavens. "In God's name, how am I ever supposed to understand any of this? My mother murdered in the hour of my birth. My body drenched in her blood. My twin . . . My brother . . . I have a brother . . ."

My brother! The hand that was one of the earliest and most comforting memories of his childhood reached out and clasped hold of him. Marcus had a sudden, startling, momentary glimpse of a face with eyes that were dark, embittered, cold and shining as the blue steel in which his twin encased himself, armoring his soul, as gallant knights armored their bodies. And for the same reason.

A hailstone struck his face. Marcus blinked at the stinging, chill sensation and came back to what passed for reality. They were out in the open, far from shelter, and the storm was worsening. Bellona seemed oblivious. She stood beside the tomb, her fingers tracing the name burned into the rock. She had blood on her fingers. The edges of the letters were sharp, cutting. Marcus pulled his cap low over his face, hunched his shoulders against the rain.

"Where is my brother?" he asked Bellona, almost yelling to be heard above the storm's tumult. "What has happened to him?"

She regarded him coldly. "That is what I have been trying to tell you. Haven't you been listening?"

"I'm sorry," Marcus returned defensively. "It's been a shock. I didn't expect this. Any of this."

Above all, he hadn't expected this terrible end from that joyous, freedom-gulping beginning. He had often dreamed of vaulting onto his horse and galloping out of the palace walls, riding up the road and into a star-laden night. The realization of his dream had been exhilarating. Then, here at the tomb, the dream had bucked and thrown him and run away, leaving him, bruised and aching, to limp back home.

Except that he didn't know where home was anymore.

"I'm listening now." Worn out, he sat down on the cairn. He rested his hand on his mother's name, felt the letters sharp and stark beneath his fingers.

Bellona began again and he realized that some part of him must have heard, for he knew the story, recognized it as it unfolded, as one recognizes a well-loved fairy tale.

Ven robbed. Ven setting off to find the robbers and win back his money. Ven hoodwinked, kidnapped . . .

"He is being held prisoner somewhere," said Bellona.

"No," said Marcus, speaking without thinking. "He is not

a prisoner." He watched the clouds, dark gray and lightning-streaked, rush across the sky. "He is not being held against his will. Wherever he is, he wants to be there."

The cold drops striking the warm rock caused steam to rise from the boulder in a ghostly mist. The water ran in rivulets down his mother's name.

"I knew it," Bellona said, and she smiled in grim triumph. "I knew you would be able to find him."

Marcus started to protest that he hadn't found anyone. He didn't know where his brother was. How could he when only an hour previous he didn't even know he had a brother? . . .

"You know now," said a voice inside the little room. "You can find me, if you want to. I've been waiting for you."

Marcus gazed north, up the river, in the direction of the distant mountains that sheltered the kingdom of Seth. The mountains could not be seen, their granite had been absorbed into the rain, but *he* could see them, for now they formed the horizon of his being.

"That way, toward the mountains. But not as far as the mountains."

Marcus frowned, concentrating. "The river forks and there's a cave . . . a drowned cavern . . ."

"Yes," said Bellona, her gaunt face glimmering with a pale, eager light. "Melisande spoke of such a cave. She said it had a 'dragon' feel to it."

"He went into that cave," said Marcus. "But he never came out."

"Then I know where to start looking," said Bellona. "Thank you for your help," she added gruffly. "I hope you won't get into too much trouble with your father over this."

Hefting her pack, she turned from the cairn and walked off through the downpour, heading toward the river. Her abrupt departure startled Marcus, caught him flat-footed.

"Wait!" he cried, bolting through the long, wet grass. "Wait, Bellona. I'm coming with you."

"There is no need. You have done enough. More than enough." Bellona gestured back at the cairn. "You have done

this for your mother and you have pleased her. It is time for
you to return to your father, to the life he has made for you."

"I am coming with you," Marcus repeated. "I want to
know my brother."

Bellona's brow creased in a frown. "I don't think he
would want to know you." Her eyes flicked over him, taking
him in from head to toe. "You are what he longs to be. He
won't thank you for that. Or love you for it."

Marcus almost laughed. "He wants to be me? If he wants
to conjugate verbs all day, I can certainly arrange it."

Bellona gazed at him through the falling rain. She seemed
about to say something, then stopped. Shaking her head, she
said something else. "The way is fraught with danger. I
won't be responsible for you, King's Son. Go back to your
books and your silk cushions. That is your life. Ven and I
have our own lives."

"You will not get rid of me so easily," said Marcus, falling
into step beside her, ignoring her scowl. "You will not find
him without me along. He and I can talk to each other, you
know." He tapped his head. "In here."

She said nothing, but continued to slog her way through
the wet grass to where the river ran, pockmarked by the rain.

"I'm very willful when I choose," he added, matching her
stride for stride. "From what you have told me, I am a lot
like my mother."

Bellona glanced at him and looked away, glad for the rain
that masked the other, softer water in her eyes. "Too much,"
was all she said, grumbling.

Edward rode hard, not sparing his horse, but the raging storm
slowed him down, forced him to seek shelter against the driving rain and stinging hail. He was off again the moment the
rain let up. By the time he arrived at the site of the cairn, the
storm had passed, the sun had come out, only to die slowly, its
last rays making liquid gold of the ripples in the swollen river.

Leaping from his near-foundering horse, Edward ran to
the cairn. He searched the ground and saw signs in the trampled grass that someone had recently been here. Their trail

led to the river. He was starting to follow after them, when a voice brought him up short.

"You're wasting your time. They've come and gone."

Edward gave a violent start, for it seemed that the voice had spoken from the grave.

A man rose up, not from the cairn, but from behind it.

"Draconas! You scared me half out of my wits!" Edward scowled, not liking this. "What the devil are you doing here? And where is my son?"

"Gone," Draconas repeated. He leaned on his staff, gazed at the gilt-edged river.

Edward eyed him. "Did he go with *her*?"

"Bellona, yes. They came here. She told him everything."

"About his mother," Edward said hesitantly.

"Everything," said Draconas with emphasis. "His mother. You. Grald. The rape, the attack, everything. That is," he amended, thinking of Ven, "she told him almost everything."

Edward looked grim. "There was no need for that. It will only confuse the boy. What does that woman want with him anyway? Why is she doing this? If it is for revenge—"

"No," said Draconas. "She wants her son back. He's run off and she knew that Marcus was the one person who could help her find him."

"But that's crazy!" Edward exclaimed angrily. "*She's* crazy! How is Marcus supposed to know anything about this woman's son?"

"The two are brothers. They were born within minutes of each other. When Melisande died, I gave one child to you and sent the other away with Bellona."

"Twins!" Edward gasped. "Melisande had twins. I have two sons—"

"No," said Draconas, and his taut voice and flashing-eyed gaze halted Edward midbreath. "Believe whatever you will, Your Majesty. Believe in a heaven, believe in a hell. Believe the earth is flat, believe it is round. Believe the sun orbits us or that we orbit the sun. Believe whatever you want. But *know* this for a fact. You and Melisande have *one* son. One son."

Edward wondered whether he did believe him. He decided that he did. Such passion could not lie.

"And the other child?" he ventured.

Draconas looked away, to the mountains in the north. "He is the dragon's son."

"Dragon? Are you mad?" Edward demanded. "How—" He flushed and fell silent, not certain where that question might end up.

Draconas made no response.

"I want to understand," Edward said finally, frustrated.

"No, you don't. Get down on your knees and thank God that you don't," Draconas returned.

He turned his gaze from the mountains, looked back at Edward, and sighed deeply. "Go home, Your Majesty. You have a wife, other sons, a kingdom to rule—"

"I had all that sixteen years ago," Edward retorted. "You didn't think about my wife or my sons then, when you took me to that kingdom." He gestured north, to the mountains. "Took me to the Mistress of Dragons. And now my son has run off—"

"—in search of his brother."

"You know where?"

"I have a good idea."

"It's a trap. You're using him. Just as you used me."

"Edward . . ."

"Admit it!" Edward said angrily.

Draconas leaned on his staff, looked away. "Go home, Your Majesty. There's nothing you can do."

"I can damn well go after my son!" Edward cried vehemently.

He turned from the cairn to follow the trail the two had left in the trodden-down grass.

A strong hand grasped his arm.

Edward swung around, fists clenched. "Back off, Draconas. I knocked you on your ass once before! I can do it again."

Draconas half smiled. "You didn't knock me on my ass.

You rocked me back on my heels, and that was only because I wasn't watching."

He regarded Edward with a look that was not without sympathy. "Go home," he said for the third time. "Leave this to me."

"You go to hell." Edward shook loose of Draconas's grasp and started off toward the river.

"And I did this to you the last time," said Draconas ruefully.

Lashing out with his staff, he struck the king on the back of his head.

Edward slumped down into the wet grass. Draconas rolled him over. Sliding his hands under Edward's arms, Draconas dragged him through the grass and deposited him at the foot of Melisande's tomb, where he propped the king up against the cold stone and covered him with his cloak.

"Take care of him, Melisande," said Draconas. "When he comes around, say to him the words I once said to you: 'I never meant for it to come this. I am sorry.'"

He picked up his staff and walked off, toward the river.

25

MARCUS AND BELLONA MADE CAMP NOT FAR from the bower where Marcus had been conceived. Bellona knew this. Marcus did not, for Bellona did not tell him. She kept silent not out of regard for his feelings—she had no care for his feelings—but because she did not want to think about it, much less talk about it. She would have camped in another area, but this was close to the drowned cave, which they had passed at dusk, and it was one of the few open patches of ground on this side of the tree-lined river.

Bellona was not sentimental. Her life was too hard for sentimentality to survive. She camped here, where she had found Melisande bleeding, ravished, half-dead, because it was practical to camp here. She slept soundly, because it is practical to sleep soundly the day before one faces a dangerous unknown. If, in her dreams, she relived that terrible night, those were dreams and were gone by morning.

Marcus lay awake, unable to sleep, though he was tired past any weariness he'd ever before experienced. They had ridden several miles along the riverbank before coming across the small village where they had left the horse in the care of a farmer and purchased a rowboat. Marcus could row a boat; Gunderson had made certain he'd learned, just as Gunderson had made certain that the king's son could handle a sword and wield an axe and shoot an arrow. Marcus was not particularly good at any of these, for he did not enjoy physical exercise, though he improved at rowing that day—it was either improve or endure Bellona's caustic comments. His arms ached and his blistered hands stung, but it was not pain that made him wakeful.

It was the cairn, the rain running down his mother's name, the blood on Bellona's fingers, the hailstone hitting his cheek. It was the story of his birth.

It was anger at Edward, his father.

"How could he treat her that way? How could he treat me that way? How could he father a child and never try to find out what became of the mother? Why did he never take me to her tomb? Why didn't he tell me the truth? He should have told me the truth. . . ." And so on and so forth.

When weariness finally overcame Marcus and he slid into a drowsy half sleep, he let go of his anger and relaxed into dreams of his brother. The brother he'd known, yet never known. Marcus had always envied the bond between his elder brothers. He watched them quarrel and squabble, compete against and fiercely love each other. Though they treated him kindly enough, there was no bond between him and them. He longed for such a bond, for love and acceptance, and secretly grieved that he would never have it. For who could understand his magic? Not even his own father and mother.

His father loved him, but didn't love the magic that was part of him. Edward often intimated that if Marcus would only try harder, he could overcome this weakness, as if he were a glutton overcoming a craving for suckling pig. Ermintrude came the closest to understanding him. He knew, however, that her prayer every night was for him to lose the magic, for him to be normal. Seeing the magic through her eyes, Marcus saw what any woman would think of it, what any woman would think of him. Dust motes wearing acorn caps. Broken crockery. A life of broken crockery. For that reason, Marcus avoided women. Avoided even thinking about women.

His brother would understand. His brother possessed the magic. His brother would sympathize.

My brother, Marcus reflected as sleep finally laid claim to his bruised and battered spirit.

He realized, as he was dropping off, that he did not know his brother's name. Bellona had never once referred to his brother by name.

Marcus woke to the smell of roasting meat and the sight of Draconas, squatting by a fire to watch over the cooking of some sort of small bird. Startled, Marcus sat up and looked about for Bellona. He saw her some distance away, whetting and polishing her sword blade. By the dark expression on her face, Marcus guessed she would be glad to use it on their unexpected visitor.

"Bellona is not pleased to see me," Draconas announced, as Marcus walked up to stand over him.

"I'm not sure I am either," Marcus said cooly. "Did my father send you?"

"In a manner of speaking." Draconas rotated the stick holding the birds so that they cooked evenly. "Hungry?"

Marcus was extremely hungry. He'd eaten next to nothing yesterday, for he had been too shocked, dismayed, elated—what have you—to think of food. His stomach thought of it, though. The meat sizzled. Juices dribbled down the spit and his mouth watered.

"I have to talk to Bellona" was all he would commit to, however.

She did not look up from her work, but continued to run the small stone over the blade with smooth, even strokes.

"What is *he* doing here?" Marcus asked her.

"I didn't invite him, if that's what you are implying. I found him here when I woke."

"Did he say anything to you?"

Bellona shook her head and continued her work. The

whetting stone scraped against the metal with a sound that jarred every tooth in Marcus's head. He left her to her work, walked back slowly across the sandy beach.

As he came close to the fire, Draconas raised the spit, held it out to him. "Be careful. They're hot."

Marcus drew his knife, stabbed one of the birds, and slid it off the spit. He squatted down beside Draconas, who was already picking apart his bird, sucking the meat from the bones.

"Why didn't you tell me I had a brother?" Marcus demanded.

"Because it would have been dangerous."

"For me?" Marcus flared, ready to be angry.

"No," said Draconas. "For him."

Marcus didn't know what to say to that. He concentrated on eating. "What is his name?"

Draconas glanced over at Bellona. "Didn't she tell you?"

"I wouldn't be asking if she had."

"His name is Ven."

"What's Ven like? Have you met him?"

"Once. Long ago. When he was six."

"Is he like me?" Marcus asked.

Draconas crunched on a bone.

"I take after my father, they say." Marcus prodded.

Draconas glanced up, looked back down.

Marcus grew angry. "I saw my brother when I was little. I told you how I saw a hand reaching out to me. You could have at least told me who he was!"

Draconas shook his head. "If you had known, you would have tried to contact Ven and you would have succeeded. That is what the dragon hoped for. That is the reason he goes prowling about your mind. He would have heard any communication between the two of you through the magic. He would have used you to find Ven."

Draconas tossed the bones into the river, wiped his hands. "Now he's using Ven to find you."

"So I was right," Marcus said accusingly. "Edward sent you. You *are* here to try to stop me from going."

"Going where?" Draconas stood, hands on his hips.

"Where? . . ." Marcus floundered. "To find my brother."

"And where is he?"

Marcus was silent.

"Where is he? Your brother?" Draconas persisted.

"He's with the dragon," Marcus said at last.

"He's with the dragon," Draconas repeated. "And you said yourself that wherever he is, he wants to be there."

"I think Ven *thinks* he is where he wants to be. I'm hoping that meeting me may change his mind."

"Because you care?" Draconas snorted. "Do you know what his true name is?"

Marcus was startled. "You said it was Ven."

"Short for Vengeance."

"Good God!" Marcus exclaimed, shocked. "She named him that? Why?"

"Because she raised him to avenge his mother. To her Ven is a weapon, nothing more."

"You're wrong. Bellona cares about him. She came all this way to find him."

"I know that. But I don't think Ven does. As far as he's concerned, he's been used all his life. Now it's his turn."

"He reached out to me," Marcus insisted. "I think he wants to see me—"

"It's a trap," said Draconas flatly.

"I don't believe you. You're trying to keep me from going."

"I'm not here to stop you," said Draconas. "If you weren't going, it would be my job to make you go. Never mind." He waved off Marcus's questioning look. "I came here to offer my help, if you want it. The dragon put Ven up to this. The dragon wants both the sons of Melisande, not just one."

"Why? What does the dragon want with me?"

"I'm not sure yet. Nothing good, we can assume."

"You're very cool about this," Marcus said.

Draconas shrugged. "We dragons have a dictum. 'A trap is a trap only if the victim doesn't know it's a trap.'"

"Victim. That's comforting," Marcus muttered.

"I don't want you to be comfortable. I want you to keep your wits about you."

"I will. I have a brother, Draconas. A brother! There are things I want to tell him. Things I want to share with him. I have to do this. I have to find him."

Yes, you do, Draconas said to himself. *A trap is a trap only if the victim doesn't know . . . and neither does the bait. . . .*

The three held a strategy meeting that morning. Bellona was not pleased that Draconas was involving himself, but, once assured that he also wanted to find Ven, she accepted his presence, if not his advice.

"I can guarantee that if you try to find this city on your own, Bellona, you won't," Draconas stated. "You'll find nothing but trees, see nothing but tree trunks, limbs, and leaves."

"His plan does make sense, Bellona," Marcus added. "If he's right about these baby smugglers, they will lead us to their stronghold. The moon is full tonight and you yourself said that they travel to Seth every month during the full moon."

"Unless they do not make the trip this month or they have already been to Seth and come back," Bellona argued. "In which case, we will have to wait until next month or the month after that. No. I say we go into the cavern and proceed from there on our own. Marcus knows how to find Ven."

"And Ven knows how to find Marcus," Draconas said patiently. "Do you sneak into an enemy camp, then announce your arrival with a trumpet blast? Or do you take the enemy by surprise, slip in silently, under the cover of darkness? At least wait until tonight to see if the baby smugglers make their monthly trip to Seth."

Bellona glowered at him, hating him for making sense. "I'll wait one night."

Bellona rowed the boat to the entrance of the drowned cave. She had muffled the boat's oars with rags and greased the oarlocks and they traveled over the water in relative silence. Marcus offered to work his magic, mask the boat in illusion. Draconas shook his head.

"You're good, but not that good. Remember, Grald's people are familiar with dragon magic. They've used it all their lives. It won't be as easy to fool them as it was to fool that jailer. You're more likely to reveal yourself to them by misusing the magic."

"How can you be sure that Ven is with the dragon?" Bellona was still inclined to argue.

"I'm not sure of anything," Draconas returned. "But it seems a likely place to start looking."

In his mind, he was sure. Ven had been born into this world for a reason, and Draconas was beginning to think he knew what that reason was. He had not mentioned this to anyone, not even to Anora, because he hoped he was wrong. He did not want to alarm her unnecessarily or set off a panic among the members of Parliament. Ven was an experiment in breeding. One that had succeeded, where others had failed. If the dragon had created one son like Ven, perhaps there were others. . . .

They hid the boat beneath an outcropping of rock, a location that allowed them to keep the cave in sight, yet prevented anyone in the cave from spotting them. The boat had no anchor and they moored it by tying it to a tree limb. This late in the season, the river ran sluggishly. The boat bobbed gently in the water with only a very slight tug on the tether.

Draconas sat in the stern, wondering what he was going to do if Bellona was right and the baby smugglers did not appear. Bullheaded as she was, she would charge right in and ruin everything.

He need not have worried. Dusk was just beginning to steal over the river when a boat slid out of the cave, quickly followed by three more. The boats were large, with several rowers in each, and people manning the tillers. Squat figures, shapeless in black garb, who sat in the middle of the boats, were the women who would tend the babies on the journey back. Draconas searched for Grald, but did not see him.

The boats carrying the baby smugglers changed direction once they were clear of the cavern. They would travel westward until they reached the fork in the river; then they would bear north toward Seth. The rowers were strong and experienced. They would make good time. Draconas calculated they would return near midnight. He slipped over the side of the boat, plunged into the water.

"What are you doing? Where are you going?" Bellona demanded.

"Keep your voice down," Draconas cautioned, treading water. "These canyon walls magnify every sound. I'm going to swim to the cave to find out if they've left a guard."

He dove beneath the water before she could start another argument and surfaced some distance away from the boat. He swam as a dragon swims, keeping his head above water, his legs and arms below. His strokes were powerful, yet he was careful not to break the surface. Silently, he entered the cave, listened, looked, searched the darkness.

No one about. Grald had not come with them this trip.

So far, so good.

"Well?" Bellona asked curtly, as Draconas pulled himself up onto the outcropping of rock. "Is anyone inside?"

"No." He wiped the water out of his face and eyes and then shook himself like a wet dog. "No guard. That makes things easier. Once the smugglers return and enter the cave, give them to the count of one hundred, then follow them. Make certain you keep them in sight. The entrance to this stronghold of theirs is well concealed—"

"But I thought you were coming with us," Marcus interrupted, suspicious. "Where will you be?"

"Believe me, I would like to come with you," Draconas stated emphatically. "I've tried to think of a way." He shook his head. "It's impossible. It wouldn't work."

"Just as well," said Bellona.

"No, it's not," Marcus returned angrily. "I want him with us, not off fetching my father. I don't see why you can't come. You can disguise yourself—"

"I am already in disguise. Look at me," Draconas added impatiently. "What do you see?"

"A man," said Marcus.

"And?" Draconas prompted.

Marcus cast a sidelong glance at Bellona.

"She knows," said Draconas. "She knows who and what I truly am. And so do you—just by looking. You see me, but you also see the dragon."

"Only indistinctly. The way I see a shadow on a hazy day. And then only because I know to look for it—"

Draconas shook his head. "I can't risk it, Marcus. And I'm not going to go after your father or anyone else. If you get into trouble, you're going to need me. I'll keep in contact with you. My thoughts will be with you, literally. Just remember this and take my warning to heart—if you use the magic, if you step outside your little room, the dragon will be waiting."

They passed the next hours in silence. Bellona was never one for small talk and Marcus was just as glad to be left to his own thoughts. Draconas pondered the magic he must use, how to best hide the boat from the sight of the baby smugglers. He could not use illusion, for he was afraid that at least some of the human males possessed of dragon magic had the ability to see through illusion, including the most powerful illusion spell a dragon could cast—the illusion that made Draconas look, feel, and act human.

But if he could not fool them with an illusion, he could try fooling them with the reverse—a deletion. An illusion spell adds the unreal to reality. A deletion spell subtracts the real from reality, makes objects appear to disappear. The spell he had in mind was complex. The humans in the center of the spell had to continue to see the object of the spell—the boat—or otherwise they would quite understandably think they were going mad. Anyone else looking at the boat and those in it must not see it. The boat would be there, but it wouldn't.

After he figured out how to cast the spell came the truly hard part—explaining it to the humans.

"I'm going to place a magical spell on the boat and on both of you. The spell will cause to you blend in with your surroundings, like a chameleon. The way I did with the window when we were fighting in the cabin." He looked at Bellona to see if she remembered.

She nodded in stoic silence. But a nerve in her jaw twitched.

"Anyone looking at you will not see you, but they can hear you if you speak or if you fall into the water or bump into them. So you'll have to be careful."

The two nodded, though both looked dubious.

Draconas gestured with his hand that, when he cast a spell, was always the clawed, scaled hand of the dragon. The magic glittered on his claws, then flashed toward the boat. The magic coursed through every fiber of the craft, from bow to stern and back, danced across the oars, and then surged into the two humans, so that in his eyes they gleamed brightly in the darkness, shining with a beatific light, as humans envision angels. In an instant—briefer than a lightning flash—darkness returned.

The spell was cast.

The humans knew nothing, saw nothing.

"There," said Draconas. "To all intents and purposes, you are invisible."

Bellona could see the boat quite clearly. She snorted in disbelief. Even Marcus, who understood the magic, was doubtful.

"Step out of the boat, Bellona," said Draconas. "Come over here with me."

She hesitated, regarding him mistrustfully, then did as he asked. She climbed nimbly from the boat, which Marcus held steady with the oars, climbed over the rocks, and came to stand beside Draconas.

"Now look at the boat," he said.

Bellona turned to face the river. She started, drew back, stared, then frowned deeply.

"I hate this," she muttered.

"I know," he answered quietly. "But it is necessary if you want to save Ven."

Returning to the boat, Bellona gripped the gunwale tightly, as if to reassure herself the boat was real, before she climbed back inside.

"He is right. From where he stands, the boat is invisible," she said.

"And so are you, when you're inside the boat," said Draconas. "When you leave it, people will be able to see you. That's why you have the disguises."

He gestured to the brown monks' robes that lay neatly folded in the bottom of the boat.

Marcus regarded the robes with a grimace. "Why don't you use the same spell to make us invisible?"

"That sounds good, but it never works," Draconas answered, adding with a smile, "someone always sneezes."

He glanced up at the moon, which had traveled a good distance among the stars. "They'll be back soon. I'm going to make myself scarce.

"Take care of yourself," Draconas added in a low voice, so that only Marcus could hear him. "Take care of Bellona. She loves Ven, though neither of them knows it."

Marcus nodded.

Faint, across the water, came a baby's wail. The boats could be seen, their black shapes crawling along the surface of the liquid moonlight like black bugs.

"Here they come," warned Draconas. "Make ready."

26

"CAN'T YOU KEEP THE BRAT QUIET, OLD WOMAN?" Demanded one of the soldiers in the lead boat. "That screeching is getting on my nerves!"

"He'll cry himself to sleep soon enough," returned the woman, holding on to the bundle of squirming cloth.

"You said that an hour ago," the man countered irritably.

The woman chose to ignore him. The baby continued to cry. The boats glided along the surface of the still water. Leaving the moonlight, they entered the darkness of the drowned cavern.

"Black as a black dog in a coal bin," complained the coxswain. "I can't see a damn thing. Stop rowing before we bash into a wall. What's keeping that light?"

The rowers leaned on their oars while the soldier posted at the front of the boat fumbled with a match in an attempt to light a lantern.

"The match won't catch fire. It's got wet somehow," he complained.

"Fancy that. Being on a river," the coxswain muttered.

He looked at a brown-robed monk, who sat silent and unmoving in the stern, his hands folded in his lap. "Pardon, brother," the coxswain said deferentially and awkwardly, "I do not like to disturb you, but the match won't light. Could you—"

The monk lifted his hand. A flicker of flame danced in his palm. He blew delicately on the flame and, like thistledown, the wisp of fire flew toward the lantern, barely missing the soldier, who hastily drew back out of the way. The wick in the oil lantern caught fire, burned steadily. The monk relapsed into the same position, hands in his lap.

A harsh glow flared from the lantern, gleaming off the damp walls and spreading like a yellow film over the water.

One of the women gave a muffled shriek. "There's someone there!"

"Guts and gore, woman!" The coxswain swore. "What do you want to go screaming like that? I nigh jumped out of the boat! It's only Grald."

"*Only* Grald," repeated the woman in a low tone, making renewed efforts to hush the crying baby.

The tall, hulking man stood at the water's edge, watching the progress of the boats edging their way into the cavern. Each boat lit its own lantern and soon four lights bobbed in the water.

All talking ceased. There was no sound except the gentle lappings of the water against the rock and the baby's wail. The woman holding the crying baby resorted to pinching his nose with her fingers and covering his mouth with her hand to hush him. The occupants of the four boats nervously eyed their master.

"You're late, Ranulf," stated Grald. "Was there a problem?"

"The Mistress kept me talking, sir." The soldier defended himself, his voice a little too loud, so that it echoed off the walls. "She wanted to know all there was to know about the Dragon's Son. She seemed to take it ill that you didn't come yourself, sir. I told her you were meeting with your son—"

Grald folded his arms across his massive chest and glared at the soldier. "I don't need you defending me, Ranulf."

"No, sir," Ranulf muttered. "Sorry, sir."

"I should have been along, it seems," Grald continued, growling. "Look at the lot of you, lit up like All Hallow's Night for anyone to see. Douse those blasted lights!"

No one dared object. One by one, the lights winked out.

"Now be off with you," Grald ordered. "I'll meet you at the landing site."

Oars splashed in the water. The boats moved cautiously, feeling their way through the darkness. Fortunately, they had only a short stretch to navigate before they reached the opening at the far end of the cavern. The boats edged their way out, the occupants forced to duck their heads as they sailed beneath the low ceiling.

"The shipment has arrived," Grald reported, mentally speaking to his partner. "I have sent them on their way. I must join up with them soon to open the gate."

"That is well," returned Maristara. "How is your son? Your man tells me you find him rebellious, uncooperative."

"That is the dragon in him." The father spoke with paternal pride. "I have the means to control him, however. Through his human frailties. A female to whom he is attached."

"Will you breed him?"

"She has no dragon blood in her, so I doubt if we'll get much that would be of any use. For the time being, he may keep her for his pleasure."

"And when will you take his body?"

"Oh, not for some time yet. This body continues to serve me well enough. And I want the people of Dragonkeep to become accustomed to seeing Ven, to paying him homage."

"And what of our army?"

"Soon ready to march. When it does, the humans of this continent will think that the end of days has come. Our army will fall upon them like the wrath of their God. And they have no defense."

"*If* your plan to kill Draconas succeeds." Maristara was openly dubious.

"It will. I have my son. I have his brother. I will have Draconas."

"Even though you have not seen him and you do not know

where he is." Maristara sneered. "He worries me. What if he doesn't come?"

"He will come." Grald was confident. "After all, he has his own trap to bait."

" 'A trap is a trap—' " Maristara quoted.

"Is a trap," Grald finished.

Bellona sat in the boat in the darkness and watched the man who had raped Melisande and forced her to bear the dragon's son climb into his own boat, take the oars, and steer himself out onto the murky water.

She meant to kill him. Not yet. Not tonight. Maybe not tomorrow. He had to first lead her to Ven. When that was done, before she left this place, she would kill him.

She made Grald that silent promise, as he rowed out of the drowned cavern, and, putting her hands to the oars, she followed silently after.

The baby smugglers had not traveled far when Grald overtook them and passed them, his strong arms propelling his craft rapidly through the water. The boats carrying the babies rocked violently in his wake.

Knowing Grald would be waiting for them impatiently at the landing site, the rowers bent to their task with redoubled effort. Oars lifted and fell, lifted and fell, now the only sounds in the night. The crying baby had either fallen asleep or been smothered; the woman holding on to him was not sure which.

27

"YOU HAVE TO ROW FASTER, BELLONA," MARCUS complained in an urgent whisper. "I'm losing sight of them! Are you sure you don't want me to help?"

"Fine help you'd be," Bellona retorted. "You have no skin left on your palms as it is. I can't row faster or I'll make too much noise."

She did increase her pace somewhat, however, and the boat slowly crept nearer to those ahead of it.

This branch of the Aston River was narrow, winding, and thickly lined with trees that hung low over the water, their branches cutting off the moonlight. The rowboat slid through thick swaths of night broken occasionally by patches of splattered light. Marcus lay prone in the bow, peering down into the black water, watching for the tell tale ripples that denoted snags or rocks below the water. The last thing they needed to do was to run afoul of something. He also kept an eye on the boat directly in front of him.

The stormy weather had left the autumn night hot and muggy. No breeze stirred the water. The thick trees hugged the humid air close, as if selfishly determined to keep it all

for themselves. Marcus sweltered in the wool monk's robes.
He threw back the smothering cowl, laved his neck and chest
with the cool water and looked with some anxiety at Bellona, who had insisted on putting the robes on over her own
clothes—wool robes over a wool tunic and a leather vest and
wool trousers. Sweat dripped off her chin, trickled into her
eyes. She refused his offer of a wet rag with a shake of her
head, kept doggedly rowing.

Rounding a bend, Marcus lost sight of the boats, but he
could hear the splash of the oars and he knew the boats were
still ahead of him. Then he could no longer hear the oars.
Someone spoke, someone answered—deep male voices.

"They've stopped," he warned Bellona.

She ceased rowing. Their boat continued on, drifting
down the stream on the slow-moving current. Marcus feared
that the boat would plow straight into the midst of the smugglers. He could not see any sign of them, however, or any
sign of their destination. Their boat slid over the smooth water and suddenly the boats they'd been following came into
view, clustered along the shoreline.

"Stop!" Marcus hissed frantically.

Bellona steered into the shoreline, beaching the boat in a
tangle of roots. Marcus tied it securely, then looked back at
the smugglers.

The monks were assisting the women out of the boats,
while the rowers hauled the empty boats up onto the shore.
Lantern light flared. Marcus could see by the bobbing lights
that several people were leaving the shore, moving deeper
into the woods.

"We're going after them," Bellona whispered, rising to a
crouch. "I'll go first."

She climbed nimbly from the boat onto the tree roots.
Marcus had more difficulty. He grasped a tree root to use it
to steady himself, but the root was wet and slimy with algae,
and his hand slipped off it.

"Here!" Bellona held out her hand.

He took hold of her arm and she wrapped her hand around

his forearm, steadying him. He put one foot on the tree root. His foot slipped. The boat slid out from beneath him. His heart jolted.

"Jump, damn you!" Bellona ordered, her grip on him tightening.

Marcus didn't have time to think. He swung his other leg up onto the tree root, found slippery purchase, and wobbled precariously. Bellona gave him a yank and he tumbled onto solid ground. As he stood panting and catching his breath, she untied the boat and cast it adrift.

"What did you do that for?" he asked, wiping sweat from his face. "Won't we need the boat to travel back?"

"We can steal one of theirs. I don't want to leave it here. If those monks found it, they would know someone had followed them."

"Of course," said Marcus, chagrined. "I didn't think of that."

If this adventure had taught him anything, it was that he was ill-prepared for adventure.

Bellona moved close to him, whispered in his ear. "They're moving deeper into the forest. They will be easy to track, what with lights and the racket they're making. But we can't take a chance on them hearing us. Watch how you walk. Tread softly."

"I can't tread softly or otherwise," Marcus returned. "Blast these robes!" He yanked on the hem of the skirt, which had snagged on a bramble. "How does anyone walk in these getups?"

"Kilt the skirt up above your knees," Bellona ordered.

"What are you doing?"

"Taking off my robe. Don't worry," she added, seeing him about to protest, "I'll put it back on when I need to."

She twisted the brown bundle under her arm and then helped Marcus hike up his robes so that he could walk without either tripping over the hem or catching it on every bush and briar. He and Bellona entered the forest, following the lights and the sound of voices.

The baby smugglers talked and chatted—the women

complaining about the lateness of the hour and the fact that they would be up all night with squalling brats; the rowers speaking longingly of cold ale. Marcus tried to walk with extraordinary caution, but his boots seemed drawn to every dry stick that cracked beneath them with a sound like a cannon shot and if there was a hole anywhere along the route, he fell into it.

Part of his problem was sheer weariness. He had taken only a few steps when he realized he was exhausted. Excitement had kept him going this long, but the tramp through the woods soon took its toll. He saw no sign of civilization—no campfires, no welcoming lights—and he began to think that they were going to march all night. He was wondering if it was truly possible that a man could fall asleep on his feet, as he'd heard Gunderson claim, when Bellona halted, holding out her arm to prevent him from plunging forward.

The baby smugglers stood huddled together in a glade, bathed in moonlight, waiting for something to happen, seemingly, for they were all of them looking expectantly at the big man.

Bellona also looked at him, looked at no one but him.

"Who is that?" Marcus asked, seeing the intensity of her fixed gaze. He knew the answer the moment he asked. "It's Grald, isn't it?"

She gave a tight nod, kept hold of him. It was almost as though by keeping hold of him, she kept hold of herself.

"So that is the dragon," Marcus said softly, trying to see some sign of the beast inside the man. Draconas had warned him he wouldn't—that by stealing a human's body, the dragon effectively hid inside it. Still, Marcus thought there must be some way to tell.

Grald raised his arms and made a banishing motion with his hands. A towering wall appeared before Marcus's eyes, its gray stone glimmering in the moonlight. Then the wall shimmered away and was replaced by forest, thick and dense, and then the wall reappeared, displacing the forest. Smells and sounds and the feel of objects around Marcus waxed and waned.

Marcus knew how to give dust motes acorn hats, but he'd never experienced an illusion perpetrated on such a grand scale, an illusion that caused his senses to go to war with each other. It was as if one eye saw trees and moonlight and the other eye saw a wall and moonlight and the conflict met in the center of his forehead. He shut his eyes, his mind wrestling with the conflicting versions of reality that seemed to wink in and wink out with every heartbeat.

He was in a forest, for he'd tripped over it, bashed into it, and been snagged on it. He could smell the moist, damp loam. Hear the fall of a tree limb. He could see it, when he opened his eyes. And in the next blink the forest was gone and he stood before a city wall and he could smell it and hear it. Smell garbage in the alleys and hear boots on cobblestone.

Reality melted and flowed away from beneath his hands and his feet. He grew dizzy and sagged back against a tree.

"What's the matter with you?" Bellona whispered, glaring at him. "Keep quiet! They'll hear you!"

Too late.

A brown-robed monk whipped around to look behind him. He stood a moment, staring intently into the night.

Marcus froze, afraid to even breathe lest he make too much noise.

The monk's hand moved to his waist. He grasped hold of something, drew it from his belt. The light of one of the lanterns illuminated the object—a small, wicked-looking dart. With a motion as gentle and graceful as if he were showering a bride with flower petals, the monk flung the dart straight at them.

Key-up, Marcus almost laughed. This was ludicrous, like a child throwing rocks. He expected the dart to flutter to the ground at his feet and then it pierced Bellona's throat.

Clutching her neck, she toppled backward.

Marcus caught hold of her, lowered her to the ground.

Dark blood welled up around the small, feathered dart. Bellona tried to speak, but there came only a horrible, gargling sound. Her eyes held Marcus fast, her gaze a death's grip on his soul. She made a second desperate attempt to speak. Her lips, trembling with the agonized effort, formed a V.

"Ven! I know!" he said, his voice shaking. "I will."

Her body stiffened. Her eyes stared at him, accepting his promise, taking it with her into death.

"I will," Marcus repeated, choked.

He didn't know what to do. One moment she had been standing beside him and now she was gone. Her sudden, brutal death left him half-stupefied. He stared in horror at the gruesome wound, at her lifeless eyes. Then the thought struck him that the killer might not be finished. The next shaft might be aimed at him. Marcus raised his head.

The monk stood alone before the wall, poised for another throw, alert to any sound. The smugglers continued on. Several glanced over their shoulders, to see what was happening, but none of them stopped. They walked up to the wall and passed through it, as if it had been made of mist, not solid stone.

Grald was gone. Only the monk remained.

Marcus crouched in the darkness, unmoving.

Hearing nothing, the monk slipped the dart back into his belt and, shrugging, turned and walked away.

Fire burned inside Marcus, a fire far different from the sparkling gaiety he used to create sprites and will-o'-the-wisps to frighten the servants. He seized hold of the flame of his rage, shaped it, molded it, as he had molded the clay on that riverbank long ago. He rose to his feet. The flames danced on his palm.

Don't use the magic. Don't leave the little room!

Draconas's warning came back to him. Marcus ignored it. His anger consumed him as the magic would consume the monk. Marcus moved toward the door of his room, started to open it.

A claw thrust into the crack of his mind.

Pain seered his brain. Marcus gasped and flung himself against the door. The claw tried to remain inside, tried to dig deeper. Marcus held fast, braced himself against the door and, eventually, the claw withdrew. Marcus gave a shuddering sigh and closed his hand over the flames, quenched them.

The monk would be the last to pass through the wall. Marcus could see no sign of a gate or even a wicket, yet somehow these people had gone inside the city. There must be a gate, hidden by an illusion so powerful that he could not penetrate it. If he lost sight of the monk, he would lose the location of the gate. Yet Marcus didn't want to leave Bellona. It didn't seem right, abandoning her like this. He looked down to see Ven's name on her bloodstained lips.

"Take her soul, Lord," Marcus whispered a hurried prayer, "and let no evil come to her."

Rising slowly and quietly, he shook down the robes from around his waist and drew the cowl over his head to conceal his face. He placed his hands in the sleeves of his robes, as he had seen the monks do, and walked toward the wall.

The monk entered. Marcus watched closely, impressing the exact location on his mind, for he guessed that there was only a small aperture, for all those who had entered did so walking single-file. He kept going, even as his eyes told him he was about to dash out his brains against solid stone. He had to keep going. He could not stop or show any hesitation, for the monk might be on the other side, watching.

Reaching the wall, Marcus gritted his teeth, plunged ahead.

The stone wafted away like wisps of fog. His next step landed on cobblestone.

Tall buildings of gray stone reared into the moonlit night, jostling each other for a place near the wall. Alleyways branched off a main street. Other streets branched off the alleys. He was in a city—a huge city, a city the size of Idlyswylde. Was this illusion? Or was this reality?

Marcus reached out his hand to touch the wall and felt stone, cold and hard. The misty gate was gone. Or did illusion mask it? He tried, experimentally, to walk back through the wall, and bumped into stone, giving himself a hard knock on the forehead. He looked up the wall and down, hoping to see an exit, a way out. The chunks of rock used to construct the wall were a darkish color, streaked with sandy white, and arranged all higgledy-piggledy, confusing to the eye. A gate was there—must be there—but it was well-hidden.

The monk had gone. The smugglers had departed. There was no sign of Grald. Marcus was alone on the street, yet he had the feeling that eyes were watching him. He'd been foolish, trying to walk back through the wall. No monk—as he was supposed to be—would have done that.

"I can't stay here," he muttered. "I have to keep moving. But where do I go?"

The street was empty. He detected the faint sound of voices fading away in the distance somewhere to his left and he began walking in the opposite direction. He walked swiftly, as though he was proceeding with his business. He had only taken a few steps when there came a noise behind him.

Marcus glanced over his shoulder.

Grald had apparently just entered through the gate, for the big man stood near the wall. If he glanced down the street he could not fail to see Marcus.

Ducking his head, Marcus pulled the cowl low over his face, and increased his pace. With every step he took, he waited tensely for the sound of the dragon coming after him.

There was only silence.

Marcus walked and kept walking. A panicked urge to look behind him came over him and he fought against it, clenching his jaw until his neck muscles ached from the strain, forcing himself to keep facing forward. When he arrived at a street corner, he ducked around a building, and halted, shaking. He decided to risk a look. Sheltering behind the wall, he cast a swift glance back down the street, the way he had come.

Grald was nowhere in sight.

Weak with relief, Marcus closed his eyes and fell back against the wall. An aching in his hands caused him to look down. He found that his hands were balled into fists and when he pried loose his fingers, he noticed something sticky had gummed them together.

Blood. Bellona's blood.

Marcus's stomach heaved. His legs prickled. He went cold and then horribly hot. Sweat trickled down the back of his neck. He tasted bile in his mouth and he realized that, unless he stopped himself, he was going to pass out.

Squatting down on his haunches, he lowered his head between his knees, and made himself breathe deeply.

The sick sensation passed. He continued to gulp in cool air. Thinking himself safe for the moment, he fled into his little room, where he could be alone.

Someone else was there, standing outside the door. Blue eyes and a child's hand.

Marcus tried to look into his brother's mind, enter his room, but all Marcus could see was glare white.

"Open the door," said Ven. "Let me in."

Marcus did not hesitate. He opened the door.

The dragon's claw lanced through his eyes, blinding him. The claw seized hold of him and began to drag him out of the room. Marcus fought, frantically, to escape the claw's grasp, but the talons pierced deep into his mind and he could not free himself.

In desperation, Marcus looked to his brother for help.

Ven's eyes watched impassively and, as the claw dug deeper into Marcus, seeking his soul, the eyes closed.

Go away! the child cried. Get out!

A burning sapling on a riverbank.

A sword, my father's sword . . .

Marcus forged a sword of blazing, molten magic. He lifted the sword in both his hands and leaving his room, he ran into the dark lair that was the dragon's mind.

In the flaring yellow light of shock, Marcus could see the dragon clearly. Grald was caught off guard, surprised beyond measure, just as Draconas had been surprised, so many years ago, by the sight of a human invading his mind.

Marcus swung the sword and brought it down with all his might on the claw that had hold of him.

The sword shattered. The claw burst into flame. The fire seared him, burned him. Marcus almost fainted from the pain, but he made himself hold fast to consciousness, for he must not fall inside the dragon's lair. He lurched back into his own quiet little room and, with his last strength, slammed shut the door.

Outside, the dragon raged, the fire blazed.

Inside all was dark and silent. Marcus let go of the sword, let go of the pain. He curled up in a ball in the darkness and shut out the noise and the heat and his brother's betrayal. . . .

"There he is."

"I don't see him."

"Over there. That lump on the pavement."

The two monks approached warily, gliding noiselessly down the street. A blade glittered in the moonlight.

"Quick and clean," one ordered. "Strike the heart."

The knife blade flashed silver . . .

"Stop!"

The monk gave a start, as if he'd been frightened out of his skin, and dropped the knife.

"Grald!" the monk gasped. "What are you doing here?" He looked behind him, bewildered. "I just saw you back there—"

"I don't recall having to answer to you for my comings and goings." Grald clenched his fist. "Be gone. I have no more need of you."

The monk raised his hands as though to ward off a blow and ventured a pitiable protest.

"But, Grald, you ordered us to slay him—"

"And now I order you *not* to slay him," Grald said angrily. "I've changed my mind."

The monks hesitated, did not move.

"What are you staring at?" Grald roared. "Be gone!" He took a step toward them, huge fists doubled. "Since when do you feeble-minded lunatics dare disobey me?"

The monks turned and fled.

Grald bent over Marcus. Placing his hand on Marcus's neck, Grald felt for a pulse. Satisfied that the young man was still alive, Grald shook his head in exasperation. Grald flung the young man over one shoulder as easily as if he were a child, the child of the little room.

"Maybe next time you'll listen to me," Draconas grunted.

28

THE SOUND OF KNOCKING WAS PERSISTENT. IT would not go away, much as Evelina tried to shut it out, but insisted on dragging her from her only refuge—sleep. Struggling against waking, she opened her eyes a slit. The room was gray with the first wretched light of dawn. The roosters weren't even up yet, if there were roosters in this godforsaken place. Evelina pulled the blanket over her head. The knocking continued.

"I brought you some food," called a voice outside the locked door.

"Go away, Brother or Father or whatever you call yourself," she yelled. "I told you last night—I don't want anything to eat!"

"You have to eat," the voice said gravely. "Otherwise you will make yourself ill."

It was not one of the crazy-eyed monks. Evelina opened her eyes.

"Ven? Is that you?"

"Yes," he said. "I've brought you bread and—"

"Are you alone?"

"Yes."

Evelina sighed deeply. Sitting up in bed, she rubbed her eyes and yawned. What was he doing up at this hour? She didn't know, but she couldn't afford to lose him. Clasping the blanket around her, she called out petulantly, "Where have you been? Why didn't you come to me last night? Don't stand out in the hall talking through the keyhole. Come inside."

He opened the door with his shoulder and entered the room. He carried in his hands a tray covered with a cloth and he had a bundle draped over his arm. Evelina barely glanced at the tray. She was far more interested in the bundle.

"A dress!" she cried. "For me?"

Ven saw bare shoulders and neck, golden hair rumpled, a face flushed with sleep and pleasure. The black habit lay in a heap on the floor. He looked away from her.

"I'll leave the tray here and let you get dressed. I hope these clothes are what you require. I asked one of the women—"

"I'm sure the clothes will be fine," said Evelina. She shifted her position on the bed, let the blanket slip a little, provocatively, and gave him a smile. "You don't need to go. Just turn your back. . . ."

"I'll wait outside." Ven placed the tray on the table, hung the clothes over a chair, and then left the room. He shut the door firmly behind him.

"Don't go far," Evelina called. "I want to talk to you."

Scrambling out of bed, she seized the clothes, shook them out, eyed them: a linen chemise and petticoat, woolen bodice and skirt, woolen stockings, a woolen cloak. Plain and shabby and dull. Her lips pursed in disgust, but then she shrugged. At least it was better than that horrid nun's garb. Evelina dressed hurriedly, her mind on her mission. She slid the chemise over her head, drew on the stockings, stepped into the petticoat and then into the skirt. She cinched the bodice tight and tugged down the chemise to better display her prime assets.

"You may come in," Evelina called, adding in wheedling tones, as he opened the door, "Next time, bring me a comb."

She dragged her fingers through her hair, toyed with a curl that lay languidly on her breast. "I must look a fright."

Any other man would have made the requisite gallant reply. Ven took her literally, said only, "I'll bring you a comb."

Evelina bit her lip in exasperation, forced a smile, and sidled closer to him.

"I have something important to talk to you about."

"And I want to talk to you. I heard you left the guesthouse last night. Where did you go?"

"For a walk," said Evelina. "You told me I was free to leave. Or have you now changed your mind?"

She was having trouble with her eyes. Ven wore different clothes: a loose-fitting shirt, open at the neck, and tight-fitting breeches slit at the seams in order to fit over his scaled, beast's legs. He wore no boots. His clawed feet scraped on the floor. Blue scales glittered. It was as if he was flaunting the fact that he was a monster, taunting her. Surely he must know how it disgusted her to look at him.

"You can go where you want by day. You shouldn't leave the compound," he was saying. "It's dangerous for you to walk the city at night by yourself."

"Danger!" Evelina scoffed. "Danger from what? Being bored to death?" Her smile slipped and trembled, her lip quivered. "There is nothing to do here. No taverns. No one singing or dancing."

She drew nearer to him and lifted her hands, as if she would touch him. He drew back a step, and she hurriedly changed her motion. She clasped her hands together, rested her chin on the fingers, and regarded him with imploring eyes. She kept her eyes on his face, not looking at his legs.

"I want to leave this place," she said.

"You are free—"

"I mean, leave this city."

He was silent.

"I don't like it here," she continued. "There's nothing to do, nothing to see, no one to talk to." She made a disparaging gesture at the nun's habit. "I might as well be shut up in a nunnery."

"What has this to do with me?" Ven asked.

Evelina flushed prettily, cast down her eyes, and said softly, "I want you to come with me."

He said nothing and Evelina was nonplussed. She had expected him to fling himself on her with rapture. He just stood there like a dolt. She fought down a desire to scratch out his eyes.

"We could leave tonight. When it's dark. Just you and I. Alone. Together."

"I don't understand why you want me to come with you," Ven said. "You despise me."

Evelina started to protest, to feed him blandishments, the honeyed words that had always seduced her other lovers. When she tried to say them to him—to those intense blue eyes—the words shriveled up, dried out.

What did I expect? she asked herself scornfully. *He's not a man like other men. He's a beast, an animal. His feelings are low and base as any mongrel's.*

"If you must know, I can't find the way out of this horrible place by myself," she said at last, sullenly. "I walked around and around the wall last night, searching for the gate—"

"There is no gate," Ven said.

Evelina gave a girlish giggle. "Oh, come now, don't tease me—"

"I'm not teasing, Evelina."

"There must be a way out!" Her tone sharpened. "There is a way in. . . ."

"True. But the entrance and the exit are both controlled by the dragon."

"Dragon?" Evelina repeated impatiently. "What dragon? What are you talking about?"

"The dragon who fathered me," said Ven. "The dragon who made me what I am—half-human, half-beast."

Evelina stared at him. She might have thought that he was jesting, but she knew enough of him to know that he lacked the capacity to jest. His father—a dragon.

Of course, that would explain a great deal.

She looked down at the scaled legs, the clawed feet, and

realized that she'd never wondered how he'd come to be this way—a beast-man.

How could I be expected to? she asked herself crossly. *I've seen so many freaks in my life: men who look like elephants, children with their heads stuck together, women with three breasts. I thought he was just another one of those.*

The question of "how" he had come by his beast-legs may not have occurred to her, but a dragon for a father? Evelina didn't believe it and she didn't *not* believe it. The truth was—she didn't care. His father could be a frog, for all it mattered to her. She had to get out of this hidden city and back to the world, a world of men with money who wanted to spend it all on her. Ven knew the way. His dragon feet could carry him there and carry her with him. She wrenched her gaze back to meet his. Her eyelids fluttered. She smiled tremulously.

"Your father the . . . uh, dragon . . . controls the exits? That's wonderful, Ven. I'm sure your father will show you how to open the gate if you ask him. If he refuses," she added, having had some experience with recalcitrant fathers, "we'll trick him. It won't be hard. You'll see—" She glared at him. "Stop shaking your head. Didn't you hear me? I want us to leave together. Together!"

"I don't want to leave," he said calmly.

"But I do!" she cried, stamping her foot. "I must leave! I hate this place! I'm in a cage— No, no! I didn't mean that! Oh, Ven, I'm sorry. . . ."

Too late. The blue eyes darkened, then caught fire. He turned away from her.

Panic-stricken, watching her freedom walk out the door, Evelina flung herself after him. Clasping her arms around his waist, she buried her head in his back and wept. Her fear was very real and, this time, so were her tears.

"I'm sorry! I'm so sorry. I'm sorry about what they did to you. I know you hate me and I don't blame you, but if I stay here, I'll die! I'll truly die!"

She felt his body quiver. He reached down to her hands and loosened her grasp, then turned around and took hold of her. His touch was gentle and tender. She thought she felt his lips brush her hair.

She whispered softly, "Help me get away from here, Ven, and I'll do anything you want. I'll sleep with you. I promise."

His arms stiffened. He let go of her and backed away.

"What's the matter now?" she cried impatiently. "Isn't that what you want?"

"Are you going to eat your breakfast?" he asked.

Evelina grabbed hold of the small table on which he'd placed the food and upended it. Food and tray and crockery crashed to the floor. "No, I'm not going to eat it. Or anything! Ever! I'll starve myself to death."

"You have the knife I gave you," he said coolly. "Stabbing yourself would be much quicker and less painful."

"I'll do it! I'll kill myself! Then you'll be sorry!" Evelina made a dart for the knife that she'd secreted under the pillow. By the time she had the blade in hand and turned around, Ven was gone. The door was closing behind him.

Evelina stood seething. Muttering curses, she tossed the knife back onto the bed and flounced down beside it. A thought came to her.

He will show me the way out, whether he means to or not. Sooner or later he will leave, and when he does, I will be right behind him. I have only to watch for my chance.

Perhaps he was planning on leaving now. True, he'd told her he didn't want to leave, but all men were liars.

Ven occupied the room next to hers. Evelina could hear him next door, moving about. She crept to the door, opened it a crack, and peeped out. He had not shut his door. It stood wide open.

She shut her door quietly. Grabbing up the knife, she bound the hilt into the drawstring that held her petticoat around her waist and pulled the bodice down over it so that the bulge wouldn't show. She wrapped herself in her cloak and hurried back to the door. She did not open it, but stood next to it, breathless with anticipation.

The door to his room closed. She heard him walk past her room, heading down the hallway. She opened her door silently, peeped out.

He wore his cloak. He was going somewhere.

Evelina waited until Ven had started down the stairs, then she glided after him, the feel of the knife reassuring against her belly. About halfway down the spiral stairs, his footsteps stopped. He was talking to someone. Evelina paused, listening.

"Dragon's Son." It was one of the monks. "You are up and about early this morning. Going for a walk? Excellent. I will come with you. I am in need of some exercise—"

There was a gasp, a crunching sound, and a thump. Mystified, Evelina stood poised on the stairs, wondering what had happened, afraid to venture any farther.

The sound of a door shutting impelled her to action.

She hastened down the stairs. At the bottom, she came to an abrupt halt.

The crumpled body of a monk lay at the foot of the stairs. The crunching sound had been bone breaking. His neck was broken. The monk did not move, and she assumed he was dead.

Gathering up her skirts so that they did not brush the corpse, Evelina detoured around the body of the monk and ran across the hall to the door.

The sun was a bleary red slit of an eye, peering over the edge of the horizon. No one else was awake yet, for the courtyard was devoid of life. Ven was already halfway across the courtyard, walking with swift, purposeful strides. Evelina knew his game now. He was making good his own escape. He'd killed the monk, who had been set there to guard him, and he was fleeing, leaving her behind.

"By the time I'm finished with you, you man-beast, you won't be a man anymore." She touched the knife at her waist. Her lip curled. "You'll just be a beast."

With this promise, she hastened after him.

29

MARCUS CROUCHED IN SEMIDARKNESS, HIS HAND pushing hard against a chill stone wall.

"You can't come in!" He was sweating, afraid. "Go away. Keep out!"

"Too late for that," said a voice.

Marcus gasped and shuddered and woke up. He found himself standing in front of a stone wall, pushing against it with all his might.

Bewildered, he backed away.

"You were walking in your sleep," the voice told him.

Still confused, but at least awake, Marcus remembered the dragon outside his room, trying to batter down the door. He drew in a breath and turned from the wall, which he could see now was just a wall, not a door. His terror was real, however, not a dream. His heart raced, he was clammy with sweat. He breathed deeply, waited for fear to subside, and looked around.

He was in a one-room dwelling that had the feel of a cave, for the walls and the low-hanging ceiling were made of rough stone blocks, irregular in shape, that had been jammed together. The floor was packed dirt. Gray dawn straggled through two crudely made windows set in the front, one on either side of an ill-fitting wooden door.

The room was bare, except for a straw mattress on the dirt floor. The mattress had a dent in it and Marcus had a vague memory of rising from it. The only other objects in the room were a slop bucket and a basin of water. A chill breeze sighed through the door, whistling a low note. The door was held shut by a leather thong attached to an iron hook on the wall.

The man who had spoken to him stood by the window.

The man was Grald.

The room was too small to hold his great bulk. He was forced to hunch his shoulders and keep his head lowered, or he would have bashed into the ceiling. He stood at the window, staring out into the street. He paid no attention to Marcus, did not so much as glance at him. Marcus might have thought he'd dreamed that voice, too, but that he could still hear the echoes in the dark hole left by his terror.

I have to calm down, he told himself. *I have to think, figure out what's going on.*

He didn't want to move, because he didn't want to draw Grald's attention, but he felt a pressing need to relieve himself. He made self-conscious use of the bucket, all the while striving desperately to figure out what was going on.

"I brought you water," said Grald, keeping watch out the window. "I thought you might want to wash the blood off your hands."

The sun's newborn rays struck the east-facing windows, brightening the room. Marcus's questions died on his lips.

Grald stood at the window. Behind Grald, clear as his shadow, was the body of a dragon—a dragon with scales of red-gold and wings of orange flame.

Marcus knew of only one human who bore the dragon's shadow.

"Draconas?"

Grald raised a thick finger in a cautionary gesture. "Keep your voice down."

"Draconas?" Marcus repeated, to make certain. He felt

his bewilderment increase, not lessen. "What are you doing in Grald's body? And where are we? Where am I?"

"Questions," said Draconas with a brooding half smile. "You're always asking questions." He shrugged in answer. "You're where you wanted to be. In a house in Dragonkeep."

Marcus plunged his hands into the cool water and laved them. "The last I remember, the dragon had hold of me and was dragging me away—"

"It's your own fault," Draconas told him, unsympathetic. "You did what you promised me you wouldn't do. You opened the door to your mind and the dragon was able to gain entry."

"I'm sorry," said Marcus, chilled at the memory. "It was foolish—"

Draconas glanced at him. "Foolish! I stopped two of his monks who were about to stab you through the heart."

"They killed Bellona," said Marcus, watching the water in the basin turn pink. He hurriedly wiped his hands on his robes.

"I know." Draconas returned to watching out the window. "I saw her die."

Marcus tipped the water in the basin out onto the floor, watched it seep into the dirt.

"I don't understand, Draconas. What's going on? You told me you couldn't come with us. Yet you were there, seemingly, and you did nothing to help her."

"Because there was nothing I could do," Draconas returned. "I told you the truth. I couldn't come with you. Those with the dragon magic see me as you see me now. The wretched monks who were going to kill you knew that I wasn't really Grald or at least suspected it. Fortunately they're so addled that most of the time they're not sure what they see or don't see and I was able to scare them off. I can't count on that with everyone I meet here, though, so I can use this body only for brief periods of time. I must be ready to abandon it if I'm discovered. You would have been safe enough on your own if you hadn't walked into Ven's trap."

"And is that where I am now?" Marcus asked quietly. "Am I in Ven's trap? Or yours?"

Draconas didn't reply. He stared out the window.

"You could have carried me to safety outside the wall, put me in a boat, and sent me back to my father," Marcus went on implacably. "But you didn't. You brought me here. You told me it was a trap. What you didn't tell me was that you were the one setting the trap. You didn't tell me that I was the bait."

Grald rubbed his chin with his hand.

"The dragon will come for you himself, since his monks failed him. He won't dare trust them again. And when he does, I'll be waiting for him."

Marcus walked over to stand beside Grald. He didn't look at the illusion. He looked at the dragon's shadow.

"All this, to avenge my mother."

"It's not about your mother," Draconas said impatiently. "It's not about you. It's about . . ."

"The dragons," said Marcus. "The dragons whose voices I heard when I was little. The dragons whose dreams I dreamed. You are old, as old as the earth, and accountable."

"We tried to fix what went wrong." Draconas sighed. "Nothing has gone the way it was supposed to." He leaned forward, staring intently into the street. "And it's not going the way it's supposed to now, either. Damn and blast it all to hell and back again!"

"What is it?" Marcus asked, alarmed. "What do you see? Who's coming?"

The illusion of Grald rippled in the air and was gone. The dragon's shadow was very bright, very vivid for an instant. Marcus stared, fascinated by the beauty, the magnificence. The dragon's head towered far above Marcus. The dragon's eyes gazed down on him from a great height. The eyes were filled with sorrow and wisdom and time.

So must look the eyes of God, Marcus thought.

The shadow of the dragon waned and collapsed into the man. Draconas. The walker. Tall, gaunt, with long black hair streaked with gray. The eyes were the same eyes, however. And behind him, enfolding him, were the wings of a red-gold dragon.

Picking up his staff, Draconas grasped the leather latch and lifted it off the hook. He gave the door an irritated push, then looked back at Marcus.

"There is so much at stake. Far more than you realize. I will do what I can to save you, but if I must let you go, I will. You are one and there are many—so many . . ."

"I've been the bait all along, haven't I?" said Marcus. "For sixteen years."

"It was the reason you were born," Draconas replied. "In a way, you are lucky, Marcus. Most humans never know the answer to that question."

He walked out the door, shut it behind him.

Marcus stood alone, a little child in his quiet room, thinking he would leave, thinking he wouldn't, confused by images of the sorrow-filled eyes and the fire of bright red-golden wings.

"—only if the victim doesn't know," he muttered, repeating the tail end of the Draconas dictum about traps. "And in this case, the victim knows."

He took a step toward the door, flung it open, and came face-to-face with Ven.

Clawed feet, digging into the dirt. Sunlight shining on bright blue scales.

30

NO ONE TOLD MARCUS. NO ONE WARNED HIM. HE had pictured a brother like other brothers.

What he saw was half-brother, half-dragon.

He looked into his brother's blue eyes and he saw himself, saw features contorted with horror, saw eyes wide with the shock that softened to pity. Ven's own eyes hardened and Marcus was reduced, in an instant, to someone very small and insignificant.

He deserved that, he knew, as he knew there was nothing he could do or say to make amends.

"I'm sorry," he faltered. "I didn't—"

Ven brushed past his brother. His clawed feet scraped on the dirt floor. His scales glittered as he moved. He closed the door behind him and turned to face Marcus.

"I take it I'm not the brother you expected," said Ven.

"I'm sorry," Marcus said again. "I don't know what else to say. I didn't know."

"Bellona didn't tell you about me?" Ven asked. The blue eyes glittered brighter than the shining scales.

Marcus shook his head. He couldn't find his voice.

"Not surprising," said Ven. "She couldn't stand the sight of me."

"That's not true," Marcus returned, finding refuge from guilt in anger. "She came seeking you. She lost her life trying to save you. You know. You saw her die through *my* eyes."

"I didn't ask her to save me," Ven said caustically, brows lowering.

"No," Marcus responded coolly. "You asked me."

"*Not* to save me," Ven countered. The blue eyes flashed. "Not to save me," he repeated.

"Then why did you bring me here?"

"Because—" Ven stopped. He cast a glance behind him, in the direction of the door, and seemed to change his mind about what he had been going to say.

"Because I wanted to meet you, Brother. I've never met a royal prince before. And, unlike me, you are exactly what I expected—handsome, comely, charming. Leading a pampered life in your 'little room' in your royal palace." Ven glanced at the door again. "Did you hear something?"

Marcus had heard a muffled noise, as of someone gasping.

If Draconas is out there spying on us, he is doing a clumsy job of it, Marcus thought irritably.

Aloud he said, "I didn't hear anything." He paused, eyed his brother, and asked abruptly, "Is the dragon coming to kill me?"

Ven raised his eyebrows. "Direct and to the point. Perhaps we're more alike than I thought."

"We are alike," said Marcus. "The dragon's scales may not show outwardly on me, but they are there, just the same. The dragon blood is in my blood. People shun me because they sense there's something strange about me. They talk behind my back. Arranged marriages fall through at the last moment. There's always some excuse, of course, but the truth is that the girls have heard stories . . ."

Marcus paused to try to find the right words. He forgot where he was, forgot the danger, thought only of how to explain what was in his heart to those blue and unforgiving eyes. "I was glad to find out I had a brother. I knew you would be the one person in the world who understood me. And then I angered you by looking at you as if you were some sort of monstrosity. I want you to know that I do understand. Or, at least, I want to try to understand. I want to be your brother. And I want you to be mine."

Ven looked at his brother. His gaze traveled deliberately downward to the normal feet, pink flesh, normal toes in monk's sandals. Ven's gaze stopped, fixed on the brown hem. Marcus glanced down, saw the stains—dark red against the brown.

"Did you know," Ven said, his voice altered, "that moments after we were born, our mother was attacked by the women of Seth, who had been sent to kill her. The midwife put the two of us under the bed, so that we would be safe from the arrows. When our mother was struck, her blood dripped down onto the floor. Onto us."

Marcus's throat constricted. Tears stung his eyes. "Yes," he said huskily. "Bellona told me."

He reached out mentally to his brother, but he was repelled. All he found was blazing white emptiness.

"The dragon is coming to kill you," Ven said. "I wanted to see you first."

"Why? If I'm to die."

Ven shrugged. "I was curious. That's all."

He turned around and loped toward the door, his movements graceful, powerful, bestial. Marcus tried to think of something to say to stop him, to bring him back, to find again that single moment they'd shared, even if it had been a moment of pain.

Ven yanked open the door. A girl bolted past him. Her arms outstretched, she ran straight for Marcus, who stared at her in astonishment.

"Save me, gentle sir!" she cried. "Save me from him!" Stumbling, weeping, the girl flung herself into his arms.

Marcus caught hold of her, more by accident than by design.

"Save me . . ." she breathed.

Her eyelids fluttered and closed. Her head lolled. She went limp in his grasp.

She was the prettiest girl Marcus had ever seen. Golden hair tumbled over her smooth white shoulders. She was tousled and disheveled, as if newly risen from her bed. Marcus stared down at her, dumbstruck, bewildered by her, so pale and languid, warm and soft in his arms.

"Who is she?" Marcus looked up at Ven.

"Her name is Evelina." Ven shut the door behind him then returned to the room.

"You don't seem surprised to see her." Marcus remembered the noise he'd heard outside the door; remembered Ven glancing that direction.

His brother smiled, faint, sardonic. "On the contrary. Evelina is full of surprises. You might want to lay her down on that mattress."

Marcus carried Evelina to the bed and started to gently lower her.

Her eyes opened. Her arms stole around his neck. Her lips whispered close to his ear, "Are you truly a king's son as he claimed, gentle sir?" Her words were honeyed breath on his cheek. "Forgive me for doubting, but you are dressed like one of those demon monks who brought me here against my will."

"My name is Marcus," he said. "My father is the king of Idlyswylde."

"And is Ven truly your brother?" she asked, her voice low and tremulous. He felt a shiver run through her soft body and his grip on her instinctively tightened. "How can that be?"

"Half brother. We have the same mother."

He laid her down on the mattress and started to rise. Her arms kept hold of him, clasping him around his neck, hugging him close.

"Don't leave me, Your Highness—" she pleaded, gulping on her tears.

"Marcus," he corrected, flushing, conscious of Ven standing there, watching and listening. "I won't leave you. I'll stay right here with you."

"Oh, Marcus," Evelina whispered, "I am so frightened. I am sorry to have to tell you this, but your brother is a monster. Not just in looks, but in deed. He killed my father and . . ."

A blush stained her cheeks. She lowered her eyes. "He . . . he tried to . . . to have his way with me. I wouldn't let him. I fought him, but he is so strong. He would have succeeded in my ruin, but my father saved me. And for that, my dear father paid with his life. Your brother hasn't tried to rape me again, but I'm afraid of him, so afraid. He came to my bedroom, just this morning. . . ."

Her tears were wet and cool on his skin. Her breasts pressed yieldingly, yet so innocently, against his flesh. Her danger, her fear, her beauty, and her tears wove a web of romance around Marcus. His skin tingled, his blood burned. He found it hard to breathe for the scent of her.

"You believe me, don't you?" she quavered.

Marcus couldn't think clearly with her arms around him. He eased his way out of her grasp and laid her—limp and unresisting—down on the mattress. He had a sudden vision of lying down beside her, and he shook his head, to clear it of such appalling thoughts.

"You should rest," he said. "And don't worry. I won't let anyone harm you."

Evelina caught hold of his hand and said hurriedly, "He'll tell you lies about me. Terrible lies. Don't believe him. He's trying to hide his own wickedness!" She dug her nails into his palm. "You won't listen to him, will you?"

"No, no, of course not," Marcus murmured, confused, soothing.

"Thank you, Your Highness." Evelina smiled at him and gave a sigh that caused her breasts to quiver beneath the thin fabric of her chemise. "I put myself in your hands."

Marcus looked up at his brother, who had not left his place by the door.

"Do you know what she has been telling me?"

"I can guess," Ven said dryly.

"She accuses you of murdering her father and of trying to rape her. Did you?"

"I did not murder her father," said Ven. "The monks did that." His eyes shifted to her. The blue flame flickered. "As to the other, what can I say? I wanted her."

"How could you?" Marcus nearly choked on his outrage. "Your father raped our mother and you were the result. How could you treat this innocent girl the same, perhaps cause her to give birth to . . ." He bit off the word that had been on his lips.

"A monster?" Ven looked at Marcus, blue eyes into hazel. "Like me?"

"Yes," said Marcus, stung to anger. "If you did what she claims you have done. Yes, you are a monster."

"Like father, like son," said Ven, and he turned his back and reached for the door handle.

"Don't let him go!" Evelina cried, half sitting up. "He knows the way out of this terrible prison! That's why I followed him! He knows where to find the gate! Make him tell us!"

"Wait, Ven," Marcus said desperately. "Listen to me!"

Ven waited, hand on the door. "Yes, Brother?"

Marcus floundered. "I . . . The dragon is coming to kill me. But you don't want her to die. Take the girl with you."

Evelina gave a shrill cry of protest.

Ven cast her a disparaging glance. "Very gallant. What I would expect of a prince. But don't worry about Evelina. She won't die. She is mine to do with as I please. You see, Brother, she is my reward. My father gave her to me in exchange for you."

He started to open the door.

A rustle of skirts, a blur of gold curls, a flash of steel. Evelina ran past Marcus.

He cried out, reached out, tried to stop her. She was too fast. She evaded his grasp.

Hearing his brother's shout, Ven half turned, raised his hands.

Snarling with fury, Evelina drove the knife into his chest.

21

DRACONAS PAUSED IN HIS WORK TO GLARE ACROSS the street at the stone dwelling.

"What are they up to in there?" he muttered.

He'd seen Ven enter the house. It had been the sight of Ven, loping down the street, that had forced Draconas to leave. Then, from his hiding place, Draconas had seen the girl come along, apparently following Ven, for she'd put her ear to the door to hear what was going on inside. Then Ven opened the door. The girl ran inside. The door shut. Then the shrill, high-pitched scream of rage, then a deep-voiced cry of pain and anger, and now there was a sound of a scuffle.

Draconas didn't dare leave his hiding place to find out what was going on. Grald might come along at any moment and he must not see Draconas until Draconas was ready to be seen.

He stood in the open doorway of the hovel across the street, staring intently into the dwelling opposite. He couldn't see anything through the window. The room was shadowy to begin with and the shadows were made deeper by the stark contrast of the early morning sun shining on gray walls.

The sounds of the scuffle continued for a moment, then

suddenly ceased. Draconas listened intently, with his dragon hearing. He could hear voices, but could not understand what they were saying. At least, someone was still alive in there.

Draconas could not afford to dwell on it. He had work to do and not much time to do it. Putting the humans out of his mind, he turned his attention back to his task of trimming the wood from the bottom of his staff.

As he whittled—the blade of his knife shaving off one curl of wood after the other—he kept one eye on the street in front of him. He'd chosen the site of his ambush with care. He stood in the doorway of a stone dwelling located directly across the street from the house where he'd left Marcus—the bait. A callous way of putting it, but accurate. This seemed his best, his only course of action. As he'd told Marcus, there was much at stake—the future of humans, the future of dragons.

"With any luck, we'll all come out of this alive," Draconas reflected. "All except Grald, of course."

He inspected the end of the staff. The butt had been worn smooth, pounded down from years of walking the paths and lanes and highways of earth. Draconas had used up many staffs in his time as a walker. This was the first one he'd ever transformed into a weapon. He trusted it would be the last. In six hundred years, he'd never killed a human. Until now.

The Parliament of Dragons had spent months crafting the spell that had transformed Draconas—a red-gold dragon— into Draconas—a human. Among the categories of dragon magic, the spell was known as a supreme illusion, one of the most difficult and complex magicks a dragon could undertake. The spell was so complex that more than one dragon was required to cast it. Humans who viewed the illusion of Draconas must not only believe in their minds that he was human, they had to believe it in their hearts and in their souls. He had to smell human, feel human, bleed human blood. He had to be human in all ways, manners, and degrees. The only way the illusion could be broken was by a single human tear.

If a human tear touched Draconas's illusory skin, the human who shed that tear would have the power to see Draconas for what he was. The Parliament had attached this "rider" to the spell not for the sake of the humans, but as a warning to the walker-dragon. Draconas must never to allow himself to become emotionally involved with humans. In other words, he must never permit a human to cry on his shoulder.

Lacking the resources to cast a supreme illusion, Grald and Maristara had been forced to steal the bodies of humans, usurp those bodies and, by means of perverted magic, take the human bodies for their own. This had certain advantages. A human—even one possessed of dragon magic—who looked at them would see only another human. No sign of the dragon. The body-snatching had one major disadvantage. The illusion spell used by Draconas allowed him to glide easily from one human form into another, thus ensuring that in most circumstances he could escape from a dangerous or compromising situation. Grald and Maristara could leave their human bodies, but only to change back into their dragon forms. As Draconas had himself witnessed, the process took a long time to complete and left the dragon vulnerable, like a butterfly struggling to escape from its cocoon; finally emerging, but with its wings wet and crumpled.

This was Draconas's plan. In order to force the dragon to reveal himself, Draconas must slay the human body. He had to kill Grald and kill him quickly, before the dragon could act to defend the body. When the human body ceased to function, the dragon would have no choice but to abandon it and, in so doing, return to his dragon form.

Draconas had no intention of fighting the dragon. To do so, he would have to change into his dragon form. A battle between dragons would destroy half this city and kill hundreds of humans. All Draconas wanted to do was to discover the dragon's true identity. Once he knew him, Draconas would report immediately to Parliament. After that, his job was done. The Parliament could decide how to proceed against the outlaw dragon and his cohort, Maristara. Draconas would then be free to rescue Marcus and return him to his father.

Draconas gave the staff that he was carving into a spear a critical once-over. The weapon was rough and crude, but it would serve his purpose. Grald should be along any moment now. He wouldn't see Draconas, standing in the doorway, hidden in the shadows. Grald would go to the door of the hovel. His back—that broad-shouldered, hulking expanse of back—would be the target.

Draconas clasped hold of his spear, readied himself. His aim had to be true, his throw swift and powerful. The kill must be quick and clean. He could not wound Grald, give the dragon a chance to think, perhaps even to recover.

Shock, the element of surprise, was crucial.

"Draconas."

The woman's voice, coming from behind him, startled Draconas so that he very nearly jumped out of skin that wasn't real to begin with. He felt a gentle hand touch his arm, felt a presence at his side. He glanced over his shoulder.

The holy sister stood beside him. He didn't recall where he'd seen her at first, and then he remembered. He'd seen her with Ven, when he was little and he'd hurt his leg.

"Get out of here, Sister," Draconas told her roughly. "This is none of your concern."

"Ah, but it is," said the nun.

In that moment, Draconas knew. He knew before he saw the shadow rising up behind the holy sister, extending its wings.

The colors of his mind splintered, shattered, crashed down around him.

"I don't understand. . . ."

"I know, Draconas," said Anora softly, and her colors were gray ash. "The pity is—you never will."

Lightning crackled from her jaws.

32

VEN PRESSED HIS HAND OVER THE WOUND IN HIS chest. Blood welled out from beneath his fingers, soaking the front of his shirt. He took a step, staggered, and sagged back against the wall.

"Let go of me! He's not dead yet!" Evelina raved, as Marcus seized hold of her.

She was frenzied, mad with rage and bloodlust. When Marcus tried to wrest the knife from her, she turned on him, stabbing and cutting. In desperation, Marcus seized hold of her wrist and gave it a twist and a wrench. The knife clanged on the floor.

Ven took a step toward them, his hand outstretched.

Marcus lunged for his brother, either to keep Ven from grabbing the knife or to help him. In his confusion, he didn't know which he meant, perhaps both at once. Before he could reach Ven, he slumped to the floor.

Ven struggled to rise, tried to push himself up. He was too weak. He collapsed and lay still, unmoving. Blood seeped from beneath him, darkening the dirt floor.

Evelina gave a cry of triumph and made a dart for the knife. Marcus intercepted her.

"Listen to me," he said, giving her a shake, forcing her to look at him. "He's not a danger to you now. You've hurt him, maybe killed him. The dragon is the danger—Ven's father. Ven told his father where to find me, and when Grald sees what has happened to his son, he will kill us both. We have to get out of here. Now! Do you understand?"

He gave her another shake to emphasize his words.

"Yes," said Evelina in a dazed voice. She stood over Ven, staring down at him. "I understand. We have to get out. Get away."

She didn't move, however, didn't seem able to move. Marcus reached out to her and she saw the bloody slash marks on his arms and chest.

"I hurt you!" she cried remorsefully. "I didn't mean to! I only wanted to hurt him—"

"I know," said Marcus, soothing her. "I know. Come with me. We have to leave before Grald finds us."

Evelina didn't hear him.

"Evelina . . ." said Marcus gently, but urgently.

"It's hopeless," she said, watching Ven's blood trickle out from beneath his body. "We can't leave. There's no way out of this horrible city."

"I know someone who can help us," Marcus said. "Quickly—" He took hold of her, tried to urge her to the door.

Still Evelina did not move.

"Is he dead?" she asked. "Did I kill him?"

"I don't know," Marcus said. "I think so."

"I hope so!" Evelina cried fervently. "I hope so—"

Brilliant, dazzling, horrific light—heaven's light—sizzled, arced, crackled and boomed.

The blast hammered the stone house, burst open the door, and rained down pain and darkness.

Marcus gasped for breath, choking and coughing. His head hurt. His wits seemed scattered to the four winds. He put his hand to his scalp, felt a tender lump rising. Blood trickled into his eyes. He wiped it away and peered through the cloud of dust, wondering why everything had gone dark. For a moment, he panicked, thinking that something was wrong with his vision. As his eyes grew accustomed to the dimness and he began to make out objects, he realized that there was no light because the windows were clogged with rubble. Shattered stone, pieces of timber and other debris filled the room. Small shafts of dusty sunlight, filtering through a few cracks in the pile, lit a scene of utter destruction.

"Evelina!" Marcus gasped, remembering. He found her lying beside him. She was covered in dust, and she stared at him, eyes wide. "Are you hurt?"

"What happened?" she asked and began to cough.

"I don't know." Marcus sat up. The pain in his head made him dizzy for a moment, but he held still and the dizziness passed. "Don't move," he cautioned her.

"I'm all right." She reached out her hands to him and he helped her sit up.

They huddled together on the floor, staring around in bewilderment.

"The door," said Evelina dazedly. "It's gone."

The door had been blown inside the dwelling and lay partially buried under a pile of broken stone.

"Stay here," Marcus told her. Picking his way through the debris, he climbed onto the pile and looked outside, into the street. Where there had once been buildings, there were now mounds of rock in which nothing moved.

The air was gray with drifting dust and silence.

"Draconas!" Marcus went inside the little room and stood there with the door open, gazing into the colors, listening for the voice to answer.

"Draconas!" he called again.

Draconas's colors were gone. His voice was gone.

It was the dragon who found him. Claws reached out to seize him. . . .

Marcus's first impulse was to run. He fought that impulse, stayed where he was, and when the dragon reached for him, he dodged around him and slipped inside the dragon's mind. Marcus was taking a risk, but he was desperate for information. The dragon's colors were red-tinged and smoke-gray: fury and doubt. The dragon didn't know what had happened but, whatever it was, it shouldn't have.

Marcus ducked out hastily, slammed shut the door to his room, and flung himself against it. The dragon raged outside, but he couldn't find the way in.

The dragon's entrance had been through Ven and Ven was dead.

Marcus knelt down beside his brother. The blue scales of the beast's legs were white with the settling dust, dark red with blood. Marcus tried to feel for a pulse. His hands shook so that he couldn't be sure if the heartbeat was there or not. Ven looked dead. His skin was ashen, his lips gray. Marcus couldn't let himself think about Ven, about Draconas. Thinking would come later. Now was for living and for staying alive.

"Well?" said Evelina, who had been watching him hopefully. "Can we get out?"

"Not that way," Marcus answered.

"That's the *only* way!" she cried. Her hands plucked nervously at her skirts. She cast a wild glance around the hovel that was more cavelike than ever. "This is a tomb." Her voice rose, shrill and hysterical. "We're sealed up in here. Trapped."

She began to choke, gasp. "I can't breathe—"

"Stop it!" Marcus ordered sharply.

Evelina jumped, startled at his tone. She fell silent, but he could hear her panting in the darkness.

"Come over here," he ordered. "Stand behind me. Keep near me. Cover your face with your hands."

"What are you going to do?" she asked tremulously, as she pressed her body close against his.

"I'm going to get us out of here."

He faced the back wall of the wrecked dwelling. He took hold of the magic, molded it, shaped it, and then he threw it.

The magic exploded against the stone wall and blew out the back of the dwelling. At the sound of another blast, Evelina screamed and buried her face in the small of his back. He could feel her shivering and he put his arms around her.

"Don't be afraid. We have a way out now."

She opened her eyes, blinked, and stared at the gaping hole in amazement. She transferred the stare to him.

"How—" she started to ask.

"No time," he said. "The dragon is still out there and he still wants us dead."

Evelina gulped and swallowed her questions and began to hike up her skirt and her petticoat, kilting the fabric around her waist. She glanced at him as she worked and she even managed a quavering jest.

"This really isn't the time to admire my legs."

Marcus felt his face burn. He hadn't been admiring her legs. Or at least, he hadn't meant to. He'd been looking past her, out through the hole in the wall into what appeared to be an alley. Across the alley were more stone dwellings, all built more or less alike. A ditch ran down the center of the street. From the foul smell seeping into the dusty room, the ditch was a gutter designed to carry away waste.

Screams and cries for help straggled inside with the sunlight, and Marcus realized suddenly that there were more people in the city than just himself and Evelina. He'd been so preoccupied with his fear of the dragon that he'd forgotten about the deadly monks.

"I'm ready," said Evelina.

She had completed her task with deft efficiency. Her legs were bare to just above the knee, her skirts bunched around her waist. Her ankles were trim and slender, her calves shapely, her thighs smooth and white. He wrenched his gaze away. He didn't move. He listened to the voices.

"What are we waiting for?" Evelina threaded her hands through his arms, tugged at him. "I want to leave this terrible place. Please, let's go now! Before someone comes!"

Still Marcus didn't move. He continued to listen. The voices came from somewhere behind the house, on the other side of the street, and they were fading.

"We can leave now. Be careful," he cautioned. "Let me go first."

The piles of shattered stone shifted precariously beneath

his feet and he was forced to move slowly. Evelina climbed out behind him, her hand clutching his hand. Each helped the other and then they were outside and the sun shone and the air was fresh. Evelina lifted her face to the heavens, drew in a deep breath.

"Thank God," she breathed. She looked up the alley and down. "Where do we go from here?"

A very good question. Marcus paused to think, to get his bearings. He had been unconscious when Draconas had brought him here. He had no memory of the journey, no idea where he was. He thought back to the early morning sun shining through the front window of the dwelling. That meant the house faced east. He was at the back of the house, now facing west. He next calculated the location of the wall that surrounded the city and the gate through which they had entered. On the trip downriver, the sun was at his back. They had sailed east. The city was on his left-hand side. North. The gate, therefore, was located on a south-facing wall.

Marcus knew now which direction to take. He didn't leave immediately, however. He turned to look back through the hole in the wall, trying to see inside the ruins of the house.

"What is it?" asked Evelina impatiently. "What are you waiting for?"

He didn't know. A call, a cry. A child's hand reaching out to him from the darkness.

"Nothing," he said to Evelina. "I'm not waiting for anything."

He took hold of her hand and they ran down the alley.

When he was certain his brother and Evelina were gone, Ven sat up. The sudden movement brought pain and he sucked in his breath, and gritted his teeth until it passed. Gingerly, he peeled away the fabric of his shirt, that was sodden with blood, to examine the wound. The bleeding had stopped. The deep gash was already closing.

Evelina had struck in haste and in panic. The blade had been stopped by a rib, scraping along the bone. Fortunately for him, her blow had missed striking any vital organs. Even dragon magic could not heal a pierced heart.

A pierced heart . . .

His father's voice called to him.

Ven paid no heed. He crouched alone in the darkness, protected by his emptiness.

33

THE ALLEY WAS STILL MOSTLY IN SHADOW. THE
sun's light had yet to reach it. Perhaps full sunlight never
reached back here, for the buildings crowded close to the alley, their ill-fitting upper stories leaning over it at precarious
angles. Marcus and Evelina hugged the shadows, avoiding
the small patches of sunlight that had managed to accidentally wander in. The alley wound and twisted among the
stone walls, so that they could not see where it was taking
them. Marcus worried that they might be going in the wrong
direction, but whenever he found a place where the sun
shone, he saw it on his left side. He looked behind them con-
tinually for some sign of pursuit, but saw no one.

The dragon had left off clawing at the door of his mind.
Marcus didn't know whether that was good or bad. Good if
it meant the dragon was distracted, preoccupied. Bad if it
meant the dragon knew that it was only a matter of time before Marcus fell into his grasp.

Marcus decided to risk opening the door to the magic a
crack. "Draconas!" he called, and waited, breathless.

No response.

"Draconas," said Marcus, the colors of his mind blazing

orange with urgency, "I need your help to escape! Draconas!"

Nothing. His colors were gone, wiped clean, as if they had never been.

Marcus gave up and kept going. He didn't have a choice.

The alley took a turn to the west, doubled back on itself, and came to abrupt end, opening into a city street, from which rose the hubbub of voices, echoing among the alley's canyon-like walls. Marcus's steps slowed. Reaching the end of the alley, he pulled Evelina to a stop.

The street ahead was thronged with people—the inhabitants of Dragonkeep, and they were not all brown-robed, magic-wielding monks. Marcus might have been looking on market day at Ramsgate-upon-the-Aston. Most of the people were dressed more or less alike, in plain and serviceable homespun clothing. Some wore leather aprons that denoted a craftsman, perhaps cobbler or tailor. Others had the sleek look of shopkeepers or the weathered look of those who farm the land.

"This is a city like any other," he said to himself, and then he saw it wasn't.

Here and there among the crowd were those who wore the brown robes of the monks.

"What are we waiting for *now*?" Evelina demanded.

"The monks," he said, and pointed. "I think they're looking for us."

Evelina shivered and shrank back against him.

Most of the ordinary citizens were roaming about in aimless confusion, shouting to each other in an effort to find out what had caused the explosion that had rocked the entire city. By contrast, the monks moved with grim purpose, shoving their way through the crowd, their cowled heads turning this way and that, staring searchingly into every face.

Evelina's grip on his hand tightened. "How far away is the wall?"

"It is on the other side of those buildings. Look, you can see it above the rooftops."

Evelina stood on tiptoe to try to see, but she was too short. "What do we do?"

"We can't stay here," said Marcus. He didn't like the fact that the monks were in the very street that they needed to cross. Almost as if they knew. He pulled his cowl over his face.

"We'll blend in with the crowd." He paused, then said quietly, "You have blood on your clothes."

Evelina looked down at her bodice, saw it spattered with blood—Ven's blood. She flushed, lowered her eyes. She felt guilty and ashamed and she didn't know why.

Ven deserved to die. He was a monster. She'd stab him again without hesitation. But she wished she didn't have his blood on her. Hastily she shook down her skirts, smoothed them, and pulled her cloak close around her blood-spattered bodice. She drew the hood up over her head.

"Can you still see it?" she asked, her voice breaking.

"Evelina." Marcus pushed back the hood to see her face. "I don't blame you for what you did to Ven. I understand. I wish . . . I wish I could make amends for what he did to you."

She risked looking up at him and found him looking at her with an expression in the hazel eyes that wrenched her heart—sympathy mingled with pain, understanding mingled with desire. No man had ever looked at her that way before.

In that moment, Evelina fell into love, plunged into it, leapt into love's chasm with all her heart and soul.

"Evelina," Marcus continued, pressing her hand. His hand was so warm and strong! "If anything happens to us, I want you to know that I admire you as I have never admired any other woman. No other woman I know would have been as brave, as courageous as you have been." He paused, then said in an altered voice, "I think my mother must have been like you."

Evelina lowered her eyes in confusion, unable to speak. She had been drawn to him the moment she saw him or, rather, the moment she had heard Ven call Marcus, "king's son." She had made up her mind then to use him. She had not meant to love him. Then had come his gentle touch, the respectful manner in which he spoke to her, the masterful way he acted to save them. Evelina stood quivering beside him, knowing exultation and terrible, chilling fear. She wanted this man as she had never wanted anything in her life and she knew that he was as far beyond her reach as a blazing star.

Especially if he found out the truth.

Then he will not find out, Evelina resolved inwardly.

She now felt no compunction over killing Ven. Thank God he was dead!

Grasping Marcus's hand tightly, Evelina sidled near and said softly, "We should go, Marcus. It's not safe. . . ."

He smiled at her and gave her hand a reassuring squeeze. "All will be well. Keep close to me."

"Oh, I will, Marcus," Evelina vowed, a vow imprinted on her soul. "I will!"

Holding fast to each other, the two ventured out into the street that was jammed with bodies. Bumped and jostled, they came perilously near being trampled by the mob. Marcus kept his destination in sight and, keeping a tight grip on Evelina, he pushed his way through the clusters of people, avoiding—if possible—the brown-robed monks. In this, he was not alone. No one liked the monks, it seemed. Dressed as a monk himself, Marcus saw people he approached cringe, avoid his glance, duck their heads, trying to get away from him. He heard muttered curses as he walked past and relieved sighs.

Pressing forward through the confusion, Marcus listened closely to what people were saying. He soon came to realize that no one knew what disaster had befallen their city, although everyone professed to.

Picking out the facts from the mishmash of rumor and speculation, he gathered that the blast had leveled several buildings, leaving scores of people dead and wounded and clogging the streets with debris. As to what had caused the explosion, everyone had a theory, ranging from lightning to alchemy gone wrong. No one mentioned the dragon, though Marcus had the impression that they were all thinking it.

He and Evelina finally pushed and shoved their way

through the crowd. Crossing the street, they reached the row of buildings that stood between them and the wall. Now they had only to find a cross street or another alley that would lead them to the wall and the illusion-concealed gate. What they would do once they got there was open to question. Marcus would worry about that when the time came. Thus far, they had managed to avoid the monks, though there seemed to be more of them all the time. They appeared to be congregating in this area, as if they knew he was here.

The street curved and sloped downhill with no outlet. The buildings that stood between them and the wall seemed to go on and on interminably. There were more and more monks. At last, Marcus saw a break in the endless expanse of gray stone. A cross street, perhaps. It was up ahead, no more than a block away. He glanced down at Evelina. She smiled up at him, brave and reassuring. His heart warmed to her. . . .

A flurry of brown robes lunged at him out of the shadows of a doorway.

Brown robes and fire.

Flames whirled about the monk's wrists and swirled up and down his fingers. The monk reached out to Marcus, sought to clasp him in a fiery embrace, grasping hold of anything he could—flesh, fabric, hair. Everything he touched caught fire.

The intense heat of the magic seared Marcus's flesh. The blazing light half-blinded him and smoke from his smoldering robes choked him. Frantically, Marcus grappled with the monk, trying to fend him off. He heard Evelina screaming, but he couldn't find her in the smoke and the agonizing pain.

Fighting for his life, Marcus used the only weapon he had available. He needed the magic to save his life and the magic was there, in his hands.

A blizzard of blue ice and white snow swirled around him, dousing the flames and easing the burning pain. He inhaled and then breathed out a blast of icy winter wind that lifted the monk off his feet, sent him flying, to slam up against a stone wall. The monk bounced off the wall, fell onto the pavement, and lay still. The flames on his hands flickered and went out.

Marcus stood over the monk, watching for signs of movement. The snow fell down upon him and then gradually ceased.

"You were on fire!" Evelina gasped. "I thought you were dead! And then . . . then it began to snow!"

She clutched her head. "I hate this place!"

"Hush, it's over now," he said, putting his arm around her.

Looking out into the street, he saw that he had lied. The fight wasn't over. It had only just begun.

The monk had not succeeded in immolating Marcus, but the magical flames—blazing through the streets like a fire-trailing comet—had drawn the attention of all the magic-wielding monks. They came from everywhere: emerging from doorways, rising up out of gutters, running down the street, all of them converging on Marcus.

The cross street was only a short distance away, but their path was blocked by three of the monks coming at them at a dead run.

"There's an alley," cried Evelina, pointing, yet holding back. "But it might be a dead end."

"We *know* this way is a dead end," Marcus said grimly. "We'll have to take our chances."

They ducked into the alley, running with all their might.

Despite his bold words, Marcus was tormented by doubt. He could not see the end of the alley, which was as twisting and tortured as every other street in the city. Glancing over his shoulder, he saw the monks in pursuit. One of them made a flinging motion with his hand.

Remembering the dart that had struck down Bellona, Marcus flattened himself against the wall, pulled Evelina with him. The dart flew past, landed in the street.

"The wall!" Evelina cried shrilly. "I see it. Oh, Marcus, I can see it! We're almost there!"

He looked to the end of the alley to see sunlight, just as another dart smashed into the stone, barely missing his head.

Marcus pointed to the buildings that stood at the entrance

to the alley. The magic rolled out of him, rumbled through the earth. Stone walls shook and trembled and, with a roar like an avalanche, two buildings collapsed in a cascade of debris that sent up a cloud of dust. He couldn't see his pursuers, but he guessed, from the screams and cries, that at least some had been buried alive. He dashed out into the alley, with Evelina at his side, and it was then he felt the weakness.

It came on him suddenly, unexpectedly—a sensation of being utterly exhausted. He could not catch his breath. His legs and arms and hands tingled. He stumbled and nearly fell. Evelina caught hold of him.

"What's the matter?" she asked frantically, terrified. "Are you hurt?"

He didn't answer. He had to use his breath for breathing. Talking required more strength than he had and he couldn't explain anyway. Nothing is free in this world. Everything has a price, including the magic.

Conjuring pixies from dust motes was a little fatiguing, but the magic had never before sent him to his bed. Bringing down stone buildings and raising ice storms was apparently different. He was so drained, he could scarcely move.

Behind him, he could hear the monks clawing their way through the rubble. He had to keep going or give up and die.

"Dearest Marcus, sweet love, we are almost there!" Evelina coaxed, her voice trembling with fear. "Please. Just a little farther, my heart, my own."

She tugged at him, pleaded with him. He nodded and stumbled forward on. He could no longer run. It took all his resolve just to walk.

"It's not far now," she urged, sliding her arm around him, supporting him.

He wearily raised his head to see the wall directly ahead. They had only to cross a street and they would be standing in front of it. Fifty, a hundred steps.

And then what? He remembered entering Dragonkeep, remembered looking back at the wall through which he'd just passed and seeing no gate, no way out, nothing but solid stone. On and on the wall ran, without end. Around and around the city. No break. No escape. A dragon eating its own tail . . .

"Marcus!" Evelina cried sharply, frightened.

He jerked his head, shook his head to clear it, and kept moving, kept walking. He concentrated on picking up his feet and putting them down, picking them up, putting them down.

The wall came closer. Solid stone. Fused with fire.

Marcus called again, one last time. "Draconas . . ."

The name echoed in the darkness of his little room. Echoed back to him.

One by one, the echoes died.

The street that ran along the wall was empty. He'd expected to find a river of brown robes. If the monks were coming to stop them, they had better hurry.

Yet why should they? Marcus asked himself. *I'm not going anywhere and neither is Evelina.*

He was at the wall, standing before it, staring at it. He poured his whole being into that stare, wishing it, willing it to give him some hint, some clue of the way out. He risked leaving his little room, risked roaming up and down the length of the wall, as far as he could see; risked using his magic to search for a crack, a chink in the endless stone.

Nothing.

He stared at the wall so long that the stones began to shift and glide in his swimming vision and he wrenched his gaze away.

He called to Draconas one last time.

When there was no answer, Marcus reached out his hand to touch the wall. He touched stone—solid and cold. He moved his hand to another part and then another. Stupid. Futile. A last desperate attempt to stave off the inevitable.

"Marcus . . ." said Evelina urgently. "The monks . . ."

He saw them rounding the corner of the building, coming for him. Some held fire in their hands. Some held steel. All of it was death, so it didn't much matter.

"Tell me the truth, Marcus," said Evelina calmly. "There's no way out, is there?"

"No," he said. "There's not. I had hoped . . ." He let hope hang, shook his head.

"I'm afraid," she said, and put her arms around him.

"So am I," he said, and held her close.

A hand thrust through the stone wall.

Marcus stared to see it, not believing. *I'm going mad,* he thought. *Like the wretched monks.*

The hand vanished and Ven stood in front of him, inside the little room.

"This is the gate," said Ven.

His blue eyes were the only color in a vast expanse of white.

"The gate!" Evelina cried. "I see it! Marcus, look!" She clutched at him. "There it is. Right in front of us. Hurry! Make haste!"

The illusion shattered and, as always, when we see the truth, Marcus wondered that he had been so blind as not to penetrate the lie at once. And he did not mean the gate, though it was also there—before him—a door constructed of wood planks, crudely built, held together with iron bands.

The gate stood open. By the rusted look of the hinges, it had not been shut for centuries. It had rusted in place.

Beyond the gate was the forest and beyond that the river. No monks blocked the way. No dragon stood at the entrance.

Marcus looked back to the little room.

"Take care of her," said Ven. He held out his hand, a man's hand, no longer a child's.

Marcus touched his brother's hand and it vanished.

The gate vanished, dissolved into the wall.

The wall vanished, dissolved into illusion.

Dragonkeep was gone, and it might have never existed for Marcus, but for the feel of his brother's hand, firm and warm, in his own.

34

VEN STOOD OUTSIDE THE WALL, HIDDEN WITHIN the illusion within the reality. Mirages, painted on the silk of his mind, wavered in the morning sunshine. Trees of lies, trees of wood, side by side. Lies and reality both solid and unyielding.

The voices were real, though dim and fading. Voices of the monks on one side of the wall, angry to have lost their prey, fearful of the dragon's wrath. Voices of his brother and Evelina on the other side of the wall growing more and more distant. The voice of the river, endlessly murmuring.

Ven rose from his crouched position and moved deeper into the forest. He had to pause frequently to rest, for although the dragon in him was able to mend his injuries, he was weak from loss of blood. The wound pained him, but then, the wound would always pain him. He had a task to accomplish, a promise to keep, and not much time to do it. Grald was occupied with the unexpected destruction of half his city, but that wouldn't last long. There would be questions asked, explanations required.

Fortunately, Ven knew right where to look for what he sought. He used the skills in tracking that she had taught him almost from the first day he could walk. He followed the trail left in the trampled grass and came upon Bellona's body.

Ven squatted down beside her, resting easily on his animal haunches. Death had relaxed the sternness of her face, smoothed out the lines of sorrow and grief and bitterness. The bloodstained lips on which his name had died were closed, composed. She looked young in death, younger than he had ever known her in life. He reached down, took hold of the dart that remained lodged in her throat, and yanked it out. He thrust the dart into his belt.

Lifting in his arms the woman who had raised him, Ven carried her body to the river.

He laid her in the bottom of one of the boats drawn up on the riverbank. Recalling her stories of ancient wars and warriors, he crossed her hands over her breast. He washed the blood from her face with river water. He broke the dart that had slain her and laid the pieces at her feet.

Ven hauled the boat into the water and waded out with it, guiding the boat with his hand. When he reached the point in the river where the current would take the boat from him, Ven looked down at the still, ashen face. He took hold of the chill hand.

"Let your soul rest easy, Bellona," he said, repeating the old ritual of his birthday. "My name is Vengeance and I will be true to my name."

His blue eyes looked away from her, looked back toward Dragonkeep. "On your blood and my mother's tears, I swear it."

He gave the boat a shove that sent it out into the swirling current, for the river to catch Bellona and bear her away to the vast and endless sea.

Ven did not stay to watch it. He had been gone too long as it was. He waded back to shore. Back to reality.

Back to illusion.

A preview of

MASTER
OF
DRAGONS

BY MARGARET WEIS

Available November 2005
from Tom Doherty Associates, LLC

LYSIRA ENTERED THE ENORMOUS CAVERN THAT was the ancient Hall of Parliament for dragonkind. The entrance was located in the tallest peak of a snow-capped mountain range. Gaping black against the white-shrouded crags, the opening had been carved hundreds of centuries ago by dragon magic. No need to hide it from humans, not this far up the mountainside; the entrance was large enough to accommodate a dragon in flight. Lysira was small for her kind, and she swooped into the entryway with ease, glad to leave behind the glare of the sun glittering on the snow for the restful darkness of the Hall.

The dragon spiraled downward, drifting on the whispering air currents, listening to the silence that was dark in her mind. The Hall was empty. Parliament was not in session. She was not really supposed to be here, but she felt drawn to this place. Disturbed and troubled, she did not know what to do or where to turn for answers, and so she decided to come here. Perhaps if she was in the Hall itself, she would be able to glean some of the wisdom of those who came before her, pick up a trace of their colors. Learn from their experience. At least, that's what she told herself.

Gliding downward on still wings toward the floor that was far, far below her, Lysira was bitterly disappointed. She saw only darkness. The cavern was empty. If there were ghosts, they slumbered in the eternal dragon dream that was death.

Upset, Lysira was not paying attention to what she was doing, and the floor came up on her before she was ready for it. She landed with an ungraceful thud, nearly going over on her nose. Recovering, she was thankful that no one was here to have witnessed such a fledgling bumble.

She was especially glad that one particular dragon was not present—the Walker, Draconas. Her scales rippled all over in embarrassment at the thought. In truth, it was because she'd been thinking of him and everything he'd said at the last session of Parliament that she had botched her landing. But she couldn't decide if it was his words that had bothered her or if it was the way his colors had so gently touched her.

Settling on the floor, tucking her wings in at her flanks and wrapping her long tail around her feet, Lysira gazed around the dark and empty cavern and sighed. She could at last admit to herself that she'd been hoping—rather unrealistically—that she would find Draconas here.

She didn't know why she expected him to be in the empty Hall.

Perhaps because he wasn't anywhere else.

Dragons communicate mentally, mind-to-mind, using images and vibrant colors to exchange ideas. A dragon may block another from entering his or her mind, just as a human can stop others from entering his house. But, just as the house is still there, so is the mind of the dragon. Though the colors are unreadable and prohibit entry, they shimmer like foxfire in the night. And Draconas's colors were nowhere to be seen.

Dragons dislike making hasty decisions. Lysira had been unsettled ever since the last meeting of Parliament—the meeting that had thrown the dragons into turmoil, the meeting in which Draconas had disclosed that the two children born to the human woman Melisande could communicate mind-to-mind, as could dragons. Not only that, but these humans could actually enter the minds of dragons! This was an awful, dreadful, catastrophic calamity. What's more, Draconas had told Parliament that one of their number was a traitor, one of them was feeding information to the rogue dragon, Maristara and her cohort. Because of this, Draconas had hidden away the two children, and he refused to tell anyone—even Anora, the wise elder dragon, the Minister of the Parliament—where they were to be found. He'd also claimed that this same traitor had been responsible for the deaths of Braun, Lysira's brother, and her father.

That meeting had taken place sixteen years ago. A long time, by human standards. A mere eye blink by dragon measuring. Lysira had spent those years dithering, wavering back and forth, trying to decide if she would talk to Draconas or not. For a couple of years, she thought she wouldn't. He was the Walker, the dragon who took human shape to walk among humans and keep an eye on them. He had, therefore, lots of humans images in his mind, images Lysira found disturbing and distasteful. And fascinating.

It was the fascinating part that bothered her. She'd seen only a few of these images the last time he'd spoken to her, and she had since discovered that they kept cropping up in her dreams, breaking her tranquility. Try as she might, she couldn't banish them. She didn't want to see any more of them. And yet, she did.

Once she had made up her mind that she would talk to him, a few more years passed before she found the courage to do so. She would start to approach him and then she would shy away and retreat back to her lair in a flutter of confusion.

This made her angry, and for the next year or so, she turned her anger at Draconas and blamed him as the cause of all the trouble. She knew she was being irrational. He wasn't the cause. Maristara had started it all by seizing that human kingdom and then breeding humans with dragons to produce humans with dragon magic. Lysira didn't like to admit that part.

At this point, she decided that she didn't need Draconas. She would find out who the traitor dragon was on her own. Lysira's investigations were half-hearted, however, and didn't get her anywhere. The other dragons she questioned were brusque and even rude. They obviously did not want to think about any of this. They were hoping it would all go away. They shut their minds to her and shooed her off.

Which brought Lysira right back to Draconas. She would talk to him. She was determined to talk to him. Boldly, trembling, Lysira reached out her colors to him.

Only to find that the colors of his mind were gone, as though they had been wiped away by a wet sponge.

Lysira crouched in the empty Hall of Parliament and, for the first time she began to be afraid. Not only for Draconas, but for herself. And all of dragonkind.

Anora felt true regret that she had to kill Draconas.

Of all the walkers who had sacrificed their dragon form to take on the illusion of a human, Draconas had been the best. One of the hazards of being a walker, of living among humans, was that the dragon tended to either become too human—in which case he forgot the reason he'd been sent to walk among humans in the first place—or he remained too dragon—in which case he moped and pouted and whined about having to put up with the inconveniences of being human.

Draconas had been the first to separate the two halves of his being, maintaining a firm division between the dragon and the human. Even now, though it appeared that was acting for the humans, siding with the humans, and protecting the humans, Anora knew better. Draconas was doing what he was doing because he firmly believed he was helping his own kind.

Admirable. Mistaken, but admirable.

She stood, masked by illusion, inside the building where she'd set her trap for Draconas. Watching him from the shadows, she pondered the idea of letting him live. She could try to explain to him that he was wrong, hoping he'd see reason. She discarded that thought with a regretful sigh.

Draconas's asset had become his liability. He was working hard to keep humans and dragons at peace, as they had been since the first human had raised himself up off all fours. Draconas would never understand why that peace had to end, and Anora knew he could never be made to understand.

He had to die.

Draconas had his back to her. She'd been spying on him from the moment he'd entered the abandoned building. He was here to set a trap for the dragon Grald, the master of Dragonkeep. Grald, disguised in his own stolen human body was heading this direction.

Grald and Anora were in contact, the colors of their minds blending, though not very harmoniously. Anora was thinking of her own lofty goals. Grald was thinking of vengeance. But what could you expect? Grald was a dragon of the baser sort. He did not come from one of the noble families of dragonkind, who had ruled the world for centuries. In human terms, Grald was a peasant.

He'd been brought into this conspiracy by Maristara, who had chosen him because he was a peasant—rough and crude and not overly educated.

The elder female dragon, Maristara, had formed a theory—a brilliant theory—that if dragons and humans bred, they would produce offspring that would look human, but would be capable of using dragon-magic. Anora remembered how shocked and appalled she'd been at first hearing Maristara's proposal, brought to her in secret. She'd been adamantly opposed to it—not only did it break all the laws of dragonkind, it could prove dangerous for dragons— creating humans with magical powers! It was not to be considered. When Maristara had defied her and seized a human kingdom in order to begin her experiments, Anora had vowed that she would do everything in her power to stop her.

Time passed. The dragons, with their usual ineptness and inability to make decisions, bungled any chance of halting Maristara. The experiments proceeded and went far better than even Maristara had hoped. Sadly, as time passed, Anora had come to see things Maristara's way.

These humans with the dragon-magic in their blood proved to be so powerful that they intimidated lesser humans. Thus, they made perfect rulers. And, because these humans had dragon blood in their veins, they were easily manipulated by the dragons. Dragons ruled the half-dragon humans who ruled the humans. Perfect all around.

Maristara needed a male dragon to start the breeding program with the humans females of Seth. She didn't dare choose one of the males of the noble houses, for fear word would get out. She selected a male from a family of lesser dragons, a young male, aggressive and ambitious and cruel.

His name was Grald.

She taught Grald the secret of ripping the heart out of a living human body and taking over that body, making it his own—a task far less complicated and time-consuming than casting the supreme illusion spell that changed Draconas into a human. Unlike Maristara, who used the human bodies she took to disguise her true form, Grald usurped the human bodies, giving them his name and taking over their personalities. He was on his sixth human right now, and this was his favorite. He had found something better however, and he was looking forward eagerly to taking over the next body— that of his own son.

Before that could happen. Anora and Grald had to kill Draconas, who had had done everything in his power to thwart them.

"I think you would understand," Anora said silently to Draconas, speaking to his back, as he stood across from her in the doorway of the building, sharpening his waling staff, turning it into a spear. "I think you might even take our side, but . . . I can't be sure. You have formed attachments among the humans. You hid Melisande's children away from us. If Ven had not cried out to us for help, we might never have discovered them."

"Quit sniveling, Anora. He should have died long ago."

Grald's colors intruded rudely into hers, and Anora, haughtily, didn't deign to reply. She saw no need to explain herself to underlings. Maristara let Grald take too many liberties. She should keep him in his place.

"Where are you?" Anora asked, her colors chill.

"I am in sight of the house. My son summoned me," Grald added with smug triumph. "He betrayed his brother, as I told you he would, to gain the female. Like father, like son." Grald chuckled.

"I don't trust him," Anora said. "Ven is devious, devious as a dragon, in many ways. I should know. I spent many weeks in his company."

"All the better for me when I take over his body."

You'll acquire a brain, at least, Anora thought, but she kept that caustic comment concealed beneath the cold flow of her colors. Dissimulation was not difficult to practice on Grald, who never bothered to look beneath the surface of any conversation.

"Don't come any closer," Anora warned. "I'm about to strike."

"Take care you don't hurt Ven," Grald said. "I need his body whole and strong."

"The only one hurt will be Draconas," Anora said softly.

She began to creep up on him as he stood, unsuspecting, staring out the door. He was in his human form, holding the spear he'd fashioned in his hand. Across the street. Anora could hear the voices of the human males raised in argument, probably squabbling over the human female. Ideal cover, for they were proving a distraction to Draconas, who looked in that direction and frowned.

"Strike now!" Grald ordered suddenly. "Strike him from behind, before he knows what's hit him!"

Concentrating on Draconas, Anora had unwittingly left her mental process open to Grald. She slammed shut the door to her thoughts and refused to answer him. He couldn't understand her strategy anyway.

It is difficult to take a dragon by surprise.

While a dragon is conscious, he can easily defend himself. Dragons must sleep, however, and when they sleep, they sleep deeply—for years at a time. There was the chance that another dragon or some enterprising human might slay the slumbering dragon. Thus, over the centuries, dragons had developed a means of self-protection. The moment Anora launched a weapon at Draconas—magical or otherwise—his dragon being would act to take defensive measures and fight back. Her plan was to reveal herself to him, let him see that the human he'd known all these years as the holy sister, was, in truth, the Head of Parliament, a venerable dragon he had long respected and trusted. She calculated that the shock of seeing her, of knowing—at the last moment—that she was going to be his doom, would suck all the fight out of him, leave him breathless, winded, amazed. Then dead.

She was quite close to Draconas now.

He was preoccupied, tense, ready for the kill. He didn't hear a sound, didn't sense her presence.

"Draconas," said Anora gently, in her human voice.

He jumped, startled, and looked over his shoulder.

"Get out of here, Sister," Draconas told her roughly. "This is none of your concern."

"Ah, but it is," said Anora.

In that moment, Draconas knew. She saw the knowledge in his eyes as she saw her own reflection, the shadow of the dragon, rising up behind the holy sister, extending its wings and its claws.

The colors of Draconas's mind splintered, shattered, and came crashing down around him.

"I don't understand . . ." He gasped, amazed, appalled.

"I know, Draconas," said Anora softly, and her colors were gray ash. "The pity is—you never will."

Lightning crackled from her jaws . . .